A PLUME BOOK

THE SPIRIT KEEPER

K. B. LAUGHEED is an organic gardener and master naturalist who has spent a lifetime feeding the earth. Her efforts have culminated in *The Spirit Keeper*, her first novel and largest contribution to the potluck so far.

"This is a sweeping and beautiful novel. The rich characters move through a frontier world that is as magical as it is raw. We hope this isn't the last we've seen of Katie O'Toole."
—Kathleen O'Neal Gear and W. Michael Gear, *New York Times* bestselling authors of *People of the Black Sun*

The
Spirit Keeper

A NOVEL

K. B. LAUGHEED

A PLUME BOOK

Plume
Published by the Penguin Group
Penguin Group (USA) Inc., 375 Hudson Street
New York, New York 10014, USA

USA | Canada | UK | Ireland | Australia | New Zealand | India | South Africa | China
Penguin Books Ltd, Registered Offices: 80 Strand, London WC2R 0RL, England
For more information about Penguin Group visit penguin.com

First published by Plume, a member of Penguin Group (USA) Inc., 2013

 REGISTERED TRADEMARK—MARCA REGISTRADA

LIBRARY OF CONGRESS CATALOGING-IN-PUBLICATION DATA
Laugheed, K. B.
   The spirit keeper : a novel / K. B. Laugheed.
      pages cm
   ISBN 978-0-14-218033-4 (pbk.)
   1. Teenage girls—Fiction. I. Title.
   PS3612.A93255S65 2013
   813'.6—dc23   2013010092

Printed in the United States of America
10 9 8 7 6 5 4 3 2 1

Set in Granjon Roman
Designed by Eve L. Kirch

PUBLISHER'S NOTE
This is a work of fiction. Names, characters, places, and incidents either are the product
of the author's imagination or are used fictitiously, and any resemblance to actual persons,
living or dead, business, companies, events, or locales is entirely coincidental.

'Tis all you, Captain.

Author's Note

IN THIS BOOK YOU will encounter variations in spelling, grammar, and syntax which were common to language usage of the eighteenth century. This variation is a result of the fact that language lives inside the heads of the people who use it, and, like any living thing, it wanders and grows and becomes something other than what it once was. The spelling of a word can change. The pronunciation of a word can change. The meaning of a word can change. Therefore, if you have any hope of understanding this story as the author wrote it, read quickly—before it all changes.

Ledger One

~ 1 ~

THIS IS THE ACCOUNT of Katie O'Toole, late of Lancaster Co., Pennsylvania, removed from her family by savages on March the 2nd in the year of Our Lord 1747.

I wish I could say this is a true and honest account, but I see no way the likes of me can make such a claim. Still, I've no reason to lie in the pages of this ledger and plenty of reason to unburden my guilty soul. Mine is such a surpassing strange story. I honestly hope by writing it all down I'll somehow see the truth of it.

I feared at first I might disremember how to write, especially in a language I no longer speak, but now that I've begun, I find my fears unfounded, as fears so oft prove to be. I wonder—what use is fear in a world where the worst catastrophes are those you ne'er see coming?

Ah, well—I'm too practiced a storyteller to fall prey to my own impatience. I'll tell my tale apace, withholding my conclusions 'til the end.

I was the thirteenth child my mother conceived—a circumstance of some significance for her, I believe, as she took great pleasure in reminding me thirteen was the number of Christ's betrayer. Her belief that I was an unlucky child was routinely cited as justification for beatings, and I grew to envy those children of hers who ne'er breathed air, believing they were, indeed, the lucky ones. Our home was always too full for comfort and there was ne'er enough of nothing—food nor clothing nor compassion—to go 'round.

By the time I reached my seventeenth year, my elder siblings had all married, thereby adding more children and chaos to our already o'erflowing household. On the morning of the attack, I was in the loft with a mob of children, readying them for the day. I cannot recall how many children were with me nor e'en which ones they were, but I recall with crystal clarity the shrill scream we heard in the distance.

At that moment all feuding and fussing stopt, and we stared at one another in stunned silence.

I peeked through the shutters and saw savages everywhere. Now I knew why various of our countrymen had warned against settling in this territory, the proprietorship of which is still in dispute, but no one ne'er could tell my father nothing, especially when he was liquored up, which he was, alas, every day I knew him.

When I was small, my gran told tales of how Father had been the son of a lord back in Ireland, how rich he was, and wanton, due to inherit the earth or such like. In trembling whispers, Gran described how her comely daughter schemed to advance herself by catching the young nobleman's eye, only to cause the ruin of them both. Instead of becoming gentrified, Gran suddenly found herself the hapless chaperon of the exiled couple as they struggled to find a place for themselves in the crude colonies across the sea.

Gran was truly happy only when recounting the many miserable failures of my father's life. Unfit for any sort of honest labor, he had, she complained, worn out his welcome in at least a dozen employments in three different colonies, eventually dragging us all into the wilderness of the Pennsylvania frontier. This, he said, was where he would at last restore his fame and fortune. For my part, I ne'er stopt longing to return to Philadelphia, where my brother James remained with his wife and children. I determined to find my way back there at the first opportunity.

Throughout my childhood, I listened wistfully to Gran's tales of the Old World—the ancient cities with stone castles, shining cathedrals, and cobblestone streets—but the only world I knew was filled with filth and toil and strife and turmoil. We siblings fought furiously o'er every scrap of food or cloth, except during those occasions when Father had a notion to school us. Then we must all sit together, boys and girls, reading as he instructed from the Bible or other books. No matter how poor we were, we always had piles of books. We soon memorized Father's favorite passages, for if any of us made a mistake, he would deny supper to us all and drink himself to sleep, grumbling o'er our shortcomings as saliva dribbled from his lips.

If liquor made our father sloppy, endless labors and disappointments made our mother cruel. I remember not a single gentle word from her lips, and the abundance of babies with which she had been blessed merely provided her with targets for her frustrations and rage. We girls were set to work from infancy, cooking, sewing, and tending to the younger ones. If we spilt a drop of stew or dropt a stitch or allowed a child to cry in Mother's presence, she immediately reached for her switch. Once when I let the cook-fire die, I ended up curled in a ball on the floor, blood seeping from the switch-cuts on my back and arms. Gran finally grabbed my mother's hand and shouted, "D'ye mean to kill that child?" But e'en with that intervention, I must still wash the blood from my shift and sew it back together myself.

After Gran died, I oft dreamt of running away to the Old World and living amongst the castles and cathedrals, but I had no means to achieve such a purpose. Instead, once my monthlies were establisht, my parents bade me follow in the footsteps of my sisters and find a husband who could save them the trouble of providing for me. The very suggestion made me shudder. Having been ill-used by men in the past, I desired no further dalliance, and e'en if I could stomach the notion of being pawed and slobbered o'er by a grunting lout, the pickings were slim in our remote community. My father spoke of wedding me off to a backwoodsman, in hopes of expanding trade opportunities for himself, but the fellow was 'round too rarely for arrangements to be made. My mother was much more interested in the bid offered by an innkeeper downriver who required a new wife to share the household burdens of his daughters, both of whom were older than I.

Determined not to be enslaved at a frontier trading post for the rest of my days, I tucked my few possessions into a leather bag, strapt a wool blanket beneath, hid this bundle under one of the beds in the loft, and prepared to run for Philadelphia upon the spring thaw. But before I could accomplish my flight, the children and I heard the aforementioned scream, and the long-feared Indian attack was under way.

Through the crackt shutter of the loft, I saw a savage knock my father on the head with a stone club and fall upon him to rip off his ragged scalp. I had not a moment to mourn because I could hear my mother and sisters struggling to secure the doors and windows down below. Encouraged thus to prepare my own defense, I latcht the shutter and snatcht the boys' musket from its hook. The weapon was useless, being old and missing several mechanisms, but I hoped it might serve 'til I could find something better. I then reached under the bed for my pack, but e'en as I drew the leather strap 'round my head and shoulder, I heard thuds from down below—wood splintering, screams, and scuffling. When whimpering children crowded 'round me, I pushed them into the darkest corner, hissing at them to be absolutely still or they would surely die. All grew quiet below as everyone was dragged outside. A long moment passed before we heard another round of scuffling, a muffled cry, another thud. The children and I waited and waited in breathless silence.

Then we heard the creak of a riser on the stairs.

I raised the musket to my shoulder as I had seen the boys do a hundred times, but my trembling disallowed me to hold the barrel steady. A shadow at the top of the stairs became a savage slowly rising into the ray of light from a crack in the shutter. He appeared to be about my age, and the fact that he was nigh naked unsettled me, but the thing that drew and held my eye was the long, sharp stone blade he held in his hand. It was dripping red with blood.

When the savage saw my musket pointed at his bare chest, he stopt cold and said something rapidly to someone behind him. His black eyes shifted from the gun to my face. He glared at me as I stared at him along the wavering barrel of the weapon.

I know not what I would have done had the savaged lunged at me, but before he could, his companion on the stairs pushed up beside him and lightly touched the hand holding the menacing knife. This second savage, more than a full head shorter than the first and perhaps a bit older, spoke with an urgency that surprised both me and my attacker. The first heathen lowered his blade, looking at his shorter companion in shock, and for a moment the children and I were forgotten as the Indians gabbled at one another in their strange tongue. Finally they both turned their eyes to me.

The short one smiled.

He spoke to me then, still smiling, as if trying to explain something very important. Of course I understood naught, so I just scowled at him, pretending I was about to shoot. The short savage extended his hand, causing me to take a step backwards. In doing so, I stumbled on a child's foot and would have fallen had not the short savage leapt to grab my arm. At that, the taller one shouted and the children screamed, but rather than molesting me in any way, the short savage was trying only to preserve me. His friend reached for my gun, but the short man stopped him with a sharp word. He then asked me something, but I was so distracted by his touch, his closeness, and his uncanny smile that the only thing I could comprehend at that moment was that I was very likely to be very dead very soon.

The short Indian released my arm and repeated his question, his breath hot upon my cheek. I looked into his dark eyes, mere inches from mine. I wanted to tell him I could not understand him, but I could not for the life of me remember how to talk. I could scarce remember how to breathe. As if in a dream, I tipt up the barrel of the musket and held it out, hoping this would move him off me. He did step back, but only because his companion grabbed the gun. The taller heathen examined the musket, smelled it, and looked at me with a flash of vexation. He said something as he tossed the weapon aside, clearly telling his companion the gun was useless. At that, the short savage actually laughed. He turned back to me and grinned—a broad, bright, thoroughly irresistible grin. He held out his hand.

I took it.

And that is the account, as true as I can tell the tale, of how I came to be a captive of the Indians.

~ 2 ~

As to the events during and after the time the children and I were removed from the loft and escorted through the farmyard, my memory is mostly darkness and terror. I clearly remember stepping o'er the body of a beastly looking savage at the bottom of the stairs, his red blood pooling across the floorboards. Outside was mayhem and I believe my two escorts were hard-presst to protect me from the madness and murder taking place all 'round.

I have an all-too-vivid memory of my brother Thomas attempting to douse the fire an arrow had establisht in a hay pile by the barn. Tom struck down every savage who beset him, swatting them aside like bothersome bees at a picnic. E'en when a flying tomahawk finally knockt him into the fire, he continued flailing, trying to put out the flames. To no avail. His clothes caught fire and soon his twitching body helpt to feed the very flames he had been trying to extinguish. As the inferno rose to engulf the barn and flames shot thirty or forty feet in the air, I could hear Tom's wife and children shrieking from their hiding place in the loft.

In the meantime, my captors directed me to sit beside the well, where my mother and sister Eliza huddled beside my fifteen-year-old brother William, who had been knockt in the head but was not dead. A few of Liza's children were there, tho' I do not recall now if they were some who came with me. I do know some of the children who had been in the loft ran off as soon as we stept outside, and at least one was grabbed by a savage and had his brains dasht out against a tree. But the fate of most of my family members will forever be unknown to me.

Tho' the particulars of my removal are vague now, I distinctly recall my two captors making it abundantly clear to their comrades-in-arms that I belonged to them and was not to be molested in any way. Whilst they suffered me to be tied with a leather strap to my sister and mother, they permitted no one to push or prod me. My brother William, wounded as he was with a great gash on his head, was forced to carry a large load of goods looted from our farm, as were both Liza and my poor mother. But I carried naught save my own pack.

I saw immediately how unlike the others were the two men who had taken me from the loft. The few Indians I had seen heretofore were uniformly savage and vile, with heads plucked bald save for a tuft atop, and odd bones and stones woven through ears or noses or lips. Most were tattooed or painted with garish designs, and all savages I had e'er seen were capable of understanding English if they did not, in fact, speak it as well as me. But the two who laid claim to me not only understood no English but clearly did not speak the same language as the others. They communicated with the main body of marauders only through an elaborate language of gestures, accompanied by grunts, groans, and a wide range of facial expressions.

Whilst we captives were marched through the woods like prize cattle, my two guardians remained always at my side. I quickly noted their peculiarities. Tho' they, like all the savages, wore only breechclouts, they carried large packs which the others did not.

Their skin was several shades darker than the others, neither wore paint (tho' the short one did have a small tattoo on the side of his face), and both wore their long black hair in a single braid down their backs. E'en at a glance I could see the muscles of their arms, shoulders, and backs bulged disproportionately, making them appear top-heavy. Their faces were wider, rounder, plumper, and, in short, everything about them was quite unlike the others. As we stumbled through the forest, I passed many silent hours wondering about these two odd fellows—who they were, where they came from, and why they had taken such a particular interest in me.

Because there was no doubt about it. My mother and sister, bound to me at the wrist, immediately saw my situation. At first Mother hoped we might benefit from the keen interest, and it was certainly true I wanted for nothing. But when I tried to share the choice bits of food my guardians gave me, they intervened, making clear my family members were dependent upon the goodwill of the other savages. As the other savages were a monstrous bunch, my relatives suffered and blamed me for it.

I remember my sister questioning me about what happened in the loft and how it came to be I had time to gather provisions. I did not want to reveal I had long hoped to run away, but when I failed to explain my preparedness, she accused me of somehow knowing my captors and scheming with them to plan this event, which was such a bizarre accusation I could find no words to respond. William dismissed the idea as absurd and told Liza to stop lashing out.

Still, the intense favoritism of my guardians did little to dispel my sister's jealousy and suspicions, and because I myself did not understand their interest, I suffered a great unease as the short savage worked to win me over. On the first night after our remove, for example, when Mother snatcht my wool blanket, the short man shyly offered me his thick bearskin. I was, quite naturally, terrified of what he might expect in exchange for this kindness, but his gentle smile and my violent shivering eventually persuaded me. I wrapt myself in the thick fur, grimly awaiting ravishment, but the short savage only smiled as he lay nearby under a thin hide. Oddly, I found I slept more soundly, knowing my peculiar protector was attending me thus. When I awoke in the morning, his smile was the first thing I saw, and after the first few mornings I could not help but greet him with a smile of my own.

I should note I was not the only captive being pampered. Three children were with us, two of whom were Liza's sons, and none were bound. Instead, certain savages claimed them, and tho' at first the youngsters naturally clung to us, as the days passed they, like me, became more comfortable in the company of their new masters. William, who understood some of the language, said the savages debated which of us they would adopt and which they would take to a French outpost for exchange.

In the two years since moving to the frontier, we had all heard tales of what happened to Christians held by the cruel and barbarous heathens—tales of torture and torments that ended in being roasted alive. As relieved as I was to hear I was not fated for the firepit, I was naturally alarmed by this unexpected alteration in my fortunes. I had ne'er enjoyed living in the wild, and had, in fact, been planning to escape it as soon as practicable, yet here I was being dragged e'er farther into the demon darkness, faced with the very real possibility of ne'er seeing the light of civilization again. But, as Gran always sighed, mere mortals must bow before God's Will.

After several days of hiking, I began to fear the special treatment I was receiving might bode particularly ill for me. One evening the short savage, smiling as always, sat down beside me so that we might eat our meal together, and Liza eyed the tender fish he gave me whilst she and the rest had naught but tough strips of dried sinew. "Y'best be careful about enticing your new beau, Katie," she said, one eyebrow raised. "He'll make ye pay for that fish!"

I stopt in mid-chew. Tho', as my mother delighted in assuring me, no one could e'er consider me pretty, I was not unacquainted with the amorous advances of young men. Throughout my youth I made friends with whate'er boys lived near us, and more than one had declared his love for me, regardless of my ruddy complexion and crooked teeth. So tho' I knew Liza's spiteful jibe was prompted mostly by the considerations I was receiving, I also knew that what she said had more than a grain of truth to it.

I was, of course, doing nothing to "entice" the short savage, yet clearly he *was* enticed by one particular part of me—my hair. Like my mother and several siblings, I had what they called "good Irish hair"—thick, curly, and red as a flame. The more I thought about it, the more I realized the short savage had been talking to his companion about my hair e'en when we were in the loft. Every morning he watched in open fascination as I retied my hair in a bun, and once whilst I braided my hair for sleeping, he reached out to take one of my curls in his hand, holding it as if it were a tiny bird he'd found fallen from a tree. When I pulled away in alarm, he withdrew his hand, smiling sheepishly.

I found this most unsettling. After all, the savages are known to be peculiar when it comes to hair, plucking their own heads clean or torturing their locks into bizarre coifs, ornamented with feathers and bones. It goes without saying the heathens are notorious for collecting human scalps, and I couldn't help but wonder if my short friend's broad smile was prompted by picturing my bright red locks as the prized centerpiece of his personal scalp collection.

But e'en as the thought occurred to me, I knew it could not be true. Whilst I fully believed his taller companion was capable of murder, I knew in my heart this short fellow was far too gentle to be plotting evil against me.

As for his interest in me—well, e'en tho' my mother snorted at Liza's warning about the fish and said she'd drown me before she'd let me entice a savage, I knew I was in no position to reject this fellow's timorous advances should they grow bolder. Not only did my life depend on his good graces, but I could not help but be moved by his many kindnesses. No one had e'er been so solicitous of me, making certain I was as comfortable as possible under such extreme circumstances. How could I not be touched, e'en flattered by his obvious admiration?

I should add that I was not like my mother, who considered savages a scourge of nature, much like rats, fleas, or lice. In truth, I knew little about savages 'til we moved to the frontier when I was fifteen, and then all I knew was stories I heard about their crimes, atrocities, and outrages. The only real thought I'd e'er given Indians was to wonder why my parents were determined to live near beings they so disdained instead of returning to the bosom of civilization where I know I, at least, would have preferred to be. Thus it was that when I suddenly found myself at the mercy of these savage beasts and understood my very survival depended utterly on their peculiarities, you may be sure I was keen to learn all I could of their ways and gratefully accept any favor I was given.

The short savage attempted to make his name known to me, but all I could discern was that it had a lot of "s," "sh," and "w" sounds. It took some effort before I could say e'en one small part of his name to his satisfaction, after which he worked to explain in gestures what his name meant. I laughed at his contrivances, and he

laughed along with me but continued trying to make me understand. Finally it dawned on me he was saying something about
"dreaming" or "seeing things that aren't there," and my smile faded
into shock.

For as long as I could remember, my mother chid me for being
a dreamer, an idler, a gatherer of wool. She accused me of wallowing in dreams the way a hog wallows in mud, saying I used day-
dreaming to escape the tedium of my work-a-day world. I ne'er
denied it, nor did I understand why the accusation was applied with
such venom, but I did understand my mother considered idle rev-
erie a sin. And now here was this man unabashedly proclaiming his
very name meant "dreamer" as if it were a mark of great distinc-
tion.

Syawa, as I came to call him, saw my shift in attitude and was
concerned. When I tried to explain in gestures and grimaces that I,
too, was something of a dreamer, he was nigh beside himself with
delight. He turned to gabble at his companion with great anima-
tion, and I watched uneasily as they discussed my shameful admis-
sion.

For his part, the taller man was quiet and aloof, quite comely in
his savage way, observing the scenes 'round him with detached curiosity, as I might watch ants on a sandhill struggling to carry off a
crumb of cake. He showed not the slightest interest in me and, in
fact, rarely looked my way if he could avoid it. His only concern was
the safety and happiness of his companion, to whom he was clearly
devoted. The bond between them was so warm and affectionate, I
at first assumed they must be brothers, but quickly concluded they
were too physically dissimilar to be closely related.

Syawa told me his friend's name, but to me it was naught but a
briar-patch of unpronounceable syllables—almost none of the

sounds have any equivalent in the English language. The best I could do was pick out an "h," a "kt," and an "r." Thus I came to call the tall one "Hector."

Once the lines of communication were opened, Syawa ne'er stopt talking. He wanted to know my name, of course, and when I told him it was Katie O'Toole, he laughed and chattered to his friend about this remarkable fact. Hector listened, half-smiling as if he understood what Syawa was saying without necessarily agreeing. Impatient, Syawa turned back to me and asked in gestures what my name meant. I was hard-presst to explain without words that my name meant only that I was my father's daughter and my family called me Katie.

Syawa went on to make me understand that the sounds of my name were very similar to the phrase in his language which means "sun setting into the sea," and because the fiery color of my hair reminded him of a sunset, he made much of this coincidence. I must have seemed as dubious as Hector, for my ear failed to hear a similarity between the sounds of his language and mine, but I did not complain when Syawa began calling me "Kay-oot-li."

Unfortunately, the more I understood my new friend, the less tolerant my mother became of his attentions. She flinched every time he approached, snarling that he stank and was ugly and was clearly mentally deficient. In truth, the frantic pace of our forced march, day after day after day, through hardships of weather, terrain, and privation, had taken a toll on my mother, who was very near the end of her endurance. Liza and I held her up between us as best we could, but the leather strap that bound us frequently tangled in brambles, which made the savages grumble. William warned unhappily that he heard talk of dispatching her.

At some point, when Liza and I had to stop yet again to pry our strap from a bush, Syawa came o'er to cut the thong that bound me to my mother. The other savages protested mightily, clearly insisting I would run away, but Syawa flashed that relentless smile of his and pointed out I was helping my mother, for which I needed both arms. Then he turned to me. I lowered my eyes and breathed heavily, keenly aware all the savages were looking at me. Syawa asked me something, but I was too afraid to look up to see his gestures.

He put his finger on my chin and lifted my face. He smiled as if an exotic butterfly had just landed on his fingertip, and with his free hand he gestured, asking if I was going to run away. I shook my head, my heart pounding as much as it did when he and his tall friend first burst into the loft at home. He turned to the rest of the savages and gestured, assuring them I would stay.

Mother immediately began whispering that as soon as it was dark, I must untie her so we could flee. For the rest of the day, as I practically carried her through the forest, she pestered me about how it was up to me to save us all. Eventually Liza joined in, and we squabbled in whispers 'til William hissed that if we kept this up, the savages would kill us all long before nightfall.

We continued in silence. I spent the evening trying to decipher Syawa's gestures as he told the assemblage of savages an elaborate story, during which my mother and Liza frequently urged me to untie them. When I continued to ignore them, they grew silent, but every time I glanced at my mother thereafter, I found her glaring at me in furious reproach.

She should have known her hate-stare would have no effect upon me; it was, after all, pretty much the same way she'd looked at me every single day of my life.

~ 3 ~

I DISREMEMBER HOW LONG WE hiked after the attack on our Pennsylvania farm, but 'twas surely a week—perhaps ten days. The most trying moments came when we were dragged 'cross rivers of various depths, but I scarce recall those ordeals, for in water I was terrified beyond reason. In any case, we eventually arrived at a savage village where we were received with much jubilation.

William was tied to a pole near the river, but Mother and Eliza were finally unbound as I. Rather than run off as they had urged me to do, they huddled with me and William as we all awaited the dispensation of our fates. Because we saw no more of our children, Liza fell into a deep despondency from which e'en the threat of pain to her own person was met with absolute indifference.

From our vantage point, we could see the village consisted of perhaps twenty or thirty squalid bark huts erected haphazardly amongst the trees on a small rise well away from the river. I cannot guess how many people lived there, for there was much coming and going, hollering, laughing, and merrymaking. The bloody scalps of our family were displayed and rejoiced o'er by everyone from grizzled grandmothers to naked toddlers. O'erwrought youngsters occasionally ran down the riverbank to beat William with sticks, at which event we women could only cling to each other, cowering, praying the Lord to preserve him.

Soon after our arrival, a group of men removed William, whilst a group of women took me, Mother, and Liza to a secluded part of the river. The women explained in garbled English we must remove our clothes and go into the water, but Mother howled, sure they meant to drown us. She had to be dragged into the river fully clothed, squawking and kicking the whole way. In the meantime, Liza and I slowly disrobed and, shivering, edged our way into the icy depths as the amused Indian women took turns plunging our wailing mother under the surface. They e'en managed to remove her clothes at last, at which point we were all scrubbed with sand.

Tho' it felt as if the women wanted to scrub the white right off us, I soon realized the cold water was intended to remove only our lice and fleas, which was accomplisht. By the time we were allowed out of the river, our clothes were gone, replaced by new French-style clothing. We quickly covered our nakedness and rejoined William, who had also undergone the indignity of a bath.

My two captors had set up their own camp alongside us, confirming my suspicion they were strangers to this place as much as we, and curiosity-seekers came to see them as much as or more than they came to see us. Syawa and Hector clearly enjoyed a certain notoriety, with the natives fawning o'er them the way my family and I might have behaved before the Royal Governor. The important men of the village met with them, and eager women regularly loitered nearby with flirtatious smiles. Occasionally one or the other of my guardians wandered off, and several times Syawa invited me to go somewhere with him, but I was too terrified to leave my family and he did not force me.

A day passed, and then two, with nothing untoward occurring. We O'Tooles comforted each other, our main preoccupation being to find food. Syawa still gave me a portion of whate'er he and Hector ate, but because no one gave my family a thing, I felt I must share what I was given with them.

Hector was unhappy about this arrangement and eventually made his sentiments known. 'Twas clear by then that he was the one who procured my food, for Syawa rarely left my side and Hector was oft gone for extended periods, returning with fish or game. A disagreement arose after I divided my portion of a fish with my family, and I remember wondering why Hector was so unhappy—he had a third of that fish, whilst I had only one-fourth of one-third! Ne'ertheless, he said something to Syawa, who said something back to him, which caused Hector to expound his position at length.

Syawa listened to this tirade with his e'er-present smile unaffected. When he replied, he did so in a cheerful and pleasant manner, as if Hector had just been congratulating him instead of complaining about my giving away food. Whate'er Syawa said to Hector was enough to cause the taller man to inhale sharply and hold his tongue. He walked off and said no more about our arrangement.

From what I now know of the Indians, I realize they expected us to trade for food—by sewing, gathering firewood, hauling water, or such like. We, on the other hand, considered ourselves helpless prisoners waiting to be fed. But the longer we went without adequate food, the more my mother suffered from hunger 'til at some point she urged me to press Syawa for more. "Tell him ye'll do what he wants if he gives ye more food," she hissed, nodding at the short savage. "'Tis the least ye can do to sustain the mother who has cared for ye all these years without so much as a word o' thanks."

I wanted to remind her that for most of those years I'd cared for her as much as or more than she'd e'er cared for me and that only a few days earlier she declared she'd drown me before she'd let me entice a savage, but I held my tongue and ignored her command, fearing that if I encouraged Syawa's interest in any way, he might be unwilling to part with me when the time came. I was, after all, still determined to make my way back to Philadelphia and enjoy the fruits of modern civilization. How could I hope to escape the godless wilderness if I entangled myself further with this grinning savage?

And then there was the fact I was not altogether sure I *could* entice Syawa in the way Mother suggested. True tho' it was he watched me all the time, he ne'er made a single lewd nor impertinent suggestion—indeed, quite the opposite. When he approacht me, he was respectful, reserved, almost in awe, greeting me with bowed head and demure smiles. But as measured as he was, he was not intimidated in the way I'd seen so many young men cringe before the girls they courted. Syawa came to me with eagerness and confidence, in much the same way I approached the dear puppy I found when I was eight. In fact, his presumption that I must be as glad to see him as he was to see me began to vex me. My past, my plans for the future—these did not exist for him. All that mattered was that we were together here and now. I felt as if he expected me to be his little lap dog—kindly used and cared for, to be sure, but subject to his will, come what may.

On the other hand, if I had just cause to pull away from Syawa's presumptions, I also had reason to use his affection as a shield. In addition to providing me and my family with what little food we enjoyed, Syawa's sponsorship also made me an object of great interest to the villagers. Tho' my brother was frequently abused and my mother and sister regularly taunted, I was only petted and pampered. Women came to touch my hair, jabbering together in excitement as they looked at my blue eyes. On one occasion, a group of elders came and consulted with Syawa, after which they all stood looking at me, nodding, discussing something at great length. For someone like me who had grown up in a cluster and for whom being singled out was usually a very bad thing, all this attention was most disconcerting.

The one heathen who continued to be unimpressed by me was Syawa's companion. Oh, Hector was respectful enough—e'en deferential in his own stoic way—but for the most part he gave me a wide berth and avoided direct contact. As noted, he protested when I gave away the food he provided, but his protestations were addressed to Syawa, not to me. Indeed, tho' we had been in close proximity for nigh two weeks, Hector made no effort to interact with me. The only time he looked my way was when Syawa talked to me through his convoluted dance of gestures, at which time Hector watched his friend with what I can only describe as amused indulgence. But if, during one of those pantomimed conversations, I happened to catch Hector's eye, he immediately looked away, his half-smile converted instantly into his usual face of stone.

Whilst Hector refused to look at me, I oft studied his interaction with Syawa, ne'er ceasing to be struck by the depth and breadth of the bond between them. 'Twas obvious Hector worship Syawa, and when Syawa chattered on and on as he so oft did—for he was quite a talker—Hector listened with a warm light in his dark eyes. When Hector felt me watching, a flicker of vexation would pass o'er his face, as if I were intruding on a private moment. And tho' I frequently saw Hector interact with other savages in a sharp and confrontational way, his words and demeanor when addressing his friend were almost always soft and deferential—with the notable exception of the time he complained about our eating arrangements. Indeed, it was the abiding affection between these men which intrigued me most about Syawa. Anyone who could inspire such devotion from a companion must be someone worth knowing—especially when that companion was as formidable as Hector.

I should add I was not the only one who found the strange men compelling. Giggling young women regularly came to lure Hector away, and tho' Syawa was neither as well-formed nor as comely as Hector, he, too, could have enjoyed much female companionship had he desired it. Slowly I began to realize why so many Indian women were pampering me—Syawa was gently redirecting their interest in *him*. Thus did my obligation to this peculiar man continue to grow.

On the third afternoon of our stay in this village, Syawa came to me with a small wooden bowl of pottage. I took it gladly for I was deeply distressed with hunger. After supping a mouthful to restore my strength, I took the bowl to William, who was still recovering from his head wound, but Mother lunged for it, causing me to drop the bowl and spill its precious contents o'er the dusty ground. Furious and crazed with hunger, she grabbed my arm and slapt me repeatedly about the face and neck as my sister fell upon the bowl to lick it clean. I was soon able to prize my arm away, but not before Mother snatcht a good handful of my hair and yanked me this way and that, howling all the while about what a wretched daughter I was to starve a mother so.

I did not enjoy being beaten in this manner, but I was so accustomed to it, having suffered such since birth, that I endured the indignity the same way I accepted the biting of fleas or the stench of the privy. My intention, as always when Mother whipt me, was simply to get away as quickly as possible and stay away 'til her choler cooled.

Before I could extricate myself from my mother's grasp, however, Syawa was upon us both. Small tho' he was, his hands were powerful and sure as he reached in to grab my mother's wrists. Startled by this sudden restraint, Mother shrieked in stark terror and collapsed, flopping and floundering to get away. My sister also screamed but managed to keep the bowl as she dove behind William, who, in spite of his bonds, had arisen to try to pull Mother away from her apparent attacker.

Finding myself suddenly released from Mother's grasp, I catapulted backwards only to have the wind knockt out of me when I hit the ground. I struggled to regain my senses, but by the time I could sit up, a crowd had collected and there was much shouting and whooping, especially from the savage children. To my horror I saw that tho' Syawa still held Mother's wrists, he was now very much on the defensive, for she was wildly kicking and biting at him as she wriggled and writhed. William was still trying to get between the two, as much now to defend Syawa as to protect Mother.

The encircling throng suddenly parted as Hector appeared out of nowhere, running at an unbelievable speed from some distant corner of the village. His face bloodless and drawn, his eyes black, his lips presst thin, he seemed to hang in mid-air for one breathless moment as he assessed the situation. Then he fell into the fray, grabbing William by the neck and tossing him aside like a limp dishrag as he snatcht Mother's arm and yanked her from Syawa. He dragged her 'round by that arm, with her all the while howling, kicking, and flailing furiously. I would have gone to her defense, but she was thrashing so hysterically I durst not approach. With a flip of his wrist, Hector tossed her onto her belly and held her down with a foot upon her back; almost immediately she stopt squirming and contented herself with sobbing into the dirt. By then I, too, was crying as I cringed beside a bush, my arms wrapt 'round my knees.

Breathing heavily, Hector scanned the scene before reaching a hand out to Syawa, who had fallen backwards and now sheepishly accepted the assistance to rise. Syawa dusted himself off whilst Hector anxiously looked him o'er, asking something repeatedly. As Syawa explained the situation, Mother quietly whimpered under Hector's foot and the rest of us cowered, waiting to see what the furious savage would do next. With his jaw clenched and nostrils flared, Hector reminded me of that awful moment in the loft when I feared my murderer was upon me, and I once again felt the thrill of pure terror.

But just as at our first meeting, Syawa began talking in that quiet, calming, steady tone of his, and the tension dissipated. Hector's brow was still deeply furrowed, but after giving my mother's back a final shove with his foot, he turned on the jeering children and shouted. E'en with the language barrier, everyone knew exactly what Hector said, and the crowd immediately dispersed.

After a long moment in which Mother moaned, I held my knees and trembled, and Syawa continued his soft, soothing placations, Hector finally raised his hand to ask a question through gritted teeth. Syawa smiled and nodded, holding out his arms as if to say, "You see? I am wholly unhurt."

Hector nodded, but before he turned to walk away, he gave me a glance that chilled me to the bone. He was angry, resentful, disgusted. But mostly he was accusative—clearly blaming me for endangering his friend. This, I suddenly realized, was probably why Hector had complained about my sharing food. He knew, sooner or later, my actions would threaten Syawa. I lowered my eyes, embarrassed and ashamed.

Syawa would have none of it. With William and Eliza consoling Mother, Syawa squatted beside me to lay his hand on my shoulder. He spoke softly, and tho' I did not understand his words, I appreciated the obvious comfort he offered. He bade me rise and come with him, leading me to a dwelling at the edge of the village. Chattering away as if I could understand every word, he pulled me inside the hut and settled me beside the warm fire therein. He solicited the mistress of that place to give me another bowl of pottage, which I ate with eyes averted, thinking of my mother so hungry and abandoned in the cold. I would have wept for her, but Syawa was making funny faces as he babbled in an effort to make me smile. I did smile, of course, because he was so relentlessly cheerful and kind, but inside I was trembling, wondering what was to become of us all. I felt so very, very guilty about my mother.

She always said I was going to be the death of her, and I was beginning to fear her little jest might just come true.

~ 4 ~

PERHAPS OUR FAMILY SQUABBLE prompted savage action, or perhaps action had been planned for some time. I know not. What I do know is that the day after our tussle, everything changed. Warriors began painting themselves and loading packs for travel.

Eliza said the commotion I'd caused must have riled our hosts, who were now preparing to finish us off. "Not that *you* have to fret," she sneered. "Your little imp will no doubt preserve you to watch the rest of us burn."

I could think of no reply to this cold accusation, especially since I was more than a little afraid Liza might be right.

A huge fire was ignited in the center of the village and the savages of that community gathered 'round. Warriors did their devilish dances, women distributed food, and children ran hither and thither with dogs yapping at their heels. The atmosphere was quite festive and gay, but my family and I could scarce enjoy the revelries. We huddled together, our enmity forgotten as we strove to pass what might be the final moments of our lives in prayer.

My guardians were nowhere to be seen, and I wondered at their absence. Had the incident with my mother finally snuffed Syawa's interest? 'Twould not be the first time my mother had driven off a suitor. Before I could linger o'er this worry, however, a group of painted warriors came to escort us to a mat before the fire. Directly across the fire from us was another mat, upon which sat a group of older men and women. With them were two men, elaborately painted and ornamented. Only after staring at these specters for several moments did I recognize Syawa and Hector.

The chattering of the crowd stopt as an old man arose to speak loudly at some length. As soon as the oration began, a fellow sitting behind us leant forward to speak in perfect English. Upon looking at him more closely, I discerned he was a white man, but he had lived amongst the heathen long enough to be nigh indistinguishable from them. He explained the speaker was reviewing a list of "offenses" committed by the colonists which led up to the "battle" of our capture. Whilst the savages reacted with glee to gruesome descriptions of the murders of our family members, my mother and sister wept. William and I exchanged nervous glances, more concerned about the future than the past. As the speaker babbled on, our translator explained we were to be taken to some fort, where we would be ransomed back to whate'er remained of our family. There followed a lengthy harangue against the colonists, as well as a declaration in support of the French.

Having little interest in politics, I allowed my mind to wander as my eyes scanned the crowd. I could feel Syawa's gaze upon me, and every time I glanced his way, I found him smiling that smile of his, as if entirely oblivious to the gravity of my position and the misery I suffered. The longer the orator's speech went on, the more excited Syawa became, as if he were a child on Christmas morning, eagerly awaiting his share of pudding. I tried not to look at him, but it was as if he willed me to do so, and every time I gave in to the urge and glanced his way, he was a little more delighted than the time before. Eventually I found I could not help but smile back, which caused him to grin with such abandon that I giggled and must clamp my hand upon my mouth to prevent another outburst.

Shortly thereafter the droning tone of the speaker changed, and our translator spoke more urgently. Tomorrow, he said, the captives would be removed. But here and now a decision must be made. William, Eliza, Mother, and I looked at each other in trepidation.

The translator told us the speaker was now recognizing the presence of two travelers, who were, he said, cousins of cousins from the Dawn of Time, participating in the ancient ritual of a Sacred Journey.

At that point, wood was added to the fire and as sparks whirled skyward and flames leapt high, Syawa was suddenly, almost supernaturally, standing before the fire. The crowd murmured, then hushed in anticipation. First he sang a song—a haunting, wistful tune in a strong, vibrant tenor. Then he began telling his tale, using his elaborate gestures. Because he moved slowly 'round the fire as he waved his hands, his actions seemed more like an exotic dance than a story, but story it was—and what a story!

The Dreamer of Dreams, the translator said, had been given a Vision upon which he was compelled to act. In his Vision he saw a Creature of Fire and Ice who would bring to his people the Great Gift of Immortality, and so he asked his friend from childhood to assist him, to fight for him and help find the creature from his Vision. Tho' the translator spoke almost too rapidly as he read the gestures, the gist of the story was that my two guardians had traversed many lands through many seasons, endured many hardships, and experienced many adventures, all to arrive at this time and this place.

For a moment I stared at the ground, thinking of what I knew

of these two young men. It had been clear Hector was serving Syawa as something of a bodyguard, and now I understood why.
What was not clear was whether these two apparently intelligent
and reasonable fellows seriously believed they might encounter and
capture a fantastical creature the likes of which can exist only in
dreams. A being made of fire and ice? Preposterous!

It was as I was thinking these things that the translator reached
out to touch my arm to renew my full attention. "On this day," he
said, speaking slowly and dramatically, "the Seer stands before us to
reveal the subject of his Sacred Vision. With our help, he has found
a Creature with hair of Fire and eyes of Ice!"

I blush now to admit how long I sat looking expectantly 'round
the crowd, waiting for someone to unveil this marvelous Creature.
I saw that Syawa was now standing directly across the fire from me,
staring at me, but because he was always staring at me, I saw no
significance in his gaze. It was only when I realized every single
other person in that gathering was also staring at me that I began to
apprehend the import of what had been said.

The Creature of Fire and Ice was me.

I swallowed hard as I slowly returned my eyes to Syawa. He
was smiling, as always, but this time his smile was different—it was
as if he had seen inside my soul and understood everything he saw
there. From another man, I might've seen that smile as almost a
smirk, but from Syawa it felt more like a hand extended in support,
a warm embrace to bolster me in my moment of crisis. I blinked
rapidly, shifting my eyes to the ground. My heart was pounding and
my stomach was rolling. What in the world was the meaning of this
bizarre declaration? I was not some mythical creature, worthy of a
Sacred Journey. I was a middling girl in a middling family from a
middling settlement which no longer existed!

Suddenly my mother, sitting between my brother and sister, turned on me, her face red and swollen in fury. *"You!"* she shrieked, showering me with spittle. " 'Twas all because of *you*! The massacre, the murder—everythin' ruined, everyone dead— all because some filthy wee savage wanted him a red-head gal!"

Eliza turned on me, too, venom in her eyes. "I knowed you was responsible, Katie! We always said you was cursed, and now 'tis proven!"

As Mother and Eliza thus condemned me, William eyed the crowd with grave solemnity, the tension in his eyes mounting. I followed his line of vision and saw Syawa coming to us, and, except for Mother and Liza, the entire populace now sat in absolute silence, watching with rapt attention. Syawa knelt before me, smiling still, compelling my eyes to meet his gaze as his hands began to move.

The translator apologized for the fact that he must insert himself into this delicate conversation, and I nodded, not knowing if the apology came from the translator or Syawa. It mattered little. I felt as if I had floated outside myself at this point, and the real me was sitting at the edge of the clearing watching this weird scene unfold as if it was happening to someone else.

With his hands, Syawa explained that because of the perilous nature of the Journey, it was essential the Creature of Fire and Ice *accept* the challenge. The translator hesitated, watching Syawa's movements closely. He then turned to me and said the Dreamer of Dreams wanted me to understand that, for the Vision to be realized, I must *choose* to go on this arduous adventure.

"Will you go with us?" Syawa's final gesture needed no translation. He let his hands fall into his lap, awaiting my reply. His smile was confident and sure, very warm, inexplicably fond of me.

I was near panic. My mother and sister were weeping now,

snuffling on each other's shoulders. I swallowed hard and asked the translator to help me make sure I understood the terms of this request. Was Syawa saying I might decide for myself whether or not to go, and that if I chose *not* to go, I could stay with my family and suffer no ill effects as the result of my refusal?

Syawa's answer was swift and short. I was free to go or stay, and in either case neither I nor my family would be harmed in any way. Regardless, my family members would embark on their hike to the French fort the next day.

The translator then began speaking rapidly, waving his hands about so that everyone would know what he was saying. "This is not a decision to undertake lightly," he told me. "I myself was taken from my white family many years ago, and I long suffered the anguish of that separation. Please understand that if you go with these men, you will travel farther than anyone could follow, and you will ne'er see anyone from your family again. You will die and be reborn, your former life reduced to a fading dream."

Syawa was still on his knees before me, but I would not look up at him, for I knew he must still be smiling with those expectant eyes. Beside me I heard Eliza whisper something, and then my mother leant across William to take my upper arm in her hand and squeeze tight. I felt more than saw Syawa tense up and heard all the spectators inhale and hold their breath as one being.

"Yer not actually considerin' goin' off with this puny devil, are ye?" Mother gasped, and the translator's hands flew. "Yer the daughter of a nobleman, the great-great-granddaughter of kings, and yer of pure marriageable age! How dare ye e'en consider abandonin' yer poor mother in her darkest hour? M'husband's gone, the only son left me here is wounded, and yer sister has lost her man an' boys both! 'Tis yer Christian duty to care for me the way I cared for my mother all her days. If the heathen says you may refuse him, refuse him you will, y'miser'ble slut!"

The crowd stirred as they watched the gestures of the translator. William whispered he was prepared to fight should the savages turn on me when I refused the offer. When I continued silent, Liza hissed, "Katie! D'you not see how unhinged this dark runt is? He grins like a cat night and day, he fumbles endlessly with his hands, and he boasts of wild dreams as if 'tis a badge of honor, not a mark o' madness! How can y'e'en consider goin' off with him?"

Mother snorted derisively. "Yer just fool enough to do this, ain't ya, Katie? So let me tell ya what'll happen if y'do. That little squirt there believes yer something y'know damned well yer not. 'Twill go hard on you when he realizes how wrong he was! Mark m'words, Katie—he'll make ye pay for his mistake! And ye'll pay dear!"

I thought of my mother's marriage, of all the marriages I'd seen through my seventeen years. In a flash, I saw the infinite hardships of my early days, the perpetual quarrels and recriminations, the constant conflicts and endless posturing for power. I saw all the potential outcomes for my life if I stayed within the bosom of my family—the struggles, the contempt, the shame, and the greed. 'Twas all so petty, so painful, and so utterly meaningless. I believed with all my heart that Eliza was right and Syawa was most likely mad, but for the life of me I could not understand why I should choose sanity o'er madness when sanity hurt so much and madness seemed so sweet. I could feel my mother's claws digging through my sleeve into the flesh of my upper arm, and I squirmed the same way I did when I was five and she was trying to keep me still in church. As I moved, my gaze shifted and I happened to see Syawa's face.

He was staring at me with such warmth, such affection, such

complete and utter confidence. Yes, he was short and strange and perhaps simple-minded and undoubtedly insane. But he made me feel so special, so treasured, so important. I'd ne'er felt that I mattered at all, much less that I mattered so much. Sad to say, I'd ne'er in my life felt appreciated in any way, and it was intoxicating, that feeling. I loved it. I wanted to keep feeling that way.

Besides, I ne'er could pass up a chance to torment my mother.

I came back to myself, suddenly, as if the me that had been watching these events from the edge of the forest floated right o'er the crowd and fell back into my body. I jerked my arm from my mother's grasp to crawl over to Syawa. I knelt before him and lifted my right hand to point to my chest. Then I made a walking motion with my fingers, moving toward him. I pointed at him and nodded.

Syawa lifted his face and whooped in joy. The entire populace joined in, like a pack of wolves howling at the moon. Only my family did not participate in the celebration—well, them and Hector, who was still sitting on the mat with the elders, apparently as shocked as my mother and sister. Only when Syawa raced o'er to gabble at him in their foreign tongue did Hector finally react. I saw relief wash o'er him as he reached out to pull Syawa's head to his, their foreheads touching for a moment in a tender testament to the bond between them.

I inhaled deeply and sighed as I turned to my family members, who were all viciously berating me for being such a goddamned fool. I smiled to myself.

I knew I'd made the right decision.

~ 5 ~

B Y THE NEXT MORNING, of course, I had completely changed my mind, but 'twas far too late to reconsider. All I could do was raise a trembling hand to wave good-bye as the same band of warriors who'd captured us led my family members off to the northeast. Only William returned my pitiful gesture; my mother and sister merely sneered. When they were out of sight, I slowly turned to my two strange companions, who stood awaiting me patiently. With ragged breath and eyes downcast, I followed as they set off to the west.

I was terrified. I have done many stupid things in my life, but none more foolhardy than this. What was I doing? Why was I doing it? Was I really willing to throw my life away, just to get back at my wretched mother? Come now, Katie—think, *think!* How will ye get back to Philadelphia? My mind raced, coming up with wild plans for escaping so I could either catch up with my kin or somehow return to civilization on my own. One way or another I knew I must return to Philadelphia.

But Syawa gave me no idle time to devise ill-fated plans. As soon as we set off, he veritably bounced along the trail, walking beside me first on one side, then the other, chattering all the while like a squirrel gathering fat nuts. I, of course, understood none of what he said, but I could not help but be touched by his enthusiasm.

Hector set a wearisome pace, trotting along a trail only he could see. I was young and hale and at first I thought I did an admirable job of keeping up, but after several hours of scurrying along I simply must rest. That's when I realized Hector had actually been holding himself back for my benefit. Whilst I rested and Syawa engaged me with his non-stop blather, Hector paced impatiently, scowling, tight-lipped, at the trail ahead. Thereafter I required frequent rests, which Syawa was perfectly happy to oblige, but Hector bestowed only grudgingly.

From the start, I worried about Hector. As frightening as I found him to be, I was e'en more puzzled by him. He clearly resented my presence—but why? If he had known Syawa was looking for someone to take back to his people, why did he resent me? Did he not expect Syawa's Journey to be successful? Or did he just not believe *I* was the person Syawa was looking for?

I had little time to spare for pondering such curiosities, as my immediate task was to learn Syawa's language. I felt sure I could accomplish this goal quickly, as my father, who spoke five languages, had forced us all to learn Latin and French e'en as we learnt English. Tho' my Latin was choppy, I was fairly fluent in French, for it was the language my siblings and I used whene'er we wanted to keep secrets from Mother. Because of my experience with languages, I was confident I could soon master Syawa's savage tongue.

My confidence proved overly optimistic.

Syawa began by telling me words for things we saw along the trail—tree, cloud, rock—but I was immediately baffled when he seemed to have multiple words for most objects. Words changed, apparently at random, depending upon how the object was used, seen, or talked about, and who was doing the using, seeing, or talking. What was worse, his language was composed of sounds unlike any I'd e'er heard—stranger e'en than the weird sounds of Gaelic my gran occasionally used—and I learnt to my dismay that the mispronunciation of a single syllable could completely alter a word's meaning. Try tho' I might, I uttered few words to Syawa's satisfaction. He repeated them again and again, but the nuances eluded me. Still, he remained good-natured about my efforts and was absolutely delighted by my determination.

I soon learnt it best to memorize entire phrases rather than simple words, and so I focused on those collections of sounds that meant "I must rest" or "I am hungry" or "I am ready." In that way Syawa and I laboriously began to communicate in words at long last.

Of course, the fact that Syawa was such an indefatigable talker meant I came to understand his meaning long before I could speak myself. Whene'er we stopt, he chattered on about himself, his family, his people, and his world through slow, oft-repeated phrases and his complex vocabulary of gestures. Using small stones to represent years, he explained he was twenty-five, Hector twenty-one. I was surprised to learn they were so much older than I'd thought, but their lack of beards and body hair made them seem young. Syawa went on to make me understand how unusual it was for any of his people to undertake the sort of Journey they were on, but added with a grin that he was very unusual amongst his people in many ways. I could certainly believe *that*—he was such a peculiar fellow, I felt certain he would stand out in any crowd.

After we supt on the first night of our journey, Hector immediately went to sleep as Syawa worked hard to explain that his people were nothing like the Indians we'd just left. Instead of living in crude bark huts, for example, his people lived in spacious wooden houses more like the one in which he'd found me. He also assured me that, unlike the Indians of Pennsylvania, who achieved notoriety through war, or my own people, who acquired power through property, his people earned status by being accomplisht artisans.

I wish I could impart how daunting it was for Syawa to explain such complex concepts through naught but gestures, but he was resolute and I was eager to learn. I frowned in concentration as he painstakingly pantomimed building, carving, painting, weaving, and I nodded as I slowly absorbed his meaning. His people, I concluded, took great pride in craftsmanship.

Once he made me understand how important these refined skills were to his people, he went on to make clear, in no uncertain terms, that he, alas, did not excel at any of those endeavors. "I—not do—building, carving, painting," he told me, shrugging in a self-deprecating way, tho' his perpetual smile was still intact. "I think, dream—alone much. No friend—but him." And he pointed to Hector, rolled up in his sleeping fur.

From this I deduced Syawa was a loner, an outcast, someone who did not fit very well within the world he knew, and this news only made him more appealing to me. "I—do much," I told him, trying hard to replicate the sounds he'd made. "But I—do much alone. No friend—no him."

Syawa's smile flickered as he sympathized, his black eyes shining. "You—alone—not now," he said softly. He took my hand and gestured from me to him to our joined hands. "You—me—together—forever."

I smiled, tears in my eyes, and slowly repeated the sounds he'd made. He grinned, and for the first time in my miserable life, I had some inkling of what it was to be wanted, to be loved. I suppose that was the moment in which it finally occurred to me I might not make it back to Philadelphia after all.

As plain as I found this declaration of love to be, it was yet unclear to me whether or not Syawa now considered us to be husband and wife; save for this one romantic moment, he continued to treat me as if I were little more than a beloved sister. I had no words to inquire as to what his ultimate intentions were, but I deduced his objective must, of course, be marriage, because, after all, that's what men and women do. I did not particularly relish the idea of being married to a savage, but, then again, I did not particularly relish the idea of being married to any man. Having no means or power to avoid it, however, I had long since concluded marriage was something which would inevitably befall me, like rotting teeth or running bowels, and I was resigned to making the best of it when it occurred. As Gran would say, "God's Will be done."

Thus, in the quiet times of our journey, whilst trotting through the thick forest at a pace which made all attempts at conversation impossible, I pondered what marriage to this odd fellow might mean. I had certainly ne'er imagined myself betrothed to such an unlikely candidate. His incessant smile, while decidedly pleasant, made him seem, as Liza suggested, simple-minded, and his admitted predilection for dreaming, coupled with his acknowledged inability to excel at everyday tasks, suggested he was probably going to be a poor provider. On the other hand, his smallish stature and unremarkable appearance no doubt prevented him from being promiscuous, which made me wonder if the real reason behind his quest to find a "certain woman" was simply the fact that it might require such a journey to find any woman willing to accept him.

And yet, I, myself, was such a peculiar girl that I found his lack of obvious advantages to be a major part of his charm, as I always was one to be drawn to the lame puppy or the runt hog of the litter. I freely admit I admired Syawa's confession of shortcomings, not to mention his lack of guile and unwavering good humor in the face of hardship, conflict, and danger—mostly because those traits were so foreign to my experience of men. No man I'd e'er known would admit to being weak or frightened or worried or wrong, for every man I'd e'er known was always locked in a self-imposed struggle to be the biggest, the brightest, the toughest, or the meanest. Hector, whose face was either entirely emotionless or set in a scowl, was much more like every other man I'd e'er known.

But e'en as I was drawn to Syawa's uniqueness, I was unnerved by it as well. Did I really want to spend my life obliged to a grinning fool, someone who seemed half-witted, a man others might well dismiss as the equivalent of a village idiot?

Which is not to say I thought Syawa stupid. Clearly he was not. The determination and dedication required to trek through miles of hostile territory to find the woman of his dreams was not only flattering and romantic, but the mark of a strong character as well. Any reasonable person might view his "quest" as half-baked and detached from reality, but I was enough of a dreamer myself to understand the nature of his obsession and respect it. He might be mad, as my sister proclaimed, but, for me, madness was far from a disqualifier. Little in life had e'er made sense to me.

Besides, there was one thing about Syawa I found utterly irresistible—his glibness of tongue. At first, of course, I understood naught of what he said, but I was tickled by the fact he ne'er ran out of things to say. He chattered on like a bird at dawn, and tho' I knew not what he was talking about, I truly enjoyed listening to him. Most evenings, both whilst we were with my family and thereafter, Syawa passed the time by telling some sort of story, which Hector—who was the only one who understood him—attended with great interest. Sometimes Hector was amused by the tales, sometimes saddened, but always he was entertained. I found myself envying the tall, silent man because he clearly derived so much pleasure from listening to his friend's words.

After the story each night, Hector curled up in his fur and went right to sleep, but Syawa always continued to sit by the fire and talk, e'en after I wrapt myself in my bearskin and lay down to sleep as well. At first I thought he did this to prevent me from attempting a nocturnal escape, for Syawa's voice had such a hypnotic effect I inevitably fell asleep long before he stopt talking, but he continued the ritual long after he must've known I had no intention of slipping away during the night.

Puzzling o'er why Syawa's stories had such an effect on me, I came to believe 'twas because he reminded me of my father, who was quite a storyteller himself. The rare occasions during my childhood when my family was happy occurred when Father was sufficiently liquored up to be chatty, but not so drunk as to be itching for a fight. Then he would sit before the fire and tell long, lingering, delicious tales of books he'd read or legends he himself had been told as a child. The only time I e'er truly loved my father was when he was telling one of his long stories, and the only time I actually enjoyed being a member of my family was when we were all gathered together on a dark winter's night, listening to father tell his tales.

So I supposed all this storytelling predisposed me to accept the peculiarities of the strange little Indian who seemed so besotted by me, and thinking about my father reminded me that e'en if I might have found a considerably more appealing companion back amongst my own people, I was just as likely to end up with someone considerably worse. Thus I found myself floating farther and farther from my former life, swept away by the relentless current of Syawa's cheerful chatter, and I snapt awake each morning to find him lying near me in his own sleeping fur, smiling, as if he, himself, ne'er slept.

It occurred to me the real reason behind the babble was to keep my thoughts from dwelling on the drastic way the course of my life had been diverted, and for that I was grateful. It goes without saying I was in desperate need of ongoing distraction from the tremendous weariness I suffered—those first days on the trail were sheer torture. Up and down we went, 'round and 'round, and on and on and on. Brambles tore at my clothing, rocks and roots tript me, my hand-me-down shoes left my feet blistered, oozing, and raw. I bowed my head each time Hector grumbled about stopping, but Syawa only laughed and said all was well. Time and again he said the three of us were exactly where we should be.

Neither Hector nor I could very well argue with that.

~ 6 ~

As my strength and endurance improved, our pace quickened, with one notable exception—water crossings. I loathed getting wet, but the invisible trail we followed forced me to wade through innumerable swamps and streams that left my shoes soggy, squeaky, and chafing my feet. Worse still, I was oft required to slog across much larger bodies of water which soaked my skirts to the skin. Oh, how much more bitterly did the March wind bite with clammy, cold cloth clinging to my legs!

Sometimes it rained, but I recall only one afternoon when a downpour actually delayed us. I enjoyed those hours huddled under the ingenious tent my companions constructed, not only because I was able to rest my throbbing feet, but also because I was able to concentrate more fully on Syawa's language lesson. Unfortunately, all that spring rain only served to swell the streams, making what was already a challenge for me become almost an impossibility.

The day came when my companions perked up and quickened their pace—I knew not why. As we topt a rise, they both whooped and ran recklessly down the hillside, shedding their packs so they could dive headlong into the water of a sizeable river. I followed them sedately and stood on the riverbank, forlorn, watching as they splashed about. Eventually Syawa came back to coax me in, but either he did not understand or could not believe I was unable to swim a lick. He told Hector to walk out to the middle of the stream to show me the water was no deeper than his chest, but I found this revelation small comfort in the face of what seemed to me to be a raging torrent.

In the end the men had to drag me across the river, each clutching an arm, whilst I kept my eyes tightly shut and whimpered the whole way. For the first time in our acquaintance, Syawa seemed unhappy when we reached the opposite shore and I fell to my knees sobbing, o'ercome by anxiety. His face was grim as he said something to Hector, but the disgusted tone of Hector's reply was unmistakable.

Still on my knees in the mud, I glanced up as Hector spoke. He was saying something about smell—something about how it was too bad the river had not washed away the smell of my clothing. At that, my tears dried up. I rose shakily and walked back into the river 'til the water was up to my waist. I knelt down and rubbed the water into my clothes, glaring at Hector, who watched in astonishment. I scrubbed myself 'til I felt sure my "smell" had been washed away, then stomped out of the water and walked to a log where I could sit and furiously wring out my skirts.

Syawa grinned at me, delight in his eyes. "You understand his words," he said.

Yes, I was learning the language, but I still despised water, and so on the day we arrived at a high bank beside a very large river, I knew I was in serious trouble. There was no way I was going to be able to walk across this one, e'en with my companions dragging me by the arms. But as I stood staring down at the watery depths in dismay, Syawa and Hector were peering at something on the far shore, which, when at last I followed their gaze, I found to be an Indian village. The more I looked, the larger the village appeared, and, preoccupied as I was with scrutinizing the huts and people, I failed to see several large canoes 'til they were in the river and coming our way. We had been spotted, which was, apparently, what my companions expected.

We descended to the riverbank to meet the occupants of the canoes, who obviously knew Syawa and Hector. This, I assumed, must be our destination, the home village of my companions. The villagers eyed me warily as they invited us into their canoes.

Grateful as I was not to be required to confront the current of this river on my own, I was far from eager to set foot in one of those wobbling, flimsy watercrafts, but before I could begin to fret and without a word of warning, Syawa lifted me up and deposited me unceremoniously in the middle of a canoe. I clung to his arm 'til he gently transferred my death-grip to the side of the vessel. Then he climbed in before me. The rickety craft was pushed into the current, and I clutched both sides with white-knuckled hands, nervous as a cat the whole way.

As miserable as I was, I took note that Hector, leaning back in the neighboring canoe, was as comfortable and relaxed as I had e'er seen him. Syawa, too, held his face up to drink in the sweet, open breeze of the water-cooled air. Sitting behind him, I could see only a part of his smile, but somehow it seemed sad to me, wistful, tinged with longing. I wondered why his homecoming should make him sad—was he sorry his adventures were finisht? Or was he sorry now to be returning with someone like me?

I quickly discovered this village was not Syawa's home at all, but only a place he and Hector had visited on their journey eastward. I believe my companions intended to stop for no more than a night or two, but we ended up staying for several days because shortly after we arrived, my monthly flow began. Aware of my situation, I excused myself to go to the bushes wherein I might tend nature's business, but an old woman came after me, jabbering away in her incomprehensible tongue. Tho' I understood naught of her words, I knew enough of reading gestures by this time to see she was absolutely insisting I follow her to a bark-covered dwelling at the edge of the village, where she literally pushed me through the deerskin-covered doorhole.

Inside the dark hut I found women of various ages lounging 'round a central fire, engaged in casual conversation. When I stumbled in, they all froze and stared at me as I crouched before them, blinking, waiting for my eyes to adjust to the dim light. The old woman came in and gabbled away, apparently explaining who I was and why I was there. I was so discomfited by the way they all stared at me that I very nigh turned and ran, but then a woman who was perhaps ten years older than I asked me something. Her voice was kind and gentle, but, of course, I could not understand her, and I told her so in English. Another moment of stunned silence passed before the woman gestured for me to come sit beside her.

This hut, I soon learnt, was the women's lodge, where all ladies go during their monthlies. In a short time, another woman entered, greeted with relief by the others. This woman could speak English, and she told me she grew up in the proximity of an English trading post far to the east. Not long ago, she said, her people had removed to this area, driven from their homeland by encroaching settlers.

My new friend, who was many years older than I, began by

explaining that amongst her people, women always separate themselves from men during their monthlies. I was, at first, appalled to find myself thus shut away from my traveling companions, held as a virtual prisoner, but once I resigned myself to my situation, I found the break relaxing and restorative. 'Twas nice not only to have a chance to recover from the rigorous hike, but also to have someone to talk to who could answer at least a few of my questions. O'erwhelmed as I was by ignorance of Indian customs and beliefs, I was in desperate need of advice on how to comport myself whilst living amongst the natives of this land.

My new friend's name was something like Ta-toe-mi. I heard someone call her To-mi, and when I called her by that name, she did not object.

Tomi told me that everyone was quite excited by my presence inasmuch as they had, as I suspected, met Syawa and Hector before and knew all about their Journey. With Tomi as translator, the women in the hut interrogated me about where I was from, how I met Syawa, and whether or not I was human. They seemed to believe Syawa might have conjured me from sheer nothingness and that I must surely be endowed with supernatural powers.

I was unnerved by my fame amongst these strangers, especially since the only reason for it, as far as I could tell, was Syawa's power as storyteller. During his previous stay, he had apparently regaled the inhabitants of this place with an elaborate performance depicting his Vision of a Creature of Fire and Ice, explaining that when he found this phantasm of his dreams, she would bring back to his people a great and glorious gift. Now, of course, all the women presst me to tell them more about the gift.

What could I say? For the most part, I understood little of what they were talking about—not because Tomi was a poor translator, but because their eager questions just seemed so stupid. I suppose I had, up to that time, assumed everyone understood Syawa's story about a Vision was nothing more than a tale he told to justify traipsing all over creation as he looked for a wife. I couldn't believe anyone had taken him seriously. After all, I knew I was not some sort of mystical creature, I believed Syawa was little more than a social misfit, and I assumed the "gift" they were so curious about was clearly a fiction. When I said as much to Tomi and she translated my words, the women in the hut seemed disappointed, but not terribly surprised. Apparently mystical creatures are rarely willing to share their secrets.

Determined not to pretend to be something I was not, I said to Tomi, "But surely you must understand that when Syawa was here before, he was just telling a story. It was a hope he had, a cherished dream perhaps, and, glib as he is, I'm sure he made it a rousing tale, but, still—'twas not real. 'Twas all just words."

Tomi's forehead furrowed as she listened to me. Then she nodded. "Yes, his words are just," she said. "And we, too, cherish his dream as a message of hope. It is truly rousing to see that you are real now, at last."

Taken aback by her complete mangling of the meaning of my words, I could only stare, open-mouthed, whilst she translated for the other women.

After a time, one of the women asked Tomi something, which she translated as an inquiry as to whether or not I was a dreamer like Syawa. From the way they all smiled, I assumed they were laughing at my companion's idiosyncrasy, mocking him for being an idler the way my mother did, and I was determined to defend him against such malicious gossip. "Well, yes," I said defiantly, speaking slowly so as not to be misunderstood this time. "I've always been one to dream a day away, if at all possible." If the women were going to mock my friend, I reckoned they might as well make fun of me, too.

But instead of jeering as I expected, the women seemed almost frightened, as if I'd just told them I'd been known, on occasion, to leap into the air and fly. At last Tomi worked up enough courage to make sure she understood me. "So you, too, are a seer?" she whispered, her head bowed respectfully.

I did not at first appreciate the extent of the misunderstanding, but o'er the course of a lengthy conversation, I finally realized Syawa's gestures to me had not indicated he was a "dreamer" in the sense of "idler," but that he was, in fact "one who sees things others do not," a visionary, or what Christians might call a Prophet. My assumptions up to this point had been entirely wrong. Far from seeing Syawa as a grinning fool, the ladies of this tribe were clearly in awe of him, viewing him the way my people might view an inspired minister of God. By suggesting I was just like him, I had not been defending his reputation at all, but inadvertently elevating my own.

I was shocked, confused, embarrassed. All this time I had regarded my companion as peculiar, a little "off," and in many ways inferior to the average man. I felt I was doing him a favor by extending my friendship, believing that, because he was so strange, he had been forced to wander hundreds of miles to find a woman whose standards were low enough to accept him. But in that dark women's lodge, I learnt Syawa was actually held in the highest esteem by his countrymen and that, because of his supernatural powers, he was revered by everyone he met. I also learnt that as the subject of his Vision, I inspired not only awe, but also a good deal of fear.

By nightfall I was exhausted, but sleep was long in coming. I lay there thinking about how my family had scorned me for tossing my life away on a worthless runt, whilst the Indians all thought there must be something terribly special about me to cause someone of Syawa's high status to undertake such a treacherous Journey on my behalf. The problem was, *everyone* was wrong. Syawa was not a worthless runt, but neither was there anything so special about me. More disturbing for me, however, was the realization of how very wrong I, myself, had been. I had totally misjudged Syawa and, based on that erroneous judgment, I had gone on to make a decision that completely altered the course of my life.

This realization begged the question: what else was I wrong about?

One additional issue of grave concern reared its ugly head in my thoughts. Whilst I had, apparently, been totally wrong about Syawa, he had also been very, very, *very* wrong about me. He did not know it yet, but he had made a horrible mistake. I was no mystical creature, no Vision, no one e'en remotely worthy of a Sacred Journey. I was nothing, no one, and sooner or later Syawa was bound to discover how dead wrong he had been.

Then what would happen to me?

~7~

I SPENT MY TIME in the women's lodge as productively as possible, asking my translator all the questions I wisht I could ask Syawa. Unfortunately, Tomi knew naught of Syawa's people, except that they lived far away and that the journey before me would be far more rigorous than the journey thus far had been. Indeed, Tomi expressed extreme admiration for my courage in being willing to undertake such an adventure, citing this as further proof of the "special powers" that drew Syawa to me.

I tried to explain that if I was undaunted by the challenges before me, it was only because I did not know what they were, and thus the quality she so admired was not courage but ignorance. She did not understand. Nor did she understand that the main reason I was not intimidated by the journey to come was that the journey I had accomplisht thus far was so much more than she could imagine. She knew of English settlements, of course, but when I tried to tell her about Philadelphia and Boston and the vastness of the Atlantic and my ancestral home in Ireland, she could comprehend naught of what I meant.

'Twas so frustrating! Here I finally had the words to talk to someone, and the words absolutely failed me. Everything I told her to try to explain why there was nothing particularly special about me served only to strengthen her conviction that there was, in fact, something terribly special about me.

The one thing I did make Tomi understand, however, was that I needed help communicating. Tho' she knew nothing of the language Syawa and Hector spoke, she was well-versed in their language of gestures, so after telling her I must learn as much of that language as I could in our time together, she signaled with her hands everything she said. In this way, o'er the course of several days, I was able to pick up a basic vocabulary of gestures.

Just before leaving the women's lodge, I asked her privately to show me the gestures which meant "marriage," "husband," and "wife." These were the words I would need in order to make my relationship with Syawa clear. As long as I was at it, I asked her to show me the gestures for "I love you." With a warm smile, she showed me everything I needed to know.

By the time I emerged from the women's lodge, I knew a great deal more than when I entered, but by far the most important lesson I learnt was just how ignorant I was.

For example, one particularly humiliating discovery I made in the women's lodge was that Indians found the odor of my clothing extremely offensive. When Tomi delicately broached this subject, I blushed, recalling the way Hector crinkled his nose at me. Back home, my family members and I ne'er bathed, wearing the same clothes day after day for weeks, e'en months, 'til they were stiff with dried perspiration. The Indians, on the other hand, wore almost no clothing, which was, of course, something my people found far more offensive than a few odd odors.

Upon being told, for the second time, that I stank, I was

tempted to retort that at least I was not a half-naked savage, but because I was the stranger in a strange land, I recognized I must do something to conform. Thus, when Tomi explained women ritually cleanse themselves after their monthlies, I obediently followed her to the secluded section of the riverbank reserved for such a purpose.

I was excruciatingly self-conscious about disrobing in front of the other ladies, but inasmuch as they were all naked or nigh so already, I soon stopt fretting. I remember some uncomfortable comments about how the hair in my nether regions was as red and curly as the hair on my head, but my companions were far more struck by the extreme whiteness of my skin, so unlike the coppery color of their own.

E'en before I was completely undressed, most of the women were diving into the river with the same delight my companions displayed. I tiptoed into the cold depths, reluctant to go farther than necessary. I scrubbed my face, arms, and legs before washing out my waist-long hair. I then turned my attention to my clothing, but the more I scrubbed the thin linen, the more threadbare it became. I laid my things across the budding bushes to dry, wondering how many more washings they would endure.

But then a young woman Tomi identified as her daughter offered me an armload of new clothing—a soft doeskin shift, two loincloths, a pair of buckskin leggings, and e'en some thick-soled Indian shoes. I accepted these gratefully, but as I began to don the shift, Tomi delicately pointed out that when a person is given a gift, it is customary to give a reciprocal gift in return.

I was stunned for a moment, embarrassed once again, but I really didn't know what to do. "I have nothing to give but my old clothes," I told Tomi. When she translated this to her daughter, the girl eagerly began snatching my damp things from the bushes. I wanted to protest, but held my tongue. No matter how hard it was to say good-bye to the style of clothing I had worn all my life, I knew it was for the best. Those things were poorly suited to the journey ahead, and Tomi's daughter seemed delighted to have them. I only hoped she would not feel cheated once she got a good look at the thin cloth.

Amongst the belongings I had packed in preparation for running away from home were a brush and comb. I sat in the sun on the riverbank, working the knots out of my wet hair, as a crowd of girls and women gathered 'round, for my fame had drawn in every female who could think of an excuse to come gawk at me. All were dazzled by my cascading curls, and each wanted to take a turn brushing my hair. Oh, how they chattered and clucked, the way I've seen chickens chattering o'er a newly hatched chick! The younger girls giggled endlessly at the way they could pull a curl out straight and watch it bounce right back into a curl when they let go.

The kindness and camaraderie I felt with those women was unlike anything I had e'er experienced. In my youth my hair had more oft been a source of pain than pride, as my brothers and sisters relentlessly pulled it or mocked me about how unkempt it was. When I was very young my hair made me look always like a ragamuffin, for my mother was too busy to tend to anything as trivial as the combing of my rat's nest and when she did make the effort, she was usually very short of both time and temper.

One of my earliest memories is that of having my mother scream at me to keep still as she yanked a comb through my matted curls. Tho' I could not have been more than three, she scolded me for failing to care for my hair myself. Every time the pain of her pulling grew so sharp that I squirmed, she jerked the comb to tear a handful of hair right out of my scalp. I can still see those wads of bright red hair rolling on the floor and I can still feel the intense humiliation of the torture as it went on and on. Thus I learnt early on to view my hair as a source of shame and suffering, which is why I wore it tied in a tight bun, modestly covered with a daycap.

How different things were in the warm sunshine on that riverbank, surrounded by mostly naked women whose touch was so gentle, whose admiration was so apparent.

E'en after the ladies had all taken a turn playing with my curls, the bulk of my hair was still wet, and I hesitated to tie it in a knot for fear it would remain damp for days. At the same time, I was reluctant to leave my hair loose, because that was, to me, tantamount to walking 'round half-naked. But when I remembered the women I was with not only left their hair loose but were, in fact, half-naked—well, I decided that if they could do it, I could. I walked to the village with my entourage of new friends, lifting my face to the sky, enjoying the cool breeze that pulled the warm sunshine into my curls.

But as soon as we began encountering other people, all immediately stopt whate'er they were doing to stand and stare at me. Conversations dissolved in mid-sentence, children froze in mid-skip, faces appeared in doorways, drawn by the sudden silence. I hesitated, suddenly as self-conscious as when the women first saw me naked.

Then I saw Syawa.

He and Hector were sitting on a log near a fire in a clearing, and when I came into view, he leapt to his feet to greet me, but as soon as he jumped up, he staggered backwards and nigh fell o'er the log upon which he had been sitting. He stood there, leaning awkwardly against the log, staring at me with an open mouth. E'en Hector, who had arisen with Syawa, stared at me openly for the very first time in our acquaintance, with a warmth in his eyes I had ne'er seen before.

I stopt walking, frightened by my own apparent power. I looked 'round the eerily silent village and saw the entire population staring at me. Syawa came forward at last, slowly, as if walking in his sleep, as if his feet were not quite touching the ground. In a squeaky, broken voice, he said something in his language, then, realizing I could not understand, he gestured that I was so beautiful, with the blue in my eyes like the blue of the morning sky and the fire of the sun reflecting off my hair—he said I was e'en more beautiful than when I appeared in his Vision.

I blusht and looked down, o'erwhelmed. Syawa reached out to take my hands in his, then leant his forehead against mine as I had seen him do with Hector. He mumbled a few words, which were the same ones he just gestured: "You are so beautiful." I began to cry.

No one had e'er said such a thing to me before.

We left that village almost immediately. I was sorry to leave my new friend, but my traveling companions were impatient to move on. Looking back on that day, I wish I had given Tomi more in exchange for all she gave me, but at the time I was too preoccupied with my own predicament. After all, now that I had learnt who Syawa truly was, I knew he must, sooner or later, figure out I was not at all what he believed me to be. I reckoned it just a matter of time before everything fell apart.

Syawa saw instantly that something had changed between us. As soon as we began hiking, he started in with his antics, trying to amuse me. I was amused, of course, but I was also terribly intimidated by his attention and quite a bit more nervous than I had been before. He asked what was wrong, and I told him 'twas nothing. I said I was just tired.

He said no more and became uncharacteristically quiet for the rest of the day. As we set up our camp that evening, Hector looked from one to the other of us, puzzled by the strained silence. Eventually he said something to Syawa, who responded at length. Hector glanced at me, nodded, and walked off into the woods.

"Your words are not true," Syawa gestured without speaking, which was unusual.

Sitting beside our campfire, I lowered my eyes and breathed rapidly. I said nothing.

He gestured again, and I looked up. "You say you are tired. You are not tired. You say nothing is wrong. Something is wrong."

I started to gesture, then stopt as tears welled in my eyes. Keenly aware of his intense gaze, I worked to control myself. "I—not good for you," I gestured. I frowned, confined by the clumsy hand-language. How could I convey the concept of "not good *enough*"? I did the best I could with my limited vocabulary. "You are good, more good, more, more, more good than me. I not good for you." I let my hands fall in defeat. All I could do was hope my meaning was clear.

It was. When at last I looked up, Syawa's face had transformed from a worried frown to an amused reproach. "You are good," he gestured, as if I'd said something silly. "You are good for me. You are as I see you in my Vision. You are smart. You are strong. You are brave."

I shook my head and sighed, looking away. "You not know me," I gestured.

He knelt beside me. "You do not know many, many things," he said, speaking softly in his language to accompany his gestures. "You do not know me. You do not know you. I know what you do not know. Trust me. You will learn." He moved so that his face was in the line of vision of my averted eyes. He smiled, hopefully, teasingly.

He almost made me smile, but I shook my head as I gestured, "You are right. I not know many things. You have Visions. I not have Visions. I not what you think. I not . . ." I froze for a moment, racking my brain, but Tomi had ne'er shown me the gesture for "worthy." "I not good for you," I finished weakly.

Syawa put his hands on my shoulders and looked me in the eyes as he said something. He waited a moment, then gestured, "You must trust me. I have seen it. You are the one in my Vision."

As I looked at him, the tears building up, he leant slowly towards me 'til our foreheads touched. We breathed each other's air for a long moment, my tears drying up, my heart beating faster and faster. He pulled back only a few inches, grinning that hopelessly infectious grin of his. "You see?" he said softly, and in my sudden delirium I scarce noticed I understood his words. Before I could reply, he leant forward again to touch his lips gently, delicately, to mine, and instantly I was o'erwhelmingly dizzy. I have been kissed many times in my life, but it was ne'er like this, nothing like this.

I remember little of parting, of sitting back to talk further, or of Hector returning with a bird of some sort, which he went on to cook. All I remember is the spinning euphoria and the absolute devotion I was beginning to feel towards this strange, very special savage man.

From that night on, I prayed almost continuously that I might, as he insisted, be good for him.

~ 8 ~

I HAVE, UP TO THIS POINT, been so consumed with explaining my predicament and describing my companions that I have completely ignored one of the key elements of my situation, which was the idyllic landscape through which we traveled.

Heretofore, as stated, I was not particularly enamored of the out-of-doors, and true wilderness seemed as dark and ominous to me as the Stygian depths. I longed for the comfort and security of the bustling towns of my childhood, the excitement and energy of the Old World cities I had oft heard of. Yet here I found myself wandering deeper and deeper into a wilderness as vast as the ocean itself, with no knowledge at all of how much longer or farther I was destined to roam. Not only did I have only the vaguest notion of where on earth I was, but by this time I rarely knew whether I was facing north, south, east, or west, so numerous were the twists and turns of our fast-paced travels.

Each day I expected to arrive at our destination, or at least to find signs that we were nearing our goal. Each evening when we stopt to make camp, I was forced to reconsider just how far Syawa had traveled in order to find me, and how far I was now being removed from the proximity of the only world I had e'er known. The distance was staggering and growing by miles and miles every day.

I took some comfort in the fact that my companions seemed to know exactly where we were at all times. I did not know if we were following the very trail they took on their eastward journey or if they were merely going in a certain direction, but Hector was an obsessive navigator, always studying our surroundings with a keen eye. Every time we so much as paused, he scanned the lay of the land, oft stopping to examine a tree, bush, or even weed. Once I found him squatting beside a delicate spring flower, curiously studying its unique features.

I asked Syawa why Hector did this, and he explained that much of the flora and fauna in this land were unknown to them. His friend, he said fondly, was always interested in new things.

Having ne'er considered the subject, I was surprised to learn plants and animals were not the same everywhere, and e'en more surprised that a brute as seemingly cold and rough as Hector might be curious about a pretty little posy.

Indeed, 'twas this interest in wildflowers that first enabled me to feel any sort of kinship with Hector, for I, too, was increasingly enchanted by the beauty of the awakening landscape. Every day brought a new crop of fragrant blooms, and e'en when the skies were gray and gloomy, the ground was glowing with glorious greens and yellows and pinks and purples. For miles and miles the three of us flew across a forest floor literally carpeted with flowers. The abundance was so o'erwhelming I began to feel as if God Himself was bestowing me with blossoms to apologize for the dismal nature of the first seventeen years of my life.

One evening shortly after we departed Tomi's village, I laid my bearskin upon a thick patch of violets and sat back to marvel at the spectacular sunset taking place across a meadow of purple and yellow flowers on the other side of the creek. The twilight sky was awash in reds and oranges, and all those fragrant blooms filled the air with an intoxicating perfume. Hector had just returned with two raccoons, which he was skinning as Syawa built the fire. They talked as they worked, but because I was too tired to decipher their words, I chose to enjoy the rare opportunity to bask in a perfect place, a perfect time. Surely, I thought, the Garden of Eden could not have been so blessed, or Adam and Eve would not've dared any action which might risk their expulsion.

I know not how long it took to realize the tone of my companions' voices had changed, but at some point my attention was abruptly wrenched from the sunset.

Syawa and Hector were arguing.

I had heard Hector complain before, but ne'er had I heard the men exchange harsh words—certainly not in the way they were doing now. I strained to make out what they were saying, but tho' my comprehension of their language was steadily improving, they spake far too rapidly for me. Ne'ertheless, I was sure I heard both say "Kay-oot-li," and assumed they were arguing about me. What else did they have to argue about?

I crawled o'er to Syawa and gestured, asking what was wrong. He ignored me as he and Hector continued to bicker, their voices raised and rancorous. Suddenly, Hector threw down the raccoon and stomped off toward the creek. Syawa watched him walk away, the expression on his face impossible for me to read. Then he looked at me and shrugged, smiling apologetically.

"Why he angry?" I gestured.

Syawa looked into the fire. A long moment of uneasy silence passed. Then he sighed and gestured that Hector was unhappy because I was not helping with meal preparation. "Among my people," he said and gestured, "men provide the game, women do the rest. My friend has never enjoyed doing women's work, but now, with you here . . ."

I nodded, the problem clear to me. Any of my brothers would rather die than be caught working in a kitchen. "I—I not know how help," I gestured. Just as when Hector complained about my body odor, I was surprised, embarrassed, and ashamed.

Up to this point, I felt my primary duty was to learn Syawa's language—a view I believe he shared. Thus, each evening when Hector was off hunting or fishing, Syawa started a fire, set up our camp, and chattered away, but he neither asked for my help nor seemed to expect it. When Hector returned, he and Syawa skinned, cleaned, and cooked the food with the clockwork precision of people who had been working together for years—wordless, efficient, companionable. It was clear to me that should I attempt to interject myself into their routine, I could only muddle things up, and, at any rate, I had no idea what to do.

The problem was not that I was untrained—indeed, no girl could be considered marriageable who was not a fair hand in the kitchen—the problem was that I had neither the ingredients nor the tools I was accustomed to using, and without them I was lost. I had no milk, no eggs, no flour, no grains. I had no pan, no kettle, no spoons, no iron spit. All I had was the knife I packed when planning to run away.

The implication that I was somehow slacking cut me to the quick. I am not a lazy person. I worked in my mother's kitchen from the day I could stand—stirring, peeling, chopping, kneading. And when it came to cleaning, well, in my life I had swept miles of floor, hauled oceans of water, and scraped up mountains of ash. No one in the world could have scrubbed more dishes in the preceding seventeen years than I.

Unfortunately, I knew nothing about the preparation of wild game nor the management of a wilderness camp. Before moving to the frontier, we kept chickens and milk cows, of course, but the only butchering I was involved with was our birds. In truth, meat was ne'er more than a small part of our diet, and when we were lucky enough to have it, we eked it out in soups, stews, or pies. For the most part we sated our hunger with pancakes, porridge, pudding, or pottage, and, of course, we ne'er ate a single meal without bread and butter.

My companions, on the other hand, ate meat, meat, and more meat, cooked in ways I ne'er imagined. They stuck it on a stick in the fire, wrapt it with leaves and buried it under hot coals, or boiled it in a pouch made from the animal's stomach. All their ingredients and cooking methods were bizarre to me—how could I possibly help?

But I had neither the words nor the time to explain all this to Syawa. He picked up the carcass Hector had thrown down and finished skinning it, all the while explaining what he was doing. The process was painfully slow because he had to keep using his hands to gesture when I did not understand his words. When he was done with that first animal, he bade me prepare the second carcass, patiently advising me how to use his stone tool. The animal he prepared was cleanly cut and ready to cook, but by the time I was done hacking away at my poor raccoon, all that was left was a pile of mangled meat scraps. Syawa laughed good-naturedly and assured me I would improve, saying the important thing was that I was willing to try.

Once we set the meat a-cooking, I found, to my dismay, my

lesson was far from over. Syawa explained that women were expected not only to turn the freshly killed game into a meal, but also to preserve all useful parts of the animal and then clean the camp of every single drop of blood. Unskilled as I was in campfire cooking, I was nigh hopeless when it came to preserving the hides, bones, and sinews, but I did my best to follow Syawa's instructions as he showed me every grueling step of the painstaking process.

By the time we finisht all my new tasks and put our tools away, the meat had cooked to the consistency of dried leather. With Hector still nowhere in sight, Syawa and I went ahead and ate our share, tho' I was so exhausted by this time I could scarce chew. Syawa ate happily, however, offering endless additional tips on how to skin, preserve, and store animal parts.

My mind was numb from all I'd learnt, leaving me incapable of following what he said anymore, so after a time he finally stopt talking to stare contentedly into the fire. I wondered about Hector's absence, but Syawa seemed unconcerned. As my thoughts hearkened back to their argument, I remembered one particular set of sounds Hector used several times—it was a word I'd heard him use before in reference to me. I looked at Syawa and shattered the pleasant silence by asking what that word meant, struggling to pronounce the sounds exactly as I'd heard them.

Syawa raised his eyes from the fire to look at me for a long moment before he said and gestured: "That word means 'not know how to do things.'"

Ah. It meant ignorant, stupid. Hector had called me stupid, and Syawa defended me. Now I understood why the argument had been so heated.

I looked at the ground with a humorless laugh. "Your friend thinks I stink and stupid," I said with words and gestures. I looked at Syawa, who was smiling sympathetically. "I told you I not good for you."

Syawa spake with both his words and hands. "You are stupid only because you do not know how *we* do things. I will teach you. You will learn."

I nodded, but my thoughts were grim. Once again I felt completely undeserving of all this attention from someone of Syawa's high status, and I worried that if the rest of his people were as intolerant of my many faults as Hector seemed to be, I was going to be in serious trouble. Syawa might be enamored of me now and therefore willing to put up with my incompetence, but once the newness wore off, he would surely despise me. How could he not? His friend clearly did.

I could almost hear my mother crowing—*I told ye so, I told ye so . . .*

When I awoke the next morning, Hector was back, but the men made no eye contact and did not speak that whole day. I was sickened by the strained silence—it was all my fault! Ne'er before had I seen a friendship like theirs, and the thought that *I* might be the cause of its demise crushed my soul. To make amends, I determined to do everything a woman was supposed to do e'en if I didn't know how to do it, which meant, of course, that I made a terrific muddle of everything.

The evening after the big argument, I immediately set about starting a fire, which I now knew was my job. I collected wood, set up kindling, and shredded dry bark as I had seen Syawa do. Smiling encouragement, he handed me the horn in which he carried a coal from the night before, but when I dumped the glowing ember into the shredded bark, it fizzled, then expired. I gasped, horrified, but Syawa only laughed and set about making a new spark, the result of which was our fire was scarce smoldering by the time Hector returned with a fish.

With Syawa's help, I did my best to scale, gut, and cook that poor fish, but my best was woefully bad and frustration quickly led to tears, which meant I had no hope of success. The fish was rendered almost entirely inedible, and Hector ended up saying the word "stupid" under his breath as he threw the charred remains into the stream, with an Apology to the Spirit of the Fish. Thanks to the mess I made, some sort of predator came snuffling 'round during the night, which necessitated Hector running into the bushes with his hand-ax whilst Syawa added wood to the fire.

The result of my first full day of doing my expected duties was that the three of us had almost no food nor sleep, which made our short tempers e'en shorter all the next day.

The next night I hurried to collect a bundle of firewood as soon as we stopt. With Hector off hunting and Syawa off filling the water skin, I looked for the hand-ax. I was confident about this chore, at least, for one of my duties at home had been to chop kindling and I fancied myself something of an expert with a hatchet. E'en my brothers acknowledged my skill, for they challenged me once to a hatchet-throwing contest and I hit the target closer to the center than any of them. Thus, when I picked up the hand-ax, I was certain I could chop a great pile of firewood in no time.

But the stone tool was strange to me, top-heavy and unbalanced, and no matter how I swung it, it kept turning sideways as I slammed it down, so that I ended up crushing the wood more than chopping through it.

Then the unthinkable happened. Increasingly frustrated by my own incompetence, I banged furiously against the wood and somehow managed to snap the stone blade in two. Terrified, I considered throwing down the ax and running off into the woods to start at last for Philadelphia, but 'twas already too late—Syawa was returning. I had no choice but to show him the ax, at which he sighed and gestured that this was most unfortunate. The ax, he said, had been a gift to Hector from his father.

I sobbed and sobbed, repeating over and over the new word I had learnt—*stupid, stupid, stupid*. With infinite patience, Syawa took the ax from me and told me 'twas not my fault. The blade had broken, he said, not because I was stupid, but because I had not been properly taught to use it. The fault, he said, was his.

And then he helpt me gather firewood that would not require chopping.

~ 9 ~

BECAUSE OF THE AWFUL TENSION in our traveling threesome, I was actually relieved when we arrived at another village. As before, I assumed this was our destination 'til I learnt it was not. Tho' the river here was larger than the one beside Tomi's village, the village itself seemed smaller, but I soon discovered it was only one of a number of hamlets in the area, all drawn to this location by a nearby French trading post. As a result, the total population in this valley was much higher than in Tomi's village.

From what I could discern, the people of this place spoke a different tongue than Tomi, but they, too, understood the language of gestures and they, too, were clearly acquainted with my companions and eager to learn of their Journey's progress. I did not fail to notice that whilst Syawa and Hector were perfectly pleasant with the people of the village, they continued to speak to one another as little as possible.

We arrived late in the day, and early the next morning Syawa sent me off with some women to bathe, as he and Hector went off to the men's bathing area. I washed my hair and tied it in a knot so I could help the women prepare food. Because of the proximity of the trading post, these women had all the utensils and ingredients I had been missing, and I was actually able to be useful. Moreover, I found a woman who spoke some English, enabling me to get invaluable advice about campsite cooking.

It was only when Syawa and Hector finally returned and I saw they were elaborately painted and adorned that I finally understood why we were preparing so much food—it was a Feast to celebrate the triumphant return of the Seer from a Distant Land. Syawa was pleased to see me working with the women, but he soon pulled me away to explain that this time I must help tell our story. "What must I do?" I asked warily.

Saying I would know when the time came, he untied my hair and smiled as he brushed it out with his fingers. "You are ready," he said warmly. "Except . . . you must be happy." He grinned, compelling me to smile back.

I had little chance to fret, for the feasting had already begun. The quantity of food was formidable, especially since I had become accustomed to a rather sparse diet during our long days of walking. After sating my hunger, I sat back, determined not to appear greedy, but Syawa and Hector continued to eat and eat and eat and eat, almost as if obliged to do so.

I later learnt this was precisely the case. Syawa told me that to refuse the generosity of another was a great insult, especially when it came to the sharing of food. I blush now to think of the unintentional insults I inflicted because I was trying to be polite.

My companions and I were seated on a mat before a large fire in the middle of a huge riverside meadow where countless people milled about. Throughout the feasting there was much revelry—dancing, singing, and the playing of rattles and drums. These activities were so interesting, with their dazzling array of costumes, hairstyles, and personal ornamentation, that I had little time to worry about what might soon be required of me.

Dignitaries gave speeches which I scarce attended, for more and more people were constantly arriving, both from the woods and from the river. All laughed and chattered as they began to form a wide circle 'round the central fire. Children ran to and fro, looking for an opening through which they could push their way to the front. In a short time, the encircling throng grew from several dozen to several hundred, and I was increasingly uneasy. All these people were here to see my companion, the Great Seer. Again and again I looked to Syawa for emotional support, and he ne'er failed to smile or squeeze my hand.

My mind reeled at the insane shift in my life's fortunes. Two months previous I had been toiling away as a virtual slave in a shabby frontier settlement; now I sat in the center of a mob of devoted admirers, alongside someone whose reputation inspired wide-eyed reverence and awe. Who could blame me for wondering if all this was naught but a weird dream I myself was having, a delusion of my own o'erwrought imagination as I lay tucked in my crowded bed in the loft?

When the sun went down, the dancing and singing reached a fever pitch. Then the singers stopt, the drums stopt, and the dancers disappeared. As several armloads of wood were added to the fire, the crowd hushed in anticipation. The excitement was contagious, and I looked anxiously to Syawa, wondering what was going to happen next.

He was already on his feet, moving toward the fire. Suddenly the wood snapt and sparks shot up in a whirlwind burst, as if he'd tossed a handful of gunpowder into the flames. I gasped along with the rest of the onlookers. He began to move 'round the fire, the black and white and red designs painted on his face and nigh-naked body shimmering in the firelight, making him look more like a phantasm than a human being. Slowly he moved at first, then faster and faster, sizzling and snapping like a flame pulled loose from the fire. We all watched in amazement.

Eventually he stopt dancing and began to sing, but because only Hector and I could understand his words, he also used the language of gestures, thus making his song another sort of dance. After the song, he told the story of his Vision by first describing a massive Earthquake that occurred just as his mother was being born. It shook the world his people lived in, toppling every building in every town, leaving everyone terrified and unsure. What did the Earthquake portend? What should the people do? In broad gestures he explained how his mother dreamt of some sort of bird just before he himself was born, and how his entire life had, therefore, been devoted to becoming a Holyman. Eventually he became the One Who Sees, and he was granted a Vision—the Vision of a Creature of Fire and Ice.

I don't know if it was because I knew Syawa better now, or because the crowd was more receptive, or because he truly did put more "magic" into this performance, but whate'er the case, this rendition of his Vision was truly soul-stirring. It was almost as if the entire performance was meant just for me, as I had finally become conversant enough with his words and gestures to understand. In any case, by the time he finisht, every mouth hung open, and Syawa was spent, dripping with sweat and trembling on his knees before the fire.

That's when Hector came in. Tho' the two men had scarce spoken in days, they worked together now as if their two bodies were controlled by one mind. Clearly they had acted out this tale many,

many times. Whilst Syawa told the story of their harrowing journey in words and gestures, the garishly painted Hector acted out the many perils and adventures they'd encountered along the way. In an impressive bit of pantomime, Hector relived a bear attack, which resulted, apparently, in the very bearskin Syawa had given me shortly after we met. Syawa joined Hector to demonstrate how they steered a canoe o'er a sizable waterfall somewhere along the way, and the two of them acted out the fear they felt when caught in the middle of some vast open field during a violent blizzard. Through it all, they were looking, looking, looking for the object of Syawa's Vision.

Everyone in the surrounding crowd was intoxicated by this story—no one more so than I. In fact, I was so caught up in the elaborate performance that when Syawa described how he and Hector joined local Indians in a raid on a family farm, I didn't e'en think about the fact that he was talking about *my* family, *my* farm. They showed how they passed through the mayhem of the massacre in the farmyard as if in a dream, looking, looking, always looking for the marvelous Creature of Fire and Ice. They showed how they cautiously entered a cabin whose residents had just been forcibly removed. They showed how a local savage tried to push past them, and how Hector thrust his stone blade into that man's heart. Then they pretended to creep up the stairs, slowly, still looking and looking, creeping e'er closer to the mat upon which I sat. Then they stood up and froze, staring at me.

Unaccustomed to being noticed at all, I was horrified to find myself suddenly at the center of a circle of hundreds of terribly excited savages, all of whom were gaping, waiting for me to do something. Silence descended as the anticipation grew. I swallowed heavily, left with no choice but to rise, trembling, before my traveling companions. I was not painted and wore naught but the simple clothes Tomi had given me, but as Syawa reached out and led me into the dancing shadows of the firelight, the encircling crowd drew in their collective breath. I suppose my white skin and long red curls did provide a startling contrast to my dark, fantastically painted companions. And, remembering the advice Syawa had given me, I smiled.

I was relieved to discover little more was required of me. My companions danced, demonstrating their joy at having found me, and before I knew it, other people were inspired to join in. I soon found myself serving as the sole spot of stillness in the midst of an enormous whirlwind of energy, motion, and emotion. And in that spot of stillness, one fact kept swirling in and out of my thoughts: Hector had killed a man on my behalf.

Because of my exhaustion that night, both physically and emotionally, I am now unable to recall much of the festivities which followed. The dancing and singing continued 'til dawn, I believe, tho' I have a vague memory of an old woman taking my hand and leading me to a dark hut where my bearskin awaited me. Grateful, I rolled myself into my furry cocoon and, despite the raging din, I slept 'til shortly after dawn.

That's when I heard Syawa cry out. I sat bolt upright, groggy, disoriented, terrified. My heart pounded as I looked 'round the dimly lit hut, trying to figure out what was wrong. Others were also sitting up, looking my way in alarm. Hector, who had apparently been lying with some young woman at the far end of the hut, had also been wrenched from his sleep and now stood nearby, naked and wild-eyed, holding his stone knife in the air as he looked for some enemy to stab. I averted my eyes, still deeply discomforted by the absolute absence of basic modesty amongst the Indians.

It took a moment to realize Syawa had, at some point, come to lie beside me and was sitting there now, holding his head in his hands, shaking slightly. Traces of paint from the night before were smeared so that he looked like a child who'd been playing in the mud. He, too, was groggy and a bit embarrassed as he looked up at Hector and said something. I knew enough of their language now to recognize key words, especially the term "Vision." Apparently Syawa had just had a dream—but not just any dream. This was the kind of dream he believed was a portent of things to come.

I put my hand on his arm, concerned by his rapid breathing and trembling limbs. My touch seemed to bring him back to himself, and he looked at me sheepishly. "I dream of you," he said, both in words and gestures. "I see you save three people. Without you, all three die. With you, all three live. Three people—three days."

I pulled back, blinking dumbly, wondering if I, myself, was having a dream. Everyone was staring at me now, and I heard hushed whispers begin. Someone got up and rushed from the hut, spreading the word of the Seer's latest Vision. Hector squatted beside Syawa, glancing my way doubtfully. He asked Syawa for more details, and as Syawa jabbered away, the thing that struck me was that this was the longest conversation these two had had in at least a week.

I lay back, still sleepy, my arm o'er my eyes. I was glad the men were speaking again, but inside I was just plain sick. Syawa said I would save the lives of three people, and now everyone would be expecting exactly that. But I had ne'er saved so much as the life of a chicken in all my seventeen years. What would happen if—or should I say *when*—his Vision failed to be realized? What would the people of this village think of him then? And what would they do?

I tried to go back to sleep, but could not. As thrilling as it had been the night before to be intimately connected with such a celebrated man, now that connection seemed like a huge mistake. Apparently there was a price to be paid for fame and glory, and the bill was going to fall due for me in three days.

~ 10 ~

As soon as my companions and I arose, we were approacht by a Frenchman inviting us to the trading post. Syawa immediately accepted, as if the invitation, like the offer of food, could not be refused. Tho' my people have always viewed the French as interlopers, I soon learnt most of the Frenchmen at this post were nativeborn, sons of Indian mothers. Upon our arrival, two young half-breeds took Syawa and Hector to one side to show them weapons, whilst our original guide led me to a platform covered with fabrics, ribbons, and beads.

As the trader strove to entice me with colorful cloths and sparkling trinkets, I remained silent and still. Having ne'er worn nothing that wasn't handed down thru multiple family members, I had no taste for finery. Traders actually made me uneasy, and tho' the young Frenchman urged me to touch this or feel that, I responded only with vague smiles. Except for my few personal items, which had little value to anyone but me, I possessed nothing to trade with, and, knowing I must carry all I owned, I had no desire to acquire nothing new anyway.

I glanced at my companions to see if they were going to trade.

Syawa was pleasant, as always, but aloof. His smile was scarce visible; his dark eyes were veiled. Hector was openly hostile, but then again he seemed always eager to shove his knife into something or someone.

My trader worked hard to win me o'er, speaking in French, English, Dutch, and several Indian tongues, but when he evoked no response, he turned in frustration to a mat hanging from the rafters, which formed a partial wall behind him. That was when I discovered two additional Frenchmen sitting in the shadows, their narrowed eyes burning into me. I stared at them and saw that one was much older, rougher, and bolder—I supposed he was in charge of the place. The other was a black-robed priest.

As soon as I saw the hidden men, I looked again to my companions, who were being shown how to powder a musket and thus were thoroughly distracted. When I returned my eyes to the traders, the older one had leant close enough that I could see the grizzle on his face. He smiled, looking me o'er in an intimate way, the way I'm sure he looked o'er most women, horses, and dogs. "How does a pretty young Englishwoman come to be in the company of strange savages?" he asked in near-perfect English.

"Truth be told, I am an Irishwoman," I said lightly.

The hearty laughter of all three men caused Syawa and Hector to look my way. Alarmed to see three hairy foreigners looming o'er me, they would've come to my rescue, but just then the trader with the gun fired the weapon, startling my companions so much that they began shouting angrily. The shooter tried to soothe the ruffled feathers by gesturing that there was no danger, for he'd not loaded a lead ball, but when these potential customers still seemed inclined to leave, the other trader recaptured their interest by pulling out a display of shiny swords.

In the meantime, the older Frenchman had arisen and stept up to the counter. "My apologies, mistress," he said silkily. "I did not mean to insult you by associating you with the lying, thieving, law-less swine who are the English."

If he was hoping to win me over by insulting our common en-emy, I'm afraid I disappointed him. As stated, I've ne'er cared for politics, and I care e'en less for smooth-talking sales pitches from unscrupulous traders.

When I failed to respond, the priest spoke up from the shad-ows, his accent thick. "But you not say how you come to be here, my child. If you are captive by these men, we shall, of course, do what we must to secure your release."

If I have no use for politics, I have an active antipathy towards religion. Religious wars are a way of life in Ireland, and my father's family had, for generations, derived great financial gain by squeez-ing out the Catholics, who make up the bulk of the population. All I know of priests is what my father always said—they're the devil's doers on earth, determined to steal the souls, not to mention the worldly goods, of all folk simple-minded enough to listen to them. I vividly recall the glee with which Father repeatedly described the burning of a priest he'd witnessed as a child.

I should add that my grandmother was an ardent Catholic all her days. I caught her once on her knees with a rosary, and, crying, she made me swear not to tell no one, lest my father throw her from his house. "Keep this wee secret, Katie," she begged, "and I'll say an Ave fer ye ev'ry day I live." I knew not what an "Ave" was, but I loved my gran and was happy to share a secret with her. It made me feel special, right up to the day she died, when I discovered she'd made similar pacts with every member of our family. It turned out everyone knew she was Catholic—e'en Father.

My point is I had reason to be wary of priests, and I smiled coldly at the one before me. "No, sir, I did not say how I came to be here, nor do I see why I should. Surely my affairs are my own."

The Frenchmen looked at one another, puzzled. The older one, handsome in his grizzled way, once again tried the smile that obviously worked with most women. "I hope we've not offended you, mistress, but we've ne'er seen a white woman this far from civilization, and we assumed, quite naturally, you are being held against your will. If we may be of any assistance . . ."

"I am not a captive," I said firmly. "Nor do I require any assistance. I thank you for your concern but would ask that you not trouble yourselves on my account."

"Ah! A runaway!" said the young trader who had failed to sell me anything. His English was poor, but his meaning was clear. He grinned as he added, "Your father, he give fortune to find you, eh?" The older Frenchman shot the speaker a warning look, which caused the younger man to turn his attention to refolding fabrics.

"My father is dead," I said simply. "The few family members remaining to me know where I am and, I assure you, would give nothing to have me back. Therefore I must ask you gentlemen, once again, not to concern yourselves with my affairs. Thank you for showing me your wares."

I rejoined my companions, hoping they were ready to return to the Indian village, but they were at this point keenly examining a large array of knives. When I asked Syawa if he meant to trade for something, he stept back and gestured emphatically that he had nothing to trade.

I was surprised. What about all those furs and hides we had been cleaning, collecting, and carrying? Why did we keep them, if not to use in trade? I thought perhaps Syawa was positioning himself to bargain, but I had no way to ask because our language of gestures offered no opportunity to speak privately. Besides, I wasn't e'en sure he fully understood the situation. He and Hector might not *want* to trade, but these Frenchmen were experts at getting what *they* wanted, and they would keep after my companions as long as they had anything the Frenchmen considered valuable—be it animal hides, information, or, for that matter, me.

Sure enough, before we could leave, the head Frenchman insisted we join them for a meal, and inasmuch as Syawa was incapable of refusing an invitation, we ate with them. I must say the food was the best I'd had since leaving home, no doubt because it was the sort I was used to. The French had taught their Indian women the Old World way of cooking, and I thoroughly enjoyed the bread and cheese and cake and pie. Syawa and Hector were less enthusiastic, but, as usual, they ate everything offered to them as if their lives depended on it.

Whilst we were eating I watched a number of local Indians come and go from the trading post. The younger, mix-blooded Frenchmen did most of the haggling, but I noticed they always consulted with the older man who was hosting our meal, e'en if the consultation consisted of nothing more than an inquiring look and a confirming nod.

Our host, whose name was something like LeFevre, got a lot more information from my companions than he had managed to get from me. Clearly LeFevre had either seen or heard about our performance the night before, and, using the gesture language, he plied Syawa and Hector for details, especially about where, exactly, I was from, what Indian tribes were involved in the raid, how many people were involved on both sides, and what sort of resistance my family and the neighboring community put up. My companions answered all of LeFevre's questions without reservation.

Knowing how traders use information as a tool in negotiations, I wisht I could urge Syawa to be less forthcoming, but because I did not want to call further attention to myself, I said nothing throughout this interrogation and did not, in fact, let the Frenchmen know I spake their language. As the men gestured on and on, silently discussing the situation on the Colonial border, I watched their discussion but let my ears focus in on what was happening at the trade tables. When the young traders negotiated with the natives, they spoke the local language, which I did not understand, but when they conferred with each other, they spoke French, which I understand well. In this way I learnt the traders were systematically cheating the Indians.

When, at last, my companions were ready to depart, I was relieved. I said naught about what I'd heard, mostly because I did not know what to say. Should I say merchants are deceptive? Who does not know that? In my lifetime, my father's livelihood came from clever deal-making and ruthless profit-taking, and the fact that Father was so bad at those enterprises helped make my early life abysmal. Considering how much information Syawa had just given the French for free, I feared he, like my father, would rarely come out on top in any trade, which made it likely I would continue to live in poverty all my days.

By the time we got back to the Indian village I was exhausted, and, still full of good French food, I curled up in my bearskin and went immediately to sleep.

Awakened the next morning by a commotion outside, I hurried out to join my companions, who were being gabbled at by a distraught young man and an older woman. Finally the young man realized

his error and repeated his frantic pleas in the form of fumbling gestures. Apparently his wife was in some sort of distress, and he and
his mother prayed the celebrated Seer from a Distant Land might
perform the magic their own healers had been unable to conjure.

Syawa stood still for a moment, an odd smile on his face. He
gave Hector the slightest shrug. Hector lifted his chin in acknowledgment and walked away as Syawa turned his eyes to me. "This is
what I saw in my Vision," he said in both words and gestures. "Now
it begins."

My stomach churned. I was not ready for this—I was still half-
asleep! Besides, I had no special powers, no unique knowledge, no
ability to help anyone do anything. The truth was, as Syawa well
knew, I could scarce assist in meal preparation and couldn't e'en
chop wood without bungling it. Yet here he was smiling at me, and
here were all these strangers staring at me with hope in their eyes. I
was absolutely petrified. How could I possibly make Syawa's Vision
come true?

I numbly turned to follow Syawa, who was following the young
man, my thoughts racing far ahead of them both. If we all somehow
survived the shame of my inevitable failure, would Syawa understand at last what a mistake he'd made? When he realized there was
nothing at all special about me, would he send me home or have
Hector dispatch me on the spot? I walked with head down, dreading the dismal end of my short, unhappy life.

We came to a hut from which a few of the roof mats had been
removed. Syawa and I entered to find a young woman clearly suffering the pangs of childbirth. She was wholly naked, sitting on a
large hide, her belly huge and tight, her face pale and dotted with
perspiration. Her eyes rolled in terror that instantly transformed
into relief the moment she saw who we were. When Syawa smiled

that smile of his and knelt beside her, I watched the tension in her taut muscles simply melt away.

The woman's husband remained outside, but his mother introduced us to the women attending the laboring girl. One explained how the young mother's pains began shortly after we arrived in the village, and how she had suffered e'er since with little to show for her efforts. With the mother growing weak, the women hoped the famous Holyman could coax the baby out into this world.

Syawa crooned a song the young woman could not possibly understand as he brushed the damp hair off her face. He gently laid her down before pulling some items out of a pouch he'd brought with him. As he began performing an incantation o'er her, I turned my attention to the young mother and the hairs on the back of my neck began to rise. Everything was eerily familiar. I suddenly realized I'd been here before—dozens and dozens of times. I knelt beside the laboring woman, becoming strangely calm, confident, and sure. I didn't know much about campsite cooking, but I knew a thing or two about having babies.

From the day I, myself, was born, I had been exposed to childbirth on a routine basis. My mother was confined about once a year, and my sisters, sisters-in-law, neighbors, and acquaintances too numerous to mention gave me infinite opportunities to learn all the problems and solutions of difficult labors. In my seventeen years, rare was the month when I was not bathed in the blood of birth—if not from a human, then from one of our many animals. I knew all about the birth process. I knew how it worked and why it sometimes didn't. If the subject of Syawa's latest Vision was childbirth, I just might be able to make a contribution.

Whilst Syawa sang and rubbed herbs on the young woman's temples, I slowly and deliberately felt her belly. I expected her to tighten up when I touched her, but I was surprised to feel her actually relax beneath my hands. Then it occurred to me—if I were being handled by someone I sincerely believed to be the embodiment of a Holyman's Vision, I suppose I, too, would relax.

My examination revealed the baby's backside was pressed down hard upon the top of the birth canal. On the other hand, the woman's pains were still strong and productive, and when I laid my ear against her belly, a strong rolling movement assured me the little one still lived. There was, indeed, reason to hope.

Hours passed as I tried to work with the pains to turn the baby 'round. Of course the women who'd been there from the beginning had already tried what I was doing, but they urged me on, sure I would have more success. I don't know how the poor woman endured all my pushing and prodding, but by late in the day I myself was beginning to flag as frustration welled in me. Remembering how I broke that ax, I struggled to remain calm, but I'm sure I would've brought the poor mother to the brink of hysteria had it not been for the cool example of Syawa, who sang sweetly through all my futile efforts, ne'er tiring, ne'er wavering, ne'er losing his encouraging smile.

Just before sunset one of the baby's grandmothers took me outside to give me food. I sat there by myself, eating numbly as I thought about what more I could do. Something was strange about that baby. I could move it, but it just would not stay where I wanted it to be.

I held my head in my hands, defeated and increasingly scared. What did I know about childbirth? Of the dozens and dozens of babes I'd seen born, probably less than half had come through the process alive, and of those, maybe half again made it through their first month. This was a grim and grisly business, and things were appearing very bleak. What right had I to be here, pretending to know what I was doing? I was no midwife! I was no one special! Fear swelled as I chid myself for e'er thinking I could save three lives.

I looked up, startled. Syawa had said *three* lives. There was the mother, the baby, and . . . oh, you stupid, stupid, *stupid* girl!

Syawa had not stopt to eat, and as I re-entered the dark hut, the flickering firelight revealed him staring at the young mother as she stared at him. 'Twas as if her mind was his now, as if he was absorbing her pain. When I resumed my place at his side, he smiled without looking at me. "Are you ready?" he asked, a phrase I knew well, for it was the very thing he asked each morning before we set off on our hike.

I mumbled an affirmation. I wanted to tell him what I had figured out, but before I could, he urged me to proceed, adding that I need not worry—all would be well. Whilst he kept the young woman focused with his penetrating gaze, I felt her belly more carefully. There it was, hiding up behind the rib cage—the second baby.

I gestured to the other women about the second baby, explaining that every time we moved the first one, the second pushed it right back where it started. Our challenge was for the grandmothers to hold the second baby out of the way whilst I pushed the first one into place.

We all took a deep breath and got back to work. I'd seen women scream and writhe under a lot less provocation, but that young mother continued to stare blankly at Syawa's dark eyes as if she felt no pain at all. Unfortunately, our efforts failed. There just wasn't room to turn the first babe all the way 'round. At some point well past the middle of the night I had to admit my plan wasn't going to work.

When I sat back on my heels, once again near tears, Syawa

turned his head to look at me. I could see the firelight reflected in his eyes, the red-orange dancing in the black. His smile was warm, encouraging, filled with love and support. No one had e'er looked at me like that. Tears filled my eyes, and I looked away, ashamed of myself. If Syawa was so sure I could do this, who was I to think I couldn't? I went back to work.

This time, instead of trying to turn the baby 'round head first, I pushed it the other way. Working through multiple contractions, I nudged the little legs 'til they were pointed straight down. When next the muscles tightened, we all saw the bulge in the mother's belly slide into place. That baby might be coming into the world backwards, but at least it was going to come out.

Once the legs were in the birth canal, things proceeded rapidly. The contractions did their job, and before long tiny feet were visible. I worried to myself that the baby's head might be too big, which happened once with a cow my father had. After the calf's body dangled from the mother for some time, my father had no choice but to push it back so he could reach in and crush its skull to save the mother's life. 'Twas a gruesome scene—not one I wanted to repeat.

I needn't have worried. With the next contraction, the baby slithered out as easy as you please. It was a boy. One of the grandmothers was ready and waiting to take him, but he was blue and lifeless, which I knew was oft the case with breech births. I sucked what I could from his mouth and nose, then rubbed him to get the blood flowing. I turned him o'er to rub his back, but nothing much seemed to be happening.

He was so very small, lying lifeless on my hand and arm.

With my palm against his tiny belly, I used my other hand to gently press the baby's back up and down like a bellows. He spluttered and choked and wiggled and kicked. Then he cried.

After tying off the cord, I gave him to his grandmother and turned my attention back to his mother. By the time the second baby was in position, the poor girl was too depleted to push, and it took much effort from all of us to get that baby out. We worked e'en harder to get the second afterbirth, for the contractions had stopt. By the time we succeeded, the young mother was bleeding so profusely it seemed, for a time, we might yet lose her.

The other women applied herb-filled pads to stanch the flow, as I piled hides beneath her legs and backside to keep her feet and legs well above her head. I also made cold compresses from river water to chill her belly. Through it all, Syawa's gentle ministrations kept the woman so calm she actually drifted off to sleep whilst the rest of us scrambled to save her. By late in the afternoon, clots had formed, and mother and both babies were sleeping comfortably.

Having done all I could, I staggered to the river to wash, my knees trembling from the strain of holding me up for so long. I had worked hard for maybe thirty-five hours, and my vision was beginning to blur. A soft doeskin appeared in mid-air before me; I stared at it blearily. When I managed to focus my eyes, Syawa was drying my hands, his smile smug. I wanted to say something, but 'twas all I could do to stay upright as he pulled me to my feet and put his arm 'round my shoulders to lead me back to the hut where we were staying. I was asleep as soon as my head hit the bearskin, but on the way down some small part of my mind screamed:

Three lives, three days. Three lives, three days.

Syawa had said it, and it had come to pass.

~ 11 ~

I FIRMLY BELIEVE I DID nothing extraordinary by helping with the birth of those twins. On reflection, I'm sure the women already there would have succeeded without me. But I doubt they could have managed without the calming influence of Syawa. He was the one who truly saved three lives.

So the question rolling in my mind was this—why did he want people to *think* it was me? Was this his way of turning me into the mystical creature he claimed me to be? Because that's exactly what happened. The villagers considered the miraculous birth to be both confirmation of the power of the Great Seer and proof of my Divinity. I would have laughed at the notion had it not frightened me so.

A gray, stormy sky prevented us from leaving the next day, but it also gave people from far and wide an opportunity to come pay us tribute. Thus began my instruction in the delicate art of Gifting.

It was so very complicated. We hauled out all the pelts we'd collected and gave these to people to whom we were obliged—those who'd given us food, lodging, or other considerations. But we also had a pile of gifts others had given us, and I asked Syawa how we could accept these things when we must travel so lightly. He smiled and said to refuse a gift insulted the giver, but once the gift was ours, we could do with it what we would. As we gave away most of the things we'd been given, he insisted the important thing was to maintain a balance between those giving gifts and those receiving them.

Oh, but there were treacherous subtleties! For example, I wanted to give the young mother a couple of soft rabbit furs, but Syawa said I'd already given her the greatest gift and to increase her obligation would only shame her. It was hard for him to explain such complex concepts through gestures, but he patiently assured me that if we gave the wrong sort of gift to someone, we might insult that person, and if we gave no gift at all, we might actually be acknowledging that person's high status or wealth, which would be a compliment. The wealthiest person, Syawa insisted, was the one who ended up with nothing.

I was confused and must ask many questions. If a gift given to me was mine to do with as I pleased, why had Hector raised such a fuss about my giving away food back at that first village? Syawa smiled and said the sharing of food was not so much a gift as an indicator of a personal relationship, but, in any case, it wasn't Hector who'd refused my family food—it was Syawa. He went on to tell me Hector had begged to be allowed to provide enough food for all in an effort to avoid a fight like the one which occurred, but Syawa, for whatever reason, flatly forbade him to do so.

I was shocked by this revelation. Why had Syawa denied my family food? Was he punishing them for the way they treated me? That seemed plausible, especially when I saw how pleased he was by the homage I was receiving. 'Twas almost as if my elevation in status was his gift to *me*. But how could I possibly enjoy such a powerful gift when, given the importance of balance in the Indian world, I knew I must, sooner or later, give Syawa an equivalent gift in return?

Thinking of balance also made me wonder about the relationship between the French traders and the natives. Every merchant I'd e'er known exchanged goods for only one reason—to make a profit. This motivation put the traders at a distinct advantage when bartering with people who exchanged goods primarily to maintain a balance of wealth and power. I wondered—how did the Frenchmen explain this contradiction to their Indian sons? And when they explained it to them, how could they look them in the eye?

The stormy spring weather continued the next day, making Hector increasingly restless. He arose in the morning from the furs of whichever girl had been lucky enough to catch his eye the night before, and he prowled the village like a cat, looking up at the gray, roiling clouds resentfully. He talked with Syawa about leaving in spite of the rain, but Syawa pointed out that our progress would be so slow and the process so unpleasant it would be just as well to wait.

Watching Hector pace, I wondered about the other news I'd learnt, that he had killed the brutish savage at the bottom of our stairs. I was not surprised to hear he was capable of murder, but I was shocked to hear he had killed one of his own comrades-in-arms. If the others in that war party had discovered the murder, they surely would have knockt out the brains of both Hector and Syawa. It seemed such a risky thing to do, so inexplicably motivated.

But then again, everything about my situation was inexplicable. How could Syawa have known I was up in that loft? Yes, he was an accomplisht storyteller, but was he truly more than that, as the Indians believed? I puzzled o'er the "Vision" about the birth of those twins. It could have been a Vision, as he claimed, or it could have been simple observation and reasoning—he might've seen the heavily pregnant woman, deduced she was having twins, assumed the birth would be difficult, and hoped that I might be of some assistance. Was Syawa truly a visionary, a prophet, or was he just an extremely shrewd man who knew how to manipulate impressionable minds?

Either way, he was special, and the more I knew of him, the happier I was I'd agreed to join him.

That afternoon, Syawa and I were checking on the young mother when the French priest arrived. He had come to bless the twins or some such thing, and when I shrank back, Syawa asked what was wrong. I gestured for him to follow me out into the drizzly day, but once there I hesitated, unable to explain in gestures how my father had harangued us all to be staunchly anti-Papist, anti-French, and anti-authority—and this priest was all those things.

I didn't get beyond explaining that the priest was from a different country than mine before Syawa stopt me to ask how many countries of people there were. I said I didn't know, but there were many, many—all with different languages, customs, and religions. Syawa frowned. He said in the two years he had been traveling, he had seen extreme differences amongst the people of this land, but now I was telling him those differences just went on and on. How, he wondered, could so many different peoples e'er achieve harmony and balance?

I stared at him, stunned speechless. For one thing, I couldn't believe he thought the differences between savage tribes were significant, because, as far as I could see, these people were all pretty much the same. But the other, far more startling thing he'd said was that he had been traveling for two years. *Two years?*

Before I could question him about this, the priest emerged from the hut and asked to speak with me. I shrugged. Syawa watched intently as I gestured a translation of everything that was said, but the conversation was difficult because the priest's English was so halting and I was still unwilling to let him know I spoke French.

He began with standard pleasantries, inquiring after my health and congratulating me for assisting in the miraculous birth, the fame of which had spread to the trading post. Then he put his hands on mine as if bestowing a blessing as he asked again if I was being held against my will. I pulled my hands away to translate his question and my answer, assuring him I was not. Syawa's eyes flashed from the priest to me and back again.

I'll say this for the priest—he was brave. He glanced at Syawa as he offered me sanctuary, promising that if I but said the word, he and his fellows would see to it that I was ransomed, rescued, and returned to the bosom of my family.

Instead of getting angry as the priest must have expected, Syawa just smiled. He looked at me, tipping his head and raising one eyebrow. "Now everyone wants you," he said. "What will you do?"

Memories of Philadelphia flashed in my mind, but only for an instant. I trusted my new friends far more than I could e'er trust a French Papist. I told the priest that Syawa and Hector were my family now, and we were returning to our people. Syawa's eyes shifted to the priest.

"I not wish make trouble, my child," the priest said cautiously whilst I gestured a translation. "But I fear you know not what is to come."

"No man can know that, can he, sir?" I interrupted. "Unless, of course, he's a prophet." I glanced at Syawa and smiled. Neither Syawa nor the priest smiled with me.

"What I say," the priest continued slowly, "uh, saying, is I hear talk—your companions come from people by the ocean—the Great Ocean."

I blinked, my hands motionless in mid-air. I knew of the Great Ocean because when I was small my father had a book with a map of the known world. He had shown us Ireland, where he was born, and the vast ocean he had crossed to come to America. The Great Ocean, called the Pacific, was easily twice the size of the one my father crossed, and it was all the way on the other side of the world.

"Did you know this?" the priest asked gently. "Did you know how far you must to go?"

"Well," I said weakly, "I, uh, knew it might take two years."

The priest bent down and picked up a stick to begin drawing in the mud. He drew the colonies, asking where I was born. I told him Boston, and he drew an X there. He drew an X for Philadelphia, adding the mountains of Pennsylvania, the great freshwater lakes, and a few of the larger rivers along the way, including the one we were on. He put another X to mark where we were on that river. His drawing covered a good ten feet of ground.

"Now, you see—this is the distance you travel already," he said, pointing along his map. He continued drawing, moving to his left as he added lines, lines, and more lines. He drew rivers and mountains, going e'er farther away from me.

By this time a crowd was gathering, and I noticed Hector had returned. He and Syawa exchanged a few words, both watching the priest warily, suspiciously, as if afraid he was conjuring something or casting a spell. I would have explained, but my gesture language included no signs for "drawing a map."

When the priest was finally finished, he put another X on the ground and stood up to look at me. He was, by that time, some forty or fifty feet from where I stood. I stared at the space between us, the distance very clear. The priest was telling me I had traveled a few hundred miles and that I had a few thousand miles to go. I swallowed hard.

"Now do you see?" he asked, wiping his muddy hands on his muddy black robe.

I nodded slowly. Syawa put his hand on my arm and asked me to translate. I sighed and gestured that the man was telling me about the journey to come.

"Is he a seer?" Hector demanded of Syawa, who passed the question on to me.

"No," I gestured. "He just a man."

The priest smiled ruefully. He dropt his stick onto his drawing and lifted his chin. "I thought you should know," he said quietly. "And my offer of protection is good. Consider it."

After the priest left, I tried to explain his visit to Syawa and Hector, but the only part of my translation they understood was that the priest wanted me to stay with him. The part of the priest's message that stuck with me, of course, was the true scope of the journey ahead, but I think Syawa interpreted my new distress as a sign that I might actually be considering the priest's offer. He reminded me that I was free to do as I would. He then told Hector to prepare to leave the next day, rain or shine.

I had a hard time sleeping. I wisht I could talk to Syawa about all that was bothering me, but my thoughts were too complicated to explain in gestures. Every time I closed my eyes, I kept seeing that huge map on the ground, the awesome distance between us and our destination. I knew Syawa and Hector had traveled a long way, but I ne'er dreamt their journey covered *thousands* of miles. And for what? For me? It simply wasn't possible. It made no sense.

And then there was the challenge of making that trip myself. What had I gotten myself into? How could I hope to cross an entire continent? And what would life be for me if I somehow managed to make it? I honestly couldn't imagine. Moreover, my companions were scarce on speaking terms, thanks to me, and if the tension of the last few weeks continued for the next two years, the journey would be unbearable.

Lying in that strange wigwam, I began to look at my parents in a whole new light. Their journey had been every bit as grand and impossible as the one before me, yet they had, after a fashion, succeeded. They made no secret of the distance they traveled, the sacrifices they made, and the suffering they endured, but I guess I'd ne'er really understood their story. No wonder my father drank. No wonder my mother lashed out at everyone who came near, threatening to beat all comers to a bloody pulp.

And then there was Gran, whose life had been a whirlwind of religious and political wars, with every scheme she concocted to improve her lot leaving her worse off than when she started. She married for love and lived in a pig-sty. She wed her daughter to a nobleman and was exiled. Every day was unending struggle, 'til her wits were addled and she died in whimpering exhaustion.

Life is very hard.

I must have slept, because then it was morning and I opened my eyes to find Syawa lying beside me, staring with questioning eyes. "Are you ready?" I mumbled. He smiled and I smiled back.

The sky was still gray, but at least it wasn't raining. We said our farewells and Hector started up a trail away from the river, but I said I must first stop by the French trading post.

For once, Syawa said nothing. Hector snapt that we would go nowhere near that place and continued in his original direction.

Neither Syawa nor I followed. Syawa nodded in assent, and he and I set off for the trading post. In a moment I heard Hector behind us, his angry breathing short and shallow. I imagined I could hear Syawa's heart pounding in his chest as he wondered if I was going to claim sanctuary from the French. I wisht I could allay his fears, but I knew I would ne'er be able to explain the details of my plan any more than he had been able to explain the subtle intricacies of gift-giving. All I could do was trust him to trust me.

The Frenchmen were surprised to see us, but masked their emotion with well-rehearsed smiles. LeFevre greeted us with what passed for genuine enthusiasm, tho' neither Syawa nor Hector was in the mood for pleasantries. Syawa was stone-faced and Hector was snorting like a shackled bull.

The priest approacht me with outstretched arms. "Welcome, my daughter," he said. "You come to us. Bless you. You making the right decision."

I smiled but side-stept his embrace as I headed toward a stack of trade goods. "No, sir," I said. "I have not come to stay with you nor ask for your assistance. I have come to trade."

The priest was nonplussed for a moment before turning to the headman, who eyed me critically. "So you want to trade, do you?" LeFevre said with a veiled smile as he slipt behind the counter where I stood. "Then by all means, let us trade."

I looked o'er the implements before me—guns, knives, swords, axes. I picked up a well-formed hatchet, the steel head thick on one side, razor sharp on the other. I weighed the handle in my fist, noting the sleek curve of the polished hickory, judging the balance. 'Twas an excellent hatchet—the finest I'd e'er seen. "This'll do," I said. "I'll take it."

LeFevre pursed his lips, his eyes amused. The salesman who'd failed with me the other day was sitting on a barrel behind the headman, enjoying this unique encounter, whilst a half-breed hovered in the shadows, made nervous by my glowering companion. E'en without looking, I knew Hector was gripping the handle of his stone blade.

"That's a fine hatchet, mistress," LeFevre said. "In fact, I fear it is too fine for you. I'm sorry to say you cannot have enough hides in that small pack to pay for it."

"I do not expect to pay for it," I said with a smile. "I expect you to give it to me."

"Now why would I do a foolish thing like that?" the hard-bitten trader asked, more amused than e'er.

"Because you have much and I have little and you must surely want to show what a great and generous man you are," I said, repeating a small part of the lesson I'd learnt from Syawa. Then I switched to French and added, "Also because you would not want me to tell your customers how you have been cheating them."

The priest's mouth dropt open as the headman's smile turned into a look of surprise quickly followed by outrage. The Frenchman on the barrel jumped to his feet, the boy in the shadows disappeared, and Syawa and Hector both stept forward, one on each side of me. Hector's knife was in his hand.

But I hadn't moved nor had I stopt smiling. LeFevre assessed Syawa and Hector, recovering his composure slowly. He signaled to his friend to sit down as he looked at me with new respect. "So you speak French," he said in his mother tongue.

"I do."

"And you have heard us say things you did not understand."

"I understood perfectly. You give the people here a reasonable exchange of goods for their furs only so long as they accept a drink or two with the transaction. When they want more liquor, as they always do, you make them pay back all the goods you gave them in exchange for the rest of the jug. By the time they sober up, one of your colleagues has taken the furs upriver to . . . New France, I suppose? At any rate, the people here generally have little more than a headache to show for all their trading."

By the time I stopt talking, the headman was furious, but the size of Hector's blade and the singular focus in his eyes kept him in check. I was amazingly calm. Just as I had been during the performance at the Feast, I was the sole spot of stillness in an emotional maelstrom.

"What are you suggesting?" the headman asked.

"I am suggesting you give me this hatchet as a gift, and I will give you the gift of leaving this place without explaining to the local citizenry what it is you do here."

The man looked into the distance, his lips in a tight line. He was angry, but he was also considering his options. "So what is your point, eh? You do not care if we cheat these people, so long as you get what you want?"

"I am not stupid," I said emphatically, immediately reminded of all the times Hector had called me so. "If I force you to stop cheating these people, I know ten more traders will swarm in to take your place. I am but a girl. I cannot change the way the world is. But I can change things for you."

The trader's nostrils flared. "And I can change things for you, too, I think. What is to stop my friends from following you into the woods and chopping you up with that very hatchet? Eh? Why should we not just kill you three where you stand?"

I looked 'round the trading post, where numerous Indians were wandering about. Some had followed us, others were there to trade, and others had their own reasons for being there. I gave the head trader a scolding look. "These people think my friend is a god. How do you think they would respond to his murder?"

The priest gasped. "Comparing a man to the Almighty is blasphemy!"

"And murdering three innocents can only lead to bigger problems," I said pointedly. "I would think you, sir, of all people, should know that."

LeFevre looked down at the hatchet, scratched his neck, and sighed. "So. You have your hatchet, for all the good it will do you. Take it and go." He spat on the ground beside the table.

Hector raised his knife, eager to avenge the obvious insult, but I gestured for him to stop. I smiled at Syawa, who was watching my actions intensely, not alarmed so much as deeply curious, and I stept o'er to pick up a leather pouch with flint, steel, and spunk. Speaking in English with my grandmother's Irish brogue, I said, "Well, now—if yer gonna be like that, sir, I'll just take this fire-starting kit, too." I smiled in my most flirtatious manner.

As angry as he was, he was still a Frenchman, after all, and he smiled in spite of himself. "Is that it, then?" he asked dryly, one eyebrow raised.

I nodded, turning to go, but the priest stept forward. "My child," he said in French, "if you are determined to go on this mad journey, I beg you, please—spread the word of our Lord amongst the heathens. Tell them of the grace and salvation available only through Jesus Christ. Make your life mean something! Tell them!"

I glanced at the knife in Hector's hand then looked back at the priest, frowning. "Why don't you make *your* life mean something, sir? You seem like a decent man. Tell your countrymen not to cheat these people. Tell them of the peace and harmony available only through a balance of wealth and power. Tell *them*!"

I turned and walked away, my pack on my back, my new things in my hands, my companions following behind.

Hector passed me almost immediately and we walked in silence 'til we reached the top of a ridge well away from the trading post. There we stopt to look back into the river valley at the tiny figures that had just been part of my daring little drama. I slipt my pack off my back to tuck my fire-starting kit inside. The hatchet I held out to Hector.

He stared at it, puzzled, then looked me full in the face, right in the eye, for the first time since our meeting in the loft. At that moment my heart began pounding as furiously as it did when last our eyes locked. This time, of course, I knew I had nothing to fear from Hector, but still I found myself struggling to control the quaver of my voice as I said as clearly as I could in his difficult language: "I gift you ax for ax I break."

Hector took the hatchet and looked at it, the cold stone of his face momentarily flushing deep scarlet. Without looking back at me, he nodded, tucked the hatchet into his waistband, and walked briskly away.

I did not yet understand the rules of Syawa's world and had ne'er really accepted the rules of my own, but, for now, at least, none of that mattered. Syawa, Hector, and I were going to be in our own little world for a long, long time, and I felt 'twas up to me to make it a pleasant one. By replacing the hatchet I broke, I hoped to restore the balance of our traveling threesome.

But when I turned to Syawa, he wasn't smiling in approval as I expected. For a fraction of a second, I saw a flash of something odd in his eyes, an emotion I did not recognize. It was akin to sadness, but it was so much more than that, filled as it was with longing, despair, and what I can only describe as excruciating pain. Then it was gone and he smiled broadly as he put his hand approvingly upon my shoulder. I grinned like a tail-wagging pup whose master has deigned, at last, to pat his head.

Our balance restored, we resumed our Journey.

~ 12 ~

THOSE DAYS AFTER DEPARTING the French trading post were the pleasantest I'd e'er known. Having become trail-hardened, I no longer suffered from aching legs and feet, and because I could communicate, if crudely, with my companions, I had some inkling of what was required of me each day. By this time I perceived Syawa was not about to press his suit upon me 'til I understood a great deal more about his world and his ways, so I focused my energies on the many lessons I was being asked to learn. And, finally, because I now had some vague idea of our destination, I knew, roughly, what to expect for the foreseeable future. The journey was bound to be arduous, but my companions had made it before and seemed confident they could make it again.

Best of all, the anger between the men was gone. Oh, I could detect a certain undercurrent now and then, a sore spot they both took great pains to avoid, but, for the most part, they talked and joked as if there had ne'er been a dispute. Knowing I was the source of their discomfort, I tried to stay out of their way as much as possible, but when I was left alone with my own thoughts, I went a bit crazy. I missed my family, my home—I fretted about being pursued by the French traders. Thankfully, Syawa ne'er let me brood for long. Whene'er he saw my eyes glaze o'er, he'd urge me to let go of the past, trust in the future, and just enjoy our Journey.

And so I did. Our days were filled with trotting through the woods and our evenings passed in amiable camaraderie. I still needed much advice about camp living, but Syawa seemed to enjoy teaching me and Hector said nothing more about me.

Some days after we left the French trading post, 'twas monthly time again, and knowing how peculiar the Indians are about this, I fretted my companions' response. Sure enough, as soon as they realized my condition, they backed away and maintained a goodly distance for the duration. Through that time they would not suffer me to touch their food nor tools nor supplies. They would not talk to me nor, for that matter, look at me. In short, tho' I was rarely more than thirty feet away, I was utterly alone for five days. At first, of course, I felt as if I were being shunned, but after a day or two I began to enjoy the break. I had no work to do, tho' they left me plenty to eat, and I no longer must struggle to communicate. In fact, 'twas almost as if I were a dragonfly perched on a nearby leaf, watching my companions without affecting them in any way.

That was when I realized how much my presence altered their relationship. When they could talk with me, I was the center of everything, but during the time they were prohibited from me, they reverted to their private language of mere grunts and glances. They were relaxed in a way they ne'er were with me, and when Syawa told his stories, Hector was as happy as e'er I saw him. I was almost sorry when my bleeding ended and, after a ritual bath and a cleansing in smoke of all my personal items, I was once again included in all activities.

One of the stories Syawa told during my isolation concerned

the creation of the world. 'Twas a fanciful tale involving a bird, a turtle, and a few other creatures I could not immediately recognize from Syawa's description. The plot involved bringing mud up from the bottom of an infinite ocean and using that dab of mud to make the world. Because I had been unable to question Syawa at the time he told the tale, I thought about it a lot. The evening after my companions and I were once again in communication, I questioned him about his story. Did he truly believe a turtle made the earth? Did he believe animals actually talked to one another?

Smiling, Syawa assured me that not only did animals talk together all the time, but trees and flowers and rivers and rocks had plenty to say as well. I smiled at his teasing. It dawned on me he was serious only when he went on to say quite sincerely that he did not presume to know how the earth was made, but someone had told him about the turtle, and it was as likely as any story.

Syawa asked how *I* thought the earth was made. I contemplated his question, realizing I'd ne'er really thought about it before, other than to accept without question the explanation in the Bible. Reluctant as I was to follow the command of the French priest, I proceeded to tell the story of Creation from Genesis, which, tho' I knew the passage word for word, was very hard to convert into gestures. Ne'ertheless, my friends attended with great interest 'til I had Adam and Eve happily situated in the Garden of Eden.

After I finisht, howe'er, Syawa looked confused. He wondered if something had been lost in translation, because he said I told two different stories—one in which a Spirit made men from mud and one in which a Spirit created man in his own image. Was I telling him this "god" of ours was made of mud?

I frowned, surprised this discrepancy had ne'er occurred to me.

Then I shrugged and said this was just the story someone had told me and I didn't presume to understand it.

We talked for a time about gods and men. Syawa thought it curious that both our stories centered on mud, but Hector said this was not surprising, considering how covered with mud we all were most of the time. At the moment it was all too true—thanks to the spring rains, the three of us were pretty much always filthy. E'en when we emerged from a cleansing bath, we must wade through mud on the bank in order to get to the drying fire, which meant we were ne'er mud-free.

The more we talked about mud and how central it was in our lives, the sillier we became. Syawa went to the creek bank to make his own little people out of mud, whilst Hector painted himself with mud and declared *he* was the Creation of the Mud God. I laughed at them both as I made mud-balls to throw at them. When one of my lobs hit Syawa's little tribe of mud-people, he grabbed up a handful of mud and tossed it at me. Laughing, I darted away from the ensuing barrage of mud-globs whilst Hector went over to stomp on what was left of Syawa's mud-people, proclaiming himself a Jealous God. Both Syawa and I then turned our mud-throwing toward Hector 'til Hector tackled Syawa and they ended up wrestling on the creek bank, wallowing in the mud.

I laughed and laughed. When my companions realized how hard I was laughing at them, they both turned to me, the whites of their eyes and teeth glowing in their mud-dark faces. Realizing my peril, I screamed with laughter and tried to scramble to my feet, but the two of them caught me and dragged me into their mucky pit. Soon I was as covered with mud as they were, and we were all exhausted from laughing.

It took a long, long time to go to sleep that night. Warm tho' the night was, I was still chilled from the bath I had been forced to take. I also couldn't stop chuckling. Then, just as I finally started falling asleep, I remembered the French priest and thought how appalled he would be to see how I shared Scripture with my savage friends. I couldn't help but start giggling again.

The next day the weather was unseasonably warm, and it just kept getting hotter and hotter as we walked. By mid-day I was drenched with sweat, but Hector kept pushing on, determined to cover a certain amount of territory. Altho' I previously attributed his urgency to the belief we were nearing our destination, I knew now that Hector was actually concerned about reaching certain landmarks along the way. At this point he was determined to reach what he called "the Great River" before it rained further.

His efforts were not successful.

By mid-afternoon huge gray clouds filled the sky and the very air felt strange. It was hot, so hot, with a strong, gusty wind blowing against us like the breath of some great slavering beast. I was not the only one who was uneasy. We stopt on an open knoll, the three of us looking up at the sky. "Those low clouds," Hector said, frowning at the white, wispy clouds racing o'erhead, "they're going north."

"But the higher clouds," Syawa said, nodding at huge, rolling gray blobs, "they're going west."

I looked at my companions, alarmed. "Wind on face *comes* from west!" I gestured. "What this mean?"

Syawa glanced at me, his face grave. "It means we must find shelter."

With the sky rapidly darkening, Syawa pointed to an enormous downed tree. Hector stuck his head into a hole in the side of the trunk and pulled back to say there was a sizable cavern wherein we could ride out the storm.

I thought he had lost his mind. I had no intention of crawling inside that black, dank, musty hole filled with dried bear droppings! When the sky turned green, however, I changed my mind.

I had seen violent storms in Pennsylvania and heard talk about cyclone winds, but I ne'er dreamt of nothing like this. Nor, apparently, had my friends. As they stufft our things into the tree trunk, their faces were enough to terrify me e'en if the wind wasn't already howling, peppering us with leafy debris. Syawa dove into the hole, pulling me with him as Hector pushed from behind.

Rank with urine, this den had clearly been occupied 'til recently, and, as Syawa wrapt a thick arm 'round my shoulders to draw me closer and thus make more room for Hector, the thought occurred to me the bear might return, looking for shelter from the storm. I asked Syawa about this, but before he could answer, the storm intensified and a theoretical bear became the least of my worries.

Tho' 'twas dark as pitch in that den, lightning flashed almost continuously, eerily illuminating the opening. I turned my face to see Hector's silhouette, his head leaning back against the den wall, his face lifted, almost in repose. He was no longer unduly alarmed, nor was Syawa, whose encircling arms were my refuge. Every time thunder crashed too closely, I flinched and buried my face against Syawa's chest.

For some time the wind and rain whirled horizontally through the forest, but then hail began pounding our tree trunk with a sound as loud as the end of the world. Hector reached out to grab one of the hailstones; it barely fit into the palm of his hand. When he tried to hold our tent cover o'er the hole to keep our den dry, the wind nigh pulled it from his hand, so he ended up wrapping the hide o'er his shoulders and shifting 'round to block the hole with his body.

"You not afraid?" I asked Syawa, having to yell e'en tho' my mouth was mere inches from his ear.

"Afraid of what?" Syawa shouted back.

"Of dying!" I wailed, then whimpered at a blast of thunder.

Syawa's chest rose and fell in steady rhythm. "We all die," he shouted into my ear. "To die here, now—would be good." He nuzzled his face in my hair.

He began to sing a soft, flowing song, and I held on to him, trying to slow my gasping to match the gentle rise and fall of his own chest. I concentrated so hard on his breathing that all else disappeared. His song went on and on, unaffected by the wind gusts or thunder blasts, and after what seemed like a long, long time, the winds howled less and the rain became a mere deluge instead of a raging tempest. Hector said something and I looked up to see that he had shifted 'round and was peering out the hole. When Syawa asked him to repeat what he'd said, Hector turned his head and said louder, "Maybe we made the mud god angry and he decided to stomp on *us*."

The thought of God being as silly as Hector had been the night before was so incongruous with the desperate danger we were in that we all laughed. The more we laughed, the more giddy we were with relief, euphoric to have survived. Syawa suggested maybe the mud god sent this storm to scrub the mud from our ears, so Hector leant his head out the hole to let the pouring rain do its job.

Almost immediately he pulled his head back to say a bear was coming. I gasped, clutching Syawa, but they both only laughed harder. Hector said a bear the size of a wigwam was coming to reclaim its den, and he described how it was doing a victory dance because it drove off the storm. When I tried to lean o'er Hector to see this crazy bear for myself, he said it ran away because it saw my hair and thought its den was on fire. We all laughed and laughed.

I knew then what Syawa meant. If the tree crumbled and we all died together right then and there, it would've been a good death indeed.

But we did not die that night. We crawled out of the tree in the morning to find a glorious, if extremely muddy, spring day. This, Hector said ruefully, was proof the mud god was indeed behind it all, because the entire world had once again turned to mud.

I was weak from hunger, for we'd had no food since the previous morning, and tho' Hector quickly pulled a fish from a stream, we could build no fire and thus had no way to cook it. Hector and Syawa shrugged and ate the meat raw, but I was reluctant 'til I tasted the warm blood on my lips. Then hunger took o'er, and I joined my friends in a feeding frenzy.

Thanks to fallen trees, debris, and standing water, we traveled only a few miles that day. We picked up sticks along the way so they might dry by nightfall, enabling us to get a small fire going. With that, we dried larger sticks 'til we had a reasonable blaze on which to cook our meat and warm our damp bones—which was good, for the weather had become quite cold.

As we sat 'round the fire, Syawa kept looking at his hand, frowning. I asked what was wrong, and he showed me a splinter between his finger and thumb. Hector rose to get a mussel shell to pry it out, but I told him not to bother. One of the things I had packed when preparing to run away was a sewing kit with steel needles, thread, and scissors. I had shown my friends these items long ago, but they had little interest in sewing. Splinter extraction, however, was another story.

I held Syawa's hand close to the fire to see the splinter, but he kept teasing me by flinching and shouting as if I were stabbing him with a knife. I started giggling, which made it harder to work, and we kept up this little charade for quite a time, with Hector repeatedly asking his friend if he needed protection from my formidable blade. I threatened to stab them both, and as I parried, they leant this way and that to avoid me. Finally I rolled Syawa onto his stomach and placed my knee on his upper arm so I could hold him still whilst digging out the splinter. He howled in mock agony, expressing terrific surprise when I was finisht, saying it hadn't hurt at all.

He sat up to look at his hand, which was bleeding slightly, now that the offending splinter was gone. He dabbed his finger in his blood and used it to paint something on the side of my face. I would've shrunk away, but he had grown quite serious. Frowning, he said he'd copied the tattoo from his own face and I was now marked as he was. He leant forward to touch my forehead with his as he whispered something I didn't understand.

He abruptly got up to wash his hands in the creek. As he was coming back, he told Hector how lucky they were to have such a great healer traveling with them. First I saved the twins, then I removed that dreadful tree trunk from his hand.

They were teasing me again, and I laughed and we played thus like children on into the night. By the time I crawled into my bearskin, I was once again exhausted from laughing. It seemed to me I had laughed more and felt more joy in the last few days than I had experienced in the whole of my first seventeen years. I slept that night as soundly as a child in its mother's arms, blissfully unaware how rare and fleeting joy truly is.

~ 13 ~

I AWOKE THE NEXT MORNING SCREAMING.

'Twas the strangest sensation. I had gone to sleep happy and secure, yet there I was, suddenly sitting upright, gasping for air, sweating and trembling, my stomach churning. Syawa sat near me, as if he had been sitting there for some time, simply watching me. I stared at him, wild-eyed, scarce comprehending where I was or how I got there.

"What did you see?" he asked quietly in his language.

"I . . . I don't know," I mumbled in English. Then I remembered myself and repeated the phrase in Syawa's language.

He nodded thoughtfully. "Be patient. It will come."

I tried to slow my breathing, but I was o'erwhelmingly nauseous. I closed my eyes and fought the urge to vomit, but closing my eyes only made things worse because I was dizzy, so very, very dizzy.

That was it! I opened my eyes. In the dream I was spinning and spinning, in a darkness so thick, so deep, I felt I could actually reach out and grab it. Spinning, spinning—as if the swirling storm had snatched me up and was spiraling me away, only there was no wind, no rain, no light, no hope. Only terror, absolute and all-encompassing, a deep, dark terror that is everything and nothing and now and forever. I lay back and put my arm o'er my eyes.

"Do not fight it," Syawa said. "Let it go and it will pass."

I nodded, swallowed hard, and stopt struggling. The spinning sensation subsided and the urge to vomit slowly ebbed.

When I finally sat up again, I was embarrassed by my childish nightmare. Syawa brought me our water pouch; I drank from it gratefully, avoiding eye contact. I saw Hector stealing glances my way as he packed up our campsite, and I started to get to my feet because I knew that was my job.

"Stay," Syawa said. "Sit. Tell me of your dream."

I thought about it. "Spinning," I said in English because I did not know the word in his tongue. I gestured and acted out the motion for him. He supplied the word. I nodded. He asked if that was all. I nodded again.

Syawa looked at me critically. Then, having reached some conclusion, he breathed deeply, slapt his thighs, and said, "If your dream was a message, the meaning is not yet clear. When you need to know more, the answer will come." He urged me to eat what they had left for me and gather my things so we could go.

The strange start to the day left us all in a somber and pensive mood. Whilst I kept hearkening back to the flood of emotions connected with that dream, Hector seemed preoccupied by something, and Syawa, well . . . something was clearly troubling him. Usually he smiled every time I caught his eye, but during our hike that morning, every time I looked his way I found him staring vacantly into the distance with a wistful expression.

As the day wore on and I moved farther from the dream, I was increasingly embarrassed by it. Obviously I had been more bothered by the cyclone than I let on, and my nerves were working through the fear I experienced whilst hiding in that tree trunk. I knew Syawa was worried about me, but I also knew he was reading more into my dream than was there. After all, I had once told him I was a dreamer as he was, so why wouldn't he now interpret my jittery nightmare as evidence of some sort of supernatural message? I blushed at the thought of misleading him, however unintentionally.

By mid-day the land we crossed was unpleasantly swampy and our forward progress slowed to almost naught. Hector stopt frequently to look 'round. At first I thought he was looking for a better path through the muck, but then I realized he was searching for something—some landmark, perhaps. Eventually he stopt to confer with Syawa before going on by himself. Syawa, looking grave, urged me to sit and rest whilst awaiting Hector's return.

"I must tell you something," he said and gestured, looking at me steadily.

I sat on a large rock and waited, tension tightening my throat and rolling my belly. I immediately thought of that strange dream I'd had. Spinning . . .

"I know how you dislike water," Syawa continued, still staring at me, "but we are approaching the largest river you will ever see. I do not mean to frighten you. I am telling you this merely so you will not be surprised. I want you to"—he gestured emphatically to make his meaning clear—"be prepared. If you are prepared, you will not be frightened."

I was strangely relieved. I don't know why, but I had thought for a moment Syawa was going to say he could not take me any farther and was going to leave me here in the forest, all alone. Compared to that, a river seemed a silly thing to fear.

I nodded and assured him I understood. I signaled that I would cross whatever river we encountered. After all, had I not conquered my fear and crossed countless streams and rivers? Did I not now bathe regularly? "I prepare myself," I said dutifully, and Syawa put his hand on my shoulder and smiled.

Ah, but nothing could have prepared me for what I saw when we arrived at the banks of the Great River. How could I be prepared for such an awful sight? It was not a river but, for all intents and purposes, a huge, fast-flowing lake whose distant shore was almost undetectable from where I stood. I stared at the vast expanse of water with a gaping mouth.

To make matters worse, e'en Syawa and Hector were surprised. From their conversation, I gathered they'd crossed this river in early winter when it was perhaps half the size it was now. At half its present size, the monstrous beast would have horrified me; at its current level, there was simply no way I would go anywhere near it. "How we go 'round this?" I broke into their conversation to gesture.

They both stared at me. Syawa took a deep breath. His eyes bored into mine as he said, "We must cross it."

"No," I said, shaking my head, my lips presst tight. "No. No, no, no, no, no. I not cross that river. I cannot. We find other way. We find a . . ." I did not know the word in their language, so I just said "bridge" in English and tried to depict a bridge with my hands.

Syawa and Hector exchanged a weary glance. "There is no other way," Syawa said in words and gestures. "Kay-oot-li, you must accept this. We are not just going to cross this river. We are going to travel on it for many days. We have a canoe."

I kept shaking my head, saying, "No, no, no . . ." as Syawa went on to explain they had buried their canoe somewhere nearby, but

Hector was having trouble locating it because the floodwaters had altered the terrain.

"Well, it's gone then, and we'll just have to find a different way!" I said in English whilst gesturing. My voice was tight with rising hysteria. "We can walk upstream. If we go far enough, there will surely be less water!"

Hector gave me a withering look and mumbled to Syawa that we had no more time to waste. In order to reach a certain village before winter, we must proceed up this river now.

I just kept shaking my head, saying "no," 'til Hector stormed off to look for the canoe. In the meantime, Syawa stood still, looking at me sadly. He waited whilst I paced and ranted and raved and raged. I reminded myself of my mother when she was in one of her red-faced screaming fits. In his language I said it was a stupid plan to cross this stupid river and I was not so stupid I would do it. There had to be another way. There had to be another way.

When I finally worked myself into tears, Syawa took my arms in his hands and stopt my pacing. "Enough," he said firmly. "You have said your words. Now you must prepare yourself. There is nothing to fear in water. It is the source of all life."

I looked into Syawa's gentle but strong eyes and struggled to match his cool demeanor. But every time I so much as glanced at that massive basin of water, I panicked all over again. I saw an entire tree bobbing along as if it weighed nothing, and everywhere were huge logs swirling like little twigs. The wind formed foamy caps upon the waves, and giant birds circled o'er the waters the way gulls circled o'er the ocean in Boston.

"I cannot do this," I gestured simply. "I'm sorry, Syawa, but I cannot do this."

Syawa's face showed no emotion as he kept looking at me. "You are smart. You will learn. I will teach you. Like talking and washing and cooking and gift-giving."

He was right. I had learnt many new things in the past two and a half months, and if anyone could teach me to embrace water, it would be Syawa. Besides—what was the alternative? If I did not calm down and do what Syawa said, he and Hector might very well go on without me, and then where would I be? Syawa was right. I was smart. I could learn.

He took me to the water's edge, telling a story about the river his village was on and how the river gave his people food and riches and life. He assured me that I, too, would learn to understand the river the way I talked about my people understanding books, and when I did, I would have access to a whole new world. Then Hector came o'er the ridge, shouting that he had found the canoe, and Syawa and I hurried to join him.

As we walked, Syawa explained they had planned to paddle the canoe all the way to my family's farm, but by the time they reached this point in their journey, the days were short and the river was freezing o'er. He said he could not wait through another winter, and so they set off on foot, determined to reach me by spring. Besides, he said, he thought the walk to the Great River would give me time to get accustomed to my new life.

I was stunned by this news. I had ne'er really believed Syawa was looking for *me*—I assumed he was looking for *someone*, and when he met me he decided I would do. But to hear him talk, he knew precisely where he was going and he was driven to get there as quickly as possible. And somehow he convinced Hector to abandon their canoe and walk hundreds of miles through strange land, just to arrive at my family's farm on that particular spring day. It was an insane story. Yet he told it in such an off-hand, matter-of-fact way that I could not doubt that he, at least, believed it to be absolutely true. And I had no way to dispute it. To the contrary, the circumstantial evidence suggested the facts were without question. But how could it be true? And why?

By the time we caught up with Hector, he had the canoe half-uncovered, and with all three of us working, it was soon unearthed. The men checked o'er their buried supplies whilst I worked on setting up our camp. Before I e'en managed to get a fire going on the soggy landscape, my companions had dragged their canoe to the water, washed it off inside and out, and jumped inside.

The sun was setting golden on the other side of the river, with all the yellows and reds and oranges and purples stretching out, shimmering, on the rippling water. I watched my friends glide into the middle of that pulsating palette and felt a thrill of horror, knowing how absolutely alone I was. I sat holding my knees to my chest, thinking of all the wild creatures and malevolent Frenchmen who might be eyeing me from the underbrush.

From the rise on which our camp was located, I could see Syawa and Hector e'en when they were far, far away. They controlled their canoe as easily as I control my own feet, and the longer I watched them, the more my dread began to dissipate. It didn't look so bad. It looked easy. It looked almost fun. Maybe I could do this. Of course I could. Why couldn't I do this?

I saw them confer for a moment before maneuvering their craft 'round. Riding with the current, they soared, and suddenly Syawa stood up in the front of the canoe to thrust a stick into the river. This was a stick they had stored under their buried canoe, and when Syawa pulled the rope attacht to the stick, a huge, writhing fish emerged from the water. I smiled. By this time I knew very well how to cook a fish.

After we ate, Syawa asked me to tell another story, like the one I told about the creation of the world. I knew he was trying to keep me from fretting about what I must do in the morning, so I obliged him by telling the story of Adam and Eve, which was, of course, the continuation of my previous tale. Tho' I hoped to restore the light mood my other story created, I failed completely. I don't know if I didn't translate well or if my listeners were too distracted or if I was just too on edge, but, whate'er the case, when I was done, I was met with an awkward silence that went on and on.

Finally Hector asked if all my people can talk with snakes. Sure he was mocking me with basically the same question I'd asked Syawa about his turtle story, I stared into the fire, tight-lipped. But his question made me think. *Did* Christians believe the snake really talked? Odd, I'd ne'er wondered about that before. When I said nothing, Hector frowned and rolled himself in his sleeping fur as if *I'd* offended *him*.

Syawa breathed deeply and exhaled very slowly. "Are you saying your people believe their own actions caused all the miseries in this world?" he asked, clearly troubled. "How can they e'er be happy, believing this?"

I shrugged, confused. "Maybe they can't." I tried to remember the good times in my seventeen years—the weddings, the successful births, the times when someone made money—and I realized how rare those moments were. Syawa was shrewd to recognize the self-loathing that fueled every aspect of a world he'd only glimpsed.

He went on to ask if this perfect place I described, this Garden, still existed. I said I didn't know, but if it did, it didn't matter—we would not be allowed back inside. Syawa glanced at me, quickly turning his eyes back to the fire. "And yet you still speak of it," he said with both words and hands. "You still yearn for it. You still seek it, tho' you believe it is forbidden to you. You torment yourself with this hopeless longing."

"Maybe we *need* believe in Garden." I shrugged as I gestured. "Life is hard, bad, much pain. With no Garden, how we go on?" I smiled feebly, hoping to tease Syawa back into a lighter mood. "Maybe you take me to Garden now, yes?"

Still staring into the fire, he quickly said and gestured, "No. Life is not perfect anywhere. People are not perfect. But my people do not seek perfection. We strive for balance. We enjoy life as we find it, the good and the bad. We are grateful for all."

When Syawa said no more, I said good night and curled up in my bearskin, pondering what he'd said. I was almost asleep when I felt his hand on my shoulder. I snapt to attention, my heart racing, sure something must be wrong. He leant over to whisper so as not to disturb Hector. "Kay-oot-li," he murmured, "you must not blame yourself when bad things happen. You are not the cause."

I thought for a second, flustered by his closeness, his warm breath on my ear. "You talk of story? Of Eve in Garden?"

"No. I talk of you, of living with my people."

I tried to sit up but Syawa held me down with his hand on my shoulder. I felt a surge of fear as I realized how vulnerable I was, but he was not threatening me in any way—he was just staring at me, staring and staring, as if trying to memorize every pore in my face. "But I *cause* my life," I said, hard-presst to add gestures from my prone position. "You say I must choose come with you, and I choose. I choose and cause my life, yes? We all are blame for chooses we make!"

Syawa smiled but seemed sad as he brusht a wisp of hair from my face. He leant so close his lips touched my ear as he whispered, "You never truly had a choice. I just said that so you would feel good about coming. What else could you do? You had to come."

I frowned, pulling back so I could see his face. "What you say? Yes, I have choice! I have choice right now. I have choice tomorrow. Tomorrow—is this what worries you? You think I choose not go with you?"

"You will go. And you will live a good life with my people. But bad things will happen. They always do. And when they do, you must not blame yourself. You must enjoy life in spite of bad things."

Then Syawa launched into one of his lectures, only a fragment of which I understood. He went on and on about rivers and currents and how they can appear one way but be another or be one way and appear another and he used words I did not understand, whispering along at such a breakneck speed I could not possibly question him or tell him I was lost. As was so oft the case, he seemed determined to throw at me everything he knew on a subject and be satisfied if I managed to pick up a few bits and pieces as I followed along.

Toward the end of this discourse, Syawa's babbling veered off into an unexpected direction. All this time he had been talking about blame and rivers and things in the way when suddenly he said there was something he wanted me to tell Hector. At this point I was only half-listening, but I remember Syawa's sudden request caught me by surprise, and I frowned at him, puzzled.

His face was only a few inches from mine, our breaths commingling. "Why you want *me* tell him?" I asked. "Why not you tell him?" I glanced at the lump on the other side of the fire that was Hector.

Syawa's smile seemed sad. "He is sleeping now. We will be busy tomorrow and I may forget. I want you to remember for me. Is that so much to ask?"

His dark eyes were right in front of mine and I was as power-less before him now as I was the moment we met in my family's loft. O'erwhelmed, I murmured, "No." His eyes warmed tho' his smile stayed sad.

"Good. Then I want you to learn the words I am going to say and remember them exactly. Can you do that?"

I nodded, thinking that memorizing a few words was nothing compared to getting into that canoe tomorrow. Syawa slowly said the words he wanted me to remember, then asked me to repeat them. When I did, he corrected my pronunciation and asked me to say them again. The only part of the message I fully understood was the end, which was an admonition to enjoy the canoe ride. He made me say the entire message several more times before inhaling slowly and deeply, apparently satisfied.

"Do not forget to tell him," he said, and before I could respond, he gently stroked my face with his hand, got up, and walked off into the darkness, leaving me to stare into the glowing embers of the fire.

~ 14 ~

I AWOKE THE NEXT MORNING screaming again.

This time I rolled o'er and vomited in the weeds before I was e'en fully awake. When I finisht, I looked 'round miserably and found Syawa sitting nearby, watching me. "What did you see?" he asked.

"Spinning," I said as soon as I remembered the word. "Spinning and spinning . . ." I stopt for a moment and thought, then looked at Syawa in surprise. "This dream I see snake."

Syawa looked up into the brightening sky, his face haggard, as if he had not slept at all. "What did the snake do?"

I glanced o'er at Hector, who was packing things up, pretending not to listen, but I knew he was. I was embarrassed to go on. "He . . . he spinning me. And he say, 'Ye'll ne'er get away from me, Katie.'" I didn't mention the snake spoke English with an Irish brogue, like my mother.

Syawa was staring at the ground, a strange, humorless smile on his face, but he said nothing.

"I think story last night . . . frighten me," I said, working hard to pronounce the foreign words. I got on my knees to begin rolling up the bearskin. "I worry about river, and I am . . ." I didn't know the word for "nervous," so I just said "frighten" again.

Syawa took a deep breath and said dreams like mine can dispel fear by giving us a chance to prepare. Such Visions, he said, cannot change the course of events—only prepare us to accept them. "Acceptance is what allows us to enjoy life," he said.

I thought it more likely my dream was telling me Christian Scripture had no place in the savage wilderness, but I said no more. Instead, I finished packing up camp and forced down my share of food left from the night before so I could steel myself to meet the challenges to come.

"Can she do this?" I heard Hector ask Syawa. I glanced at Hector, who was looking my way skeptically. I resented him talking about me as if I still couldn't understand what they were saying, but I suppose I had given him plenty of reasons to be skeptical.

"She will be fine," Syawa said.

Hector thought for a moment, then ventured a question he seemed reluctant to ask. "Did *you* dream anything?"

Syawa smiled, but his eyes were sad. "My dreams these days are all of home." As they talked briefly about their home, I felt a surge of guilt, knowing I was the reason they were not there. Then I remembered what Syawa said about not blaming myself, and I wondered if this was what the snake in my dream was talking about. 'Tis all well and good to say I'm not to blame for things; 'tis something else altogether for me to stop feeling guilty.

The two of them began to carry the canoe to a stream which fed into the Great River, where they would teach me the basics of handling a canoe. I was not eager for this lesson, but I understood the need for it.

Hector also understood the need for it, tho' the delay clearly vexed him. Moreover, the trek to the creek was insufferable, through a long stretch of swamp and bracken. Mosquitoes swarmed us, and after a short time I began to think the plan was to make me so miserable on land that I would eagerly jump into their boat just to get away from the voracious insects. I was relieved when we reached the creek.

Normally this tributary stream was shallow, but the floodwaters had filled its banks, creating a fierce current. I was as tense as a bowstring when Syawa helped me into the front of the canoe, but knowing I had no choice, I gritted my teeth and complied.

I should say this canoe was wholly unlike other Indian canoes I'd been in. Those were made from bark, and I despised the sensation of water roiling under that flimsy membrane. This canoe, however, was made of a section of a tree trunk that had been hollowed out in a most ingenious manner. Solid and sturdy, the wood was also amazingly light, so that e'en when heavily loaded the canoe rode high on the water.

I settled into the front, clutching the sides as the craft rocked. Syawa climbed in behind me and Hector pushed the canoe out into the current before jumping in at the back. They paddled rapidly upstream. At first, I held on to my panic as tightly as I held the canoe, but in spite of my pounding heart, I knew Syawa would let no harm come to me. Before long I did with my fear what he had advised me to do with my dizziness—I let it go and it passed. Soon all that was left was excitement and energy, because it truly was sensational to be skimming along above all that water.

When I stopt staring down into the churning brown ooze and began looking up into the pretty blue sky, Syawa asked me to turn 'round so he could show me how to paddle. I soon became absorbed by the lesson. For the past two and a half months he had been teaching me one new skill after another, and I responded now to his slow, steady instructions the way a well-trained dog responds to its beloved master. When Syawa said it was my turn and gave me the paddle, I wasn't e'en worried. I wanted only to make my teacher proud.

'Til I grew confident with the paddle, Syawa leant o'er me, guiding my hands and pulling with me. As I think back to that moment, it occurs to me I should have been distracted by the nearly naked man presst up against me, but all I remember is the comfort I derived from being encircled by Syawa's strong arms. It was, in fact, this physical closeness that prevented me from reverting to my old fear. Because I knew Syawa would protect me, I was able to relax and enjoy myself. I e'en laughed when he leant back and said now he finally had what he always wanted—two servants doing all the work whilst he enjoyed the scenery.

Of course, our progress slowed considerably when I took the paddle, but the farther up the creek we went, the less furious was the current. At first I had to pull with all my strength just to keep the craft from going sideways, but Hector, pulling in the back, was able to correct most of my mis-strokes. I quickly realized my main task was simply to complement his expert paddling.

In no time at all I understood why my friends had such huge arms and well-developed shoulders. Paddling was hard work, and long before I was proficient I was exhausted, hoping Syawa would say we could stop. We kept going, however, 'til my weariness caused me to make mistakes which made the canoe wobble. When I overcorrected and the canoe turned sideways, Syawa leant forward to talk me through my panic, explaining what Hector was doing to turn us right again, guiding me 'til we were once more gliding smoothly. After this sort of thing happened several times, I no longer panicked whene'er the canoe wobbled.

Finally Syawa said we should turn the canoe 'round. My stomach tightened, but I followed his instructions through the nerve-wracking turn. Before I could congratulate myself on my success, however, the canoe caught the current and our speed rose precipitously.

Syawa had warned me this would happen, but as our speed picked up, so did my heart rate. We were moving so very quickly that I couldn't respond to the rocks and trees and o'erhanging limbs which were so easy to avoid during our slow trip upstream. E'en as Syawa told me what to do to avoid an upcoming rock, we slammed against it, turning sideways. The current pulled us backwards and I panicked, but Syawa told me to relax and let Hector turn us 'round, which he did. In his calm, steady voice, Syawa assured me we'd be fine e'en if we turned over. "What's the worst that can happen?" he soothed. "We will get a little wet, that's all."

No sooner had he said it than it happened. I steered us almost directly into a dangling branch that scooped the canoe over like a giant hand. I splashed and spluttered and gasped and choked in the waist-high water, terrified beyond measure, but as I collected myself, I saw Syawa and Hector were both just standing in the water laughing. Whilst I had been trying not to drown, they had collected the canoe and paddles and were waiting patiently for me to stop floundering.

I stood there dripping and shivering, feeling like a drowned rat—and a useless one at that. Syawa smiled and said, "You see? We are only wet!"

I wanted to scream that I knew this would happen, that it was all my fault, that I was stupid and useless and a danger to the both of them . . . 'til I realized 'twas my mother's voice shrieking in my head. She was the one who always told me I couldn't do nothing right, that everything bad was all my fault, and that I would, inevitably, be the death of her. I looked at the men standing in the creek, joking and laughing, and I took a long, slow, deep breath. What was I so afraid of, really? Hector squatted down to dunk his head in the water, then stood up to comb loose wisps of his long, black hair off his face with his fingers. He was smiling broadly, the water dripping from his face down to his chest. I stared, transfixed by the droplets dribbling down, down, down, and suddenly my fear of water evaporated. I raised my eyes to Hector's face. For an infinite moment our eyes locked, and I forgot all about the water, forgot my fears, forgot my mother's voice, forgot e'en how to breathe . . .

"Are you ready?" Syawa asked, and I flinched, startled. I nodded, blushing, and as he helped me climb back into the canoe, I stared down at the gurgling water, wondering what in the world just happened. Before I could figure it out, we were flying down the creek again and I had no time to think of anything but avoiding the looming rocks and tree limbs. I was relieved when Syawa reached 'round to take the paddle, saying it was his turn again. Shortly thereafter we passed the point at which we started, and with the current rushing us along, we soon gushed into the Great River. I clutched the sides of the canoe again, instantly tense, but was surprised to find that once we were in the larger body of water, the ride actually smoothed out.

The men steered us back to our campsite, where Syawa showed me how to load the canoe and tie down our gear, and because the canoe was small—about eight feet long—it was quickly filled. After settling me atop our packs, he stept into the front of the canoe and I turned to look at the woods behind us.

This was the point of no return. Once I crossed that massive river, I would ne'er be able to come back on my own. I lifted my chin and turned my face resolutely to the west, praying my mother's critical voice would not follow me further. That's when I found Syawa also looking back at the woods, with that same sad, wistful expression I'd seen several times since arriving at the river. But when I caught his eye, he smiled fully for a split second before the canoe shot forward and Hector hopped in.

As we slid into the open water, I was pleased to discover my fear of water truly was gone. For a long time we stayed to the side of the river as we worked our way upstream, but by mid-afternoon, Syawa began angling into the stronger current. I could feel the canoe hesitate between the force of the river and the pull of the paddles, but this sensation did not alarm me. I looked at the woods on the eastern shore, watching it grow smaller and smaller, remembering how I felt the night before, when I was all alone. I was glad I wasn't alone anymore.

By the time we reached the middle of that vast expanse of water, I felt euphoric. Oh, the exhilaration of riding all that raw power! I knew I was impotent before those raging forces, wholly subject to the whirling whims of the current, but I also knew I was perfectly safe, nestled between two pairs of strong, highly skilled hands. I laughed at the huge logs swirling helplessly whilst we rode steady and sure. I sneered at the debris eddying in our wake. As mighty as that river was, we puny humans were controlling our own fate, plotting our own course, going our own way.

I wanted to tell Syawa how wonderful this experience was and how right he had been, but he ne'er turned 'round. I occasionally turned to grin at Hector, who always looked away but seemed mildly amused by my newfound enthusiasm. When we were more than halfway across, I turned my attention to the looming western landscape, wondering if it was different from the one we'd left behind. It didn't seem to be. I saw trees and bushes and the occasional swollen tributary, just like on the other side.

We rode upstream for a long time, 'til at a certain point, without conferring, my friends steered a course up a small creek. It seemed to me they were communicating through the canoe itself, which made me remember how much time they had spent in it. And for what? For me?

They steered the canoe to the deep-shaded shore of the swollen creek. Syawa jumped into knee-deep water, squishing through mud in the shallows before turning to look at me. I expected him to grin and say, "You see? Nothing to fear!" But he didn't. He just walked backwards through the mire, pulling the canoe as he went. His face was expressionless, like stone.

I was peering down at the mucky water, hoping Syawa would get the canoe all the way onto dry land before I had to get out, when I heard him yelp. Out of the corner of my eye I saw him fall backwards as, at the same moment, Hector leapt from the canoe behind me. Hector's feet hit the water hard, shooting mud up into my face so that I was momentarily blinded. Worse still, Hector's wild leap shoved the craft back into the creek, where the current immediately caught it.

I could hear shouting as I wiped the mud from my face, but my eyes were thick with it and I could not see. When I reached o'er the edge of the canoe to get a handful of water to wash out my eyes, I felt the canoe moving at an alarming rate. Faster it went, and faster, and then it began to turn.

With my face in my hands I felt a huge wave of nausea as my dream came back to me full force. Spinning and spinning, all was darkness, all was terror, and when I finally got my eyes clean enough to see, I found the canoe was already at the mouth of the creek, slipping back into the river, where the current caught it and spun it 'round. Spinning and spinning, I turned to see if my friends were coming for me, but I saw nothing save drooping tree branches.

I was alone.

I screamed, but the very act of screaming took me right back to my dream, intensifying my terror. I screamed and screamed, just as I had whilst awakening, and nauseating dizziness o'ercame me just as it did in my dream. I leant o'er the side of the canoe to vomit.

Then I remembered. Syawa said dreams could prepare me, dispel my fear. I had already vomited this morning, so I need not do it again. Now I must do what Syawa had taught me.

I saw his paddle lying in the canoe, and I grabbed it and stuck it into the water. The canoe immediately wobbled violently, water splashing in at my feet. I fought my rising panic—after all, I was only getting wet, and I had already been much wetter today. This wasn't so bad. I could do this. I could do this.

I could not do this. The more I tried to paddle, the more I caused the canoe to spin. But e'en tho' I could not control the direction, I quickly realized my flailing was slowing my forward motion considerably, keeping the current from having me. I thought perhaps this was the message of my dream, if, indeed, message there had been—to keep the canoe spinning so I did not get sucked into the middle of the river where I would float helplessly 'til I crashed and drowned. Frantic, I slapt at the water, making the canoe spin more and more.

During one of my revolutions I saw something in the water behind me. I turned my head this way and that against the spinning, straining to see more clearly. One of the men was swimming after me, his head buried in the water as his arms pulled rhythmically. I couldn't believe how fast he was moving, but, then again, he was using the current as much as I was fighting it. Now it was a race to see if he could catch me before the river pulled me out of his reach forever.

'Round and 'round I went, but with each revolution, my pursuer drew closer and closer. When he raised his head to take a breath, I saw it was Hector. His arms pumped whilst I spun 'round and 'round; soon he was close enough for me to hold out the paddle, hoping he could catch it. But when I stopt paddling, the canoe straightened and picked up speed, so I had to use the paddle to re-start the spinning.

Hector's hand grabbed the lip of the canoe just as his strength gave way. I clutched his wrist and held on because his arm was trembling so much I feared he would lose his grip. Luckily, the current pushed his body up against the canoe, and for a time he held on to the side with both hands, spinning with it, holding his head back as he gasped raggedly. I held his wrists, crying out his name over and over, unable to help in any way.

As soon as he was able, he made the supreme effort to pull himself into the boat. The side tipped precariously, but he had clearly done this sort of thing before and knew how to use the rock-ing to roll into the craft. Once inside, he tossed his head to get his loosened hair out of his face and yelled for me to give him the pad-dle. From the moment he put the paddle in the water, the canoe was once again under control. Hector wearily steered it toward the wa-ter's edge and slowly turned the craft 'round. Then he began the arduous task of pulling against the current by himself.

It was a long journey, during which I felt useless and stupid. I turned and looked at Hector, but he was so thoroughly depleted it was all he could do to keep paddling. Thereafter I kept my eyes on the shoreline, straining to catch sight of Syawa.

We arrived back at the point in the creek where we started just as the sun was setting. There was no sign of Syawa. Hector paddled the canoe onto the bank, but when I prepared to jump out as Syawa had done, he shouted so violently I flinched and shrank from him. I was desperate to get out of the canoe, but Hector made it clear I must stay where I was 'til he said I could get out. He slid into the mucky water, pulling the canoe with me inside past the worst of the mud on the bank. Then he nodded and I got out and waited whilst he secured the canoe between two bushes. As soon as the canoe was situated, Hector turned to walk briskly inland, leaving all our things in the canoe.

"Where Syawa?" I asked, struggling to keep up.

"I do not know," Hector said through clenched teeth, his face grim.

"What happen? He hurt?"

Hector glanced at me, the exhaustion in his eyes dwarfed by a looming fear. "He was bitten by a snake."

~ 15 ~

I T WAS GROWING DARK in the woods, and Hector frowned as he followed Syawa's trail. For a time I pestered him with questions—what sort of snake was it? where was the bite? how deep was it?—but he was in no mood to answer questions. All he said was that Syawa ordered him to get me.

When we began climbing a rise, I stayed close behind Hector, so much so that when he reached the top and abruptly stopt, I actually stumbled into him. Then I heard Syawa singing in the distance, and relief swept o'er me like a cleansing breeze. I stept up to glance at Hector, expecting to see him as relieved as I, but what I saw in the deep shadows chilled my blood. His face was contorted in pain. I had no chance to ask what was wrong before he was running through the dark undergrowth at breakneck speed. I followed as best I could, emerging into a grassy clearing where Syawa sat before a small fire. Hector knelt beside him, holding his head in his hands. I saw Hector's shoulders heave, but Syawa did not stop singing.

As I stared at this scene, my arms and legs began to tremble. Just as at that Indian village when it was decided I would come on this journey, the me that was me left my body and simply stood there, quivering, as my body walked slowly forward. I was sure it was still morning and I was still asleep on the other side of the river, preparing to wake up screaming and puking. But I did not wake up. I watched as my body knelt beside Hector. Syawa did not look at me nor did he stop singing. "What wrong?" my hollow body asked quietly.

Hector did not look up but I knew his face was wet with tears. "He sings his Death Song." Hector's voice wavered.

I snapt back into my body the way a trap snaps shut when a creature steps into it. I could not comprehend what was happening. I knew that many, if not most, snakebites are not fatal, and tho' Syawa might be made gravely ill or even lose an appendage, he was strong and healthy and I saw no reason to assume he wouldn't recover. Moreover, he seemed fine, sitting there singing, and what was a Death Song anyway? In my experience, people are oft sure they're going to die 'til the crisis passes, at which point they begin to get better. Surely all this was an over-reaction.

Then I saw Syawa's leg. From the way he was sitting cross-legged before the fire, I thought at first there was a shadow near his knee. But upon looking more closely, I saw his left calf was dark purple and twice the size it should be. I scooted o'er to get a better look.

That's when I saw his arm.

It, too, had been bitten, somewhere near the wrist. His forearm was swollen and purple. I stared at it, my insides liquefying as fear flooded my own veins. I slowly raised my eyes to Syawa's face. He stopt singing. He smiled.

He looked terrible. His skin was drawn and pale; his eyes were sunk within dark circles. Tears filled my own eyes as I started to speak, but Syawa stopt me by looking at Hector and asking him to go get water as well as our things from the canoe.

Hector put a shaky hand on Syawa's shoulder and asked in a stricken voice, "Can you not heal these wounds?"

It was the very question I was going to ask. Syawa shook his head. "I've always known my Journey would end here, at the Great River. I am sorry, my friend."

Hector bowed his head, then rose to disappear into the darkness. Syawa turned his eyes back to me, smiling sympathetically.

"You say you come on Journey, knowing you die?" I asked, working hard to pronounce the difficult words.

Syawa shrugged, looking sheepish. He closed his eyes for a moment, and I was not sure whether he was struggling against the physical pain or some emotional one. He did not open his eyes as he said quietly, "Do you remember when you said you are not good for me?"

I nodded, recalling the conversation that seemed as if it happened years and years ago, tho' it had been only a few weeks. Syawa opened his eyes to look at me wearily. "I did not tell you then, but I should have. You were never meant for me."

I swallowed heavily, fighting back tears. "Syawa, stop! You are wrong! Of course I am meant for you. Your Vision . . ."

He grimaced slightly. "There is much you do not know." He looked at me, sadder than anyone I'd e'er seen in my life. "Kay-oot-li, I have allowed you to believe things that are not true. I wanted to tell you. But you were not yet ready to hear me. You do not understand my Vision."

I frowned, my mind reeling. "What? What do I not understand?"

He stared down at the fire, apparently oblivious to what must have been horrific pain throbbing in both his arm and leg. He spoke quietly, hesitantly, and I concentrated, desperate to understand his words. He told me, once again, about the Great Earthquake that occurred when his mother was born, and how after that his people lived always in fear because they believed the Earthquake was telling them something, warning them. The Holymen worked to understand the Earthquake's message, but could not. "Just before I was born," Syawa said slowly, "my mother dreamt of the Thunderbird. Because of this, she knew I was destined to be a Holyman. Others did not believe her, but I knew. I *knew*. Through my youth, I studied and learned. I fasted and prayed. I offered my life in exchange for understanding. The Holymen saw my dedication, trained me in their ways. And then the Vision came to me. I became the Seer. I saw it all. I understood."

There followed a long, long pause during which Syawa's face twitched with spasms of pain. I still could not tell whether the pain came from his injuries or his memories. In any case, he fought against it for some time, finally controlling it enough to go on.

"It was you," he said at last, so quietly I could scarce hear him.

I shrank back, stunned. "What?"

"It was your people." Syawa closed his eyes and seemed to slip into unconsciousness, tho' he remained upright and steady.

I stared at him with an open mouth. "What . . . what you mean it was my people? You think . . . you think my people cause earthquakes?"

He smiled without opening his eyes. "Your people *are* the Earthquake." His breathing was becoming slightly labored, and I could see he was hard-presst to continue. He took a deep breath and let it out slowly, still with eyes closed. "There are so many of you. So many. I saw them, saw them all—all colors, all kinds, all crowded, all suffering. So many. Like leaves on the trees, like drops of rain, like stars in the sky. All fighting, all struggling, all pushing against one another, helpless, hopeless. All coming this way."

Syawa opened his eyes, which warmed when they looked at me. "And then I saw you. You were so lonely. So sad. I saw you lying on your stomach on top of round wooden boxes, your clothing sliced on your back, blood seeping from long, thin wounds. You were crying. You had flowers in your hair. The flowers were the color of the sky, the color of your eyes."

As I listened to this slow and soft description, my face crumpled and tears rolled down my cheeks. Well I remembered the scene he described. It happened on a lovely day in May when I was fifteen, when we were on our way to the parcel of land in the wilderness where we were going to build a farm and recover all the riches and prestige and power my father had lost. We were traveling with at least a dozen other families, and one day my new friend, Abigail, made me a crown of bright blue flowers to wear on my red curls.

After we stopt to camp, I went to the creek to get some water, accompanied by a man at least twice my age who said he'd lend a hand. He kept saying how pretty I looked with those flowers in my hair. The creek bank was high and the only way he could reach the water was to lie on his belly, but the bucket snagged on an underwater branch and he could not pull it up. I knew my mother would beat me if I lost a bucket, so I lay down and reached to unsnag it. Whilst I was reaching, the man rolled atop me, threw my skirts o'er my head, and forced himself upon me. I struggled mightily, to no avail.

I had ne'er been used by a man and it was brutal. After he ran away, I wiped the blood from my legs with a handful of weeds.

Then I staggered back toward our camp, carrying the two heavy buckets of water.

On the way I passed some boys, two of whom were my younger brothers, playing at chopping wood. I should have told them they were too small to be swinging that large ax, but I didn't. I just kept walking. Before I made it back to camp, I heard a scream and dropt my buckets. I joined the others running toward the scream, only to find Edward's hands had slipt and he had cut off his great toe.

As the midwife tended Edward's wound, Mother was hysterical, raging 'round in circles as she looked for someone to blame. Accustomed as I was to her red-faced fits, this one was truly formidable. When her eyes fell upon me, she demanded to know how I could have passed those boys without taking the ax from them. I had no answer. She pulled a pliant limb off a bush and began striking me with it, the switch slicing through the thin fabric of my dress like a whip . . .

As I sat beside Syawa, remembering that trauma, I was stunned by the accuracy of his description. Whilst everyone else fretted o'er Edward, I climbed into our wagon and lay on my stomach across some barrels. I cried 'til I had no more tears to cry. I prayed for relief, for protection, for salvation. When my prayers were not answered, I went out and threw the crown of flowers into a ditch.

"I heard you call," Syawa said softly. Momentarily lost in the painful memory, I looked up, startled. "And I pitied you. You are so smart, so strong, so brave. How could I leave you in that meaningless life when it was in my power to save you?"

I opened and shut my mouth several times but could think of no English words at that moment, much less any words in Syawa's language.

It was about then that Hector returned, carrying everything we had, as well as the loaded waterskin. He gave Syawa a drink whilst I laid out his bedding. The two of us helped him lie down. At that point I was able to get a good look at the bites.

The purple on his calf was turning black, with dark streaks climbing up his thigh. His arm was, if possible, e'en worse, swollen to twice its normal size, with the purple stains creeping to his armpit. His arm was hot and so tender that he winced when I touched it.

Hector rolled some hides to put under Syawa's head and shoulders. I could not bear to look at Hector—his desolation was too dreadful to behold. I went to collect firewood and heard them talking, but by the time I returned, Hector was preparing to go off with his bow and arrow, saying Syawa thought he might be able to eat. I glanced at Syawa, then turned my dubious eyes to Hector. He must have known Syawa would not soon be eating.

I went to Syawa to ask if I could put a damp compress on his arm, but he told me not to bother. He said he must finish before Hector returned. His voice was getting weaker, his breath more ragged, but he was determined to go on. By this time I had thought of numerous questions to ask, but he grabbed my arm and gave me no chance to speak.

"The Holymen would not hear me," he said slowly. "I tried to tell them the meaning of the Earthquake, to make them understand. But I failed. I failed. I wept in frustration. I prayed for help. That was when I heard your call. And then I understood, at last. I could help you—you could help me. I knew you were going to die, so I had to find you, to save you, even tho'—" He stopt abruptly, turning his head to look off into the dark woods.

"You come for me, e'en tho' you know you die!" I finisht for him. In the whirlpool of emotions spinning me 'round, I suddenly recognized a new one—anger. "Why you do that? Why come for me, knowing it kill you? I not ask for that! If I know this, I not come with you!"

Syawa smiled vaguely. "That is why I could not tell you. It was best you did not know."

"But *you* know. And you do it anyway."

"Of course." Syawa concentrated on breathing a moment before offering me another weak smile. "It was a gift, Kay-oot-li. I know you do not yet understand Gifting, but you will learn. You will learn."

I looked down for a moment, still fighting my resentment, still o'erwhelmed by how quickly the day had gone from glorious to tragic. "You save me, I bring gift to your people—is that it?" I struggled to think of the words in his language, using gestures when I got stuck. "But, Syawa, how can I do that when I not understand, when I not know what gift is?"

He assured me I would know the gift when I needed to know it, then smiled sadly as he added, "Ah, Kay-oot-li, believe me when I say you should not struggle so hard to understand. I understand— I *know*—but knowing changes nothing. Life is good, even if you do not know, even if you do not understand. Life itself is a gift—please accept it and be happy."

I tried to smile, tho' tears were rolling down my cheeks as I shook my head with certainty. "I ne'er be happy before you. I ne'er be happy without you."

Syawa's face went through a range of emotions. I had the strong impression of a little boy caught in a lie. He finally looked up at me, tipping his head apologetically. "I knew you were becoming attacht to me, and I should not have let you. I just wanted to know . . . how it felt. I am sorry I did not tell you sooner."

I raised my tear-soaked face to the sky, breathing through my open mouth. When first I met Syawa, I thought he was odd, an outcast, a loner. Then I learnt he was held in the highest esteem by his people, revered and celebrated. Now I was finding out that all along he believed he was soon to die and yet did not tell me. A thought whirled through my mind: there might be other things he hadn't told me. But I could not think of that now—I could think of naught but that I loved him with all my heart, and he was dying.

Hector returned with a raccoon, which I skinned and cleaned with trembling hands. I set about heating some water in the stomach the way Syawa had shown me, hoping he could take some broth.

Whilst I worked, Syawa and Hector talked. I tried not to listen to their private conversation, but from what I heard they talked mostly of family matters—Syawa's mother, Hector's father, other people back home. At first Hector was, understandably, extremely upset, but after Syawa discussed mundane things like the river and the canoe, Hector was able to restore his usual face of stone.

When the broth was ready, I could not get Syawa to take more than a few mouthfuls. Neither Hector nor I had much appetite either. We sat, one on each side of Syawa, watching him slip farther and farther away from us.

Well into the night Syawa urged Hector to get some sleep, so Hector wrapt up in his furs and almost immediately began to snore lightly. As Syawa rested fitfully, I continued to sit beside him, watching the dark spot on his arm slowly spread. I kept mulling all that he'd said to me, but the more I thought about it, the less sense it made. How could Syawa have known about that May day in the wilderness? And why would he come on this incredible journey to "save" me, dragging Hector the whole way, if he truly knew he was going to die before it was accomplisht? I wasn't worth it. He shouldn't have bothered.

As the light of dawn began to fade the stars from the sky, I whimpered aloud, "It's not fair!"

"Make it fair," Syawa croaked hoarsely in his language. I looked at him and saw the whites of his eyes had turned yellow.

I could not believe he understood me. "What?" I whispered in his tongue.

"You have been given the gift of a life. You must give a life in return."

"But how I give you life if you are gone?" I whined, causing Hector to stir in his sleep.

"Kay-tee—I gave my life for the Vision," Syawa struggled to say. He laboriously turned his head 'til he could see Hector's slumbering form. "*He* is the one who killed your murderer. *He* is the one who saved you from a pointless death. *He* is the one you must re-pay."

I looked at Syawa, who was working to turn his eyes back to me. "No," I said tearfully. "No!" I made the gestures Tomi had taught me which meant "I love you," and Syawa's eyes crinkled in a pale version of the smile that had captivated me in the loft of my family's farm.

He blinked very, very slowly and whispered, "Not me."

"You!" I wailed. "I want to give my life to you!"

The noise brought Hector upright, and he groggily resumed his place on the other side of Syawa. By that time I was being wrackt by such violent sobs I could barely breathe, and when Syawa and Hector exchanged some words, I couldn't e'en hear what they said. I sat holding my face in my hands, rocking back and forth, retching in a despair that shredded my miserable soul.

Suddenly I felt a strong hand grab my arm and jerk me roughly. I looked up, startled, to find Hector reaching across Syawa. He was furious as he leant o'er and growled, "Do not send him on his Journey this way!"

I gasped, frightened by the wild look in Hector's eyes. I gulped, nodded, and bent down to wipe my face on the hide of Syawa's bed. When I was back in control of myself, I returned to sit by his head and give him a feeble smile.

He had been talking to Hector, but he looked at me now with warmth. "Fire and Ice in one Creature . . . now they will believe me." He looked from me to Hector and said, "My time with you has been beautiful. Thank you . . . both."

He closed his eyes for a long, long time, his breath coming slower and slower. Finally he opened his eyes again and looked at me. He managed a faint smile as he said a few words I didn't understand. I would later learn those words meant: "It was worth it."

"Don't leave me," I mumbled, and when I could see he did not hear me, I bent o'er him and said again, "Please don't leave me. Please, Syawa . . . don't leave me!"

I could feel Hector glaring at me, warning me not to break down again, and, somehow, I did not. Syawa was trying to respond to me, and tho' his breathing had become nigh impossible, he struggled to shake his head and mouth the words "I will not . . ." Through an act of sheer iron will, he lifted his hand and put it on my heart. He closed his eyes briefly, then opened them. I nodded and smiled through my tears. We had communicated by gestures for so long, I knew exactly what he meant.

I once again made the gestures to say "I love you," then leant o'er and put my trembling mouth on his dry, cracking lips. I almost sobbed again, but stopt myself in time, afraid of what Hector might do. I could feel Syawa's lips respond, and for an infinite moment we hung there, breathless, in the space between life and death. Then his lips relaxed, his breath seeped out of him and into me, and he did not inhale again. I pulled back, horrified. His eyes were open, but they had rolled up slightly and were blank and lifeless.

I cringed as Hector lifted his face to the brightening sky and screamed in abject agony.

$\mathcal{A}$s all-consuming and unendurable as was my own grief, 'twas a drop in the ocean beside the infinite anguish of Hector. I've ne'er seen nothing like it and hope ne'er to see nothing like it ne'er again.

He shrieked, he howled, he wailed, he raged. He suffered—oh, God, how he suffered! For an endless span of time whilst Hector thus lamented, I huddled beside Syawa's body, holding my knees to my chest, trembling, rocking back and forth, still too stunned by all that had been said and done e'en to think. My mind was frozen solid, like a pail of water left out in the cold.

At one point I thought Hector had recovered himself, for his sobs subsided, but when I dared look up I saw he had gotten out his knife. I gasped and screamed for him to stop, please stop, certain he was preparing to plunge the stone blade into his own heart and leave me stranded in the wilderness with two dead bodies!

But no. He ignored me as he grabbed his long black hair and began hacking it off close to his head. I stopt screaming, shocked. Hector was proud, e'en vain, about the length and beauty of his sleek locks. Now they lay lifeless, abandoned in the dirt.

But he was not done. After cutting off all his hair, he made incisions all o'er his arms. He chanted and lifted his face to the sky, weeping as blood oozed from the cuts and trickled down to his palms. He lifted the knife and made similar slices on his chest. In a very short time his entire upper torso was bright red with blood.

Panic-stricken, I looked at Syawa's body, wishing so much he could turn and tell me what Hector was doing and what he was going to do next. But my dearest friend lay lifeless, his lips forever still. I laid my head upon his chest and held him tight, abandoning myself to my own tears. I cried 'til there was not a drop of liquid left inside me.

I may have swooned. I know not. But I do know that time kept moving, carrying me farther and farther from Syawa, and, at some point, I realized Hector was gone. I slowly sat up and blearily looked 'round, surprised to find I was still alive. I was actually rather disappointed.

The fire was as dead as I felt inside. I set about rekindling it. My hands moved, but my mind was not connected. I felt as if the me that was me was lying dead on the ground from snakebites. I started a fire. I watched it burn. At some point I heard a noise in the woods and wondered dully if some predator was coming to finish me off. But it was only Hector, returning with an armload of vines and the refilled waterskin.

With his hacked-off hair, blood-encrusted body, and the glazed, violent glow in his eyes, he looked like something that should be kept in a cage. He handed me the skin and gestured for me to drink, which I did without thinking. Then he pointed at Syawa's body, gesturing I must prepare him for his final Journey.

I swallowed hard, nodded, and found a soft rabbit skin, which I dampened with water before gently wiping Syawa's forehead, his cheeks, his chin. I closed his half-opened eyelids for the final time and leaned o'er to kiss each one. Then, for the last time, I kissed his mouth, so unnatural now it was no longer smiling. I stared at his mouth and remembered.

It had been my job to wash my grandmother's body when she died. I was fourteen at the time, beside myself with grief. Gran had been failing for about a year, and in that time she gradually lost her wits and began hearing voices. Then she began responding to those voices. By the time she died, she was engaged in almost constant conversation with people only she could see—her husband, her sister, her mother. Oft she was visited by her own grandmother, and I marveled at the way time and space melted away. I wondered if one day I would be talking to Gran whilst I myself lay dying, sometime far in the future. What are time and space, I wondered, compared to love?

'Twas strange to handle Gran's dead body. The soft skin I'd loved so much was cold and stiff; the rosy cheeks were white. She'd been my only source of solace and security throughout my childhood, and without her, I knew life was going to be much harder than it had been before.

And it had already been pretty hard.

I remember washing her fingers, her hands, her arms, puzzling o'er the way a person could be alive one minute, and then gone—just absolutely gone. The body was naught but dead meat, like any butchered animal, a carcass waiting to be consumed by the rotting forces of the earth, but Gran had somehow slipt away. Was she in Heaven, I wondered, benevolently watching o'er me? Had she joined the throng of dead relatives she claimed were always watching from above, those hovering specters visible only to those slated soon to join their ranks?

As I washed Syawa's body, I wondered if Gran was watching

o'er me now—lost in the middle of a strange continent, heartbro-
ken as I prepared the only man I'd e'er loved for burial. It was cold
comfort, but all I could find in an otherwise unendurable situation.
I had to believe Gran was watching o'er me. The only time I'd e'er
felt anywhere near as safe as when I was in Gran's arms was when
I was in—

Syawa's. Oh, God, I wondered, where are you? How could you
leave me like this, just as we were learning about each other, just
when everything seemed so promising? Here I was, thinking I
knew at last what my life was going to be, thinking I finally understood some things, and then in the space of one awful moment I
discovered I knew nothing, I understood nothing. How was it possible for me to be so very sure and yet so very, very wrong?

I washed Syawa's wounds, the angry purple-black no longer
spreading. Suddenly I remembered the dream I'd had—was it yesterday or years ago?—about a snake, something about a snake.
Syawa had said dreams like mine could help prepare us for what
was to come, but if that was the case, the system failed miserably. I
was in no way prepared to face this horrific situation nor to consider
the possibility of life in the wilderness without my love.

I simply could not consider it.

When I was done with the washing, Hector laid Syawa's personal items beside the body and gave me a sharp bone awl and some
sinew, gesturing for me to wrap the sleeping fur like a shroud and
sew it up securely. I numbly did as he instructed as he went back to
constructing something on the other side of the clearing.

The day wore on. About the time I finisht sewing, Hector hauled
o'er the contraption he'd made. It was something like a giant cradle,

loosely woven from vines. He bade me help lift Syawa's wrapt body into it, then set about twisting the vines further to create an open-weave cocoon. When he was finisht, Hector told me in gestures I must help pull this cocoon-contraption through the woods.

I stared at the awful apparition that was Hector—blood-covered, hack-haired, wild-eyed—and it occurred to me my situation might be e'en more dire than I feared. Not only was the love of my life inexplicably taken from me, but the only other person in my world, the only thing standing between me and certain death, was the creature before me who had clearly gone completely mad.

What could I do? I had no intention of getting between Hector and his grief, so I wordlessly followed his commands.

We dragged Syawa's body back toward the river, covering a mile or more. It was a difficult trek, with bushes snagging the vine-cocoon and swamps forcing detours, 'til at last we arrived at a small promontory on which stood a huge tree. Hector pointed up, gesturing that he was going to pull Syawa's body to the top.

I stared at Hector, more than a little afraid. I said nothing, but when he gestured, increasingly impatient, asking if I understood, I nodded, still staring with wide eyes.

He climbed a smaller tree near the large one, dragging along the vine rope attached to the cocoon. I fed the vine up as he climbed, gaping as he worked his way out on a rather precarious limb to cross, like a squirrel, from the smaller tree to the large one. Dizzied by the dangerous display, I lowered my eyes and hunched my shoulders, fully expecting to hear Hector come crashing through the branches to land with a hideous thud right beside me.

But he did not fall, and when the cocoon began rising slowly off the ground, I grimly helpt get it started. By this time the light of day was dimming and I could no longer see Hector when the cocoon caught on a branch of the lower tree and would not budge. I heard him yelling, his tone tight and rising in despair. I yelled back that I would help.

Tho' I always feared water, I have no fear at all of heights, so up I climbed, limb by limb, 'til I got to the spot where the cocoon was caught. Inside the woven vines, the hide containing Syawa's body was slumped and sagging. I loosed the entangling branches and shouted up to Hector to pull again. I watched as the cocoon containing my beloved slowly rose and disappeared.

I was alone and it was nigh dark. I sat on the limb to lean against the trunk and watch the stars pop out, one by one.

For the first time since Syawa died, I thought about what he'd said before he passed. He said he had seen me—how was that possible? It wasn't possible, was it? Surely not. Surely he'd just imagined me, or imagined someone, and when he found me I happened to fit the bill. There was no way he could have seen me on that day in May. Yet he described the scene so perfectly, right down to the color of the flowers in my hair. How was that possible?

And he said he'd taken pity on me, that he came to save me from a miserable life and a meaningless death. He said that if he hadn't come to get me, I'd be dead already. With the dark of night deepening 'round me as I hovered in the middle of the forest canopy in the middle of a vast wilderness, I wondered—is this what it's like to be dead? Lost in darkness, floating, aimless, alone.

I heard Hector coming down long before he reached me. When he lowered himself onto my branch, I startled him so that he very nigh fell, which infuriated him. He said I should not be there and we must leave now. I did as he told me, and when we reached the ground, I silently followed him through the black forest to our camp.

We must've eaten something, but I really can't remember. What I do remember is sitting bleary-eyed before the fire with Hector on the other side, doing the same. I was so far beyond exhaustion I could not think straight, especially since my thoughts kept circling 'round and 'round this wild refrain: "I am supposed to be dead. I am supposed to be dead."

I heard Syawa chuckle as he leant o'er my shoulder to whisper in my ear, "Sleep now, Kay-oot-li."

I said, "No! I am afraid!"

Hector said, "What?" in a tone tight with alarm.

I tried to look at him but could not focus my eyes beyond the fire. I glanced behind me for Syawa but found only darkness. I would've cried had I any tears left. Instead I mumbled, "He tells me sleep, but I am afraid of dreams."

Hector inhaled sharply. "If he tells you sleep, then you must sleep. In the morning I will take you back across the Great River and return you to your people."

I tried again to look at Hector. The shadow I could see of him did not look at me. I nodded as I crawled to my bearskin and unrolled it on the very spot Syawa died. My last thought as I lay down was, "Well, yes, maybe that would be best."

'Twas the only thing that made sense. I would go back to my family and this entire excursion into the forest would be as if it had ne'er been. These months I'd spent with Syawa would be naught but a memory, a weird and wonderful dream.

~ 17 ~

AGAIN AND AGAIN THAT NIGHT I was jerked from sleep just as my throat was being sliced open with a sharp knife. I was back home in the sleeping loft with the children, and, as before, when we heard the mayhem outside I got the musket and the children cowered behind me. But in these repeating dreams, it wasn't Hector and Syawa who crept up the stairs—it was the savage I'd seen lying dead on the farmhouse floor.

In my dreams he was very much alive, his scalp plucked bald save for the stiff brush atop his head. His war paint was hideous; his black eyes gleamed in murderous rage. He sneered at the musket I pointed at him, knocking it from my hand before I could lift it to swing. In one smooth motion he grabbed my arm, spun me 'round, and pinned my back against his chest as, with his other hand, he drew his razor-sharp blade from left to right across my throat. He released me and I crumpled, the light of life fading from my eyes as he threw the children down the stairs, one by one.

Every time I felt that knife slice into my flesh, I jerked myself awake, so that the last glimmer of life in my dream was also the last glimmer of the dream as I awoke. But I was so exhausted that I kept falling right back to sleep e'en tho' I didn't want to, e'en tho' I knew the dream would happen again and again and again.

Finally it didn't. Finally I slept deeply and well and as I awoke, I could feel Syawa beside me, his hand resting lightly on my arm. I heard him breathing and I smiled, knowing that when I opened my eyes, he would be lying there, smiling that smile of his, about to ask if I was ready.

But he wasn't.

I opened my eyes to naught but woodland, and I sat up with a start. Like it or not, I was still alive and Syawa wasn't. He was gone, gone, and I would ne'er see his smile again. As I looked 'round the camp, all my dreams dissolved and the enormity of reality piled on top of me like a million invisible blankets. I was sure I would suffocate under the weight.

Hector had packed and was waiting impatiently for me to arise. I slowly rolled my bearskin and tied it to my pack. I accepted the cold food he gave me and ate slowly as we hiked through the woods. I felt numb. I could not taste the meat, nor could I feel the earth beneath my shoes. Everything about me was numb.

We neared the spot where Hector had pulled the canoe into the bushes. I stood on the muddy creek bank, staring at the mucky remnants of a large snake that had been chopt to pieces, apparently by Hector's paddle. I began to tremble. Then I began to scream.

Startled, Hector spun 'round, his hand on his knife, bracing himself against the canoe as he looked for trouble, but I was just standing there screaming, staring at the pieces of snake. Hector must've assumed the sight of the snake terrified me, but it wasn't that—it wasn't that at all. It was what the snake represented, what it meant, what it was saying to me. This precious interlude in my life was finished, irrevocably gone, lost forever. As sweet as it had been to have a few brief weeks in which I wasn't miserable and suffering, the respite was done and the misery could begin again, a million times worse than before.

How could I not scream?

Hector sighed before coming to take my pack from me. He strapt it in the canoe, then said something, clearly urging me to get in. But I couldn't. This was the spot where it happened, where everything changed, where my life was ruined. I fell to my knees crying, my heart broken, bleeding. Without another word, Hector leant over and picked me up the way Syawa once did. I felt his arms shake as he carried me to the canoe and knew his heart, too, was broken. I wanted to reach out to him somehow, to comfort him, but I could not stop crying.

Once in the canoe, I struggled to control myself, to stop making things worse for Hector. He ignored me as he pushed the craft into the water, jumped in, and began to paddle. The other paddle was in the canoe, but Hector needed no assistance from me. In no time at all we were in the Great River, and shortly thereafter we were half-way across, angling with the current.

I was quiet now. I sat staring at the eastern shoreline, watching the woods loom gradually larger and larger. That woods was the way back home, to my family, to my life. My meaningless life . . .

I did not want to go back to that life. Suddenly I knew I would rather drown, right here, right now, than return to that life. How could I go back to being nobody, nothing, to being tortured and tormented, to being miserable, when I had experienced what it was like to be somebody special, to be loved and cherished, to be the object of someone's sacred dream? I picked up the paddle at my feet and stuck it into the water. The canoe immediately wobbled. I began pushing the paddle against the water in a movement exactly the opposite of what Syawa had taught me. The canoe jerked into a hard spin.

Hector yelled, startled. "What are you doing? Stop that!"

"*You* stop!" I shouted back, turning to glare at him. "Why you do this?"

Hector leant back, his forehead furrowed. I hadn't really looked at him yet that morning, but now that I did, I was appalled. His skin was gray, his eyes were sunk in dark circles, his short hair was sticking out in all directions, and he was still covered in dried blood. "I am taking you back to your people!" he exclaimed. "I will take you to the village of trade. From there the Black Robe will help you."

"No!" I shouted as he put his paddle back in the water to pull the canoe out of the current. "No! I not go back there! We go that way!" I pointed to the west.

Hector ignored me the way he'd ignored me earlier, so I turned 'round and began paddling furiously against him, which nigh upset the canoe. "Stop that!" Hector screamed, hard-presst to steady the canoe. "You'll turn us over!"

"Good!" I screamed back, slapping the water so that a great wave washed o'er him.

"Stop!" Hector shouted again, trying to grab my paddle. I swung it at him, narrowly missing his head. He leant back again, his eyes now filled with fear. "What's wrong with you? You cannot swim! Do you want to die?"

"Do I want to die?" I repeated, then laughed at the thought. "I cannot die! How can I die? I am already dead!" I laughed again, and the more I laughed, the more hysterical I became. I laughed and laughed and laughed.

Between my bouts of laughter, I heard the eerie silence that accompanied Hector's horrified stare, and that silence eventually reached me, sucking all the humor out. When I recovered myself, I sat breathing heavily, staring into the depths of that deep, dark river as we drifted slowly 'round and 'round.

"What did you say?" Hector asked, his voice low and quiet. His eyes were narrowed, and he held the paddle in mid-air, forgotten. The canoe righted itself, and we rode backwards with the current—smooth, steady, picking up speed.

I swallowed thickly before turning to Hector to use a combination of words and gestures. "You must take me to your people. That is what Syawa wanted."

"That is not his name."

"That is what I call him."

"You do not know his real name."

I sighed impatiently. "Well, I know *him*. And I know Syawa says I must—"

"Do not speak of him!" Hector snapt. "We do not speak the names of the dead!"

I raised one eyebrow. "I thought you said I do not know his name."

Hector breathed heavily, clearly at wit's end. "Please do not disregard my beliefs."

"Well. Then let us speak of you. You promise him you take me to your people."

"I did not."

My mouth fell open. I thought for a moment, then shifted 'round to gesture more clearly, for I was sure we were just failing to communicate. "Of course you promise him you take me to your people! *He* taking me to your people! Before he die, he ask you— take care of me, yes?"

Hector shook his head, his face blank. "No."

"But . . . but his Vision!" I stammered, completely undone. "You two come on Journey looking for me, and you find me, and I take gift to your people! You know his Vision more than me!"

Hector looked to the west, his focus a couple thousand miles away. "Seers can be wrong." I saw him blink several times, swallowing hard as he worked to keep his face stony.

I saw something then, something I had not seen up to that point because I was so absolutely blinded by my own pain, my own tragic loss. I saw Hector. I saw so much suffering in his eyes, so much sadness, so much betrayal. If I had been shocked to lose Syawa in the way I did, how much more terrible must have been Hector's shock, Hector's loss. Hector was devoted to Syawa, sworn to protect him, and yet . . . he had failed.

"He not tell you he die on Journey?" I asked slowly.

Hector continued to stare to the west. "No." He suddenly turned his eyes to me. "Did he tell you?"

"Same time he tell you." I pondered for a moment as Hector turned his face away again. "You not think, not ask him—does his Vision show you two returning to your people?"

"I thought to ask," Hector said sharply, "but I chose not to. No man should know the time and place of his own death."

I sighed. Whether I wanted to know or not, I was now keenly aware of the precise time and place of my own death—after all, I had experienced it a dozen times in my dreams. Alas that my time and place had come and gone without bothering to take me with it! Now, as humiliating as it was to have to force this angry, unhappy man to let me stay with him, the truth was, as Syawa recently assured me, I simply had no choice. I had nowhere else to go.

Nor was I the only one with no choice. I considered my companion and the loneliness that loomed before him—well, it was unimaginable. Whether he wanted to admit it or not, it would be very difficult, if not impossible, for him to proceed on his perilous journey and successfully arrive at his extremely distant destination by himself. Suddenly I understood he needed me every bit as much as I needed him.

"Hear me," I said softly, "I know this is bad for you. It is bad for me, too. All I have now is he say I must go to your people. So you must take me with you."

Hector glanced at me, his eyelids heavy, his mouth twisted in a terrible frown, his nostrils flared. He said nothing, but his doleful gaze spoke volumes. He lowered his eyes to the canoe and shook his head. "It is too far, too dangerous. I cannot promise your safety."

"No, but *he* can." Hector's eyes shot up to my face and I decided to build a fire from this spark of a response. "Hector, you not see—he is not gone! How is he gone? He is here!" I put a hand on my heart, thinking of Gran and her hovering relatives. "He is always here, watching o'er us."

Hector's frown melted into uncertainty, then puzzlement, then a dark and naked fear. His eyes narrowed as he said in a low, tense voice, "He gave you his _____?"

It sounded like a statement, but it was clearly a question. In either case, I did not understand the word Hector used. I knew I'd heard the word before, or a word very much like it, but I could not recall exactly what the word meant. I was sure it had something to do with spiritual things, and I deduced it must mean something like "sacred vow." I was certain that was it. Hector was asking if Syawa had given me his sacred vow, and tho' Syawa did not, perhaps, use that exact word, his intent was beyond doubt—he said I would live with his people.

"Yes," I said to Hector, lifting my chin to meet his gaze confidently. "Yes, of course."

Hector's narrowed eyes narrowed e'en further as he studied me. Then he abruptly nodded, shifted his eyes to the river, and put his paddle back into the water. He slowly turned our craft and began paddling steadily upstream. He would not meet my eyes further, so I turned 'round and put my paddle into the water. Remembering all Syawa had taught me, I handled the paddle well enough, and we actually began moving forward.

Looking back on that moment, I shudder to realize just how stupid I was, how naïve, how blissfully unaware of all the things I did not know. I said, "Yes—yes, of course," as if I understood Hector's question perfectly, as if I knew exactly what I was talking about. But I did not know—*I did not know!* The only thing I knew for certain was that there was no place for me back in the world of my family. I was dead to them. The person who had once lived with them was dead to me. I was someone else altogether now.

I was Syawa's Creature of Fire and Ice.

~ 18 ~

The thing I remember most from the days immediately following Syawa's death is pain—huge, rolling waves of excruciating pain. Pain from the loss, pain from the loneliness, pain from uncertainty, pain from struggling to understand, pain from paddling. So much pain from paddling.

As we slowly made our way upstream, Hector and I strove to work together, to communicate with one another. He oft yelled at me, demanding I hold the paddle this way or that, constantly criticizing my efforts and ne'er being satisfied with the results. Quickly exhausted, I must soon ask him to land the canoe to let me relieve myself, and when I jumped from the canoe before he did, he screamed furiously. Only after he made it clear with wild gestures I was never, *ever* to get out of the canoe first did I realize he was thinking of what happened when Syawa jumped from the canoe, and he did not want the same thing to happen to me.

I sat on the shore with my arms wrapt 'round my legs, my head upon my knees, unwilling to look at Hector as he paced back and forth. I asked why he kept hollering at me and told him I could not understand his words. Because he also had trouble understanding me, I must repeat myself several times, then ask him to repeat himself, and only through this laborious process did I figure out he was merely telling me to switch sides with the paddle to avoid straining myself unnecessarily.

But there was no way to avoid straining myself. Tho' he was amazingly adept at choosing the channel with least resistance, I was wholly unaccustomed to this particular form of physical labor, which meant I immediately shredded every muscle in my arms, shoulders, neck, and back. Indeed, the challenge of paddling was almost as severe as the challenge of accepting Syawa's sudden disappearance from my life.

Hector expressed little sympathy for my suffering, but, then again, I expressed little sympathy for his. Whene'er he wasn't yelling at me, I sat in the front of the canoe, staring straight ahead, feeling utterly alone in all the world. Blinded by my own thoughts and feelings, I scarce remembered Hector e'en existed, much less that he was sitting not eight feet behind me.

My thoughts and feelings were completely consumed by Syawa. Did he truly have supernatural powers? Was such a thing possible? I wanted to believe it, and I was sorely tempted to believe it, but part of me always resisted, part of me always wondered, part of me always reasoned it away. He was a shrewd man—this I knew—and, as I myself had experienced, he was keenly capable of reading people and making intimate connections. But was he able to "see" events from afar? Was he able to "know" what the future would bring? Surely no man could do that. And yet . . .

I knew how close I'd come to dying in my parents' house. And I knew Syawa was offering me a chance to start o'er with a life of meaning and purpose. More than anything, I knew he loved me and I loved him. But I did not understand why he had to leave me. I did not understand what "gift" he expected me to bring to his people. And I did not understand why he suggested I was meant to be with Hector, not with him.

It's not that I didn't care for Hector. For all his bluster, Hector was a decent fellow, capable of great loyalty and depth of feeling. But he just wasn't the sort of man who would e'er appeal to me. He was bold and brash and belligerent and self-obsessed. As well-formed as he was, he was used to getting whate'er he wanted, and I preferred men like Syawa, who had to work to be noticed and were less likely to be surrounded by eager young girls. I had no desire to compete for someone's attention and, besides, Hector didn't e'en like me and had made his views plain enough on several occasions. The more I thought about it, the more I decided Syawa's deathbed declaration that I was meant for Hector was, frankly, offensive. Hector certainly required no one to procure ladies for him, and I did not appreciate feeling as if I had been deliberately procured.

I concluded Syawa's final wish was simply that—a wish—which would expediently resolve the rather messy situation left by his untimely demise. He did not want to leave me in the lurch, nor did he want to abandon his lifelong companion; naturally he hoped we might find comfort in one another.

We did not.

Once I got the hang of what I was supposed to do with my paddle, we traveled in silence, speaking only to convey essential information. Hector occasionally gave me paddling advice, and I told him when I needed to relieve myself. In the evenings we said nothing, avoiding eye contact. We performed our chores the way I once saw a pendulum clock perform in Boston—the brass disc swinging relentlessly back and forth, back and forth, heedless of anything going on in the world 'round it.

On the first night after Syawa died, we did have one brief conversation. Rather than set up our lean-to as Syawa had done, Hector made a shelter by pulling the canoe far up the bank, rolling it onto its side, and bracing it with the paddles. After we ate, I began unrolling my bearskin under the canoe, eager to rest my weary muscles, but Hector stopt me.

"You slept last night," he said bluntly, "and I did not. Tonight you must watch first. I will get up halfway through the night. Then you can sleep."

I was astonished. "Must one of us always be awake?"

"One of us always has been awake," he said as he spread his own sleeping fur under the canoe. "You are the only one who has slept all night every night." He rolled himself into his fur.

"But . . . but what I watch *for?*" I asked, suddenly very aware of the vast darkness surrounding our tiny circle of light.

"Bears, panthers, wolves," Hector mumbled from within his fur. "People who might harm us. If anything threatens our camp, wake me."

As Hector's breathing slowed immediately into sleep, I looked at the vast darkness with wide eyes. All this time Syawa and Hector had been taking turns watching o'er me, and I didn't e'en know it, nor did it occur to me such watchfulness was required. Once again, I felt like a fool. I crawled to Hector's pile of belongings to pull out the French hatchet. I clutched that hatchet to my chest for hours, jumping at every rustle in the darkness. I kept the fire well-stoked and kept myself company by crying.

I soon learnt I might as well stay awake half the night because when I did sleep, I did naught but dream of Syawa. Every time Hector poked me with a stick in the morning, which is how he woke me, I jerked upright, startled, torn from some deep, deep dream discussion with Syawa. I did not mention these nocturnal conversations to Hector because I did not mention anything to Hector, but they always stuck with me for a good part of the day, giving me much to think about as I paddled.

In spite of the comforting companionship of those dreams, I still broke into tears almost as regularly as that clock pendulum used to swing. Whilst we were paddling it did not matter that I cried, either because Hector did not notice or did not care, but in our camp he was discomforted by my regular breakdowns.

"Why are you crying?" I recall him asking one evening in exasperation.

Surprised I must explain why a woman with a broken heart cries, I tried to shrug, but my shoulders were so stiff and sore I couldn't e'en do that. I whimpered that I was in pain and showed him how the blisters on my hands had popt and oozed, leaving my palms as little more than two huge, open sores.

"Does crying help?" he demanded.

I admitted that it didn't, then cried all the more.

I should mention at this point that tho' I have perhaps made it sound as if Syawa, Hector, and I were alone in a vast, deserted wilderness, such was ne'er the case. The truth is we frequently encountered other people as we hiked through the forest, sometimes stopping to exchange information, sometimes merely acknowledging each other's presence, and sometimes steering clear of others altogether. I have not mentioned this aspect of my travels primarily because I, myself, ne'er interacted with strangers and my thoughts were always so preoccupied with my own situation that I took little note of the predicaments of others.

Whilst Hector and I paddled up the Great River, however, we encountered other people almost constantly. The Great River, it seemed, was the main thoroughfare through the continent, and rare was the hour when we did not pass some habitation, campsite, or fellow canoeists. Hector sometimes had trouble finding a campsite not already occupied or situated so close to others as to make him uncomfortable.

In the past, of course, Syawa was the one to speak with strangers, whilst Hector hung back with his menacing scowl. Now it was up to Hector to respond to those who hailed us, and he did not accept this new responsibility with enthusiasm. At first he tried glaring and waving people off, but we were, after all, a very unusual pair, and everyone who saw us was naturally curious. Every single stranger stared, most chattered, and some e'en followed us, shouting repeatedly for us to stop. A few canoes pulled alongside us, the strangers interrogating Hector as they stared at me.

I ne'er got involved in these exchanges but thought Hector made things more difficult than need be. Whereas Syawa was always open and pleasant, perfectly willing to go into the whole story of his Vision, Hector tried to share as little information as possible and get away as quickly as he could. I knew the reason he didn't want to talk was that he was loath to speak of the death of our friend, but I believe many people wondered what he was hiding.

One evening just at dusk three strangers appeared at our camp, asking if they could share our fire. I could see Hector despised the idea, but his savage commitment to hospitality precluded a refusal. I divided our supper five ways, using large leaves as plates, working silently, feeling as if Syawa was watching o'er my shoulder. I wanted to make him proud. After our meal I told the strangers my basic story in gestures, which they attended with great interest. They stopt me as soon as I told about the snake biting Syawa, because they could tell from Hector's ragged hair and mass of shallow wounds how the story ended.

Hector took the first watch that night, then failed to wake me for my turn so that when morning came, I was well-rested and he was more irritable than ever.

We followed the men to their destination, which turned out to be our destination as well—a sizable Indian community on the east side of the Great River. For several miles we had passed numerous small settlements on either side of the river—sometimes a hut or two, sometimes a cluster of twenty or more. I e'en saw some wooden houses built in the Old World style. When our companions turned their large canoe to the eastern shore, I was surprised to see an actual dock, and tho' I could not at first see much of the town itself because the terrain rose well away from the river, the fact that the bank was covered with dozens of canoes, rafts, and other boats suggested this place served as a trade center as much as a permanent town.

We reached the place just about noon. There was much shouting as we neared, as people were gathering on the high ridge to watch our approach. I was terribly self-conscious, but there was nothing I could do to stop attracting attention, so I just put my head down and paddled 'til the canoe bumped on the bank. When Hector jumped out to pull it out of the water, he caught my eye. "This will be very hard," he warned quietly, his jaw clenched.

Before I could ask what he meant, I began to find out.

One of the men from the night before stood on the ridge and shouted something, then began to wail—a high-pitched keening that pierced the ears and echoed mournfully across the river valley. Others picked up the cry, and in a moment the air was vibrating with anguished howling. I looked at Hector, who was ashen, stricken, and trembling from head to toe. He fell to his knees in the mud as he, too, lifted his head and keened.

It was Syawa.

I immediately understood Syawa and Hector must have stopt here on their way eastward, as they stopt at other cities. The lamentation was in Syawa's honor, and it swirled 'round like an endless whirlwind of human desolation. It roiled and rumbled from earth to sky and back again, with me and Hector in the middle, waiting for the horrible storm to pass.

Not knowing what to do, I knelt beside Hector with my head down, his words echoing in my head: "This will be very hard. This will be very hard."

My memory of the ensuing events is hazy, but I'm sure we were given food and lodging, as was always the custom. Immediately the inhabitants of this place began preparing for the typical Indian gathering, which included food, dance, and a recounting of our adventures. As the day wore on, more and more people arrived, and I could see Hector was immeasurably miserable, clearly dreading the evening e'en more than I. When I managed to ask him, at one point, what was expected of us, he just grumbled that I should know—we had done it before.

By evening the crowd had become a colossal mob, the likes of which I ne'er saw—not e'en in Philadelphia nor Boston. Whereas we had previously attracted a crowd of a couple hundred individuals, what I saw gathering on the encircling hillsides and in crafts on the river was a collection of as many as a thousand. I also saw numerous Europeans in the crowd, their fluffy beards, white linen shirts, and knee-length breeches offering a stark contrast to the mass of semi-naked savages. The Indians in this place came in every size, shape, color, and configuration. They settled 'round us like an ocean of people, yet maintained a respectful distance so that no one was closer than about thirty feet to the mat upon which Hector and I sat.

As usual, official speeches were made. One of the Europeans spoke—a Spaniard, I deduced, tho' he spoke the local Indian tongue. Of course I understood nothing, and I believe Hector not only did not understand what was being said, but did not care. Tho' he had painted himself, as usual, he sat near me in an unhappy daze, staring blankly into the fire.

Eventually some sort of Holyman had his say, and because he used the general language of gestures as well as his own tongue, I understood he was telling about the previous visit of the Seer from a Distant Land, about his Vision and Journey, and how the people here had wisht the travelers well. Tonight, the Holyman explained, the rest of the story would be told.

The crowd hushed. The silence spread from the center outward, 'til gradually all was still. Hector looked at me expectantly.

"What?" I asked him, astonished.

"The people want to know who you are and why you are here."

"Well, tell them!" I hissed, wishing I could find a rock to crawl under.

"*You* must tell them!" Hector growled, his painted face frowning furiously. "Tell them now and be done with it!"

What was I supposed to say? That I was the thirteenth child my mother conceived, a bad-luck baby suckled on misery and weaned on despair, a misfit nothing of a nobody who died almost three months ago but didn't e'en have enough sense to lie down and leave her wretched husk of rotting flesh?

I got up and walked forward on shaking legs. I stopt before the fire. I raised my hand above my head to get everyone's attention and waited 'til all eyes were on me. And then the strangest thing happened. A log on the fire snapt, tumbled, and sent a great gust of sparks spiraling up into the night sky. Everyone gasped and trembled. I sighed, closed my eyes, and shook my head.

I gestured as big as I could so everyone could see: "The Seer was on Journey to fulfill his Vision. He was looking for a Creature of Fire and Ice. I am the One the Seer was seeking. I go now to his people to give them great gift. I have nothing more to say."

A stunned silence followed as I turned 'round and walked back to the mat.

"You cannot stop now!" Hector gestured, appalled. "These people have been generous and kind. You cannot accept their hospitality and give nothing in return!"

"Tell them what you will. I am done." I flopt down on the mat, my eyes on the ground.

Hector seethed, then got up to begin walking the open space 'round the fire, gesturing broadly as he filled in the details of our story. I did not watch too closely because, after all, I already knew the details of our story and because I was so horribly uncomfortable before that enormous crowd. As time passed, however, I became aware Hector was going on and on, sharing details I found irrelevant and strange. He told, for example, about my removing the splinter from Syawa's hand and how the Seer had painted a symbol on my face with his blood. He told the crowd about my dreams of spinning and the snake and how both dreams came true. He told about my last kiss with Syawa—how I inhaled his final breath. He e'en told how hysterical I became when I saw the snake that killed him.

I was perplexed. Hector had told me I could not say Syawa's name, but here he was, telling strangers every intimate detail of our friend's final days. He may not have used Syawa's name, but he sure was morbidly dwelling on each painful memory. I could stand it no longer. I got up and headed to the river.

The crowd parted, hushed and awed, as I walked by. I saw toddlers clutch their mothers' legs, grown men stagger backwards in obvious fear. I lowered my head and tried not to look anymore, because the more I saw, the more hideously uneasy I became.

It was so hard to know what to do without Syawa.

I found our canoe in the midst of what seemed to be hundreds that were lying on the high bank. I sat beside it, leaning my cheek against it, taking comfort in the knowledge that Syawa had touched that wood, that he had used that canoe to come for me.

Time passed. I know not how much. All I remember is that at some point I was startled by a quiet voice beside me. It was a woman saying something I could not understand. When she saw my blank stare, she asked if I spoke French. I said I did.

"Your companion asked me to find you. You are welcome to sleep in my lodge." The woman was clearly very nervous, but she smiled, trying to be friendly. I could see she had some quantity of European blood and wondered what her story was, who she was, and how she came to be there.

Ultimately I didn't really care. I lowered my eyes and shook my head. "I'd rather stay here a while, if you please."

The woman nodded, eager to be agreeable. She looked toward the village, then back at me a few times as if reluctant to fail in her mission to fetch me. Finally she decided to try a conversation. "I remember the Seer when he passed through last fall," she offered. I said nothing, so she went on. "He was very nice, charming, sweet.

I am sorry to hear he died." When I continued to say nothing, she added, "Ah, but at least you are left with the handsome one, no?"

I looked up sharply. I had not hit anyone for a while, but I had an almost irresistible urge to smash my fist into this woman's face.

"I mean no offense, because I know your loss is great," she babbled on in panic, afraid of the way I now stared at her, "but surely you take consolation in the fact that you now have the best of both worlds—you travel with the handsome one while the Spirit of the Seer lives on inside you."

My urge to hit the woman vanished as my stomach suddenly lurched. I looked up at her. She was smiling nervously, desperate to please me. "What did you say?" I asked, my heart pounding.

"The Seer's Spirit, his Soul . . ." she said, hesitating before what must have been a terrible expression on my face. "This is what your companion says—that the Seer gave you his Soul, thereby making you his Spirit Keeper."

I began to tremble uncontrollably. Spirit—*that* was the word Hector had used during our conversation on the river, the word I had not understood. He did not ask if Syawa gave me his sacred vow; he asked if Syawa gave me his Spirit, his Soul, his Eternal Life Force. I said yes and now Hector believed . . .

Oh, sweet Jesus in Heaven! When the woman leant over to ask if I was ill, I brushed her aside, saying I must be alone, that I needed to, um, pray. She stared for a moment, then nodded and walked off slowly, frequently turning to look back at me. I seriously considered running down to the river, throwing myself in, and trying to drown before Hector could come find me.

My mind raced, reviewing everything that had transpired. Hector saw Syawa mark me with his blood when I extracted that splinter from his hand, and that marking, for Hector, meant Syawa gave me his ability to dream, to see the future. Those silly dreams I'd had, dreams caused by the storm, my stories, the stress—Hector believed they were evidence of my new supernatural power. What's worse, Hector believed Syawa had breathed his Spirit into me as he lay dying, and the only reason Hector agreed to take me with him to his people was that he believed I'd told him Syawa had given me his Spirit, his Soul. And the truth is I *did* tell him Syawa had given me his Spirit! Oh, God, sweet Jesus Christ—how was I ever going to be able to explain the truth to Hector without causing him to believe I had deliberately lied to him?

Because I *didn't* lie to you, Hector—I *didn't*! Or at least I didn't mean to. I swear, *I swear* I gave an honest, truthful answer to the question I thought you asked. But the question you asked was not the question I answered! Don't you see? What I said was not a lie! It was a simple misunderstanding . . .

I SLEPT THAT NIGHT CURLED UP beneath our upside-down canoe. When I awoke in the morning, I saw a pair of dirty little feet in front of my face. Behind those feet were other little feet, and others and others, and then there was a pair of large feet and I heard Hector yelling, shooing the children away. When I poked my head out from under the canoe, I found at least a dozen youngsters who had, apparently, been daring each other to peek under the canoe to steal a look at me.

Hector's shouted words in a language they did not understand moved the children back a bit, but when they saw my face, they gasped and scrambled away. This made me feel terrible for many reasons, not the least of which was that I suddenly realized how much I missed my younger brothers and sisters. Since I was old enough to watch others, I had ne'er had a single day of my life when I was not caring for children, and I was surprised how sharply I missed them. Besides, these children were adorable. Naked, save for a few breechclouts, they stood off in clusters of twos and threes, gawking at me and whispering together. I crawled out from under the canoe and leant against it, watching the youngsters watch me.

I asked if anyone spoke French, and when a lad who was perhaps twelve nervously said he did, I asked if he and his friends
would like to play a game. He wasn't sure what I intended 'til I
explained how my siblings and I used to pretend to be bears or bun-
nies. If a bear caught a bunny, that bunny became a bear, too, and
the chase went on 'til there was only one bunny left, who was the
winner. It took a while for my translator to explain the game, but as
soon as the children understood they were supposed to pretend to
be a bear or a bunny, they began acting out their parts with great
aplomb. Soon we were chasing each other up and down the riverbank, hiding behind or under boats, teasing one another, acting
silly. It was such a relief just to play, and the children and I laughed
and laughed.

Throughout this game, Hector stood motionless, his face blank
as he watched. Eventually I ran away from a "bear" child and hid
behind Hector. By this time all the children were after me, and
when they descended, I told them this man was my Guardian who
would drive off any beast who threatened me; therefore, our game
was done. As the children wandered off, I looked at Hector and
remembered the revelation from the night before. I dropt my eyes
to the ground.

"Why did you sleep under the canoe?" he demanded. "It is an
insult to refuse an invitation to stay in someone's lodge."

"I not want insult someone. But I . . . I not want you leave without me."

Hector was deeply offended. "Why would I leave without you?"

"You say you take me to village of trade, leave me. I fear you
leave me here."

Hector tightened his jaw, clearly trying to control his anger.
"That was before. I will not leave you now." He stared off across the

river, his dark eyes full of pain. His voice was so low I could scarce hear him, but it mattered not. I knew he was speaking to Syawa, not to me, when he added, "I will never leave you."

This was the moment. This was my chance to explain to him somehow that we had had a misunderstanding, that it was innocent and harmless, and that we could get beyond it and move on to a whole new understanding, but first he had to accept that Syawa was gone and I was not actually in possession of his Spirit—I was just a simple girl caught in a maelstrom she couldn't control. This was the moment in which I must make all of this clear.

I knew I should tell him. I wanted to tell him. I had to tell him. I opened my mouth to tell him.

But I didn't tell him.

I couldn't tell him. How could I tell him? I tried to tell him, but no words of any language came to me, and my hands, which I desperately commanded to move, remained hanging on the ends of my arms, stubbornly silent and still.

Hector broke the awkward silence. "I made no promises concerning you, but before we left our village I vowed I would protect the Seer always and bring him safely home."

So that was that.

If I told Hector that Syawa had not given me his Spirit, Hector would turn 'round, get in his canoe, and be gone, and I would be left in a place where I knew no one, with no alternative but to go back east to live with people who abused me in a life that was hollow and meaningless. Syawa's Vision would be forgotten, for it, apparently, lived and died with him. The only way to keep his Vision alive was to keep him alive in me, and I knew that at all costs I must keep Syawa's Vision alive. It was, after all, the only reason I was still alive.

I know this sounds fantastical, but I owed my life to Hector and, because of what Syawa had taught me, I believed I could not let Hector go 'til I gave him an equivalent gift in return.

And so I said nothing.

As we stood in uncomfortable silence, my twelve-year-old translator came running back to say his mother—who was, it turned out, the woman I'd met the night before—had food for us. Hector and I followed the lad to his home.

After we ate, Hector fell asleep in the French-speaking woman's lodge, leaving me to play with her son and his friends. We went outside so as not to disturb Hector. Late in the afternoon, I looked up to see a mass of European men approaching, all elegantly dressed in black suits with shiny buttons and lace and long woolen stockings. The children and I stared at this entourage 'til it arrived before me, at which point the armed men shooed the children away. The gentleman who had spoken at the gathering the night before stepped forward with a flourish, as the others formed a human wall behind him. I stared at this curious display.

The man said something in Spanish. I shook my head. He spoke again in French, asking if I could understand him now. I nodded.

In French he went on to explain that he was the Ambassador of New Spain, here to meet with the Ambassador from New France, who had not yet arrived. He said, "You know, of course, you are in New France. I perceive you are planning to cross the river, where you will travel through Spanish territory. I am here to discuss granting permission for your passage."

I smiled at the jest 'til I realized no one else was smiling. "Oh, my heavens—you're serious!" I exclaimed, immediately bowing my head before the glare of the Spaniard. I bit my lip and looked back up at him. "Please excuse my outburst, sir, but I am confused. Do the people who live in this land know it is New Spain or New France or New Whatever?"

The Spaniard raised one eyebrow. "Do they know you are not at all what you claim to be?" I must have blanched, for he smiled as he continued: "The people here know exactly what we want them to know—nothing more, nothing less. Now you will tell me everything you know."

"Of course." I had no wish to tangle with this or any other individual, so I cooperated to the best of my ability. After briefly recounting my story, I was interrogated about the situation on the Colonial frontier, the state of politics in the Colonies, and the condition of the Indian tribes I met along the way. Whilst I muddled through what little information I could provide, the Spaniard twirled his long mustache with his fingers, staring at me in an appraising way.

"This is all you can tell me?" he demanded at last, clearly frustrated by my ignorance. "This is nothing!" He presst his lips into a thin line as he stared at the ground, twirling his mustache and thinking. At last he looked up again. "And what is this game you are playing, this business of keeping a dead man's soul?"

I glanced 'round to see who might be listening. No one was within earshot, but I lowered my voice nonetheless and looked the man in the eye as I answered. "I am playing no game, sir. I am merely responding to circumstance."

The Spaniard narrowed his eyes as he smiled vaguely. "They believe all this nonsense about spirits and visions, you know. If they find out you have been lying to them . . ." He raised one black eyebrow significantly.

"Why would you assume I don't believe what they believe?" I asked coldly.

The Spaniard gave a little chuckle. "Because you are not a half-wit. These people are like children. They know nothing of the world. You and I do. We can ne'er explain it to them. Believe me, my dear, it is a kindness not e'en to try."

I stared at the ambassador, grinding my teeth as I fought the impulse to shove him backwards into the dirt. I said nothing.

He stept closer to speak emphatically. "Listen to me, child. I have a daughter near your age, and I would kill her with my own hands before I would allow her to live amongst these heathens. But I know how headstrong girls can be, so if you are determined to keep up your pretense, I will not stop you. I will permit your passage on one condition: if at any point in your travels you discover any gold or silver—any quantity at all—you must immediately send word of your discovery back to this place, addressed to me. Do you understand?"

I tried not to look skeptical as I nodded.

"Do not disappoint me, my dear," he warned as he reached out to grab my wrist. "There is no place you can go that a Spanish force cannot follow. But if you make me rich enough, I will return the favor. I can make you a princess—maybe e'en a queen!"

I looked at the bejeweled fingers grasping my wrist, then shifted my eyes to meet the Spaniard's intense gaze. "I appreciate your offer, sir, but what use have I for royalty or riches when I have been given the soul of a god?"

Before the Spaniard could respond, there was a flurry of activity as his hand was torn from my wrist and Hector was between us, his stone blade raised in front of the ambassador's chest. The wall of Spaniards drew weapons, but I raised my hands to hold off the swords and guns as I pleaded desperately in French.

Unruffled by the uproar, the ambassador twirled his mustache and smiled. "Ah—now I see how it is," he grinned. "But this is a dangerous course you are on, my dear. Take my advice—be careful what you say about gods and souls, lest you begin to believe it yourself!"

After the ambassador departed, Hector demanded I tell him what the Spaniard wanted, but I simply could not explain because everything about the situation was absurd—the man's alleged authority, his lust for gold, his belief that he could in any way alter the course of my fate, which was so clearly beyond all human control. But then again, my situation with Hector was already so absurd that I was beginning to accept being unable to explain, or even understand, anything affecting the two of us. I told Hector it was nothing, assuring him he should not worry about it.

"Do not lie to me," Hector snapt, his eyelids heavy. "I want to know what that man said!"

"And I want tell you, but I not have words!" I replied, getting angry myself.

"You would've told *him*," he said, referring, of course, to Syawa.

"And *he* would understand me."

Hector's eyes narrowed further as he raised his chin. "You think I am stupid." It was a statement, not a question.

"No, Hector," I said in both words and gestures as I met his bitter gaze. "*I* am stupid one, yes? And I am stinky, lazy, insulting— I not talk right or start fires right or cook right or paddle right. I do nothing right. You are right one—you criticize me and shame me and complain I wrong, always wrong. I am not perfect, Hector, but I am not *petty*."

Hector looked as stunned as if I had slapt his face. "How do you know that word?" he asked in a tight voice.

I thought about it and realized I didn't really know. It was a complex concept, one Syawa would have had to explain to me, and I had no recollection of him ever doing so. "I not know," I said wearily. "You want tell me I use word wrong?"

There was a long pause as Hector stared at the ground, his jaw working as he strove to control his emotions. "It is what he sometimes reminded me. He said I must not be so . . . petty."

I closed my eyes, o'erwhelmed by the memory. Yes—I heard Syawa use that word during their big argument, and I guess it somehow stuck in my brain. But Hector, of course, assumed Syawa was speaking to him through me. I opened my eyes to apologize for berating him, but he beat me to it.

"Please forgive me," he said, his face lowered. "I will try to be less petty." He glanced at me, then stared off at the river. "I think we should leave in the morning. It is difficult being with people now, talking . . ."

I agreed. Things between us were confusing enough without adding the complication of other people and their inexplicable issues. It was time for our Journey to resume.

~ 20 ~

SHORTLY AFTER LEAVING THE Trade Center, Hector turned our canoe west, entering a smaller (tho' still formidable) tributary of the Great River. I soon learnt the Indian name for this river was something like "Misery," and tho' I know not what the word means to the locals, to me it meant God has a wicked sense of humor. I was *in* misery *on* the Misery—floating on misery, bathing in misery, drinking in misery, and listening to misery whisper in my ears all night long. I wisht I had someone to talk to about the irony of the river's name, but Hector and I had once again lapsed into silence, which was familiar, if not exactly comfortable.

Little about my situation was comfortable. Tho' my neck and shoulders had benefited from our rest at the Trade Center, the blisters on my hands returned with a vengeance. They burst and oozed and by the end of the second day on the Misery I could scarce hold my paddle.

When we camped that evening, I asked Hector if I could use a scrap of hide to make myself something. He said the hides were mine as much as his, to do with as I pleased. After we ate, I began sewing, and by the time Hector rose to take his turn at watch, my new paddling gloves were finisht. When I put them on in the morning, he lifted his chin in acknowledgment, which pleased me greatly. So hungry was I for any sign of approval from him that I interpreted e'en this slight gesture as a great triumph.

But that afternoon he started hollering again, and for the longest time I could not figure out why. When I adjusted my paddling, he only hollered more. Finally he steered the canoe to the bank and dug in his pack for a small pouch of grease, which he gestured for me to smear on my neck and face. My neck and face *were* very hot, for the sun was fierce and there was no shade on the river, but the grease didn't help at all; it made me feel like a chicken rubbed with butter, sitting in a frying pan. By evening, any place my white skin had been exposed was red as a beet and throbbing.

This, I eventually realized, was what Hector had been yelling about—he saw my skin reddening and thought I should do something. Because the grease was no good, the only solution I could come up with thereafter was to tie our old tent cover o'er my head and shoulders as we paddled, which not only protected me from the sun, but also shielded me from the prying eyes of passers-by, much to Hector's relief.

Like the blisters and sunburn, the forced intimacy between us also caused me great discomfort. Having grown up in very crowded quarters, I was not troubled by the lack of privacy, but Hector made me uneasy, for I e'er expected him to grumble, yell, or otherwise express his enormous disapproval of me. I could ignore him well enough during the day, e'en tho' he was sitting only a few feet behind me, but when evening came I made an effort to stay as far from him as possible, preferably with the fire between us. For safety reasons, of course, he rarely let me out of his sight, but when he saw how I shrank from him, he went to great pains not to touch me, refusing e'en to make eye contact if he could help it.

Thanks to our physical proximity, he knew immediately when the time came, shortly after we started west, for my monthly. Our forward progress promptly came to a halt because Hector would not get in a canoe with me whilst I was in that condition. Therefore, we camped 'til my infirmity passed.

Being prohibited from speaking or e'en looking at one another proved to be no problem at all, because that was how we interacted all the time anyway. The truth was, our grief was still so raw that all we could do was feel it, live with it, and wait 'til we somehow became accustomed to it. I cannot speak for my companion, but I spent most of my waking moments during this time curled into a tiny ball inside my own head, crying and crying in unceasing sorrow.

At least I rarely cried aloud anymore, which must have been some relief for Hector.

To occupy myself during my monthly, I gathered a great armload of grass stalks and set about twisting the straws to make a broad-brimmed sunbonnet like those my gran used to make. Whilst I thus busied myself, Hector plucked his whiskers and worked on arrows or fish spears. I know not where his thoughts went during this silent time, but as I worked, I thought about Syawa, only Syawa. I basked in my memories—every word, every look, every touch, every smile—for I could not afford to forget a single precious moment, so few were those we shared.

As the shock of Syawa's sudden death slowly faded, I found myself inundated by a flood of new emotions. In addition to being devastated, I was also hurt, angry, and increasingly bitter. I had assumed Syawa wanted to marry me, but it turned out he only wanted someone to fulfill his stupid "Vision." And all those crazy things he told me—why had he not warned me about this Spirit Keeper business? He must've known Hector would view me as such. In fact, the more I thought about it, the more convinced I became that Syawa had gone out of his way to encourage Hector to believe that very thing.

But why would Syawa want Hector to believe something that simply wasn't true? It felt like some sort of trick, as if Syawa was setting me up the way I might set up pieces on a chessboard. Everyone I'd e'er known had used me in some way, so why should Syawa be any different? And while I was perfectly willing to honor his last wish by trying to convince his people of his Visionary powers, still—'twas hard not to feel as played as a hapless pawn.

No sooner did I think these ugly thoughts than I was swirled into a maelstrom of guilt—guilt for thinking badly of Syawa, guilt for allowing Hector to believe this Spirit Keeper nonsense, and, more than anything, guilt for being here in the first place. The only reason I'd come was to vex my mother; now my mere presence had completely changed the world. Of course, the moment I started blaming myself, I remembered Syawa's admonition, but that only made me feel guilty about feeling guilty, at which point I knew I must stop thinking altogether or I would go mad.

Ah, well. If my days were long and lonely, filled with questions and self-recriminations, my nights, at least, were short and sweet, filled with dreams which gave me brief relief. I dreamt of Syawa obsessively, going all the way back to the beginning of our acquaintance, when he was chattering on and on and I understood naught of what he said. As I revisited those days in my dreams, I gradually began to understand his words, or at least to imagine I did, and in this way I committed to memory every conversation we e'er had, right up to the cyclone storm. At that point my dreams inevitably whirled me back to the beginning, as if my slumbering mind durst go no further for fear of the agony embedded in more recent memories.

'Twas a curious sensation, this vivid reliving of past events. I know it was happening only because my thoughts were so entirely fixated, day and night, on Syawa, but I was grateful for the phenomenon, whate'er the reason. As long as I could dream of him, I still had him in my life.

Near the end of my monthly, as I took my turn at night-watch, a movement behind a bush caught my eye and I watched a shadow with increasing alarm. When I threw a rock at it, it disappeared, but before long it was back, circling our camp. E'en when I added wood to the fire, the shadow didn't run off. I lifted the hatchet, my mouth set in a determined line, and when I had a clear shot, I hurled the weapon, sending the shadow screaming off into the darkness.

The scream brought Hector to his feet, knife in hand. Knowing I mustn't talk to him, I pointed, and he rubbed one eye sleepily as he trotted into the bushes. I fretted o'er a commotion in the distance 'til Hector returned, carrying the hatchet distastefully between two fingers, the carcass of a bobcat draped o'er one shoulder. He said nothing and would not look my way, but he did jerk his head toward my bedding as if to suggest it was my turn to sleep, which I was glad to do.

By morning my monthly was done and everything I'd touched whilst bleeding must be washed or purified in smoke to Hector's satisfaction. I continued to be offended by these odd rituals, but I knew it was useless to argue, especially since I didn't know Hector's language well enough to make my position clear.

When we were finally permitted to speak again, he stared for a moment at my hat and I trembled, expecting him to tear it off my head and declare it somehow unacceptable. Instead, to my surprise, he almost smiled, and as we set off in the canoe, I was very pleased with myself.

Thanks to my new sunbonnet, I need drape a hide only o'er my shoulders, which enabled me to look 'round more freely as I paddled. Near the end of that day, I remember looking up to watch an odd bird fly by, only to find myself suddenly floundering in the river, for my looking up had somehow upset the canoe. Luckily, the water was only a few feet deep at that point, so as soon as I realized I could just stand up, I stopt splashing hysterically. In the meantime, Hector collected the canoe and our things—everything except my hat, which was floating in an eddy not far off. I started slogging toward it, only to have the earth fall out from under me as I stept off a shelf into much deeper water.

Because I immediately tried to scream, my lungs filled with water, causing me to panic. The harder I strove to arise, the farther down I went.

It seemed like hours, but 'twas only a matter of seconds before Hector was tugging my arm to drag me to the surface. The moment my head popped above the water, I coughed and coughed, clinging to him as he swam us to shore. He left me on the riverbank, still spluttering, still gasping, as he leapt back into the water and swam downstream to retrieve my hat.

When he returned, he stood staring at me as I miserably wrung out my hair. I waited for him to yell at me, but he just asked if I was hurt. I said no. He said, "Well, then. It is time for you to learn to swim."

I looked up at him, horrified. "I cannot!" I protested. "I cannot!"

"You can and you will," he said. He reached out his hand to me.

I turned and began scrambling up the bank to where he'd laid our things to dry. He came after me to grab my arm just as he'd done a few minutes earlier, when I was under water. This time, instead of clinging to him, I struggled to get away, screaming, inordinately terrified. "Let me go! Let me go!" I shrieked, but he pulled me back down the bank, a determined look in his eye.

With my free hand I hit his arm repeatedly with a tight fist 'til he abruptly released me, sending me flying backwards onto the muddy bank. From there I started scrambling away again, screaming, "No touch me! No touch me!"

I was sure he was coming after me, enraged, but when I finally dared look back I saw he was just standing there staring at me with narrowed eyes and lifted chin. I sat in the mud, breathing heavily, defiantly glaring up at him. For a moment our eyes locked exactly as they did when we first met in my family's loft. Then Hector broke the silence. "You must learn to swim." It was a statement, not a question.

"Why? He say if I fall in water, the worst that happens is I get wet."

"That was before, when there were two of us. Now there is just me."

I glowered at Hector, my head lowered, my eyes still locked on his. I had absolutely no intention of getting back in that water, and I was about to tell him as much when he spoke again.

"Sometimes the canoe tips," he said, his words slow, tight, and clipt. "It just does. And sometimes you will fall in. I will try to save you, but if I cannot get to you in time, you will drown. Please—do not make me watch you die . . . again."

Oh, sweet Jesus, what was I supposed to say to that? I rolled my eyes, sighed, and stared into the water, wishing I'd ne'er made that damned hat. "Well," I said at last. I sighed again as I slowly got to my feet. "Well. We do this quick—be done. What must I do?"

"Take off your leggings." I gasped and reared back, but my indignant reproach was lost on him because he was staring at the ground. "They will weigh you down," he said apologetically.

I rolled my eyes again, muttered voluminous curses in English, and angrily stript down to my short shift and loincloth. "Now what?" I snapt.

"I will have to touch you," he said, still not meeting my eyes.

I sighed again, enormously. "Well. Do not let me drown!"

We walked into the river and Hector showed me how to wave my arms and legs to stay afloat, treading water. I was surprised by how easy it was. Then he showed me how to take breaths by turning my head to the side. With great discomfort, apologizing again for having to touch me, he held me up as I practiced paddling and turning my head. Finally he made me swim up and down in the shallows near the bank, with him walking along to monitor me. He was pleased with my efforts, saying that was enough for now, but hereafter he would require me to swim every morning.

We ate, as usual, without speaking. As Hector laid out his sleeping fur, I sat by the fire, still drying my soggy hair. Having had time to reflect on the incident, I was thoroughly ashamed of my behavior. In my defense, all I can say is I was so accustomed to ill-treatment, I e'er expected to be hit, screamed at, or otherwise abused. Knowing how Hector disapproved of me, I was particularly suspicious of him, and I cringed to think my childish fit must have only confirmed his poor opinion of me. I owed it to Syawa to make amends. I mumbled, "Hector?"

He stopt spreading out his bedding and turned 'round.

I looked at him meekly as I mumbled, "Thank you for teaching me swim."

He lifted his chin in acknowledgment, but his face remained stone.

"And I . . . I am sorry I hit you. People hurt me before."

He nodded and turned away, only to stop short and turn back

to me. "*I* will not hurt you," he said, speaking slowly so I would be sure to understand.

I gave a humorless laugh. "People tell me that before, too." I stared at the fire, but I knew he was still kneeling there, staring at me. I kept brushing out my hair. Then I heard him crawl into his sleeping fur.

The next day we resumed paddling as before, but I remained uneasy, expecting always to be reprimanded for my many faults, ne'er knowing when the next awful "lesson" might occur. But when I noticed a large, dark bruise on Hector's arm where I'd hit him, I felt terrible. My guilt o'er that bruise kept me from fighting against the swimming lessons I must endure each morning.

Our silence continued, but I had come to realize that e'en when Hector made a big show of not looking at me, he was watching me all the time from the corner of his eye—wary, worried, wondering what stupid thing I might do next. Sometimes when I set up camp or prepared our meal, he watched me openly, as if making sure I followed the proper procedures. I was very self-conscious about this scrutiny, expecting him to criticize my every move, but when I met his gaze, defiantly, he looked away, jaw muscles tight, as if I had caught him doing something he shouldn't.

Sometimes he couldn't stop himself from offering suggestions about an easier way to do something, and sometimes I had no choice but to ask for help. I expected him to respond to these requests with a scolding for my stupidity, but he was ne'er nothing but polite and respectful, if a bit terse and impatient. He tried always to say as little as necessary as quickly as possible, as if it pained him to speak to me, and this way he had of talking through clenched teeth made it very difficult for me to understand his words. I decided he spoke this way because if he allowed himself to speak freely, he would ne'er be able to stop pointing out my many flaws.

It didn't help that I spoke his language so poorly. Hector had a much harder time understanding me than Syawa e'er did, and he was oft puzzled by my meaning e'en when he could understand my words. I knew I must improve, but how could I learn his language if I did not practice? Sometimes I was desperate to talk—simply desperate—but I was determined not to bother Hector more than I must.

The loaded silence began to grate on me. I remember complaining about the heat one day, because the weather had turned brutally hot, but Hector said nothing. I asked if the summers were always this hot, and he shrugged, saying it was ne'er this hot where his people lived. Stunned that he'd voluntarily said more than three words in a row, I asked him about the place he lived, the place I would soon live. He shrugged again, saying there was nothing to tell. But what about the weather, I asked, the land, the plants, the trees? What about the people, their houses, beliefs? I peppered him with questions, to no avail. The moment had passed and his answer to all questions was essentially the same: I would see for myself when I got there.

I refused to give up. There were so many things I wanted to know, so many things we needed to discuss. One evening after eating in silence I finally had enough of his wordless shrugs and halfhearted grunts, and said, "Hector, why you refuse talk with me? We were friends, before . . ." I stopt and exhaled sadly. "Now you not talk."

He looked at me blankly, as he always did. "I talk," he said. He turned his attention back to the pile of berries we'd gathered, picking through them with his finger.

I sighed. "Yes—you talk. Well. Then I ask you something. You now . . ." I paused, considering carefully how to word my thoughts. "You believe in his Vision—same as before, without him?"

Hector did not hesitate. "Yes."

"But I think . . . I think you not like me." I was not coyly fishing for compliments, and I knew Hector would not take it that way. "If you believe I am one he sees in Vision, then how you not like me?"

"It is not for me to like or dislike. You are not what I expected."

"What you expect?"

Hector looked at the fire and pursed his lips, considering. "Someone like . . . White Buffalo Woman maybe, or maybe the Corn Maiden."

I waited for him to continue, but he was finisht. I thought for a moment, then smiled and said, "I see. You expect someone not stink, someone not stupid."

Hector raised his chin and lowered his eyelids, staring at me in a calculating way. "I expected someone who doesn't cry all the time."

I tipt my head apologetically. "You expect story-woman. You get crying girl."

Hector tossed several of the berries into his mouth and chewed for a moment before shrugging and saying, "Not anymore."

I held my breath. Was he talking about my not crying so much anymore or about my being Syawa's Spirit Keeper? Either way, this topic was too charged for me, so I steered the conversation in a new direction, to a question I had been dying to ask. "You remember my family house?"

"Of course."

"I saw man at bottom of . . ." I pantomimed stairs, Hector gave me the word, and I repeated it. "Yes, stairs. I saw dead man at bottom of stairs. You kill that man?"

"Yes."

"But men you are with know that man! He one of them. You not afraid you kill him, they kill you?"

Hector finished the berries, wiped his hand on his leg, and shrugged. "The Seer said I must kill that man. He said it was part of his Vision. I did as he told me."

I numbly watched as Hector unrolled his sleeping fur. "I owe you my life," I said quietly.

He grunted an affirmation as he lay down on his fur. He started to wrap himself up, then stopt to look at me. "Are we done talking?"

I grunted a mocking affirmation and watched as he curled up under his covers. I added wood to the fire and picked up the hatchet before sitting down to ponder what I'd just heard. Only slowly did I perceive the full import of Hector's words: Syawa had given me an awesome power. Hector always did whate'er the Seer told him to do and he would continue to do whate'er the Seer told him, only now the commands would have to come to him through me.

I wondered—was this, then, why Syawa set me up as his Spirit Keeper? So that I could make Hector do my bidding? 'Twas possible. But the more I thought about it, the more I realized it did not matter where my newfound power came from. E'en if this strange situation was naught but a curious side-effect of a gross misunderstanding, the end result was the same.

I needn't be afraid of Hector anymore.

As we paddled west on the Misery River, we stopt at a few—but by no means all—of the villages along the way. They blend together in my mind now, for they were all small and similar, nothing like the large towns east of the Great River. The people, too, were different. Whilst the Indians of Pennsylvania were warriors, the people along the Misery were mostly fishermen who had little to do with the world beyond their small stretch of riverbank. They were all, needless to say, astonished by me.

We stopt at these places because Syawa and Hector had stopt on their journey eastward, and Hector felt duty-bound to let the people know how their Journey turned out. At each place, he gestured a summary of Syawa's Vision, then reviewed the adventures the two of them had on their way to my family's farm. From that point, I gestured a description of our hike through the forest and a brief explanation of what happened after we crossed the Great River. I was compelled to tell the villagers the Seer gave me his Spirit, because if I didn't, Hector would. At least if *I* told them, I could keep the story short and simple.

Tho' my white skin, red hair, and blue eyes were viewed as

wonders in the Indian world, it was the fact that I was a Spirit Keeper which inspired the greatest awe. I disliked the pretense, but saw no graceful way out of it. The benefit to being a Spirit Keeper was that most Indians were deathly afraid of me, which meant they left me alone, and because no one seemed to know what sort of supernatural powers a person with two souls might possess, any odd behavior on my part was always excused as "being the sort of thing a Spirit Keeper might do."

Whereas I had, at first, been uneasy about stopping in strange villages, I soon realized the advantages. Indian villages were islands of safety and security in the midst of the vast, ominous wilderness, places where people could watch out for each other, love one another, and live comfortable lives. They could also entertain each other, which is where Hector and I came in. As traveling storytellers with a real-life drama to share, we were welcomed and celebrated like royalty. Not only were we given ready-to-eat food in payment for our story, but both Hector and I were able to sleep the whole night without worrying about taking turns at watch.

In addition to food and lodging, we were also given gifts at every place we stopt, but because we gave most of these gifts to other villagers in exchange for gifts they gave us, we mostly just recirculated the wealth of each community. Thanks to these exchanges, I acquired two soft deerskins and thereafter spent my hours at night-watch huddled by the fire, sewing new garments.

For the top I made a laced bodice with roomy armholes for ease of paddling, but because of my fear of sunburn, I left broad shoulder flaps draping o'er my arms like wings. For my lower half I saw no choice but to make breeches like my father's, tied at both the waist and calf to keep the sun off my legs and the mosquitoes away from my nether regions. I knew my outfit, once completed, would be strange to everyone who saw it, but most people I met were mostly naked most of the time, and Hector rarely spoke to me, so was unlikely to comment on my appearance.

The land we paddled through as we headed west on the Misery was as different from the eastern woodland as were the Indians. Instead of huge, dark forests, we passed scrubland, then open meadows, then more and more wide, rolling grasslands. The grains in the fields were ripening at this time, so one night I made a stuffing for our fish. When Hector, unprompted, said the stuffing was good, I almost fainted from shock. Thereafter we spent many evenings walking the meadows, stripping seeds, which we stored in skin sacks.

During one of these walks I encountered a snake slithering on the ground and nigh jumped out of my skin. I screamed, dropt my seedbag, and ran back to the canoe in the time it took Hector to blink. I was certain he would be disgusted by my cowardice, but he gathered up what I spilt and brought it back to camp where I was cowering. "I will stay closer to you," he said quietly, "and make sure you see no more snakes."

Pretty much the only time Hector initiated a conversation was when we were in a village and he needed to confer with me. I found it curious that when we were with others he made it very clear we were a team, a partnership, but when it was just the two of us, we were completely separate, isolated, alone. The breakthrough came one evening when I was preparing dinner and had to ask Hector something—just what, I cannot recall. At any rate, I said, "Hector?" and asked my question, which he answered before adding quietly, "And that is not my name."

I jumped on the opportunity to start a conversation. I apologized for still not being able to pronounce his name, but pointed out he ne'er used any name at all when addressing me. If he wanted my attention, he usually just grunted. I told him my name was "Katie," not "Huh!"

He almost smiled at that, but caught himself in time.

Seeing an opening, I told him that "Hector" was actually a famous name amongst my people, an honorable name, the name of one of the greatest warriors of all time. He looked me full in the face for a moment, his interest clearly piqued. "Tell me," he said, lifting his chin.

I smiled to myself, pleased I had broken through the formidable wall of silence. "It is a long, long, long story," I warned.

Hector nodded as he returned his gaze to the fire. "We have a long, long, long way to go."

I must have been about ten when Father made us read the *Iliad* aloud. It took the entire winter because he made the boys read the passages in Greek after we girls read them in English. Times were hard for my family, but listening to the trials and tribulations of the ancients somehow made our troubles more bearable. 'Twas comforting to know the same sorts of jealousies, quarrels, and misfortunes that plagued us had been plaguing people for thousands of years and would no doubt continue to plague people for thousands of years to come.

With Hector waiting expectantly, I feared the story of the Trojan War was too complicated, full of abstract concepts which would be difficult to translate. I looked at him doubtfully. "I not speak well. You must help with words." He shrugged and nodded at the same time, still looking into the fire.

I started by describing the strategically placed city of Troy and the group of city-states that was ancient Greece. I told about King Priam, and his sons Hector and Paris. Then I ran into trouble, because I must explain the involvement of the Greek gods in the lives of men, but Hector readily accepted the notion of powerful beings in some other realm who affected things in our world. Thereafter I had to stop many times to describe objects or ideas I knew no words for, but the challenge became almost a game, with Hector trying to figure out what I was talking about so he could supply the word. He oft corrected my pronunciation or changed my phrasing, but he did so politely, gently, reluctant to break the flow of the story.

After we ate, I explained how Aphrodite rewarded Paris with the love of Helen, a woman already married to someone else, and Hector nodded, saying he knew of a situation where a man from one village stole the wife of a man from another village and the resulting discord led to a big fight. "That's exactly what happened in Troy!" I exclaimed.

That's about as far as I got the first night. The next night Hector bade me continue, so, with his help, I explained how the Greeks gathered together, got into big canoes, and went to besiege Troy. There I ran into trouble again. I could explain the concept of "besiege" well enough, but I knew no number-words in Hector's language. I counted in English on my fingers. Then I picked up some pebbles on the riverbank and counted them out. "Give me the words," I said to Hector.

He was puzzled. I counted my fingers again. I counted the stones. I counted some sticks. I counted some leaves. Hector finally got it, telling me the words in his language as I counted. I repeated his words, but once we got to ten, the numbers became mere equations—eleven was ten-one, twelve was ten-two, and so on. There were new words for twenty, thirty, forty, etc., but the term for one hundred was simply "ten-ten." All words beyond that were mere sums of previous numbers.

I frowned, frustrated. Somehow I needed to get Hector to understand a much larger number. I went to the river to gather more pebbles and rocks. I made ten piles of ten, counting each pebble with the words he had given me. He watched closely, curious. When I reached one hundred, I gestured at all the rocks and said "ten-ten" in his language. Hector nodded. I took a bigger rock and gestured to the ten piles of pebbles. "Ten-ten!" I said again, referring to the larger rock. He nodded again.

I collected ten of the larger rocks and lined them up before him. "*Ten* ten-ten!" I said. "That's how many canoes the Greeks sent to Troy!" Hector's eyebrows shot up. I went on to explain the Greek canoes were much, much larger than ours, each holding more than "ten-ten" warriors. "Ten-ten warriors in *ten* ten-ten canoes!" I said, pushing all my pebbles into one pile with the ten larger rocks. "That's ten-ten, ten-ten-ten men!"

I lost him. He looked amused as he stared at the rock piles. "No village could gather that many warriors!" he said, clearly convinced I was exaggerating.

I sighed and held my chin on my hand as I stared into the fire. "This war happened many, many years ago," I said quietly. "Maybe *five* ten-ten-ten years ago. There are many, many more men in that land now. Many, many more. And there are many, many other lands in that world, each with many, many, many more men than that. They are like leaves on the trees, Hector. They are like stars in the sky."

Our eyes met and held for a moment. Syawa's words echoed in my brain, and I had to look away to keep Hector from seeing my tears. He could not understand why I was suddenly upset, but he could see that I was. "That is enough," he said, trying to make light of it. "You need not talk to me if it is too hard to make me understand. I am not smart, like you."

"Oh, Hector—the fault is mine, not yours. I just . . . I remember something . . . something *he* told me. But I want talk—I *need* talk."

Hector nodded, managing a feeble smile. "Talk more tomorrow, then. For now, I leave you to your memories."

For many evenings thereafter I plodded through the tale of the Trojan War, explaining how the Trojan Hector held off the massive Greek force for nine long years, and how his name became synonymous with loyalty, courage, and steadfastness e'en in the face of certain defeat. I hesitated to tell the end of the Trojan's story for fear the ignominious death he suffered might offend the man I called Hector, but my fears proved unfounded. My Hector concluded Achilles had an unfair advantage and was, therefore, not an honorable warrior. He also thought the mutilation of the Trojan's body, tho' shameful, was the sort of thing men do in war, which was why war was best avoided, and, of course, he was glad to hear Achilles eventually paid for his deeds.

All in all, the story was the perfect ice-breaker, not only because it forced Hector to teach me many new words and phrases, but also because it gave us something to talk about that wasn't charged with painful personal emotions. Knowing I must speak his language in order to learn it, I was delighted I'd finally found a way to get him to talk with me. But the best part of telling this story came when, after weeks of my halting, garbled delivery, my companion sat staring into the fire, nodding thoughtfully, and after a long pause he said he guessed he didn't mind if I called him Hector.

The day after I finished telling the tale of the Trojan War, my monthly returned and, once again, we camped in silence.

Hector and I worked on our separate tasks, near one another but entirely alone. I don't know how things seemed to him, but for me, at least, the silence felt very different than it did the previous month. It was less strained, less miserable. As I sat sewing, I marveled how quickly time passed—it was already six weeks since Syawa died. I mourned the steady passage of days pulling me farther and farther away from him. Six weeks gone—and the total time of my life with him not twice that. Yet those precious days had changed everything for me, and the six weeks since . . . well, I assumed that e'en if I lived to be a hundred, I would still be trying to figure out exactly what happened during those glorious days I spent with the Seer.

Shortly after my monthly we came to a place where the river looped in an enormous oxbow. To paddle the loop, Hector explained, would consume more than a day, time we could save by carrying the canoe o'er land. He steered our craft to the shore.

By this time my arms and shoulders were strong, but the canoe, filled with our things, was heavy. On the other hand, I had long since decided not to argue with Hector if I could help it, so we got out and began lugging our load o'er a well-trodden path. 'Twas not an easy haul for me, as we walked for a couple of hours, the land sloping steadily upwards the whole way. I tried to keep a steady pace, but before we were done I was calling for a rest every few minutes. I knew the frequent stops were frustrating Hector, but, to his great credit, he said not a word.

During one of our breaks, I saw a flock of ducks in a marshy area, sitting on a grassy hillock, watching us walk by. "Look!" I said, hoping to distract Hector from my repeated need to rest.

"Those ducks are like the ones Coyote tricked when he was carrying his grass bundle. They watch us now as they watched him. Shall we sing for them, to see if they'll dance?"

Hector half-smiled at the ducks, and I silently congratulated myself for having gotten a response from him. Then he picked up the front of the canoe and I stooped to pick up the rear.

Suddenly he stopt and dropt the canoe, nearly jerking me off my feet. I dropt my end as well, assuming he must've stumbled, but he had turned and was staring at me with a very peculiar look on his face. "How do you know about Coyote and the ducks?" he asked in a strained voice.

I reflected. "*He* told that story—remember?"

"I remember exactly when he told that story, the only time he told that story in your hearing. It was right after we found you, when we were with your family on our way to the warriors' village."

I lifted my face, remembering. "I think you are right. That was when I heard it."

Hector stared at me, his eyes frightened. "But you could not speak then! You could not understand our words. Do you share his memories?"

I looked down at the rocky pathway, inhaling slowly and deeply. I shrugged as I looked sheepishly up at him. "I . . . I dream of him. Every single night since . . . well. I dream it all over and over—every gesture, every word. That's how I know the story. He tells it in my head."

After studying me with narrowed eyes, Hector nodded curtly and turned to pick up the canoe. I did the same, feeling a huge wave of guilt. I knew he was interpreting my knowledge of this story as further proof I was Syawa's Spirit Keeper, but to me it was merely evidence that I was mentally unstable, fanatically obsessed with a dead man. Either way, this was not a conversation I was eager to pursue.

But later, after we had eaten one of those nosy ducks and Hector was unrolling his sleeping fur, he suddenly turned to me. Because Hector ne'er initiated a conversation unless he had some vital information to convey, I stopt poking the fire to look at him expectantly. He seemed reluctant to speak. He forced himself. "Will you talk with him tonight, do you think?"

I shrugged, blushing scarlet. "I always do," I said quietly.

Hector nodded, his eyes averted. "Will you tell him . . ." he said haltingly, "will you tell him I'm grateful?" His voice broke on the last word.

I knew it would bother Hector for me to cry, so I tried very hard to hold back the tears. "Yes, I will tell him," I said in a shaky voice.

Hector nodded again and rolled himself into his fur, his back to me. I tried to cry quietly as I built up the fire, but I'm sure he heard me. I could tell by his breathing he didn't fall asleep for a long, long time.

Thereafter Hector seemed calmer somehow, less tense, more comfortable with me. When he had a chance to catch another duck the very next evening, he did so, saying I'd done such a fine job of cooking the first one, he was hungry for more.

Stunned by the compliment, I plucked the new duck happily as I explained my family always kept birds—ducks, chickens, turkeys—so I had plenty of experience cooking them.

Hector wasn't sure how my family could keep birds the way Indians keep dogs. "Do they follow you in day and sleep with you at night?" he asked, trying not to smile.

"No!" I giggled, then went on to explain about pens and roosts. He was interested to learn we had a steady supply of eggs, intrigued by the notion we could butcher and eat a bird whene'er we wanted, without hunting. I then told him about a pet chicken I had when we lived in Boston—a pretty white hen I called Fluffy.

"You gave a bird a name?" he asked, unable to suppress his smile any longer.

"Oh, yes!" With him supplying any words I needed, I told all about Fluffy—how she hatched eggs for other hens, and how cute the chicks were when they peeked out from under her. When Hector chuckled at my pantomimes, I jumped up and acted out my mother's favorite way of killing a bird—grabbing it by the legs, flopping its head on the ground, putting her foot on the head, and yanking the body off. I acted out what happened one day when she killed a dozen birds to sell at market—pop, pop, pop, pop. Each time she threw a body down, it got up and ran 'round so that our garden was full of headless birds running into each other, their wings flapping frantically. Finally, one by one, they stopt and stood still for a moment, as if surprised to realize they were dead. Then they fell over.

As I ran 'round our fire acting out this scene, Hector laughed more than I have e'er heard anyone laugh about anything. He laughed so hard I thought he would choke; he laughed 'til tears rolled down his cheeks. I laughed with him, working the story for all it was worth, well aware that this was the first time I had heard him laugh since Syawa died. What a joy it was to see him as something other than angry, gloomy, or sad!

Later, when he was unrolling his bedding, he glanced at me, still smiling. "You have learnt how to talk," he said, clearly pleased.

I nodded, ready to thank him for all his help, but before I could, he spoke again. "It is good he is teaching you in your sleep." I drew in my breath, but Hector was still smiling. He lay down, enwrapping himself in his fur.

I sighed. All this time Hector had been teaching me to talk, but now he was giving the credit to his dead friend and there was naught I could say to convince him otherwise.

I sighed again.

~ 22 ~

ABOUT THIS TIME the Misery turned north, and on one side of that turn was the largest village since the Great River. As we walked up from the riverbank, I felt again the familiar discomfort at being surrounded by so many gawking strangers, but this time, with Hector walking beside me, I no longer felt so vulnerable, so alone. He had fastened some duck feathers in his hacked-off hair, and the bright colors emphasized his strikingly handsome features, which helped draw attention away from the wonder of my red hair, white skin, and blue eyes. For that I was grateful.

At this village, as always, we were warmly received, and tho' we were forced to endure, once again, the public outpouring of sympathy that always accompanied the discovery of Syawa's death, Hector and I had endured it so many times we no longer wilted beneath this public sharing of our very private pain. In fact, when the keening began at the Big Bend village, I remember exchanging a glance with Hector for just a fraction of a second before we bowed our heads, and I felt a bond I'd ne'er felt before. It wasn't just *my* sorrow anymore—it was *ours*. And that's when a strange thing happened.

I discovered the grief did not hurt so much when it was no longer mine alone.

Later, as the local speaker wrapt up our introduction, I remember exchanging another glance with Hector. This time I felt a wave of encouragement, support, and trust. I had long since vowed ne'er to let him down the way I did at the Trade Center. Knowing him as I did now, I understood Syawa was the storyteller and all along Hector participated in the performances in much the same way I participated in swimming; it was simply something he had to do.

By the time we reached the Big Bend, I was getting the hang of this storytelling business. I knew enough now to wait under a cloak whilst Hector gestured the summary of Syawa's Vision, their Journey, and their arrival at my family's house. I waited as he acted out his death-struggle with the bald savage, and I waited as he showed how he and Syawa slowly climbed the stairs. Then I jumped up, pretending to point a weapon at him as he pretended to point his bloody knife at me. The crowd always gasped when I appeared.

It was at the Big Bend village that Hector and I truly connected during that critical moment in our tale. Our eyes locked and I felt again all those feelings of terror and despair, but I also felt all the trust and affection we had built in the ensuing months. It was a strange sensation, to feel so many diametrically opposed emotions at exactly the same time. I remember sort of smiling at him as we stood brandishing our imaginary weapons, and I remember seeing him sort of smile back at me in the exact same way. There was a new unity between us, an interdependence I'd ne'er experienced. We had become a true team, two oxen working together to haul a heavy load.

I went on to tell the rest of the story. The audience listened with rapt attention as I described hiking the eastern forest, learning to live in the wild. To them, I must have seemed some sort of other-worldly creature who dropt out of the sky and must learn to be human, and, to some degree, I suppose that's exactly what I was. When I got to the part where the Seer was bitten and the canoe went spinning off into the river, I screamed and spun 'round the fire as Hector pantomimed swimming after me. We made several circuits, during which the crowd went wild, roaring for him to save me, which, of course, he always did.

By this time I had e'en become resigned to the resolution of our story, wherein I became Syawa's Spirit Keeper. Tho' I knew 'twas not true, I also knew that without that ending, the story was just too tragic to tell.

After our performance at the Big Bend village, I did not glance Hector's way again 'til after he sang the traveler's song and the community dancing began. At that point men were gathering 'round him as women were gathering 'round me, and our eyes met across the crowd. He gave me one of his half-smiles and I smiled back, glowing inside.

At that moment I wisht Syawa's Spirit truly *was* inside me, or at least watching from above. I knew he would be pleased his friends had finally befriended each other.

Hector and I had turned a corner in more than just the direction of the river. Tho' we still remained mostly silent during the days, it was now a companionable silence, a comfortable one, and during the evenings, more and more, we enjoyed pleasant conversation.

I told various stories to amuse him, but nothing entertained him as much as genuine descriptions of my early life. I told him about the sweet brown cow with a crumpled horn who always

mooed plaintively whene'er we were late to milk her. Hector looked
skeptical from across the campfire. "This cow of yours," he asked,
"it was like those we see sometimes drinking from the river?" He
was referring, of course, to the great wild cows of America, the buffalo.

I admitted Bossie wasn't nigh as big as a buffalo cow, but I pantomimed how big she was and assured him she seemed huge to a
twelve-year-old girl who was milking her. I described how her wet,
nasty tail smacked my face if she thought I tugged her teat too hard,
but how she always licked me with her big, rough tongue to thank
me when I was done.

Hector shook his head in amazement, asking why I took her
milk from her.

"To drink!" I exclaimed, then told about cream and butter and
all the delicious cheeses we made from milk. He listened to my babbling descriptions, his eyes shining with the same rapt attention our
audiences always displayed, and on his face he wore the same half-
smile I'd seen whene'er Syawa told a story. He was a wonderful
audience.

But if I say Hector was interested in my stories of our cows, I
cannot begin to describe the wonder with which he attended my
explanation of how and why we gelded our bulls.

And so the evenings passed as pleasantly as the days. Once we
turned north, the wind was behind us, which meant we fairly flew
upon the water. Occasionally it rained, but unless there was lightning, we kept moving. When weather did stop us, we sat on the
riverbank under our upturned canoe, each concentrating on handi-
works. He made arrows and fish spears; I sewed. I oft wisht I had a

book to read. Sometimes we chatted, but mostly we kept our thoughts to ourselves, tho' I suspect our thoughts went to the same place more often than not.

I remembered watching Hector and Syawa sit together like this, remembered how amazed I was by their almost supernatural connection. I had ne'er seen nothing like it, but now, because Hector fully believed Syawa's Spirit was living inside me, he was letting his guard down, relaxing, interacting. 'Twas thrilling to experience e'en a faint reflection of the deep bond between those two men.

Mind you, I have had deep and abiding friendships in my life. I had a friend in Philadelphia—Mary—who was like a twin from whom I had been separated at birth. Whene'er we were together, we chattered endlessly about everything and nothing. Her father owned a stable, and the two of us rode together whene'er we could slip away from our families. We rode bareback, both on one horse. 'Tis a wonder to me now we did not break our necks on those rides, for we were oft thrown and were always at the mercy of the large beasts, who trotted, cantered, or galloped as they pleased. Mary's father encouraged us to ride, for it was good for the stabled horses to get fresh air and exercise, but we were whipt more than once for being careless with other people's property when we ran a horse too hard or brought it back limping.

Some of the happiest moments in my early life occurred when I had my arms wrapt 'round that dear girl as we rode along the Delaware River.

My point is that I knew how good it felt to have a true friend, but any experience I e'er had with friendship paled beside the bond I was beginning to enjoy with Hector. Unfortunately, my good feelings were riddled with guilt, as I knew the only reason Hector was nice to me was that he believed some part of me was his own childhood friend. I tried to temper my guilt by reminding myself it did Hector good to have Syawa back in his life, if only in this once-removed way. I assured myself it was a good thing I was doing, that by letting him believe Syawa's Spirit was residing in me I wasn't lying to him so much as offering him a way to cope with his awful loss. If I just happened to benefit from the deception by stepping right into the friendship the men had establisht and enjoying it for myself—well, that was not my intention. I ne'er meant to take Sy-awa's place in Hector's life, but once I felt it happening, it felt good, too good to stop.

Back at the Big Bend village, the elders had warned of a band of ruffians somewhere to the north. At first we little heeded this warn-ing, inasmuch as the danger was far away, but because the winds were with us and we were now working together like wheels on a cart, Hector and I made excellent progress, traveling great distances every day. As a result, the threat to the north loomed e'er closer. Soon every traveler we encountered could speak of naught but the ruffians.

A week or more after passing the Big Bend, we stopt at a village where the people were so distraught they scarce had any interest in our story. They said a group of fishermen had headed north two months earlier and were now long overdue. A search party had gone to find the missing men, but no word had yet come from either group.

Hector processed this news grimly before insisting we must go on. He was determined to reach a certain village by winter, and that village, he assured me, was still a long, long way away. But the far-ther north we traveled, the more uneasy he became. Each afternoon he looked for a small settlement or occupied campsite—exactly the sorts of places he previously avoided. Hector did not like camping with strangers, but he liked e'en less the risk we might be taking if we continued to camp alone.

Most people held us off with spears or nocked arrows 'til we explained who we were and what we wanted. Then they told the story we'd already heard—a band of miscreants up north was harassing travelers, hunters, fishermen, taking whate'er they wanted. When asked about the search party sent from the downstream village, most people said they had seen canoes or talked with the searchers, but that was all anyone knew.

At one small settlement we met a man who said he had escaped the ruffians. He said their leader was a young man expelled from a village far to the north, and this ne'er-do-well had attracted a band of outcasts from many neighboring villages. The trouble-makers now roamed the countryside, killing or enslaving everyone they met.

This news so vexed Hector he said we must stay where we were 'til the threat to travelers was somehow resolved. He, like everyone else, reckoned the missing fishermen and/or the search party would be returning any day now with news of a peaceful reconciliation.

I wasn't so sure. I could see the idea of adding months to our journey made Hector as miserable as a swarm of biting flies, and I felt awful, knowing that, were it not for me, he would be living a life of comfort and ease back home. I told him and the people of that settlement the story of Robin Hood—another social outcast 'round whom a band of criminals collected. When Hector understood Robin Hood's men robbed and harassed travelers for many years, he decided we'd best just keep moving.

So off we went at dawn each day, paddling as if the Hounds of Hell were baying at our backs, covering incredible distances, breathing a huge sigh of relief each afternoon when we found someone to camp with.

One day we realized that whereas we had, up to this point, regularly met canoes coming or going on the river, suddenly there was no one. No one. The entire day we met not a single traveler. That had ne'er happened during the entire time we paddled up the Misery.

What a deliverance it seemed that afternoon when we found an extended family group just wrapping up a hunting expedition! There were eighteen of them, including four women and six children. With all their weapons trained upon us, they flatly refused our request to join them 'til Hector told them I was a Spirit Keeper. Then they welcomed us, presuming, I suppose, my supernatural powers would protect us all from earthly peril. Far from providing protection, however, my presence only increased our vulnerability, for almost as soon as we joined them, my monthly began. Thus I found myself isolated with the women whilst Hector conferred with the men.

When we arrived, they had been packing to leave the next morning, but Hector convinced them to remain by pointing out that if they did not finish drying their meat, much of it would be ruined and the Spirit of the Buffalo would be displeased. Reluctant to offend the Buffalo Spirit, the hunters stayed to finish their work. Hector helped, hoping to convince them to stay through my time, but each day the men were increasingly agitated, and after three days, they would wait no longer. They left some meat in exchange for Hector's help and pushed their heavily laden canoes into the current.

Hector was stone-faced as he watched them depart, but I knew he was feeling wretched. I, myself, could not have felt worse, keenly aware I was the one putting us in danger. At least if we could travel, we could hope to out-paddle any pursuers. As it was, we were sitting ducks. And, thanks to the ridiculous rules of his people, I couldn't e'en talk to Hector about it, to ease his mind.

As he paced the riverbank, anxiously trying to look in all directions at the same time, I finally decided this unique circumstance must surely merit an exemption to his hard-and-fast separation requirements, so I urged him to let us get in the canoe and go, regardless of my condition. I explained my people ne'er observed monthly prohibitions and nothing bad e'er happened to us. When Hector refused e'en to acknowledge he heard me, I was infuriated. I ranted and raved in English, calling him every foul name I knew.

Eventually I gave up and sat by the fire glaring at the flames, trying to convince myself that all the rumors we'd heard were surely exaggerations. People tend to let their imaginations run wild, and my sense was that the "band of ruffians" was probably nothing more than a group of young men flexing their muscles.

When we lived in Philadelphia, my older brothers became well-known as hooligans, and the more people feared them, the more they swaggered and bullied. What started as petty theft and minor vandalism soon escalated into grand larceny and deliberate arson. As their reputation for violence grew, so did their power and influence, and before long the townspeople were actually paying my brothers and their gang not to cause trouble. That was the main reason James stayed in Philadelphia when the rest of us moved to the wilderness—he had a good thing going and didn't want to give it up.

I reckoned the ruffians we'd heard so much about were in a similar situation, which meant the more people talked about how terrible they were, the more terrible they became. Our best hope, I knew, was to slip swiftly and silently through their territory whilst they were occupied with something else—such as the search party we were following. If we were waylaid by the ruffians, we'd just have to pay whatever tribute they demanded, after which they'd let us go. Tribute was all my brothers e'er wanted.

The sun set and it came time for Hector to sleep, but he remained on the riverbank, looking back and forth. I told him it was stupid to go without sleep—he would wear himself out so that if the ruffians *did* show up, he would be too tired to offer a defense. Tho' he was ignoring me, I could see my words had an effect. Then I got an idea.

My brothers ne'er got into a fight they weren't sure they could win, and if the odds were against them, they'd wait 'til they had the advantage. So as Hector paced nearby, I collected piles of grass and weeds. I spread our extra hides atop these piles so that it looked as if there were two people sleeping near our fire. Tho' Hector ne'er looked at me, he joined me in collecting four more piles so we seemed to have *six* additional people sleeping in our camp. Satisfied, he lay down amidst the "bodies" and went to sleep.

Holding the French hatchet in my hand, I sat under my bearskin with my hat on my head so that it was not obvious I was a woman. Thankfully, nothing unusual occurred during my watch, except when Hector snorted in his sleep, woke himself up, and nigh stabbed one of our sleeping "bodies" with his knife. I would've laughed at him had he not been so obviously anxious for my safety.

I slept undisturbed that night, and tho' Hector paced like a caged cat all the next day, nothing happened. When nighttime rolled 'round, we rearranged our piles and hoped for the best, both aware we should be free to travel on the morrow. All we need do was make it through one more night.

The second night was more tense than the first, but, once again, nothing occurred. When the second morning came, I got up, tied back my hair, and picked up my pack, preparing to go to the river to perform the purification rituals Hector insisted upon before we resumed normal communications, but just as I turned to leave, Hector suddenly spoke.

He was standing by the canoe, facing the surrounding brush, casually collecting his fish spears. "If I had someone to talk to," he said quietly, clearly addressing me, "I would say we are being watched."

I froze, considering. I tried to look unconcerned as I went back to stand near him. I bent down beside his pack, looking for the hatchet. "If I could talk to someone," I murmured, "I would ask how many people are watching us."

A long moment passed. Hector continued to fumble with his spears. "I would tell someone I see at least ten, maybe more," he said softly, apparently to the canoe.

"Can't we just get in the canoe and go?" I asked, dropping the pretense as fear took over.

But it was too late. There was a whoop from the river as two canoes whizzed into sight, and at that signal, the people hiding in the brush stood up and revealed themselves. All of them—those in the canoes and those in the brush—were wildly painted as if for battle. They howled in victory.

We were surrounded.

~ 23 ~

Our attackers encircled us, howling in delight. A few rummaged through our things, snatching up Hector's knives, arrows, spears, and the hatchet. Others stabbed the hide covers of our grass piles, sneering at the deception. I was surprised to see how many had European weapons, including at least one sword.

They all "ooo"ed and "aah"ed o'er me, walking 'round and 'round, eyeing me up and down. When one reached out to touch my knot of hair, Hector shoved away the offending hand and was immediately knockt to the ground, pinned there by two large warriors. E'er since he intervened when the Spanish ambassador held my wrist, Hector suffered no one to touch me. In the villages we visited, he scowled e'en when I let the women brush my hair.

I trembled to see Hector assaulted and struggling on the ground, but there was little I could do to aid him. As his attackers bound his hands, he shouted in his language, which, of course, only I could understand, "Someone must tell them she is a Spirit Keeper!"

In spite of the dire circumstances, I felt a flush of exasperation. "E'en now?" I demanded, looking down at him. He would not look at me. "E'en now you will not speak to me?" I sighed heavily and raised my hands to gesture as Hector advised. The effect was immediate and sensational. Every one of the marauders froze. They all stared at me, then turned to see what their leader thought of this revelation.

He was a tall man, probably in his mid-twenties, wearing a fantastic cape of feathers. He had come in one of their long canoes, and whilst his minions pillaged our campsite, he walked slowly and majestically toward us. His entire body was painted a bright blood red, save for black marks on his face, but the most striking thing about him was his eyes. They were black and shining, wide-open as if he was startled. They made him look like a lunatic.

He walked to me slowly, looking me up, down, all 'round. He stopt with his face a few inches from mine, and for a long moment our eyes locked, not unlike the way my eyes had locked with Hector's in my family's loft. This time, howe'er, Syawa wasn't there to disarm us.

Or was he? As soon as I thought of the man whose Spirit I purportedly carried, I became calm. I remembered his Vision, just the thought of which comforted me, as if it wrapt 'round me like an invisible cloak. Suddenly I knew—*I knew*—I was completely safe.

The wide-eyed savage before me hissed something in his language; I could feel his breath moist upon my lips. I smiled the same way Syawa always did and said in English, "Well, you're quite a cock-of-the-walk, aren't you?"

Somehow the leader's wide-open eyes opened wider and he grinned like a gurgling half-wit. At the same time, Hector began struggling again, which caused the leader to turn, as I'm sure Hector hoped. The befeathered leader walked over to sneer down at

Hector, then turned and shouted orders to his men. At that, the underlings resumed their pillaging, whilst the leader and his party got back into their canoes. Two others pulled our canoe to the water, got inside, and followed the two larger canoes.

In a short time Hector was yanked to his feet and dragged up the riverbank. No one touched me, but I followed along, and as soon as I stept beside him, Hector stopt resisting. Thereafter we walked side by side, surrounded by our captors.

In some ways, the ensuing hike reminded me of the days right after leaving my family's farm, only this time Hector was the one who was bound. We walked for hours, and in all that time he ne'er looked at me directly. I remember wondering if his dogged adherence to superstition was so strict he would not look at me e'en if these men ravaged me or tore my flesh asunder. Strange to say, I was more vexed by his behavior than by the fact we were now captives of the fabled ruffians.

In truth, I was almost relieved. For so long we had dreaded the ruffians, worrying about them and wondering what they would do; now I no longer need wonder. It was like the time my gran had a rotten tooth, which she complained about for months 'til my mother finally had enough and fell upon her with a pair of tongs. "Well, that was no fun," Gran grumbled after the tooth was removed, "but at least 'tis done!"

So, tho' I was not exactly having fun as we marched in the hot sunshine, I reckoned 'twas no worse than having a tooth pulled and 'twould soon be over.

As time passed, I began to regret my earlier vexation with Hector. To cheer him, I sang a song Gran used to sing—a long, tuneful ballad about going to a fair. Because my singing seemed to unnerve our captors, who exchanged glances with increasing consternation,

I sang other songs as well. The more I sang, the more I saw a slight softening in Hector's stony face.

By mid-day we arrived at the outlaw camp—a filthy collection of hide tents set beside a shallow, muddy tributary of the Misery. The canoes had beaten us back, and the leader awaited us in the central clearing of his grimy little village. Besides the twenty or so warriors who participated in our capture, there was a handful of additional guards, half a dozen slatternly women, and something between fifteen and twenty cowering captives, bound in various ways, who were clearly being compelled to perform the basic maintenance of the camp whilst the warriors were otherwise occupied.

There was much whooping and hollering as we arrived. The "warriors" were mostly very young men—several younger than I. They reminded me of my brothers when they first started carousing all night with their friends.

The warriors took great pleasure in screaming in our faces and brandishing their weapons in a menacing manner. Hector's face remained non-responsive through this posturing, tho' his black eyes flashed rage. I, myself, was little perturbed because I know how boys behave, and besides—I knew none of the warriors would do a thing without direction from their leader. Therefore, the only truly dangerous individual in the whole camp was the man with crazy eyes.

This madman was no longer wearing feathers; now he wore a European jacket of some sort—perhaps part of a Spanish soldier's uniform. I noted that in addition to a large metal knife strapt to his waistband, he also had Hector's hatchet.

He circled me again and again, seemingly determined to figure out what sort of creature I was. He stopt to stare me down the way he did in our camp, but this time he stood far enough away so that he could gesture. Without blinking, he moved his hands, asking if I was afraid of him.

Now that was a tough question to answer.

I knew he wanted me to be afraid—the women in his camp were all cowering—but I also knew he used fear as a weapon. I saw no need to give him ammunition. Holding my hands low to force him to look down whilst I gestured, I said, "I have been captive before. It is not a pleasant experience."

Surprised, the leader lifted his face and laughed. Others obediently laughed with him, tho' I'm sure they had no idea what was so amusing. I saw Hector actually glance at me, his eyebrows contracted; he immediately looked down, breathing heavily.

The leader gestured that he was called Three Bulls, a name he earned by killing three bull buffaloes in a single day. Seeing he meant to impress me, I smiled, but my response disappointed him. He frowned, still studying me, before turning his attention to Hector.

Three Bulls did to Hector exactly what he'd done to me, circling 'round, looking him up and down, smiling vaguely as he stopt to breathe in his face. Hector met his gaze steadily and did not otherwise react, tho' his jaw was clenched so tightly I feared he might break a tooth. When Three Bulls slowly pulled Hector's hatchet from his waistband, the surrounding crowd held its collective breath. I had no idea what the lunatic intended, but I decided not to find out.

"Excuse me!" I said in English, which made everyone look at me—everyone save Hector, who kept his eyes on Three Bulls. "Sorry to interrupt," I gestured, "but I am new to this land and oft do not understand. Please explain. I am a Spirit Keeper—does that mean nothing to you?"

Three Bulls reared back as if I had spit in his face, his wide eyes now so enormous I feared they might pop like fat tossed on a fire. If the people in the crowd were tense before, they were literally quaking now. The madman stept slowly back to me, his thin lips twitching. "That depends," he gestured as he walked. He stopt before me, his eyes flashing. "What Spirit do you keep?"

I tipt my head, puzzled, looking 'round at the cringing villagers. "This is why I am confused," I gestured. "At every other village, I am welcomed and respected. My Guardian is welcomed and respected. We are given food and lodging in exchange for our story. Do you expect me to tell my story here, now, with my Guardian bound?"

Three Bulls snorted in amusement. "Do you expect me to untie your snarling dog, Spirit Keeper?" He laughed at the thought, looking to his cronies. They chuckled obligingly.

I chuckled, too. "Yes," I gestured with a smile. "Unless you are afraid of him."

Three Bulls returned my smile, but I could see his irritation. He directed his minions to untie Hector, then turned back to me, his face in my face. "I fear nothing, Spirit Keeper," he gestured. "But I have something you will fear. Let us test the bravery of this Spirit you keep."

Hector was rubbing his wrists and tho' he still would not look at me, I saw a flicker of concern on his face—a concern I shared. The two of us, along with everyone else, dutifully followed Three Bulls as he walked to the edge of his village. Some of the lesser-bound captives came, too, all wearing the same doleful expression of despair.

From the edge of the village, we stept into the wide-open prairie. We walked for half a mile or so, and as far as the eye could see, from the river on our left to the horizon on our right, there was naught but an ocean of golden grass, hip-deep and waving in the breeze. I looked across the vista in awe, but when I looked back to the river, I saw something that ruined the magnificent view. At the edge of the prairie the grass had been trampled, and five corpses were staked out in the sun, each in a different stage of decomposition. Hector and I stared at these horrors in alarm. When Three Bulls saw our reaction, he smiled.

He then said something to his men which prompted one to scurry down the riverbank to a clump of trees. In a moment the man returned, and as he topped the bank I saw he was leading a brown horse by a rope tied 'round its neck.

I felt as much as heard the crowd whimper. People actually backed away as the horse was led up to us. E'en Hector flinched, bothered by the way the horse bobbed its head and blew through its great nostrils. But he held his ground, and by the time the man with the horse reached Three Bulls, the only people who had not backed away were the crazed leader, Hector, and me. I was smiling at the horse in delight.

This was clearly not the reaction Three Bulls expected. He frowned, perplexed. He reached out to take the rope from his lackey, pulling the horse 'til its face was right in my face. "It is a big dog!" he gestured triumphantly.

I could not help myself—I laughed. Whilst I laughed, everyone stared, stunned. Finally I gestured, still giggling, "That is *not* a dog!"

Three Bulls looked from the horse to me, then back again. "It is *like* a dog!" he gestured, somewhat defensively.

"It's nothing like a dog!" I insisted. "Dogs eat meat—this animal eats grass!" I remembered I had a bag of grain in my pack, which I began digging for as Three Bulls frowned at the horse.

"Well, still," he gestured after a moment, "this is a fierce animal who will kill you if I command him to!"

I shook my head knowingly and pulled out a handful of grain, which I held up to the horse, clucking my tongue the way Mary and I used to do in her father's stable.

The horse was a beautiful chestnut stallion, obviously raised by someone from my world. When I held out my hand, he perked up his ears and sniffed the air, then my face. He took a step forward to eat from my hand. With my other hand I scratched his ears and petted his neck, murmuring endearments in English. When I kissed his soft snout, the horse snorted and I laughed.

An ominous silence descended.

If Three Bulls was crazy-eyed before, I know not how to describe what he was now. He turned his stunned face to Hector and waved his arms wildly, demanding to know what was wrong with me. Hector gestured that the Spirit I keep is that of a powerful Holyman, known to have many supernatural gifts.

Three Bulls shouted a variety of orders to his underlings, who scurried away. He turned back to me with a smile so broad it seemed his head might break in half, like an egg, and he gestured he was going to give the Spirit Keeper and her Guardian the best celebration they'd e'er seen. He was, he said, eager to hear our story.

Accompanied by two large guards, Hector and I were allowed to go to the river to prepare for our performance. Only after I finally completed my prescribed cleansing ritual would Hector, at last, look at me. I stood on the riverbank clad only in my bodice and loincloth, my hands on my hips, glaring at him. "So?" I demanded. "Will you speak to me now?"

He exhaled loudly, his face still stony. "Please do not disregard my beliefs."

I was livid. "Why not? You disregard *my* beliefs!"

He frowned, confused. "I do not disregard your beliefs. But we are no longer in your world."

"If I am in a world, it is my world!" I declared furiously. Hector's brow furrowed deeper as he considered, but I went on: "Because of *your* beliefs, we are now captive and you were nigh hacked to death before my eyes!"

"He was not going to kill me. At most he would have cut off a finger or two. He just wanted to see how much pain I can take."

I stared at Hector in disbelief. "And you thought I would just stand there and watch that happen?"

"Now he knows how much pain *you* can take," he said unhappily, "and how to inflict it."

I inhaled sharply. "You're suggesting I've made a target of you? I beg your pardon—I saved your life! You and I both know I'm in no danger, because, well, look at me! I'm a prize. Everybody wants me! But you—he'll keep you alive only so long as he thinks he can use you to control me."

"You think you are protecting me, but please believe me when I say you will not save me by enticing him."

I gaped at Hector in much the same way everyone had gaped at me earlier. "*Enticing* him? Exactly how do you think I'm *enticing* him?"

"You speak to him. You smile at him. You look at him."

Shaking my head in outrage, I raised both hands. "I . . . I know of no way to answer that, Hector. Maybe . . . maybe the Seer got the wrong girl. Because I am someone who *will* look at people. I will smile. I will speak. And if that offends you, or if it violates some of your stupid rules, then that's just too bad."

Hector opened his mouth to say something, but I was on a tear and he had to concentrate to follow my flood of words, blurred as they were by my thick accent. "Stop. Just stop. It was better when you wouldn't talk to me. I think you're all"—I made a gesture because I couldn't remember the word in his language, and Hector supplied it for me—"yes, crazy. You people, you're all crazy. I'm tempted to walk away right now and let you all kill each other. You accuse me of enticing Three Bulls—how dare you? What would you have me do? Bow my head before him, get down on my knees? I'll ne'er bow before a crazy person! If I let a little crazy bother me, I ne'er could have survived growing up with my mother! So I will thank you not to worry about me, Hector! I can be every bit as crazy as that madman—maybe more. If you must offer someone advice, go tell *him* to bow down before *me*! In the words of the man whose Vision made all this possible—what's the worst that could happen?"

Hector had been waiting for me to take a breath. "You are right. Maybe the Seer *was* wrong. In that case, the worst that could happen is Three Bulls will kill you."

I made a disparaging noise. "I've been killed before and it didn't take. So that's not really much of a threat, is it?"

Hector stared at me, rendered momentarily speechless. "He could . . . take your freedom. He could bind you, like those others—force you to do his bidding for the rest of your days."

I glanced at our guards, who had been alarmed by my ranting and were now watching us suspiciously. I snorted. "How can he take from me something I've ne'er had? I've ne'er been free, not for a single moment of my life. When I was young, I did what my parents told me, went where they told me to go, thought what they told me to think. Since I've been with you, I do what you tell me to do, go where you tell me to go, think what you tell me to think. I can't imagine what it would be like to be free to choose my own way, to

do what I want to do. I don't e'en know what I would want to do."
I paused, thinking, then smiled ruefully at Hector. "So I guess captivity is not much of a threat either."

Hector was troubled by my words, but determined to make me
see the danger I was in. He looked at the guards uneasily, quite
uncomfortable about what he was preparing to say. "He could force
you to become one of his wives. He could *use* you, violently, as a
woman." Hector would not lift his eyes as he said these words.

I raised my face to the sky and laughed. I waited as the flood
of memories poured o'er me, washing away my amusement, before
turning my eyes to smile sympathetically at my friend. "Oh, Hector. I've been violently 'used as a woman' before. It was awful. But
hear my words—it was that very experience which brought me to
the attention of the Seer. That was when he 'saw' me and that was
when he resolved to save me. It's crazy, I know, but that's what he
told me."

I paused for a moment, lost in thoughts of that grinning little
Indian who set me up, who brought me here, and who was still, I
was sure, pulling all our strings. My hysteria was gone. I took a deep
breath, let it out slowly, and glanced sheepishly at Hector. "I'm sorry
I yelled at you. I have no right to speak to you that way."

Hector would not look at me. He was staring at the riverbank,
deeply disturbed. He swallowed heavily before speaking. "Do not
apologize. It is I who have no right to speak to you."

I sighed. I walked to stand as close to him as Three Bulls had
stood to me. I put my face in his line of vision, forcing him to look
at me. "Hector, I *need* you to speak to me. I need you to look at me;
I need you to smile at me. I know that's not your way, but it's *my*
way, and when you ignore me—don't you see?—I go crazy." Hector's eyes were swallowed by his frown.

I turned to get my pack to finish getting ready for our performance.

The festivities which followed were not unlike those we had experienced in many villages. As usual, there was dancing, singing, speech-making, but the speeches all came from Three Bulls, and tho' I could not speak his language, I suspected most of what he said was rambling nonsense. He reminded me of an old woman I knew in Boston who wandered the streets screaming that the rats in her hair told her Judgment Day was nigh.

As darkness fell, Hector and I told our story, keeping it short and simple so as not to soil Syawa's memory. It mattered little; the only part of the story that made any impression on Three Bulls was the part in which we said I was to give a great gift to Syawa's people. As soon as Hector and I returned to our mat, the madman came to question me about this gift, but I feigned illness, claiming I was too exhausted from our performance to engage in conversation. Three Bulls stormed away, posting a circle of guards 'round our mat.

Seeing he expected us to spend the night right there, I urged Hector to get some sleep. He flatly refused, saying if I was ill, I was the one who must sleep. I gave him a withering look. "Hector, I'm fine. I just wanted Three Bulls to go away. I always take the first watch, so you must sleep now."

Hector frowned as he considered. "Tonight I will watch first."

I gave him that look again. "You think I am stupid? You will not wake me up."

Through clenched teeth he said, "I will not sleep as long as we are here."

"What if we're here for days? Will you ne'er sleep again? Do you not trust me? Have I not been watching as you sleep for months now?"

Hector raised only his eyes to meet mine. "Chasing off an animal is not the same as fighting a man."

I chuckled. "I've fought men before. I've killed a man. If I must, I will do it again."

This was not a complete lie, but it was a gross exaggeration. The May morning after I was raped, the man who'd raped me offered to let me ride on his horse with him, but I preferred, of course, to walk. Thereafter, whene'er he caught my eye, he winked or licked his lips. I stopt at one point along the trail to break off a twig with several large, needle-sharp thorns, and later, when we all stopt to rest and my attacker was off behind a bush passing water, I tucked my thorn-twig under his saddle.

As soon as the man returned to his seat, his horse threw a bucking fit which tossed him down a ravine. I watched indifferently as people scrambled to help him, and I listened with cold detachment to his agonized cries as the midwife worked to set the shattered bones jutting through the flesh of his arm. Only when rot set in a few days later did I begin to feel a little uneasy, and by the time the whimpering man finally died and was buried beside the trail, I was praying fervently that no one would ne'er figure out what I'd done.

So tho' I did not kill the man outright, I certainly felt responsible for his death.

Recalling that incident as I sat beside Hector, my smile faded and I bowed my head. "This morning you thought I was stupid, telling Three Bulls how to inflict pain on me, but, Hector, I was really telling *you* something." I looked up to find his eyes watching me warily. "I will not stand idly by as someone hurts you. I will not. So if that is what must happen for the Seer's Vision to be realized, then I say again—he got the wrong girl."

Hector looked away, blinking repeatedly. It took him a long moment to turn his face back to stone. At last he said quietly, "The Seer did not get the wrong girl. His Vision brought us here, and I am sure it will see us safely away."

Our eyes met and we both half-smiled. Then he lay down beside me and went right to sleep.

~ 24 ~

THE NEXT MORNING THREE Bulls came to sit beside me—very close beside me. He looked me up and down, asking again and again what gift I was taking to the foreign land. I told him again and again the Seer said I would know what it was when the time came for me to give it. 'Til then . . .

Three Bulls pouted. "I give you a feast, and all you give me in return is a story?"

I looked at him, his face mere inches from mine. Keenly aware Hector sat on my other side, seething, I lowered my eyes and gestured I would think about what sort of additional gift would be most appropriate for Three Bulls. Pleased, the lunatic bade us rise and follow him and his people, once again, to the prairie, where he would thrill us all with a demonstration of his bravery and daring as he sat atop his big dog.

Things started badly. It took two warriors holding the skittish horse and another to boost Three Bulls up before the demonstration could e'en begin. Then the madman clutched a wad of the horse's mane, clearly irritating the animal, so that when the warrior with the rope walked, the horse reared and Three Bulls fell off. Everyone gasped as several warriors ran to help their fallen leader, but Three Bulls was unhurt and insisted on getting right back on the beast.

As for me, well, I had to keep my hand on my mouth to stop myself from laughing. I knew nothing was truly funny, as the five rotting corpses constantly reminded me, but Three Bulls looked so silly, bouncing about on the animal, that I oft had to look away just to stay silent. To me the most impressive part of his demonstration was not that he mastered the angry animal but that he somehow managed to fall off only twice.

Actually, 'twas three times. The last time was when he came trotting in our direction and the horse abruptly stopt, causing Three Bulls to fly forward and land at our feet. At that, I could not help it. I laughed aloud.

Three Bulls got up, dusted himself off, and laughed along with me for a moment. Then he stopt as abruptly as the horse and became downright sinister as he gestured he had skinned alive people who dared laugh at him.

I gestured that I laughed only because I was delighted he was unhurt. I also said I knew he would not harm me or my Guardian in any way because then he would not receive the special gift I had decided to give him.

His demeanor shifted again as he beamed like a child about to be given a dripping honeycomb. He wanted to know what his gift was. I gestured that I could give Three Bulls his great gift only after he agreed to allow my Guardian and me to go our way unharmed.

Three Bulls glared at me, his face in my face. He said something in his language, and when I did not react, he gestured: "No one tells Three Bulls what to do!"

I whispered in his ear in English, "You are a nasty little turd!"

but gestured that I was confused again. "I plan to give you a gift—is it not customary for you to give a gift in return?"

"Of course I will give a gift!" Three Bulls spluttered. "Now tell me what you will give me!"

I smiled as I gestured broadly I would give him the gift of control o'er his big dog.

His wide-open eyes opened wider and the crowd murmured. He looked at his friends, who were all surprised and hopeful. "Give it to me!" Three Bulls demanded, gesturing for his men to bring me the horse.

I took the horse's rope and scratched behind his ears. As I gently petted the part of his neck where Three Bulls had been tugging on his mane, the horse leant against me, swishing his tail at a fly. I murmured endearments in English, then turned to Three Bulls to gesture: "Tomorrow!"

Three Bulls was not pleased. He had a bit of a fit—screaming, stomping, flailing his arms about—and everyone, including Hector, shrank before his wrath. But I had been raised by a woman who regularly had red-faced screaming fits, so histrionics have little effect on me. When Three Bulls stopt to take a breath, I gestured again: "Tomorrow!"

At that Three Bulls grabbed Hector's arm and threatened to slit his throat right now if I did not give him his gift immediately.

I know an empty threat when I hear one, so I forced myself to smile as I gestured: "Three Bulls—nothing would give me more pleasure than to give you your gift right now. But the Spirit of the Big Dog is strong and the power I intend to give is dangerous, requiring many rituals before it can be safely passed on. Were I to give it to you now, without taking the proper precautions, the big dog would turn and trample you into a pile of bloody flesh."

I was making this up as I went along, but it worked beautifully. The truth was, I needed time to prepare my "gift," and I knew the Indians well enough by now to know that e'en an imbecile would not knowingly violate the sanctity of a sacred ritual. It would ne'er occur to any of them I was lying to stall for time.

Three Bulls immediately gestured that we would all return to the prairie in the morning so I could give him his gift.

"And then my Guardian and I will leave," I gestured, making sure everyone saw what I said.

Three Bulls stared at me. He nodded curtly. Then he took the horse and left.

A liar can always tell when another liar is lying. My only hope was that after I gave Three Bulls his "gift," he would ride far out in the prairie, giving us a chance to slip away.

With two guards following, Hector and I returned to the river so I could "perform my rituals." On the way I bade Hector help gather an armload of prairie grass, and then we sat under a shady tree whilst I twisted and braided the stems into a rope, singing hymns to make my actions seem more ceremonial.

Hector and the guards watched me for a time, 'til the guards got bored and started talking to each other. I noticed our canoe was there on the bank, along with the two large canoes we'd seen before and several smaller crafts. I wondered aloud if one of the big canoes belonged to the missing search party, and Hector said he believed it did—and the other must have come from the fishermen the search party had been looking for. Some of those men, he said, were no doubt amongst the captives; others might be tied to the stakes on the prairie.

Since the guards didn't seem to care if we talked, Hector went on to say he remembered seeing animals at my family's lodge—were some of those the same as this big dog?

"Yes," I said, smiling. "But I call it a horse." I used the English word, which, of course, meant nothing to Hector.

"Can you talk to it?" he asked, his eyes grave but hopeful.

I stopt braiding for a moment to stare at him. "Yes, but not in the way you think."

Hector was puzzled. "What do you mean 'not in the way you think'?"

I waggled my head as I braided. "I mean you do not understand what I mean."

"How do you know what I understand? Can you hear my thoughts?" Hector looked at me, suddenly worried.

I tried not to sound superior as I said, "No one can do that, Hector."

"*He* could."

"Could he?" I glanced at my friend, considering. Could Syawa truly hear Hector's thoughts, or did he simply deduce them, as I did? Either way, it was a handy trick to keep in mind. "Well, I have not yet mastered that skill. All I know is that when you say 'talk to the animal' and I say 'talk to the animal,' we mean two different things."

"What do *you* mean?"

"I mean, 'tell it what to do.'"

"That's what I mean!"

"No, it's not!" I insisted, frustrated. "Look, you mean you think I can talk to it the way I talk to you, like a conversation."

Hector raised one eyebrow. "If you cannot hear my thoughts, then how do you know what I think?"

I stopt braiding and sighed. "I'm sorry. I guess I cannot explain it to you. I do not have the words."

"I just want to know if your magic can control the animal," Hector said through clenched teeth.

I shrugged as I resumed braiding. "I think so. It depends. I'm sure I can control him better than that madman." I explained to him about the halter I was making.

Hector nodded, staring down at the creek. Suddenly he looked at me in alarm. "You do not mean to sit on that animal, do you?"

I gave him an exasperated look. "Hector, stop worrying. For me, sitting on that animal is like swimming is for you." I continued to braid, then grinned as I added, "Besides—what's the worst that could happen?"

"I wish you would stop saying that," he said, looking glum.

We spent the night on the mat in the village center again. I was jerked awake early the next morning when Hector grabbed my arm, but before I could sit up, two guards pinned him to the ground whilst Three Bulls jumped on me and breathed into my face. "It is now tomorrow!" he gestured. "Give me my gift!"

Instantly terrified, I forced myself to inhale slowly as I racked my brain for a way to get the crazyman off me. I got an idea and gestured with trembling hands: "I was just dreaming about you."

Three Bulls sat up, surprised. He had surely expected me to scream and struggle against him, not blithely begin a story. "What were you dreaming?" he gestured with a leer. "About becoming one of my wives?"

I started to gesture, then stopt. I made it clear that he was in my way, and if he wanted to know more of my dream, he would have to move.

He moved. I gestured that I saw him in the center of a large group of people. They were all shouting and waving their arms. There was much excitement, and then . . .

I acted as if I simply could not continue to gesture from my prone position, which caused him finally to get off me. Pleased that my little ruse worked, I sat up and gestured that in my dream the people 'round Three Bulls were angry, terribly angry. One of his most trusted friends—no, two of his best friends—turned against him. I stood up and repeated my gestures, turning slowly so that everyone watching—which was nigh the whole village—could see what I said. I gestured that when his friends encouraged the angry people to rebel, someone untied the captives, who joined in the fight. Someone threw a rock, which hit Three Bulls in the head. Then someone else threw a rock. Then another. And another. I described Three Bulls being buried beneath a rain of rocks as the people cheered. "And then you woke me up!" I gestured.

Three Bulls did not like this dream. He brushed it aside with his hand and once again demanded his gift.

"I cannot give a sacred gift 'til I have had food and water," I gestured with a shrug, and he sighed and commanded his women to feed me.

The guards released Hector as soon as I finisht telling my "dream," but when Three Bulls turned to yell at his two main guards, I knew my little invention was doing its job. I remembered how suspicious my brothers always were of their friends, e'er afraid those closest to them might betray them. It was a simple thing to sow the seeds of discord, especially in the fertile ground of a mad mind.

The women brought us food, cringing because they were as afraid of me as of their leader. I nibbled what they brought, then gestured that what I really wanted was green corn, like the stuff they gave us during the feast. They said they would cook some, but I said no—I preferred it raw and in the husk. Exchanging surprised glances, they scurried to bring me three good ears, which I promptly tucked inside my pack. The women exchanged another glance, but were too timid to question me. I explained to Hector why I wanted the corn, and he nodded unhappily.

I'm sure he wanted to argue some more about my plan, but we could scarce speak because by this time Three Bulls was loudly berating the two warriors who had been guarding us. One of the guards clearly resented whate'er Three Bulls was saying. The other was denying whate'er he was being accused of. I smiled at Hector, but he was too preoccupied with worry to smile back.

As soon as we had eaten, we all tromped out to the prairie. The horse was led to me like a big dog, but e'en before I could unwind the reins I carried under my arm, he was nuzzling my pack because he could smell the corn inside. I cooed as I dug out an ear and peeled back the husk to let him nibble on the kernels. The entire populace watched with great interest.

Now that I had the horse's attention, I slipt my pack behind my back and held up the halter. The horse lifted his ears and sniffed the contraption suspiciously, but decided it posed no danger. He went back to nibbling the corn.

This would be the tricky part. I asked Hector to come hold the corn. He was not eager to have his fingers so close to the animal's huge teeth, but I believe if had I told him to go lie down in the fire and chew on the flames, he would have done so without question or a murmur of complaint. With the corn thus distracting the horse, I was able to slip the headgear o'er his nose. When the horse pulled back and whinnied, I purred soothing words both to him and to Hector, who had also pulled back. Reassured, the horse soon came back for more corn.

I gestured to the warrior holding the leash-rope that he must link his fingers to give me a boost. He looked to Three Bulls, who nodded, and up I went.

Several things happened at the exact same moment. The horse snorted and reared, Hector fell backwards, the crowd gasped and jumped, the man with the leash dropt it, and I pulled the reins to turn the horse's head toward the prairie. The horse ran and I held on for dear life.

What a beautiful animal! I let him have his head 'til I was sure I could keep my seat, then gently directed the way he ran. As I suspected, he had surely been trained, for the slightest touch of rein caused him to veer right or left. I swear he appreciated having a rider who did not bounce up and down, yanking at his mane. I urged him on 'til I almost couldn't see Three Bulls's village, then let him walk whilst I untied the rope 'round his neck and threw it away.

A thought occurred. I could turn the horse east and ride, and no Indian would e'er be able to stop me. I raised myself up and gazed 'round at the distant horizon. Everywhere I looked was wide-open prairie, rolling out in all directions 'til it fell off the edge of the earth. I could go anywhere, do anything, and I thought to myself, "This is it—this is what freedom feels like!"

Oh, it was sweet.

But then I remembered Hector and all I owed him, and I remembered how worried he was about me, and I remembered how Syawa told me I ne'er really had a choice, and I remembered seeing Hector fall backwards when the horse reared. What if he was hurt?

I turned the horse and nudged it to a full gallop again. I leant forward 'til we neared the clearing, at which point I sat up to slow the horse to a walk. I was relieved to see Hector standing in no apparent distress, watching my approach with his usual face of stone.

Just to show what I could do, I made the horse trot 'round the crowd, weaving in and out between Three Bulls, Hector, and the guards. I stopt him and sat smiling down at Three Bulls.

The lunatic wasn't exactly happy. He clearly resented having anyone get attention besides himself, and now that he could see how easy it was to control the horse with the headgear, he didn't consider my gift much of a gift at all. Still, when I slid off the horse and handed him the reins, he took them and began speaking to his men.

I walked to Hector, sure Three Bulls would want to ride the horse, but suddenly he was beside me again, grabbing my upper arm with one hand whilst gesturing with the other: "In exchange for this gift you give me, my gift to you is that your Guardian is free to go. But you must stay. I have no Holyman in my camp and require the one you keep." He dismissed Hector with a wave of his hand.

As two guards shoved Hector backwards, he gestured wildly he would not leave without me.

"If you will not leave without her," Three Bulls gestured with a smile, "then you will not leave at all." He nodded to the guards, who grabbed Hector, one on each arm, and began dragging him toward the rotting corpses.

That was when I noticed a new set of stakes had been set out, awaiting a new victim.

I have been in many fistfights in my life. I won some and lost more, but I learnt a lot from every fight I've been in. The biggest fight I remember was shortly after we'd moved to Philadelphia and my brother Thomas took offense at the way a neighboring family of London scumrats kept calling us "Taigs." Thomas rallied the

O'Toole clan and friends, and we fought hard, we fought dirty, we fought with everything we had. We fought for the pure fun of letting our frustrations and rage run free.

I was probably ten at the time, as thick in the action as any of the two dozen or more children rolling in the street. I punched, kicked, scratched, pulled hair, bit, gouged, and used all the same tactics that had e'er been used against me by the very brothers and sisters alongside whom I was now fighting. I don't remember if we won that particular fight or not, but I do remember the camaraderie I felt as we nursed our wounds and recounted the highlights of battle. And I remember that no one on that street e'er called us "Taigs" again.

So when the guards began dragging Hector away, I didn't hesitate. I pulled my free arm back and punched Three Bulls full in the nose, feeling the satisfying *crunch* and *splat* of my fist in his face before he fell backwards like a sack of apples falling off a cart. In less time than it takes to blink, I stomped on his groin with my heel, and when he rolled into a ball, I reached down to yank the French hatchet from his waistband.

When Three Bulls went down, Hector broke free from his distracted captors and pushed them both to the ground as he grabbed a metal knife from one of them. By that time, I was swinging the hatchet at every man who approacht. Hector slashed his way toward me, but someone grabbed him from behind and he became involved in a wrestling match with first one, then two, then three of the warriors. When I saw them piling on, I began hacking my way to him, but two men tried to grab my arm, and I ducked down and chopt off their toes—three small ones here, a great one there. As those men crumpled, I dove forward and hacked at the backs of the legs of the men atop Hector. Two rolled off, clutching their gushing calves, which left only one for Hector to worry about. He and his opponent were flopping too wildly for me to get a clean hit in, so I rolled and jumped to my feet.

By this time Three Bulls had recovered enough to be shouting orders in spite of his broken nose, tho' he was still on his hands and knees, with one of his men trying to help him rise. I ran o'er and kicked him hard in the temple, which shut him up once and for all, but his assistant grabbed my kicking foot and yanked me back-wards. E'en as I hit the ground I swung at the man's knee, desperate to keep him from falling on me, but he dived for the hatchet, en-abling me to roll to my side and kick him in the kidney. I still would've lost the hatchet to him had not someone come up from behind to hit him o'er the head with a big rock. When my assailant toppled, I gaped up at the grinning fellow who saved me, recogniz-ing him as one of the captives. I looked 'round and saw all the cap-tives were loose now, fighting Three Bulls's warriors. It had become a complete melee.

I jumped up and for a time hacked and smacked at random, leaving a path of destruction in my wake 'til someone finally man-aged to grab the wrist of my hand that held the hatchet. Just as I was about to bite the restraining fingers, I discovered they belonged to Hector. His face was pale and he was breathing hard, but, except for a few cuts and bruises, he was unharmed. "We must go now," he said as he pulled me from the fray.

Some of Three Bulls's men were bleeding on the ground, some had fled, and the ones left standing were fully occupied with venge-ful captives. Hector had left the metal knife in the chest of the war-rior who had his stone knife, which he was now carrying. As we ran to the creek, I saw the sharp stone blade was again red with blood.

A screaming young man intercepted us. He held a wooden club

with both hands, raised to knock one of us in the head. He should've chosen his victim more carefully, because as he went for Hector, I stept up and punched him hard in his unguarded gut. I've been punched like that before and I know how completely it takes the wind out of you. The poor fellow froze in mid-air for a long moment before falling sideways, his club still raised above his head. After looking at me with wide eyes, Hector bent down to slit the man's wrists. It was my turn to look at him with wide eyes. Then he grabbed my arm again and off we ran.

We raced down the riverbank. Hector pushed our canoe down to the water as I hacked holes in the two larger canoes. There were only four other boats, so I hacked a hole in each whilst Hector grabbed up all the paddles he could find and threw them into the front of our canoe. Then he shouted for me to get in. With a dozen or more paddles in my usual spot, I had nowhere to sit, but Hector pulled me into the back of the canoe with him. From that position, I couldn't very well paddle, so he bade me lean back and let him reach 'round as he changed the paddle from side to side.

I'd seen Hector paddle hard before, but now that we were going *with* the current, we truly flew. It reminded me of being on the horse, only this time Hector was the animal, and I had to move with him as he pulled, up and back, up and back. I don't know about him, but for me this intimacy became nothing short of pure torture. I tried not to notice his powerful muscles pulling as I leant against his chest, enwrapt as I was by his strong arms, but try tho' I might to ignore it, I felt his mouth right beside my ear, his heavy breath warm upon my neck. I had to force myself, again and again, not to turn my face to meet his, not to let my cheek rub deliciously against his chin. I wanted to so badly, but I knew I must not. This was Hector, my only friend in the world, and I could not risk putting him in an awkward position or embarrassing him with a momentary whim. I turned my face away and held it there through an act of sheer iron will.

What had been a half-day's hike on foot was a canoe ride of less than an hour. We arrived at our campsite and gathered what was left of our things. I packed the canoe as Hector threw the extra paddles into the Misery, where the current quickly carried them away. I jumped into my usual seat in front and picked up my paddle. As Hector pushed us into the river, I asked, "Do you think they will follow us?"

"I think they are afraid of you," he declared. He jumped into the canoe and slid his paddle into the water as he added, "I think *I* am a little afraid of you!"

I turned to look at him, taken aback. He smiled at me then, his whole smile, unlike those stingy little half-smiles he usually gave. I'd ne'er felt the full force of Hector's smile before, and I inhaled sharply, feeling as if I'd just been punched hard in the gut. Something inside me melted.

I turned back to the front of the canoe, o'erwhelmed. Syawa's smile had warmed me, but this—this was something else altogether. This was a white, hot, pulsating blaze that rivaled the sun in intensity. Maybe it was the leftover exhilaration from the fight, or maybe it was the heat generated between us as we rode presst together in the canoe, but . . . I suddenly knew it was not. My hands shook as I put my paddle into the water. After everything we'd just been through—the captivity, the fight, the escape—the only thing I could think about was the fact that despite my best efforts I had fallen desperately in love with Hector.

And so Syawa was right after all.

HEADING NORTH ON THE Misery once again, we paddled determinedly 'til darkness prevented us from seeing. Then we pulled under the cover of an overhanging tree, keeping the canoe in the water. Hector propt a large rock beside it and showed me how to kick it aside to push the canoe back into the river should pursuers appear.

In darkness we gnawed some dried meat and the two ears of corn I carried, listening to the loud babble of the river as it beat upon a nearby sandbar. Then Hector surprised me by speaking, his voice so soft I could scarce hear him. "Did you . . ." He stopt and I leant toward his end of the canoe. "Did you think you were captured that day, at your family's lodge?"

I sat back, surprised. "You mean the day you captured me?"

I heard his sharp intake of breath. "We did *not* capture you! We *saved* you."

I laughed a little, softly. "You pointed a bloody knife at me whilst my family was being slaughtered. I was bound and forced to march for days with the constant threat of death hanging o'er me. I know now that all was not as it seemed, but Hector—I was your captive."

"But those men had already planned their attack! We went along only to save you. For two years, he talked of nothing but saving you." Hector sighed. "I . . . I did not realize how it seemed to you." There was a long, long pause during which wild dogs howled in the distance. "You know you are not my captive now?"

"Yes," I said, wishing I could see him.

"And you are free to do as you will?"

Now it was my turn to let the croaking frogs fill the silence. I thought about that moment on the prairie, how good it felt to believe I could do anything, and how quickly that moment passed. "I am not free, Hector," I whispered at last. "And neither are you. We're bound together, you and I—to each other, to his Vision, to this canoe." Silence wafted like the light fog arising from the dark water. "But I'm not complaining. I'm rather enjoying it. Aren't you?"

I heard him chuckle and my pulse quickened. He told me I should lie down and sleep, but I insisted he must sleep first, as was our habit. When he hesitated, I dug out the hatchet, still crusty with blood, and said I could do what must be done.

Dark tho' it was, I knew he was frowning. "That ax will not stop an arrow," he said bluntly.

"Nor would anything stop an arrow from hitting *you*," I pointed out. "Either way I am dead. So, as a free woman, I tell you this: I sleep only after you do."

He had no choice but to curl up in his end of the canoe whilst I sat at my end with the hatchet in my hands. Now that all the excitement was o'er, my hand was aching from the fight and I rubbed it absent-mindedly as I gazed at the thick darkness of the surrounding trees, the pulsating darkness of the river in both directions, and the twinkling darkness that was the moonless sky. But no matter where

I looked, again and again, my eyes were pulled back to the dark shape curled up in the rear of the canoe. All my thoughts were of Hector, and I stared at him the way our cat used to stare at a mouse hole—intent, unblinking, hungry.

I watched as he woke up. It was still very dark, but I saw him move, heard his breathing change. Finally he sat up and leant over the canoe to splash water in his face. With arm outstretched, he asked for the hatchet, and at the last moment I purposely moved so that he grabbed my hand instead of the handle. It was a silly thing, but I wanted him to touch me. He jerked his hand back as if it had been burnt. The second time he reached more carefully.

I slept curled up in my end of the canoe, enjoying the way it rocked with the passing current. When I awoke we were already moving. I sat up slowly, trying to get my bearings. "How long have you been paddling?" I asked.

"Long," Hector said, and because the sun was scarce o'er the horizon, I knew he must have started well before dawn.

Shortly after noon we encountered four large canoes heading downstream, all heavy-laden with furs, four men to a canoe. They told us they were going to the Big Bend to trade; we told them about the ruffians. Hector explained how we fought our way out of the camp and said it was possible some of the miscreants might be following us. The traders listened with growing displeasure. One man apologized for what we had been through, saying his son may have been one of the marauders. The unhappy father assured us we need not worry about pursuit—no one would get a canoe past them.

After that, Hector was less tense. Late in the day he suddenly dived into the water and killed a fish with his knife, for the ruffians had broken all his spears. I was amazed, but also a little frightened— it was up to me to paddle the canoe to shore.

This was the first time in a long time we camped alone. Tho' we were silent as we set up camp and prepared the fish, everything felt different to me. Any time we happened to catch one another's eye, a split second passed before we turned away. Whene'er this happened, something in me flared up, like grease dripping on a log.

As we waited for the fish to cook, Hector sat across the fire, staring into the flames. I felt as if he was working up to something, and, sure enough, after a time he said, "Did *he* give you that dream?"

I blinked rapidly, looking at the ground. "What dream?" I finally had to ask.

"About Three Bulls and the people turning against him. How they hit him with stones."

My eyes opened wide. I had not really had a dream, of course, but I said, "Oh, uh, yes . . . I suppose he must have." Hector started talking about how quickly the dream came true, which I scarce understood because few details of the alleged "dream" were matched by what happened, but I was no longer listening because another thought had come to me, a strange and startling realization: I had not dreamt about Syawa the night before. Nor had I dreamt about him when we were in the outlaw village. Now that I thought about it, I had not dreamt about him since . . . since before the ruffians captured us. Before that, I had dreamt of him every single night since the day he died, but now the dreams were gone.

After remarking on the accuracy of my dream, Hector went silent again, staring into the flames. I wisht I could tell him the truth—how it wasn't a prophecy at all, but the result of my understanding of human nature and his own conviction that my dream was bound to come true. But how could I tell him that? He had his beliefs, and I had mine.

We ate in silence, but the more I thought about how impresst he was with my prophecy, the more it bothered me. As I was cleaning up, I took a deep breath and said, "Hector . . ." but when he looked at me from across the fire, his eyes thrilled me to distraction and I forgot what I was going to say. I blinked, keeping my eyes on the ground, berating myself for being a soppy fool. "Hector," I tried again without looking up, "you do realize, don't you, that *he* wasn't the one fighting yesterday? I wasn't using some sort of special Spirit Keeper powers, you know. Not everything I say or do is because of him."

"I know," he said. He was staring into the fire with that familiar half-smile, but then he looked up at me and briefly graced me with the full one. "He knew nothing of fighting. That is why he needed me. But you—well . . . I remember your mother."

I bowed my head, o'erwhelmed by both his smile and the embarrassing memory.

"You fight well," he added. "A true warrior. You are smart, strong, and brave." I was just beginning to swell before these compliments when he added, "You are everything he said you would be."

I felt as if I were an ocean vessel whose sails had just gone limp. I sighed. How could I get Hector to see me as a person, not just the object of Syawa's Vision?

Before I could pursue that thought, Hector himself went on. "Among my people, women do not fight."

"Only the men?" I asked, eager to talk about anything but Syawa.

"Even the men prefer not to fight," Hector said slowly. "It is better to talk than to fight." He looked into the fire, his thoughts miles away. "My father thinks I fight too much. He says I am too quick to anger, too quick to act. He said this Journey would teach me restraint."

"How goes that lesson?" I couldn't help but tease.

Hector laughed and my heart thumped. "I still have much to

learn." A long moment passed. His face grew serious as he glanced across the fire. "You have been in more fights than I have." It was a statement, not a question.

I shrugged and looked away. I told him about the first big fight I could remember, when I was out with a gang of kids on the streets of Boston. I couldn't have been more than four, maybe three, and for some reason two kid armies were lined up on opposite sides of the street, throwing rocks, sticks, and anything else we could find. A mud-ball hit me square in the eye, knocking me backwards. One of my siblings eventually led me home to Mother, who shrieked and dragged me down to the river's edge.

"The river was enormous," I continued, "as much salt water as fresh, and when my mother dunked me, head first, I was terrified. I suppose she was trying to wash the mud from my eye, but I thought she was trying to drown me. It was awful."

Hector listened to this story with an expression of sympathetic horror. "No wonder you dislike water," he said. I shrugged and said he could be right, or perhaps it was the time my brothers built a raft and put me on it to see if it would float and when it didn't I ended up in the bottom of the river looking up through the water as they stood laughing on the bank 'til one of them realized I wasn't coming up and dived in to pull me out. Or maybe it was the time my sister and her friend stole a rowboat to go visit a boy up the creek and had to take me with them because they were supposed to be watching me but ended up capsizing and I had to hold on to a tree limb 'til a fisherman came and rescued me and helped me find my sister but by the time we found the other girl, she'd drowned.

I had plenty of reasons, I said, not to like water.

Hector stared into the fire, stunned. "You have suffered much." Another statement.

I shrugged again. "It wasn't as bad as I make it sound. We didn't know we were suffering. We didn't know any other way to be. We were all in the same situation."

"And your mother—did she always treat you the way she did when . . . when I saw?"

I cringed before the memory. "Sometimes worse. She beat us fairly regularly. But she wasn't the only one. We beat each other. Complete strangers beat us sometimes, and we beat them back. That's just the way it was." I thought for a moment, then looked at Hector, who was still staring at me. "Didn't your mother beat you?"

Hector's smile was immediate and vastly amused. "My mother would kill anyone who beat me," he said with certainty.

"What about your father? Did he beat you?"

Hector's smile became a sneer. "My father would kill anyone who *threatened* to beat me."

I stared into the fire for a long moment. "I can't e'en imagine what that would be like," I said, as much to myself as to Hector. "I honestly cannot imagine what it would be like to have parents who would protect me. Nobody e'er protected me from anything, 'til . . ." I looked up, our eyes met, and fire sizzled between us. "'Til you saved me."

Hector looked off down the river. "Your father, he beat you, too?"

"My father was too . . ." There was no word in Hector's language for "drunk," so I said, "Too distracted to care much about his children. He did beat us, but it was different with him. Mother used to hit us all the time for no reason, but Father . . . he made a ritual of it, to teach us a lesson. If he caught one of us lying, for example, then he'd line us all up and beat us one at a time. It wasn't easy, waiting for your turn. You had to watch the others get theirs, and you had to listen to them scream and cry, and you just knew that would soon be you."

Hector was watching me openly now, as he'd ne'er done before, that look of sympathetic horror still shining in his eyes. "And did you learn not to lie, from his rituals?"

"No, I did not," I said, keenly aware of just how dangerous this particular subject was. Still, I went on. "If anything, his beatings achieved the opposite effect. We learnt how to lie well enough not to get caught, and we learnt how to cover for each other when we did lie. We learnt how to be really good at lying."

A shadow passed o'er Hector's face. "Have you ever lied to me?" he asked.

I looked at him, trying to assess why he would ask such a question. My heart was pounding and my lips were dry. I lifted my chin. If this was it, so be it. I was ready. "Yes," I said.

He smiled his half-smile. "If you had said no, I would have known you were lying." He tipt his head as he shifted his eyes back to the ground. "But that was when you did not know me. Now that you know me, you will not lie to me anymore."

I suddenly thought I might vomit. "But Hector—surely you've lied before. Everyone lies. You must have lied to your parents at one time or another. Didn't you?"

Hector looked at me gravely as he said, "I would die before I would ever deliberately lie to my parents."

"God in heaven!" I exclaimed in English before switching back to Hector's language. "You're a man of extreme views, aren't you? Do you have any opinions that don't end in someone dying or being killed?"

Hector smiled into the fire. "My parents gave me life. I respect them and honor them. I would not lie to them." His eyes shifted up to me. "And I will not lie to you. Please do not lie to me."

The warmth I had been feeling toward Hector iced o'er like a pond in winter. He really hated lies. If he e'er found out I had been lying to him all along about Syawa giving me his Spirit, I believed he might just kill me. After all, his people apparently responded to the slightest provocation with cold-blooded murder, and he himself just told me he was impulsive and violent. Besides, if e'er anyone deserved to be killed it was me.

I had ne'er liked myself very much. But at that moment on that riverbank I truly despised everything about myself and the world I'd grown up in. I was embarrassed, ashamed, and immeasurably sad. Hector was so open, so honest, so trusting. I suddenly understood the cruelest thing I could e'er do would be to encourage him to love me.

And so I resolved to leave him alone.

A strange thing happened later that night. Hector unrolled his sleeping fur whilst I got the hatchet for my turn at watch, but instead of lying down as I expected, he went back to the fire and poked 'round it for a moment. He finally pulled out a small stick, the end of which was burning like a candle. He came to me and held that light up between us, nervous, as if afraid of the stick he held.

"What is it?" I asked, trying to see if there was something on the stick he wanted to show me. "Is something wrong?"

"I just wanted to see if you . . . if you want anything more," he mumbled.

Puzzled, I stared at him and his stick and said no, no, I was fine, thanks—he could sleep now. I thought he must be remembering all the things I'd told him about my childhood and just wanted to make sure I was taken care of, which was such a sweet gesture I started to melt again. Then I remembered my resolution and forced myself to say no more, to smile no more, to resist the urge to throw myself on him and start rolling 'round in the mud.

He nodded and started to pull away, then held the glowing stick in front of me again. "You are sure?" he asked, moving the stick back and forth, as if daring me to take it.

"I think I'm sure," I said, laughing in spite of myself.

When I laughed, he smiled and slipt away, tossing the glowing stick onto the fire. He crawled under the canoe and rolled himself in his sleeping fur. I shook my head at his strangeness and stared at his back.

I sighed and spent most of my watch that night imagining what would happen if I jumped on him and we began rolling 'round in the mud. Leaving him alone was going to be the hardest thing I'd e'er done.

O'er the next few days I tried not to look at Hector if I could help it, but I couldn't resist sneaking peeks whene'er he wasn't looking my way. I responded if he spoke, but I did not trust myself to initiate a conversation, fearing I would become a stuttering simpleton again if he smiled. Luckily, we soon arrived at a village. When we told them of the ruffians, they were so outraged they didn't e'en care about our other story—they just wanted to go after the outlaws. Someone who said he was related to Three Bulls gave Hector a new bow and arrows, to replace those he'd lost, and everyone assured us the people here would see to it the ruffians harassed no more travelers.

As we continued north, the river grew smaller, with portages growing more and more frequent. When I said I longed for a wagon to carry the canoe, Hector asked what I meant, and I explained it was like a canoe with wheels. I drew an example in the mud, but Hector thought it looked like more work to build such a thing than just to carry the canoe. I didn't disagree, but still—I got sick of carrying that canoe.

Hector made new spears, and the fishing was as good or better than e'er. In the evenings we talked about our families. He told me his was a large one—an older brother and two sisters, one older, one younger. I smiled to myself as I said that before the attack on our farm, I had two sisters and three brothers who were older than me as well as two brothers and two sisters who were younger. I told him I couldn't e'en remember how many others had died or how many stillbirths and miscarriages my mother had.

Hector was astounded, wondering if such an enormous family was normal amongst my people. I said it was. "But how do they feed all those children?" he asked.

"Not well," I smiled ruefully. "Before I met you, I think I was hungry every day of my life."

"Now you eat well." It was a statement, not a question, said with a certain pride.

"Now I usually have too much to eat!" I declared, and he looked concerned 'til he realized I was teasing. "If I ate all the food you provide, I would be as big and fat as my old cow!" He tried not to smile, but I could see how this pleased him.

Oh, it was so hard not to put my arms 'round him and thank him for taking such good care of me! But I didn't. I gritted my teeth and stared into the flames.

One evening he asked me to tell a story, and I considered my options. My people tell a lot of stories, from the Bible to fairy tales to histories to literature. Then I remembered my father's all-time favorite story, the play we must perform at least once a year: Shakespeare's *Hamlet*.

Hector leant back on one elbow, watching with his head cocked sideways in exactly the same pose he'd always assumed whene'er Syawa told a tale. I took a deep breath and started. I've read this play at least a dozen times, but it ne'er occurred to me before that evening how similar was my predicament to Hamlet's. He was haunted by his father's Spirit; I was haunted by Syawa's. Hamlet and I both wrestled with guilt and uncertainty, and neither of us could figure out what was the right thing to do.

Hector was fascinated, right from the start. I began by summarizing the story and describing events, but before I knew it, I was pacing the riverbank, trying to translate the lines as I remembered them. I used different voices and mannerisms for the different characters, talking to myself or arguing, as the case required.

Hector watched me, but I tried not to look at him, for e'en his half-smile was intoxicating. He had to stop me during the "to be or not to be" soliloquy, because he wanted to know who Hamlet was talking to. When I said he was talking to himself, Hector asked if Hamlet was crazy. I laughed and said no—these were just thoughts going on inside his head which he had to say aloud or we wouldn't know what he was thinking.

Satisfied, Hector sat back again and watched and listened. He got impatient with Hamlet's indecision, but he loved the sword-fight in the end, when I used a stick as a sword and jumped back and forth between the characters. He considered each death with a frown of concentration.

When I was done, I bowed and sat down by the fire.

"That was a good story," he said as he sat up to rest his arms on his knees. His dark eyes were warm as he studied my face. "Thank you for telling me."

I nodded, smiling, but couldn't look at him because I wanted so much to crawl o'er and kiss him. I'd always felt sorry for Hamlet, but now his problems seemed simple, compared to mine. All Hamlet had to do was avenge his father's murder. I had to pretend to carry inside me the soul of a man I once loved so that his best friend, the man I was now hopelessly in love with, wouldn't be alone.

Thus conscience does make cowards of us all.

The next day we made camp early because we had seen some huge deer-like creatures run from the river and Hector was eager to try out his new bow and arrows. The deer—he had some other name for them—were so large I couldn't imagine what we would do with all that meat, but naught I said could dissuade him, so off he went.

I set up camp and wandered about gathering herbs and roots as I found them. This was the first time I had been alone for any length of time since leaving my family's farm—and e'en before then I was pretty much ne'er alone—so the sudden solitude was strange and more than a little unnerving.

My thoughts began swirling. I thought about Hector and how kind he was and how accepting he'd become and I thought about myself and what a liar I was and what a monster I was because on some level I secretly agreed with the Spanish ambassador in thinking the Indians were all like children and I was so much smarter than them—e'en Hector. The more I thought about it, the more I convinced myself I wasn't really lying to Hector so much as I just couldn't explain it all to him. If I couldn't get him to understand what a wagon was, how could I get him to understand that a simple mistake in translation had led to this huge misapprehension between us? Hector would think I was saying he was stupid, but that wasn't it at all. It was just that I couldn't explain.

I thought of Syawa on his deathbed and his apparent inability to explain his thoughts. I was beginning to understand why it had been so difficult; translation requires something much more than just an exchange of words.

The sun set. I sat and waited for Hector. It got dark. I was still alone. More time passed. I added wood to the fire and paced the riverbank, holding the hatchet in my hand. The moon rose and moved steadily across the sky. I waited and waited, imagining all sorts of calamities that might have befallen my friend. I imagined a bear attacking him. Then a panther. Then the outlaws. I imagined a terrible accident befalling him, wherein he broke his leg or his arm or got his foot caught under a rolling rock. I imagined him lying out there somewhere, helpless and dying, with no one to protect him from blood-thirsty scavengers. I swung the hatchet back and forth as I paced, wishing I knew where he was and how to help him.

I heard a noise in the brush. I froze and peered in that direction. I heard another noise. I took a few steps that way, squinting through the darkness. I saw a shadow, then recognized Hector's familiar walk as he approacht, carrying a large, heavy pack on his back.

I dropt the hatchet, cried out his name, ran to him, and threw my arms 'round him before I knew what I was doing. He dropt his pack and held me lightly, clearly very surprised. "I think you missed me," he muttered as I presst my face hard into his neck.

"I did!" I laughed, pulling away, embarrassed. "I'm sorry, but I was so worried! You were gone so long!"

He covered his own embarrassment by kneeling before his bundle as he explained he had killed one of the big deer, but the pursuit had been long and tricky. "I kept asking myself, 'Should I shoot my arrow or not?'" He opened the hide to display an unbelievable quantity of meat.

I looked down at him, baffled. He seemed quite serious as he added, "I finally shot my arrow and saw it hit, but then the deer said, 'To be, or not to be . . .' It took him a long time to decide not to be."

I laughed, and as I got the full scope of the joke, I laughed more, and then more, and then more. I laughed so hard I actually had to sit on the ground, but Hector continued teasing me, saying the real delay was that he kept having all these complicated thoughts he had to stop and say out loud to himself.

"You did not!" I screamed, but he assured me he did, and after we began peeling the meat into thin strips, which we hung o'er a blazing fire, we each performed numerous silly soliloquies just to make the other laugh.

Neither of us slept that night, so we took turns sleeping most of the next day as well as the next night, whilst our meat dried. We were lucky no predators came to steal our meat because, during my turns at watch, I could do naught but stare at Hector's sleeping form, remembering how good it felt when he held me in his arms. Oh, I wanted him to do that again . . .

The next night, just before he went to his sleeping fur, he once again approacht me with a burning stick. He asked, once again, if I wanted anything else. This time I was e'en more puzzled than before because we were no longer in imminent danger and he surely knew he needn't keep checking on me.

I assured him, once again, I was fine, but he withdrew slowly, as if making certain of my response. I wisht I could think of something for him to do, just to make him happy, but I couldn't, so he threw the stick on the fire and went to his fur.

As soon as he fell asleep, I stared and stared at his unconscious body as I alternately smiled and cried. It was actually becoming painful to keep my feelings to myself.

~ 26 ~

AFTER DRYING ALL THAT MEAT, Hector was anxious to make up for lost time. We paddled hard 'til the river turned west again, at which point there was another large village. Shortly after we arrived, my monthly began, and so I once more found myself cloistered for several days with a group of women I did not know.

The women were kind, but different from those I'd met so long ago at Tomi's village. Their homes were ingeniously constructed hide tents—similar to those used by Three Bulls, but much more elegantly constructed and maintained. The women wore more clothes than the eastern Indians, and they were fascinated by my garb. We talked about sewing quite a bit.

But the main topic of interest was my story. Sometimes every inch of the women's lodge was crowded with curious women and children, all eager to get a first-hand look at the Spirit Keeper. It was an excruciatingly uncomfortable situation, trapt as I was. I have said I no longer dreamt of Syawa, which was still true, but whilst in that women's lodge, I dreamt of Hector wickedly and repeatedly. More than once I woke with a start, longing to see him, to talk with him, to touch him. Then I remembered I was surrounded by strange women and I curled up under my bearskin, wishing I was done with my time so I could go.

When I was finally able to walk in the village, I felt his eyes upon me long before I knew where he was. I scanned the area, looking for the source of heat I felt, and there he was, staring at me. He did not smile as I approacht—in truth, he looked rather sad. But by the time I reached him he did smile, and I melted like butter on a hot skillet.

We left the next day at dawn and paddled hard for several days.

Before long the river veered north again. Not only did the terrain continue to change, but the weather was beginning to turn as well. There was a chill in the air at night, and the vibrant green of summer was fading fast into the yellowing hues of fall. Finally, after so many days of good weather, it began to rain. It rained and rained and rained and rained. For the most part we paddled in spite of the constant dribble interspersed with heavy downpours, but we stopt early on those days to dry out before sleeping. Hector fastened a hide jutting out from the upturned canoe, under the edge of which we could keep a small fire going.

Those were deliciously intimate evenings and I was happier than I'd e'er been, sitting side by side with Hector under the canoe, watching the rain drip into the fire. We enjoyed many long, lingering discussions. I remember, for example, talking about how we made the metal used in hatchets and knives. I was hardly a metallurgist, but one of my brothers spent a lot of time at a blacksmith's shop, so I shared as much information as I remembered.

Hector found my story amusing. "They make rocks from trees which burn hot enough to melt other rocks?" he asked. "The rocks where I come from are not so interesting. Or maybe my people do not have the same magic as yours."

I tried to assure him that neither the rocks nor the people where

I came from were in any way magical, and that, in fact, charcoal kilns were horrible places where men frequently burnt to a crisp and blast furnaces were e'en worse, rendering most men who toiled there either dreadfully disfigured or dead. I also tried to explain it was the Spanish ambassador's lust for a certain rock that had been the subject of our conversation back at the Great River, but I fear my explanation made little sense to Hector. In any case, I loved to hear him laugh, and if he was amused by my Story of Melting Stones, that was fine with me.

During those rainy nights, one of us slept curled under one end of the canoe whilst the other sat at the other end, keeping an eye on the fire. The fishing was generally bad, so Hector taught me how to cook the meat we'd dried. We discussed ways of cooking and preserving food, but sometimes Hector seemed disinclined to talk, and that was also fine with me. I was content to enjoy the comfort of his companionship.

As the rainy days wore on, Hector seemed increasingly distracted, but I knew him well enough by now to know that sometimes he had to work himself up to sharing his thoughts. So I waited. Eventually he asked about the rituals my people observed. I wasn't sure what he meant, so he explained about his people's Manhood and Womanhood Ceremonies. I listened, fascinated, then told him my people had no such rituals. I thought our birthday celebrations were the closest thing to what he was describing.

I suddenly realized my birthday had come and gone. I was born in July, and by now it must be mid-September. I was eighteen. I tried to explain this to Hector, but he tipt his head, puzzled. "How can you know what day you were born? Seasons change, and the moon marks the passage of days, but one day is pretty much the same as the next."

I explained calendars, with our months and weeks and names for days. He was stunned by the complexity of record-keeping required just to know when our birthdays were, and I tried to explain it was more than that—so much more. But it was almost impossible to discuss such huge concepts without the necessary words, so we both ended up frustrated.

The next day the rain was so heavy Hector said we should not keep fighting the sky, and I heartily agreed. So there we sat, side by side, staring into the fire. Again I could sense Hector wanting to say something, so I waited, my curiosity growing. He brought up rituals again, and for a time we talked about funerals and births, neither of which interested him.

It was mid-day before he managed to work 'round to his real interest. "You have told me many things about the way your people do things," he began stiffly. He was choosing his words carefully; I could not understand why. I waited for him to continue. "One thing you have not told me is how your people _____."

The word he used was not familiar to me, so I asked him to gesture. Without looking at me, he moved his hands the way Tomi had shown me so long ago. Hector was asking me how my people marry.

My heart began pounding. Why would Hector want to know such a thing? "Um, when two people . . ." I tried to pronounce the word he used; he corrected me and I said it again. He nodded and I went on: ". . . marry, they generally go to a . . . a Holyman, who performs a ritual to unite them." I turned my face to see if this was what Hector wanted to know, but he was looking at the ground, listening intently.

He nodded and without turning his head asked, "But who decides when it is time for a man and woman to marry? How do . . . how are the choices made?"

I looked into the fire, trying to keep my breathing steady, but it was already fast and shaky. "Oh, uh, sometimes parents choose, but usually a man chooses a woman and begins visiting her. If he decides to marry her, he asks her father or perhaps asks her."

Hector listened, staring at the ground, and, after a long, long pause, he said, "Among my people, it is the woman who visits the man to show interest. If she wants him, she makes a pair of shoes and leaves them at his door. Then, if she sees him wearing them—"

"Wait. So a woman chooses a man?" I interrupted. A glimmer of understanding was beginning to dawn on me.

"Yes," Hector said. "It is always up to the woman. Unless . . ." He paused and inhaled deeply, clearly forcing the next words out of his mouth. "Unless a man wants to encourage a woman to think of him in that way, and then he goes to her after dark with a lighted stick. If she is interested, she takes the stick and extinguishes the flame, to show she trusts him e'en in the dark. If she does not take the stick, he knows she is not interested and then she—"

"Stop!" I said, my heart pounding so hard I could scarce hear his soft, halting words. "I understand. I understand!" In English I added, "Oh, sweet Jesus, I am so stupid! Stupid, stupid, stupid!!" I was rocking back and forth holding my head in my hands, horrified to realize Hector believed I had rejected him. I knew all too well the pain of rejection—e'en Syawa had rejected me in the end—and the very last person in the world I wanted to suffer such a bitter blow was Hector. I could feel him beside me, watching me with that puzzled expression he so oft had. I suddenly crawled forward and grabbed the small stick we had been using to poke the logs in the fire. I held the end in the sizzling flames 'til it caught, then crawled back and held the stick out to Hector. "Here!" I said. "Try again!"

Hector reached for the stick slowly. He took it, looked at it, then looked at me. I was on my knees beside him, waiting. He thought for a moment, then held the stick out to me.

I grabbed it from him, leant out from under the canoe, and shoved the stick flame-first into the wet mud. I pulled it out and shoved it into the mud again and again 'til it was not only extinguished but would most likely ne'er burn again. I looked at Hector.

He was watching me, his eyebrows raised. "This means . . . you trust me?"

I couldn't help it. I started to cry. "Oh, yes!" I whimpered. I held my face in my hands, not wanting him to see me like this.

His voice was perplexed. "Then why are you crying?"

"Because I don't know how to make shoes!" I sobbed.

Hector laughed. When I looked at him, my tears dried up. He was gazing at me in that way he had—silent, stone-faced—but in his eyes I saw wonder, longing, love, and I returned each of those sentiments a thousandfold. We stared at one another for an infinite moment before he looked away. "We need a Holyman," he said. "Both your people and mine require—"

"But we have one!" I said brightly, holding my hand on my heart. "It was really all his idea anyway. He wanted us to be together. It is what he told me at the end. He said I was ne'er meant for him—I was meant for you."

Hector's head turned so swiftly I felt a little breeze. "What did he say, exactly?"

I looked into the river, remembering. "I . . . I told him he should not have given his life for me, and he said he did not—he gave it in exchange for his Vision. He said *you* were the one who saved me, the one I owed my life to."

Hector turned his face back to the ground. "I release you from the debt. You are under no obligation to me."

I got on my knees and put my hand on his shoulder. Lightning flashed between us, and he lifted his face, shocked. "I *will* give my life to you," I said firmly, "whether I owe it or not. Now give me the words." I made the gestures Tomi had shown me, the same gestures I once offered Syawa, which he refused with a shake of his head. Hector watched me now, and as he watched, his stone face turned to mush. "Give me the words!" I demanded.

His eyes were wet as he said "I love you," and I made him say the words again. He said them with feeling, and I tried to repeat them, and he corrected me, and I said them again and he said them again and he rose to his knees and I rose to mine and our foreheads came together and we said the words to each other at the same time, soft and slow, our lips mere inches apart.

Hector pulled back, smiling faintly. "Come," he said, and I followed him out from under the canoe. It was raining only lightly now, but the day was still gray and cool. "Leave your clothes," he said as he removed his breechclout.

Altho' I had been naked in Hector's presence before, I knew this time would be different. This time he would look at me. His eyes were on me as I unlaced my bodice with trembling fingers and slowly took it off. He watched as I untied my breeches, let them drop, and stept out of them. He stared as I unfastened my own loincloth and tossed it, with the rest of my things, under the canoe. Then he took my hand and led me to the river.

I ne'er liked water, but I had long since learnt to accept the Indian obsession with it, and so I had gritted my teeth and endured the required bathings and swims. But I need not grit my teeth through the ritual cleansing I was about to receive.

Hector led me slowly into the water 'til it was just above our knees. I began shaking pretty violently. He turned to me, concerned, asking if I was afraid of him. "No," I said.

He leant over to whisper in my ear, "I am still a little afraid of you." I smiled broadly and he smiled back. Then he began to wash me.

I have noted that in the past men have used me—violently, painfully, disgustingly. Hector's gentle, loving touch was as unlike the rough handling I had previously received as the sun is from a speck of dirt. He scooped the water of the river into his hands and trickled it upon me, starting with my face, my neck, and my shoulders, working his way down. Once I had been entirely baptized by him, he slowly, delicately, began rubbing the water against my flesh, exploring every inch of my body. In this way he touched every part of me. My body, he said, was now his.

It was an exquisite experience.

When he was done, he said his body was now my body and I must wash him the same way. I trickled the water o'er him with shaking hands, keenly aware of his eyes upon me. When I began rubbing the water into his skin, he closed his eyes and raised his face to the gray sky. The light raindrops trickled down his body, and I traced their passage with my now-bold fingers.

When I was finisht, he opened his eyes, took my shoulders in his hands, and looked deeply into my eyes. "You are now my wife," he said.

"You are now my husband."

We embraced.

Modesty prevents further description of the afternoon. Suffice it to say that I experienced an ecstasy I ne'er knew existed, forging a bond which completely obliterated any lingering tie I had to my unhappy past and my miserable childhood. If I was meant to die in that farmhouse in Pennsylvania, I was destined to be born again there on the banks of that wild river.

As usual, I took the first watch that night. Hector fell asleep immediately, but I would not have been able to sleep if I tried. I wanted only to sit beside him and watch him sleep, to enjoy the feelings he had awakened in me and bask in the bliss that was now mine.

When he stirred in the middle of the night, I slipt into his sleeping fur and we once again celebrated our new union. This time he left me there to sleep whilst he rose to stoke the fire and take his turn at watch.

I awoke in the morning from a deep, dreamless sleep. I smiled at the smell of Hector in the fur beneath my cheek. I opened my eyes, so happy, and touched the place where he had lain beside me. I sighed.

The rain was done and the sun was well up—Hector had let me sleep too long. I sat up, tied back my hair, wrapt his sleeping fur 'round me, and crawled out from under the canoe. He was standing at the water's edge, throwing rocks into the water. His face was stone, but I could tell by his stance and furrowed brow that he was deeply troubled. I walked quickly in his direction, concerned. Tho' his eyes softened when he saw me, there was a definite cloud hovering o'er him. "What's wrong?" I asked as I approacht.

He turned from me to hurl the rock he was holding into the water, the power of his throw belying the emotion he was working hard to conceal. But Hector would not lie to me. "I should have waited," he said simply, looking out across the river.

"What?" I exclaimed, stunned. "Why? What's wrong? Did I . . . did I displease you in some way?" My thoughts raced across the events of the previous day, desperately searching for whate'er it was that had caused this apparent change of heart. I wailed in English, "I've disappointed you! Oh, God in Heaven! I've disappointed you!" Then I switched back to his language. "You thought I was . . . something I'm not . . . and I've disappointed you!" I felt as if I had been punched in the stomach, and I fell to my knees, doubled o'er under the fur. I was sure he had somehow discovered I was lying about being Syawa's Spirit Keeper and now he hated me as I knew he would. "I'm sorry, Hector!" I sobbed, "I'm so, so sorry!"

He fell upon me, grabbing my shoulders, shouting for me to stop, stop, it wasn't that at all! "No, Kay-tee, no!" he whispered in my ear as he held my body against his. The fur fell to the ground and I was now fully bare in his arms. "It is not you—you are perfect, you are beautiful, you are far too good for me. It is me. I am disappointed in myself."

"What?" I pulled back to look at him. "Why? Because you married me?"

"No! Well, yes." Hector sat back on his heels and sighed. "It is my duty to protect you, to see you safely home, but . . ." He looked at me so sadly I almost started to cry again. "We have a long, long, long way to go. It is a difficult, almost impossible Journey in any case, sure to take at least another year. But if you are . . ." He gestured a big belly on me and said a word in his language which I assumed meant "with child." He stopt and looked down in anguish.

Relief washed o'er me like a cleansing rain. "Oh, Hector—is that what worries you? That is nothing. Women have babies all the time in all kinds of places under all kinds of conditions. My mother had a baby in a big canoe on the ocean. She had another in a . . ." I said the English word for "wagon," reminding him of the device I wanted to use to carry the canoe. "A baby might slow us down, but we will still be able to go on!"

Hector looked at me hopefully, then stood up and turned his face to the river again with a mournful expression. "You do not know how far we must go, the dangers we will face. I do. I should have been stronger. For your sake, I should not have done this."

Still on my knees, I pulled the fur back o'er my shoulders and looked up at him critically. "You know this conversation is about a day too late, yes? Because what's done is done. What I don't understand is what's different. You didn't seem to have any doubts yesterday. You're the one who first spoke of marriage."

Hector literally hung his head. "I did not think you would accept me."

My mouth fell open and the fur fell to the gravel again. It took a long moment to recover my senses, close my mouth, and pick the fur back up. "Why would you think I would not accept you?"

"You rejected me twice."

"But I did not know you were . . . approaching me!"

Hector shrugged unhappily, looking at the ground. "It was wrong of me to approach you. You are a Spirit Keeper. I am just a man. I am not . . . good enough for you."

My mouth fell open again. "Oh, my heavens!" I said slowly in English. I looked up at Hector, remembering when I had the same conversation with Syawa, or at least tried to. The absurdity of my being on the other side of this conversation made me want to laugh. I said, "Hector, you *are* good enough. You are much, much better than I am."

He stood facing the river, still looking down, tight-lipped, shaking his head. A long moment passed. "You do not understand. My father will say I took advantage of your . . ." He said a word which I had to ask him to define. It meant "vulnerability." He went on to remind me his father thought he was impulsive, brash. "Now I know what he means."

I sighed, looking up at the glistening leaves in the trees. I may have broken with my past, but Hector had not and ne'er would. "Your father will not approve of our marriage?"

Hector glanced at me glumly. "Marriage is a sacred thing. It is not just between a man and a woman. It is a bond between families, between communities, between generations. Marrying you now, like this, is an insult to all."

Oh, wonderful. If we e'er made it all the way to Hector's home, everyone there would hate me right from the start. Huzzah.

But no, that was not the case, Hector assured me when I said as much. He mumbled about the complex social rules of his people. Apparently being a Spirit Keeper elevated me beyond the reach of his class or clan or some such thing, which meant he had no right to approach me. The fact that I did not know it was wrong only compounded Hector's responsibility and subsequent misconduct.

Class, society, la, la, la—these ridiculous concepts had tormented me my entire life. Because my father married below his class, he was expelled from his homeland, denied his inheritance. Because my mother married above her station, she was always frantic, frazzled, and furious. Because my siblings and I all must struggle to improve our positions, we constantly fought each other and everyone we met. But the truth was, were it not for the social misconduct of my parents, I would not exist. Therefore, who could blame me, as I sat naked in the midst of that wild land, if I decided once and for all I no longer had any use for social rules?

"Look, Hector—I do not know your father," I said slowly. "But I do know you. You saved my life. You defended me. You fed me. You protected me. You cared for me. I have told you about my life and you must understand this: no one else I have e'er known has e'er truly wanted me. No one was e'er even kind to me 'til I met you and the Seer. You think I am something special. I am not. *You* are.

You gave up a life you loved for me, you traveled across this entire land for me, you risk your life every day for me. You are the most glorious person in the world. How could I not accept you?"

He tipt his head, more miserable than e'er. "This is what I mean when I say I took advantage of your vulnerability."

I sighed and stood up, naked before him, hands on hips, one eyebrow raised. "Truly? After what you've seen me do, after knowing what I'm capable of, can you honestly say you think I'm vulnerable? I'm pretty sure I could beat you in a fight." I lifted my chin and stared at him, a challenge in my eyes. His eyes went grave as he met my gaze, and for a moment we were in my family's loft again, toe to toe, eye to eye, weighing each other, wondering, calculating our next move.

Hector inhaled deeply and turned back to the river. "We should not fight."

I walked to him, breathing on his neck. "I agree. We should be married instead."

He raised his eyebrows as he turned his face to me. "You think married people do not fight?"

"I think married people have a strong reason to stop fighting." I could see my breath on his shoulder was affecting him, but he turned his face away, still unconvinced. I stared at him, saw his suffering, and a new thought occurred, a disturbing thought, a nagging doubt which began to grow and fester in my brain. "But, wait—something makes no sense. If you believed you and I could not marry, then why did you ask me to marry you in the first place?"

Hector hung his head again. "I did not," he mumbled. "Because I could not."

Stunned, I reviewed our conversation from the day before, that sick feeling spreading from my brain to my stomach. Was Hector saying he ne'er meant to marry me at all, that I had assumed things that were not true, that this was just another huge misunderstanding? "But you gave me a burning stick! Three times! Why would you do that if you believed we could not marry?"

Staring at the riverbank, he inhaled and exhaled a couple times. Finally he spoke without looking up. "I should have explained it all to you. I was trying to. If I had explained, then you would have known how wrong my actions were. You would have known you must reject me. But I . . . I wanted you more than I wanted air to breathe. And when it seemed you wanted me, too, I could not stop myself. I knew you didn't understand and I knew I should explain, but I also knew this was my chance, my only chance. So I took it."

I stared dumbly into the river. "So . . . so you're saying you *did* take advantage of me. You knew I was stupid and you gave me the stick, knowing I wouldn't understand, knowing I would assume . . ."

"I did not intend to trick you into marrying me, but that is exactly what I have done. I ne'er dared hope it would work, but it was the only way . . ."

A single laugh shot from me. "Hector, did you plan all this, just to get 'round your people's rules?" When he shrugged, head still hanging, I became vastly amused, and, quite frankly, impressed. He hadn't exactly lied to me, but by withholding vital information he had allowed me to believe things that weren't true. "But I still don't understand. If you had explained everything to me, what was I supposed to do? Slap your face, push you away, threaten to tell your father?"

"That is what others in your position have done. We are people who could ne'er marry, so you should have ignored me, and if I approacht you as I did, you should have apologized for enticing me and stopt torturing me with what I could never have."

"I should have *apologized*?" I shook my head, staring into thin air. For a moment I was back in Philadelphia, watching my sisters entice the men they met. They wore their bodices low, breasts bulging out the top. They batted their eyelashes, smiling coyly, licking their lips or running their fingers seductively across various parts of their body. They breathed heavily as they presst their loins against the swollen breeches of the men they teased. They laughed and got the men to do whate'er they wanted.

And then I thought of how I behaved with Hector. I had, on countless occasions, stood before him in various stages of undress, including complete nudity, and he had not reacted in any way. But apparently whene'er I smiled at him, or talked to him, or—God help me—*looked* at him, he was unbearably aroused. Why is it that knowing this only made me love him all the more?

"Very well, Hector," I said slowly, turning back to him, "if you want an apology, here it is. I am sorry. I truly am sorry. Because I am not going to stop enticing you. I will ne'er stop enticing you. I plan to entice you as much as I can every single day for the rest of my life."

Hector looked at me with a worried frown. "Well, then it is a good thing we are married."

I laughed. "I think so, too." He finally smiled with me—a sheepish grin, with face downcast. I thought for a moment, trying to choose my next words carefully. I sighed. "But because of all you have said, I must ask you something. Why in the world would you want me so much? Is it because you are forbidden to have me? Is it because I am the Creature of Fire and Ice? Is it because I am his Spirit Keeper? Hector, I need to know—is there any part of you that wants *me*, that married *me*?"

Hector pursed his lips, considering. Knowing he would be

nothing but honest, I awaited his answer in great trepidation. "It is not possible to"—he gestured so I would understand the next word—"*separate* those parts of you. You *are* all those things. But I have been with you for a very long time now. I have seen you. I have heard you. And I love you, Kay-tee." He looked at me with such a fiery affection I melted before him. "I think you know I love you."

I nodded, smiling. "I do. And you know I love you, too."

We came together passionately, 'til suddenly I pulled away. "Oh, but wait! My husband will be very unhappy if we do not travel a great distance today! He hates it when I delay."

Hector would not release me. He growled, "Your husband will be very unhappy if you do *not* delay!"

And so we delayed.

~ 27 ~

I WISH I REMEMBERED every tiny detail of the days which followed, but alas, I do not. My memories are a blur of bouts of unbridled passion interspersed with periods of recovery from and build-up to e'en more passion. We traveled slowly through those glorious days of autumn. We tried to move quickly, for Hector was still determined to reach a certain village before the full force of winter set in, but no matter how determined we were to get an early start or to keep paddling as long as possible, our impulsive natures frequently got the better of us.

One thing I remember is that he did, finally, teach me to say his name. It took a great deal of coaching and laughing and trying again as we rolled together naked, but eventually I could replicate the sounds exactly as he made them. Thereafter, all I need do to start a fire in his loins was whisper his name. Because of this reaction, I continued to call him "Hector" most of the time, saving his other name for special moments. E'en if I could write a rough equivalent of his name in English—which I cannot—I would not do it, for his name is far too precious to sully it with ink.

I remember, too, how much I missed just talking with him. I

had enjoyed talking with Hector so much after our long period of silence, but after marrying we entered into a new period of silence. It was not that we did not want to talk; it was just that whene'er we were not paddling, hunting, cooking, or cleaning, we were too entangled with each other to talk. In a peculiar way, I missed Hector. No matter how intimate we were physically, I wanted more and more and more of him—his words, his thoughts, his feelings, his soul.

We still understood so very little about each other.

At one point, shortly after we married, I complained it wasn't fair I had to sit in the front of the canoe because I must turn if I wanted to see him. The river was smooth and easy at that point, so I twisted 'round and played at paddling backwards. Hector smiled at my silliness, but replied I had it easy—it was far more difficult, he said, to sit in the back of the canoe, as he must do. "I stare at your hair, your arms, your back," he said wistfully, "and at times it has taken all my strength not to reach for you. I do not know why we have not run into more rocks!"

I stopt playing with my paddle and stared at him, surprised. "Is that so? Since when have I distracted your paddling?"

"Since the moment you got into my canoe."

I sat there watching him paddle for a while, knowing I was distracting him, but I was too hungry for the mere sight of him to stop. Thereafter I was oft a distraction for him. Once I insisted on sitting in the back of the canoe with him, the way we did when we escaped from Three Bulls. I leant against him, so happy, surrounded by his strong arms as they pulled through the water again and again. After a short time of this sort of stimulation, however, I found myself insane with desire, unable to do anything but insist we pull over and yield to my rabid need immediately or I would die. Hector was surprised by the extremity of my passion, but he obliged me without complaint. Afterwards, I apologized for the delay, saying I guessed I could not sit in the back of the canoe with him. He laughed and said I had the appetite of a man—which I'm sure he attributed to the Spirit I kept. Concerned, I asked if it was bad for a woman to be so lustful. Hector grinned at the sky and said, "Not for me!"

Unfortunately, I found the more I had of him, the more I wanted, and I swear if I could have crawled inside his skin and bedded down like a parasite amidst his internal organs, I still would've wanted to get closer to him somehow, to have more of him, to become more inseparably intertwined.

Occasionally I felt guilty, horrendously guilty. I hated the fact that everything about our relationship was based on a lie, a miserable mistake, but I simply saw no way to undo what had been done. I knew, sooner or later, I must tell Hector the truth, and I thought of a million ways to say Syawa had not given me his Spirit and I was not, in fact, a Spirit Keeper, but long before I could push any explanation to my tongue, every single word withered in my brain and washed away in my pulsing blood. I couldn't tell him. How could I tell him? I simply could not tell him. Not yet. Not whilst I needed him so desperately. And so I learnt to live with my horrific guilt the same way I learnt to live with my insatiable lust.

One evening as we lolled naked together, Hector asked what had caused a scar above my knee. He had been touring my scars—which are many—asking about each one, and when he came to this one, I smiled. "That's my brother's mouth," I said and proceeded to tell the tale.

A girl who lived near us in Boston had been born with a club-foot, causing her to walk with a considerable limp. The girl was older than I—perhaps twelve to my eight—but she was frail and easily frightened and rarely left her house save when her mother sent her to the market with eggs. Then a gang of little boys would follow after her, cruelly mocking her uneven gait.

I could see the boys were a torment to her, and tho' the girl meant nothing to me, I despised bullying, especially since two of those boys were my own little brothers. One day when the girl passed by, out the boys ran, and I marched out behind them to demand they have done. Tho' the other lads ran off, my brothers were not inclined to take orders from me, reckoning, of course, they had me outnumbered. I had righteous indignation on my side, however, so when fists began to fly, I gave as good as I got, and in a moment I was sitting atop one brother whilst holding the other by his arm and slapping his face. With both my hands busy, the brother below took the opportunity to sink his teeth into my leg just above the knee, and when I jumped up to shake him loose, both boys escaped.

In the meantime, the crippled girl cowered in a doorway, terrified by the sudden flurry of violence. I dusted myself off and walked her to market, tho' I fear anyone who saw us must've thought I was mocking her as much as the boys had been, for my bleeding knee made me limp. We laughed about that, and, thereafter, 'til we moved away a year or so later, I walked her to the market many times.

Hector listened to this story with a fond glow in his eyes, telling me afterward he wisht he could have been there to fight beside me. He said he could just see me as a little girl, my red curls bouncing as I battled my brothers. Then he got a sort of faraway look in his eye, saying he also could not abide bullies. "Someone must defend those who cannot defend themselves," he said with conviction.

We went on to discuss other scars, and that was the end of that.

But the next morning I awoke with a start, my ragged gasp bringing Hector to my side in a heartbeat. "What is it?" he asked, far more concerned, I thought, than a simple gasp deserved.

"Just a dream," I mumbled. "But such a strange one . . ."

He wanted to know what I dreamt, but, like most dreams, it was fragmented and fuzzy. "We were somewhere, you and I, where there were people. Boys. A gang of little boys. And they were picking on me, mocking me about something. They called me names— they chanted. One threw something . . . and you . . . you came out of nowhere. You pushed the bullies back. You hit them. It was strange, because it was you, like you are now, but you were younger than those children somehow, and there were so many. They piled on top of you. I wanted to help you, but I couldn't, I just couldn't . . . then someone was coming, and the boys ran away. You were on the ground, blood on your face. That's when I woke up."

It was a silly dream, clearly caused by the story I had told the evening before, but that was not how Hector saw it. When I looked at him, he was sitting back as if I had pushed him, his face ashen, his eyes haunted. "Hector?" I said. He did not seem to hear me, so I sat up and touched his arm. "Hector—it was just a dream!"

But when he turned his face to me, I saw that odd look he got when he spoke of Syawa. "It wasn't a dream," he said, his voice shaky. "That truly happened. Exactly as you described. Except, it wasn't you—it was him. The others picked on him. Because he was small. Always. They followed him, chanting. They never did it when parents could see, but they did it whenever they could."

"And you defended him," I prompted gently, for Hector was lost in the memory.

"Yes. One boy always hated him. He led the others. That boy

threw dirt in his face, just as you said. I stopt him. I stopt them all."
I saw Hector's face transfigured by the same sort of rage he'd felt for
Three Bulls. I felt the muscles of his arm tighten.

I remembered what I'd seen in my dream—was it possible I
was sharing Syawa's memory, as Hector assumed? Preposterous! It
seemed obvious my dream was sparked by my own memories, by
the conversation we'd had, and by my obsessive closeness to my
husband, both emotionally and physically. But it was peculiar, I'll
own to that.

Then I thought about what it must've been like for the two of
them as kids—Syawa, small but smart, endowed with incredible in-
sight and perhaps e'en supernatural gifts—and Hector, younger but
fearless, willing to do whate'er it took, fighting in spite of the fact his
culture frowned upon fighting, risking not only his own well-being
but also his personal reputation and his father's respect, all to defend
someone who needed defending. I thought I loved Hector before,
but now, seeing him as the champion of the downtrodden, my love
for him swelled 'til I feared my heart might explode.

Once again I felt the awful enormity of the loss he suffered
when Syawa died, and tho' I was certain my dream was just a dream
into which he was once again reading things that were not there, I
was not about to snatch whate'er comfort he derived from believing
his lifelong friend lived on inside me.

"I wish I had been there to fight beside you," I said gently, and
Hector took me in his arms. We held each other for an infinite moment before our passions once again o'ercame us.

Thereafter I sensed something troubling Hector. He said nothing,
but I could feel it—a barrier between us, some sort of obstruction I

could not get 'round. It occurred to me he might feel odd about bedding me now that I'd reminded him of the Spirit I purportedly kept, but our passionate encounters continued as enthusiastically as before. Still, something was troubling him.

On occasion he e'en grew testy.

Since teaching me to swim, he had required me to join him each morning, but I ne'er enjoyed the water, e'en after our swimming turned into aquatic coupling. My problem was that when my hair got wet, it stayed wet, and so I slept always with damp hair. This was not a problem when the nights were warm, but now that the evenings were increasingly cool, I needed to keep my hair dry.

When I awoke one morning to find my hair covered with frost, I told Hector I would no longer dunk my head. He argued, insisting his people regularly broke through ice to swim, but I pointed out my hair was not like his, as my skin was not like his, and he must make allowances for the differences between us. He grumbled at me, then turned his grumbling on the frost, which, he said, was a warning. It was just as well I would not swim, he snapt, because we must pick up our pace in order to reach our winter destination.

A day or two after this disagreement, we passed a fairly large village, and I was surprised when Hector put his head down and kept paddling. I saw people on the shore pointing and shouting, and soon a large canoe was following us, the four men inside paddling with deep, hard strokes. As I looked back at the pursuing canoe, I saw Hector's face was stone.

The larger canoe easily o'ertook us. The men seemed friendly enough—concerned, even. They remembered Hector and were eager to renew their friendship. With broad, welcoming gestures, they invited us back to their village, but Hector responded with short, impatient signs, telling them he was sorry, but he must push on to a certain village before the snow came. They reluctantly accepted his explanation, but kept looking at me. When they finally asked who I was, Hector bristled like a dog with a bone, saying he had said all he was going to say.

The men were shocked by Hector's rudeness, as was I. After they left and we set off, I paddled without looking back. Something was very wrong.

We spoke not a word all day, my imagination running wild. Why did Hector refuse to tell those men I was his wife? Was he ashamed of me? I kept going back to the fact that he had not asked me to marry him in the first place—what if he had changed his mind about the whole thing?

When Hector speared a fish late in the afternoon, he pulled it into the canoe and said we must keep going. We paddled 'til almost dark. After we camped, Hector worked on fish spears as I prepared our meal, but as soon as it was cooking, I turned to ask the question I'd been asking myself all day. "Why did we not stop at that village?"

Hector froze, his eyes on the ground, his lips tight, his nostrils flaring.

I continued: "It's been a month since we stopt. We've skipt at least one other village, haven't we?" The accusation hit him like a slap in the face. "That's what I thought. So all day I've been wondering, asking myself why. It's not that we're in such a hurry. We've always been in a hurry, yet we've always stopt. The only difference now is that we're married."

The fish spear fell, forgotten, onto the riverbank. "It's not what you think," he mumbled.

"Indeed? How would you know? Can you hear my thoughts?"

His eyes shot up to my face. "I want to explain it to you," he began, then stopt, looking pained. "But it's . . . complicated!"

Complicated. Aaaaaah, yes. How well I knew that frustration, that inability to explain a concept because it was so complicated it simply could not be translated. I sighed. "This is a problem we have, you and I. Our worlds are very different. But no matter how hard your thoughts are to explain, you must try. I will try to understand."

He nodded, his arms on upraised knees, his head hanging between them. I could see him swallow hard as he considered. "It's his Vision," he said in a meek voice.

"His Vision?"

"I have forfeited my right to tell the story. I can no longer help fulfill his Vision."

"What?" I exclaimed, staring at him in disbelief. "Why?"

Hector launched into a slow, miserable explanation of how he was responsible for Syawa's death.

I stopt him right away. "How can you possibly believe you are responsible? I was there. I saw what happened. There was nothing you could have done!" I softly said his real name as I put my hand on his shoulder. As something of an expert on guilt, I knew what it was to carry a staggering burden, and because my own guilt arose from the very same event, I desperately wanted to relieve him if I could. There was no reason both of us should suffer on account of Syawa.

"Of course I was responsible," Hector insisted quietly. "I should have gotten out of the canoe first. But I accept my failure. We all fail. What I can't accept is—"

"Listen to me!" I interrupted, grabbing his upper arm with both hands. "You did not fail in your promise to protect him—you didn't! Your promise just shifted to *me*. That's why he didn't make you promise to take care of me. He didn't need to! You had already promised to protect *him*, and he is *here*, safe and sound." I put my hand on my heart, but Hector would not look at me.

"I understand all that. But you do not understand. I . . . I *caused* his death." Hector let this shocking statement hang whilst he swallowed thickly. Then he went on: "When we began our journey, I did not understand how far we must go. I thought we would just cross the mountains. When he kept going and going, I wanted to turn back. Many times I threatened to leave him, but he said he would go on without me. I couldn't let him do that. To distract my thoughts, he spoke of you, endlessly, through all our hardships. The things he said about you—I didn't believe you were real. And then I saw you, and . . . it was all true. You are like no other woman. You are so smart, so strong, so brave. So beautiful." He stopt to glance at me as I stared at him with an open mouth. "I did not expect to love you, to want you so much. I knew it was wrong because you were for him, but I couldn't help it. I couldn't help it."

"But . . ." I mumbled, my thoughts spinning with the flood of memories, "but you *hated* me at first! You resented me! You were always so vexed . . ."

He shook his head, his face a tragedy. "I was afraid of you at first. I still couldn't believe you were real. But then I saw you begin to respond to him, and, well—it was *him* I resented, not you. I was jealous. I wanted to be happy for him. I *was* happy for him. But when I saw you were falling in love with him, I couldn't bear it. I said he was stupid, I said you were stupid, I said his Vision was stupid. We argued . . ."

I was staring again, my mouth still open, my eyes narrowed, remembering. That argument they'd had back in the eastern woodlands—that was because Hector *wanted* me?

He still couldn't look at me. "Every time he touched you, I wanted to kill him. I was petty and childish. I said things I never should have said . . . unforgivable things. I wisht him dead, Katie. And then he died."

"Oh, Hector," I moaned, leaning my forehead on his shoulder, "things don't happen just because you wish them."

"Sometimes they do." He turned his unhappy face to me. "I wisht you were mine. And now you are."

I drew in my breath sharply. It broke my heart to hear the pain in Hector's voice, and it was all because of me . . . *me?* How could it be because of me? I was nothing, less than nothing, one of millions and millions, but I knew I would ne'er be able to explain that to him. To him I was special, unique, endowed with supernatural powers. I suddenly understood that just as Syawa had set me up, he had set Hector up as well, priming him like a pump so that he must fall in love with me.

"Hector—do you not remember he said he knew he was going to die on this Journey?" My voice wavered, the memory still so painful. If it was this painful for me, I wondered, what must it be for Hector? "He knew everything, so you must believe he knew how you felt about me and he wanted you to feel that way. It was important for you to feel that way, because . . . well, otherwise you would ne'er have had the patience to put up with me. I needed time to learn your language, to learn your ways. Don't you see? He was preparing you for me, me for you. Because I was meant for you, Hector. He told me so."

Looking down at the ground again, Hector shook his head. "He loved you. You loved him. By marrying you in the deceitful way I did, without his permission, without his approval, I insulted you both. I should not have done that. I betrayed the trust he put in me and violated the most sacred beliefs of my people."

"If anyone did anything wrong, it was *him*," I snapt. Hector looked up sharply, a flash of anger in his swimming eyes. He was still protecting Syawa—e'en from me. I met his gaze defiantly, but my voice was shaking, my own eyes filling. "Yes, Hector, I loved him—I did—but he would not accept it. He told me he was wrong to make me fall in love with him. He apologized and said . . . he said he just wanted to know what it felt like. Maybe you were jealous of him, but the truth is he was far, far more jealous of *you*. He was jealous of *us*, of what we have now, of what he knew we would become. You can't blame him for that. Because what we have is so good . . ." I leant into him, devouring him with my eyes.

He turned his face to me, amazed. "How can you still want me, after what I just told you?"

"What can I say, Hector?" I murmured, shaking my head. "I could try telling you again how special you are, but you will not understand me any more than I understand you when you tell me the same thing. It makes no sense, any of it. Maybe we're both just stupid."

Hector wanted to smile, but couldn't. "You are not stupid, Katie, but I think you still do not understand what I am telling you. I married you without his permission, without his blessing, and the rules of my people are clear. I cannot go home. If you truly want to stay with me, after all I've said, then we must find another place to live, maybe up in the mountains . . ."

He cannot go home? *This* was Hector's horrible secret, the source of his mortifying shame—by marrying me without Syawa's permission he had thrown his life away, a life he loved, a life he longed to return to. What's worse, he had destroyed Syawa's Vision. My mind reeled. But . . . but how could he do that? And how could I let him? I knew with absolute certainty that, sooner or later, he'd come to hate me for all he'd given up because, after all, my mother told me so, she told me so . . .

"Hector," I whined, "you have to believe me when I say he told me I was meant for you! He did! He *did*!"

"But he did not tell *me*!" Hector's face contorted in pain. "All that time we traveled together and not once did he say you were for me. If he told *you*, why did he not tell *me*? E'en as he lay dying, all he talked about was . . ." and then Hector started going on and on about the river and currents and how the way things look on the surface can be caused by things underneath and how the surface may be still e'en tho' there are obstructions below, and he used words I didn't understand but then I started to realize I'd heard those words before in this very context, in reference to blame and guilt and acceptance, and then I frowned and then I remembered and then I knew . . .

"God Almighty!" I exclaimed in English, which made Hector stop and look at me, startled. I jumped up and staggered along the riverbank, my head in my hands, shouting, "God! Oh God!" over and over. Finally I stopt and stared at Hector, but I was not seeing him at all. I was seeing Syawa.

Syawa was kneeling beside me there on the banks of the Great River, going on and on about how a river can appear one way but be another and how important it was not to blame myself for things that were not my fault, and I thought he was talking about my story of Adam and Eve, but he wasn't, he wasn't, he was giving me a message, a message he said I must pass on to Hector, e'en tho' I did not understand all his words at the time and what I did understand made no sense and so I had completely forgotten his instructions because of all the other things that happened but now the memory flared up and I blushed scarlet, remembering.

I held up my hand to Hector and said, "Wait! I am supposed to tell you something! Let me think!" I closed my eyes, concentrated, and told him, sound for sound, the first part of the message Syawa bade me memorize after making me promise I'd tell it to his friend.

When I was done, I opened my eyes and saw Hector had blanched and was staring at me with wide, frightened eyes. "How do you know these words?" he demanded, his voice cracking with tension.

"I don't. What do they mean?"

Hector looked down, o'ercome with emotion. He closed his eyes and shook his head, and then, to my amazement, he chuckled. He opened his eyes, smiling in wonder. "What you just said is something we say when a canoe becomes lodged on an obstruction in a river. Some obstructions are invisible, unavoidable, but if you struggle against them, try to push backwards, you will flip your canoe. To break free, you must lean forward, move *into* the obstruction." Hector smiled at me. "It is something he said to me many times on our Journey."

This "saying" was as hard for Hector to explain as it would be for me to explain to him the meaning of the phrase "Ne'er look a gift horse in the mouth." These were river people, for whom flowing water was the basic metaphor of life, and the message Syawa bade me tell Hector was one only he could send. E'en without understanding the message, however, I could see the effect it had on Hector: he was transformed.

I told him there was more, and when he asked what it was, I said I must first know the meaning of a certain word. I told him the word, which he defined as "items held within something else"— that is, contents. "Contents!" I exclaimed. "*Contents?* I think I'm offended!" Hector stared at me, perplexed, 'til I recited the second half of Syawa's message: "I leave the canoe and all its contents in your capable hands—enjoy the ride."

Hector laughed and laughed as I went on a bit of a tirade, proclaiming myself the Creature of Fire and Ice, not some small part of a canoe's contents, but eventually I, too, had to laugh. Tho' I did not appreciate being handed off along with the tent cover and paddles, I could not very well remain offended because these words were, apparently, all the permission Hector needed in order to feel our marriage was legitimate.

With this blessing, we could go home now and Syawa's Vision could still be realized.

As our fish burnt to a crisp, Hector and I sat side by side on the dark riverbank, silent, staring into the flowing water, lost in our separate thoughts. I cannot say what Hector was thinking, but as for me, well, Syawa's intoxicating smile just kept flashing in my brain. My God, what a mastermind! Somehow he had set all this up, playing both me and Hector the way I'd seen Hector play a fish—slowly, methodically, watching and waiting 'til just the right moment, knowing exactly when and where and how to strike the lethal blow. How had Syawa done it? I didn't know, but I knew he had done it and I knew he had done it quite deliberately.

It was obvious now why Syawa had sent his message through me rather than just telling Hector himself. By sending this particular message in this particular way, Syawa had made damned sure I could ne'er tell Hector I was not a Spirit Keeper—if I did, my marriage would be invalidated. I looked up at the bright stars in the black sky, awe-struck. I had once seen myself as a hapless pawn in Syawa's hand, but now I felt more like his puppet, my stiff lips smacking nonsensically as he supplied all the words.

And yet . . . e'en as I resented being cast as the long-suffering Judy in Syawa's traveling Punch 'n' Judy show, still, I could not be as furious as I thought I had a right to be. The simple truth was I loved Hector with all my heart and soul and so could hardly complain about the way things had turned out. What's more, because I now knew Hector was willing to throw his entire life away for me, I would ne'er again be able to doubt his love or deny it as I was wont to do. Now I knew beyond a shadow of a doubt *he* loved *me* with all his heart and soul.

But there was something else. The most unnerving part of this unnerving situation was not that Hector thought I was something I was not; it was that Syawa knew exactly what I was—or, at least, he said he did—and he had made his plans based on that knowledge. My arms prickled with goose-flesh as I suddenly realized it wasn't over between us. Not by a long shot. The Seer had set a series of wheels in motion, and e'en tho' he was, unquestionably, gone from this world, and his soul, as I knew all too well, was off doing whate'er it is dead souls do, I was still being spun by his whirling circles.

Thus the real question I had to worry about was not so much *how* Syawa had managed so deftly to keep playing me long after he was dead, but *why*.

~ 28 ~

Now that Hector's remorse had been relieved by Syawa's belated message, my husband was the happiest man who e'er lived. I envied him the relief which came from confessing his sins, but I reconciled myself to ne'er receiving a similar absolution. In exchange for this glorious life I'd been given, I knew I must play the part that had been thrust upon me—I must dance to the tune of the puppet-master. To me it seemed a small price to pay for the intense joy I received in return.

After long days of paddling, playing, and loving each other, Hector and I arrived at another village and prepared to tell, once again, the story of Syawa's Vision.

We soon found ourselves seated on the mat of honor, waiting for the local dignitaries to finish their harangues. Tho' I had seen Hector "painted up" for our performance many times, this was the first I had seen him thus as my husband, and he was so adorable it was all I could do not to fall upon him and smear myself head to toe with his paint. I, myself, continued to rely only on my red hair, white skin, and blue eyes to capture the audience's attention. It ne'er failed me, and the farther we traveled, the more startling was the impact of my Irish complexion.

The locals introduced us, then added wood to the fire. With a quick intake of breath, Hector leapt to his feet and began his pantomime of the long Journey eastward. The story proceeded 'til I, too, jumped up, but this time, when we confronted each other with our imaginary weapons, the terror was gone, simply gone. As we stood staring at one another, breathing hard, eyes shining, lips parted, our passion was undeniable. The onlookers exchanged glances, surprised by the plot twist.

It quickly became clear that our relationship transformed the story of Syawa's Vision from a Holy Quest to a much more complex human drama—a romance. When I included details I had previously omitted, such as Syawa's declaration that I was meant for Hector as well as the belated message, the audience easily saw what I had failed to see—our marriage was inevitable, an important part of the Seer's Vision.

This revelation nagged at me e'en as we performed the rest of our adventures. I wondered—what would have happened if I had told the whole story all along? Would I have accepted my fate sooner, or would the thought of marrying a savage brute have sent me screaming back east? As I puzzled o'er this, I began to understand what Syawa tried to tell me about the river on the last night of his life—struggle tho' we may against the current, sooner or later we all let go and drift to the exact place the swirling forces always meant for us to be.

Hector and I acted out our capture by Three Bulls, the fight, and the escape in our canoe, then ended our story by simply turning to face one another. I smiled as I gestured he was now my husband, and he smiled as he gestured I was now his wife. The audience whooped in triumph.

As always, Hector closed our performance by singing the traveler's song, but this time, shortly after he started, I joined in, adding a harmony to his strong baritone notes. He turned to look at me in surprise, his voice faltering. When I smiled and arched one eyebrow, he recovered and sang with feeling as I added my harmony.

And so the story of Syawa's Vision was made e'er more powerful.

After the general singing and dancing, and after receiving the usual accolades from well-wishers, Hector and I had the opportunity to do something truly special, something we'd ne'er had a chance to do as husband and wife. We slept together. Ah, with what eagerness we raced to the lodge where we were staying! Onlookers surely assumed we were hastening to copulate, but the truth was we could do that whene'er we desired—to sleep together was a rare and precious thing! Giggling, we rolled ourselves into an intertwined bundle inside our sleeping furs and shared hour after delicious hour unconscious in each other's arms.

The evening after we left that village, Hector said he had a confession to make. Considering his last confession almost ruined our lives, I regarded him warily as I asked what it was.

Before we went to that village, he said, he had worried very much about something he'd ne'er told me—he was afraid how he would react to having people boldly looking at his wife. It was hard enough before, he said, when I was just a woman, but now . . . well, he feared he might lose control and hurt someone. Shocked, I asked why.

"You know why," he said, somewhat impatiently. "Because I am petty and jealous. I want no one looking at my wife but me!"

"That seems a little extreme," I observed, sure he was joking.

"I told you I was unsuited to be married to a Spirit Keeper," he replied glumly. He went on to explain that back home he had been in love with an upper-class girl who promised she would find a way to bend the rules so she could marry him, but then she continued to flirt with other men. When she saw how much her teasing bothered him, she did it all the more. "I hated it when she looked at other men the same way she looked at me!" he grumbled, the anger still raw. "I hated the way they looked at her and then at me, openly, boldly, because they knew there was nothing I could do!"

Apparently Hector got himself into more than one fight because of this girl, and his uncontrollable rage was the main reason his father was willing to send him off with Syawa.

"Well, everything turned out for the best," I soothed, sipping broth from the horn we used as a cup. "This girl sounds like a female dog to me."

Hector laughed. His people did not curse or call each other bad names, and the ease with which I was able to come up with verbal insults struck him as terribly clever. Finally he went on. "Loving her was hard because she showed me something about myself I did not like to see, something that made me afraid to love again. From the day I met you, this has bothered me. I've always hated it when men look at you, but because you are a storyteller, I must accept it."

"Wait—are you saying that if I wasn't telling a story, men would not look at me?"

"Not if they are decent, respectful men. But because you are telling a story—"

"Wait. So is that why you've always wanted me to tell you stories?"

Hector squirmed. I was snuggled up beside him under the canoe, sharing his warmth as we sat before our fire, and I tried to catch his eye, but he wouldn't look at me. I bumped his shoulder with my own, 'til he grinned sheepishly. I said, "So you ne'er cared a bit about the Trojan War, did you?"

He grinned more broadly. "I cared that you cared."

I laughed, but as I slowly sipt my broth I started thinking about the implications of his revelation and I lost my sense of humor. "Is this going to be a problem for you? I mean, if you didn't like men looking at me before, when I was 'just a woman,' you must really hate it now."

Hector looked up at the starry sky, contemplating. "This is what I am telling you. I worried about that. I feared I would lash out again, the way I did before. But it's different with you. You don't seem to notice the men watching you."

I leaned on him, playful again. "Are men watching me?" I looked 'round as if searching for an audience. "I don't like men," I said in mock confidence. "In fact, I don't like people. People are vexing."

"You like *me*, don't you?" He grinned, bumping my shoulder.

"Who told you that? Are you some sort of seer?"

"No," he said, trying not to laugh. "I just remember what we were doing earlier. You seemed to like me then."

"Was that you? Oh, yes, I remember now. I *do* like you." I bumped his shoulder coyly, then finished my drink and turned to put the horn away. "Or at least I *did* like you 'til I found out you don't care a bit about my stories—that all along you just wanted an excuse to look at me!"

"I love your stories," he protested, still grinning broadly, "but I also love to look at you."

"Hmmm. I notice you haven't asked for a single story since we married."

"Will you tell me a story now?"

"Ha!" I scoffed as I wrapt a fur 'round my shoulders. "I'll tell you a story about the husband who got himself into trouble and tried to get out of it by asking his wife for a story . . ."

And so we passed our time in silly repartees like this that went on and on.

The way I put words together or expresst ideas oft amused Hector, and many of my ideas themselves seemed bizarre enough to make him smile. One of my favorite jests was to sit beside him and say hello in the formal way we greeted strangers when we first arrived in a village. This was a mistake I'd made soon after we married, and he thought it hilarious, because it was totally inappropriate within the context of our intimate relationship. Thereafter I frequently made such verbal errors on purpose, just to hear him laugh. Thus we had a great deal of fun as we sat, night after night, shoulder to shoulder, under the canoe before a warm fire.

From the village where we first slept together, the river turned due north again, and each day seemed markedly shorter than the day before. I won't say Hector was panicking, but he was more determined than e'er to cover as much ground as possible each day. We pushed ourselves but still managed to enjoy almost every moment.

The terrain was unlike anything I'd e'er seen. Long, rolling vistas turned into dark bulges in the distance, and I stared at the foreboding landscape uneasily. To distract me as we trudged o'er long portages, Hector oft stopt to point out a flower, to watch some birds, or to spy on a colorful spider weaving an intricate web. He saw things I ne'er noticed, and I loved it when he brought them to my attention.

Unfortunately, the increasing chill was a growing problem for me. Some days I shivered constantly and Hector, who continued to wear naught but his breechclout, was troubled by my complaints. He once again bade me rub my skin with the grease he rubbed on his, but just as it did not protect me from the sun, it did not protect me from the cold. Tho' he assured me I would soon grow accustomed to the air, I assured him I would not. Like my skin that burnt and my hair that ne'er dried, this, I said, was a way in which we were different. During my turn at night-watch, I sewed myself a long-sleeved shift to wear o'er my laced bodice and a thicker, longer pair of breeches to wear o'er the ones I already wore.

One afternoon snowflakes began to fall, and tho' they melted as soon as they hit the water, we knew they were harbingers of things to come. That evening I strode back and forth on the riverbank, waving my arms to warm up. Hector suggested I dance, whereupon I immediately launched into a high-jumping Irish jig, the kind my father did when he was drunk enough to be silly but not so drunk as to be mean. Hector found some sticks and banged on a log to make a beat, chanting as I danced.

We laughed and laughed. Soon I grabbed his hand to make him dance with me, but he pulled back, saying men and women do not dance together. I gave him a reproachful look, saying men and women do not swim together either, but that ne'er stopt him from pulling me into the water.

"You know men and women do not swim together?" he asked, clearly surprised.

"It took a while to figure out, but at some point I asked a woman, and she told me."

Hector was embarrassed. "I should have told you. But you had to learn to swim, and there was no other way. I'm sorry I did not tell you sooner. You were right to stop swimming with me."

"That's not why I stopt swimming with you! I stopt swimming with you because I was freezing! You should know by now I don't mind breaking rules. So break a rule with me now, my love, and let us dance together!"

He was hesitant but willing, and in a moment we were jumping and spinning and flailing about as if we were attending one of our performances. Because I had watched Hector dance many times, I was able to copy his steps exactly, which tickled him to no end. Then I taught him some of my Irish dances, and that also made him laugh.

So this was another way we passed many an evening—wildly dancing together under the stars as we laughed and laughed.

When gray skies brought more snow, Hector decided e'en *he* needed clothes, so he stopt one afternoon to pursue more of those enormous deer-like creatures. I asked if I could go with him and he said yes, as long as I was much quieter than I had been in the eastern woods. I promised to try.

I wasn't really interested in hunting; in truth, I just didn't want to be left alone. I remembered how crazed my thoughts had become the last time Hector went off hunting, and I dreaded going through that again.

At first I was glad I went, for it was a revelation to see Hector as predator. The way he trotted along the big deer's trail, intensely focused, was just the way I'd seen dogs back home trot along a rabbit trail. I was hard-presst to keep him in sight without making any noise. Finally he stopt, and I stopt as well, watching as he sank into a crouch. Up ahead I saw the deer—six of them—climbing a slope on the other side of a gully. I remained utterly motionless whilst Hector nocked his arrow and I watched without breathing as he crept slowly, slowly forward. Finally his arrow flew, swift and sure, slicing through a young buck's neck as easily as a hot knife slices through butter.

I was startled by the frantic motion which ensued. I assumed a deer fatally shot by an arrow would simply fall down and wait to be retrieved, but apparently that was rarely the case. Not only did all the deer bounce away in panic, but Hector bounced through the brush behind them to reach the wounded deer as quickly as possible. By the time I caught up with him, he had wrestled the deer down, slit its throat to end its suffering, and was offering thanks to the Spirit of the Deer.

He left me to eviscerate the animal, remove the hide, and cut up the meat whilst he went off after a second one. I saw no need for all this killing, but he said we needed the hides, and I could not dissuade him. So I got to work and off he went.

I'm sure an Indian woman would've had no problem with the task Hector left me, but I am not the sort of person who should e'er be left alone. As soon as he was gone, I began imagining all sorts of predators circling in the brush. I heard things, saw things, conjured things. I clutched my knife as I eyed the wavering shadows. I knew Hector was not far off and would soon be back, but . . .

The blood on my hands began to bother me; the pool of blood I stood in bothered me e'en more. As I looked down at it, the pool of blood seemed to deepen and spread, expand and grow, 'til suddenly I saw it was pouring, not from the deer, but from the sliced-open belly of my would-be murderer on our cabin floor. I backed away, but the pool of blood quickly followed me, merging with the pool of blood flowing from my father's scalpless head where he lay in our garden. It was all the same pool of blood, rising and rising like an irresistible red tide, and I backed away from it but it caught up with me and gurgled 'round me 'til I fell backwards and scrambled away from it on hands and knees.

I staggered to my feet, determined to get control o'er my sudden fit of insanity. "I've got to get this off me!" I said aloud in English, then turned to run to the river. Within seconds I was hopelessly lost, and the harder I tried to find my own trail again, the more turned 'round I became. How could I not find the river? It was just right there! I had no choice but to sit down and wait for Hector to find me.

It felt like forever. I sat on a large rock, weeping, holding my face in my hands as my tears washed salty streaks down the red stains on my arms. I wept for my father in his pool of blood and for my mother in her captivity. I wept for all the family members I would ne'er see again. I wept for Thomas, who died defending his family, for William, who offered to fight for me, and for my little sister Susannah, whom I always slept beside. So far from me, all of them, in time and space. I would ne'er be able to tell any of them the story I had told countless strangers, and that thought made me sad, so horribly, horribly sad.

I didn't hear Hector coming, but then he was there, staring at me in astonishment. "Why are you crying?" he asked, worried almost beyond expression.

I shook my head and held him off, sniffling, ashamed of myself. "I don't know—I just . . ." and I wept again, helplessly.

"But what happened? Why did you come here? Why are you sitting here?" Hector was completely unable to comprehend my behavior.

"I'm lost!" I snapt, inexplicably angry. "I'm useless and stupid and the only thing I knew for sure was that you would find me. And you did." In spite of my resistance, Hector put his arms 'round me and held me whilst I sobbed like a little girl. He thought I was scared because I was lost, and I let him think what he would. The truth was that I was beginning to suspect my real problem, and I was not yet ready for him to figure it out.

He had failed to kill another deer, but we got the meat from the first one back to our camp, and o'er the next few days we stript and dried it as quickly as we could.

Then we were paddling north again, soon to arrive at another village, where we gave another rousing and well-received rendition of our story. But that night, after we hurried to our sleeping furs, Hector reached to pull the bearskin 'round us and when his arm brushed my breast, I gasped in pain. He pulled his arm back and looked at me, alarmed. "Did I hurt you?" he asked anxiously.

I swallowed heavily and looked up at him, crinkling my nose. I put his hand gently on my swollen breast. I could see his face in the dim firelight of the lodge; he was frowning, uncomprehending. I took his hand and moved it down to my flat, hard belly, which would not be that way much longer. I bit my lip and shrugged. I heard him inhale sharply.

I wisht I could see his face more clearly, but all I could see was that he was staring down at my body. Finally he lifted his eyes to mine and tried to smile. "Your mother . . ." he said slowly, "she had a baby in one of your big canoes? And another in a . . ." He tried to say "wagon," and I nodded in agreement to both questions. I didn't mention that one of those babies was stillborn and the other died within hours of birth, but I reckoned such an omission was surely not as bad as an outright lie.

Hector nodded, as if to himself, then smiled at me, his eyes sparkling in the firelight. He leant o'er to kiss me, but I winced at the weight of him on my tender breasts. He pulled back and leant so that the only parts of us touching were our arms and foreheads.

In truth, I was terrified at the thought of being pregnant out in that foreboding countryside, but I knew it was far too late to start worrying about that now. Seeing Hector was also terrified did not soothe my fears, so I tried to console us both by reminding him the Seer had said I would live with his people. "We just have to trust in his Vision," I said softly.

Hector nodded but said nothing. I started to fall asleep only to jerk awake, startled by something in my head. I could've sworn I heard Hector's thoughts. He was thinking that sometimes seers can be wrong.

The next day, after I was in the canoe ready to go, Hector stufft a large new bundle in amongst our other things. "What is that?" I asked, turning 'round to look.

"It is a buffalo hide. Very thick. Very warm. I traded much of our meat for it because my wife is always cold."

I looked at him and could not help it—I began to cry. He had to push the canoe quickly into the river so the people who had come to see us off would not be alarmed. When we were out of their sight, I glanced back and said I was sorry for crying all the time, but he said now that he understood why I cried, he did not mind so much.

At that, of course, I blubbered like a baby.

~ 29 ~

During my turn at night-watch, I wrapt myself in the buffalo robe and sewed clothes for Hector, happy to have something to keep my thoughts occupied. I made both a warm shirt and thick breeches, and tho' they were unlike any other Indian's clothes, Hector was delighted with them, touched by my determination to give him something special.

I finisht the clothes just in the nick of time. He had worn them for only a day or two when the sky grew dark and snow began to fall in a way it hadn't snowed before. The wind blew hard against us. After steering 'round a rather large sandbar, Hector turned our canoe to the riverbank. The sandbar was surrounded by and covered with dried-out rushes, which rustled and rattled in the wind like the hissing whispers of a worried rabble.

'Twas full dark and our dinner was nigh ready when we heard a hail from the river. Two large canoes were rounding the sandbar, headed our way. The canoes were tethered together, with two men in the lead canoe, one in the other. None of them wore shirts and the animal hides that covered their heads were white with snow. A man in the first canoe said something we could not understand, then gestured, asking if they could share our camp.

Normally there would have been no question. Since we escaped from Three Bulls, Hector ne'er allowed other campers anywhere near us. He hesitated e'en now, but the cold and dark gave him pause. He turned and said that if he sent them on, they would no doubt camp close by; at least if they were here with us, he could keep an eye on them.

I shrugged. I always left such decisions up to Hector.

The lead man was nondescript, identical, in my view, to the hundreds of Indian men I had met o'er the previous months. The one in the rear of the first canoe had a wide, flat forehead, and when Hector saw this, he spoke to him in a language I did not understand. The man eagerly responded. The man in the tethered canoe was very light-skinned, and his hair, instead of the jet-black I was accustomed to, was dark brown. His eyes were brown as well. When he saw me, his eyebrows contracted, and he tipt his head to ask in a thick accent if I spoke French.

For a time the five of us engaged in a most confusing and cacophonous conversation. Hector spoke with the flat-headed man, who then conveyed information to the others, whilst I spoke with the light-skinned man, who conveyed my conversation to the others, at the same time that Hector and I turned and filled each other in on what the two strangers were telling us. The effect was dizzying.

The two darker men were traders who had, in the spring, taken a large load of furs all the way to the Great River. There they met the light-skinned man and one other, who teamed up with them to bring a massive load of trade goods to some village well to the northwest of here. We must have passed them on the river, they said, but, at any rate, they knew all about us, because throughout their return trip they heard stories of us at almost every place they stopt. They were delighted to meet us, e'en awed, and this flattery had an unfortunate effect: we let our guard down.

When the traders went on to explain in an off-hand way their fourth partner was killed at some point in some sort of altercation, we should have paid more attention, but Hector was too busy playing host and I was too distracted by the mountain of trade goods. The man who spoke French bade me come to the canoes and take what I wanted from his kettles, pots, pans, spiders, tongs, but because I knew I must carry everything I owned for perhaps another year, I complimented him on his nice things and said I myself wanted for naught.

Encouraged by my interest, he dug down for a secure-looking hide satchel, from which he extracted a beaver-skinned pouch. He opened this to show me two leather-bound ledgers, which, he confided eagerly, he was going to use to prove to his father that he could be as successful as he. His father, it seems, was a French trader who traveled up and down the Great River, and this young half-breed was determined to impress him by establishing his own trade route on the Misery. "Do you know how to read and write?" I asked, amused by his youthful exuberance.

"Enough to keep records," he said with pride.

I had no more than smiled at the man before Hector was beside us, demanding to see what we were looking at. Because I could not explain it quickly, he waved his hand to dismiss the subject as he gruffly said it was time to eat. Knowing Hector would be bothered if I paid attention to anyone but him, I served the food silently, no longer looking at the strangers. When the half-breed tried to re-engage me in conversation, I just grunted and kept my eyes averted the way Hector always used to do. Frankly, I was too tired to be sociable anyway and saw no reason to make Hector unhappy.

After we finished eating and I was cleaning up, the strangers pulled out some tobacco and all the men smoked. Hector regularly smoked when we were in a village, but because I found the odor noxious, he abstained 'round me. This particular evening the smoke actually made me nauseous, so when I was done with my work, I went back to our upturned canoe and wrapt myself in my warm furs. I had our usual fire in front of the canoe to keep me warm, but the strangers had started a fire of their own about thirty feet away, and this was where the men sat smoking. Knowing Hector would not sleep with strange men 'round, I reckoned I might as well enjoy some extra sleep, so I closed my eyes and quickly drifted off.

Sometime later loud laughter woke me up. I lifted my head to look o'er at the men only to see one of them raising a jug to his lips. I was immediately alarmed and called out Hector's name. He did not respond, which alarmed me all the more. Only when I shouted his name loudly did he turn his head and slowly rise to come to me. He left behind a wobbly line of footprints in the two-inch-deep snow.

He stank of rum. "What are you doing?" I hissed.

He was taken aback by my tone. "We are smoking. They have a strange water they wanted to share with me. Why are you angry? All is well. You should sleep." His speech was slurred.

"It's not 'water,' you dog!" I snapt. I had ne'er called Hector a name before, but my outrage was beyond all bounds. I saw my words wounded him deeply; I did not care. "It is . . ." I did not know the word for "poison," so I said, "Bad, bad, bad water! Do not drink it! It will make you sick!"

Hector hesitated. "They said this water is like tobacco. They said your people use it to make friendship."

"My people use it to make stupid dogs of themselves!" When he still seemed uncertain, I became e'en more agitated. "Who knows more about my people—them or me? I am telling you not to drink this water! It is bad for you, Hector!"

"It is a gift," Hector mumbled defensively. "To refuse a gift of food or drink is an insult."

"I don't care if it's an insult! You must refuse it! And don't let them drink it either!"

Hector's face turned to stone as he said, "Who knows more about the ways of my people—you or me?" He rose to walk unsteadily back to the men's fire.

I was shaking in fury. I pushed myself upright under the canoe and pulled the buffalo robe 'round me. I watched Hector flop back down beside the flat-headed man, who laughed and handed the jug to him. My husband took it and paused, considering. He looked in my direction, a bit blearily. Then, whilst looking directly at me, he raised the jug to his lips and swallowed deeply.

I felt as if my head exploded.

I was back at home—at the farm, in Philadelphia, in Boston. In every place we e'er lived, my father drank himself stupid whene'er he had the chance. Every scheme he e'er had to make money ended in a keg of rum. Every dream he e'er dreamt drowned in a keg of rum. Every sincere effort he e'er made to reform floated, face down, in a keg of rum.

And every time my father got good and drunk, he turned on my mother. He screamed at her and abused her and called her whore and cunt and slavering bitch, and he blamed everything— everything—that had e'er gone wrong in his life on her. "'Twas all yer fault!" he always slobbered, weaving unsteadily, "and now ye've burdened me with this goddamned batch o' goddamned bastards, half o' which I'm sure ain't even mine! I ought to kill ya, y'witch— I ought to push ye right into the fire and watch the flames consume yer cursed flesh!" And we children would scream as he lunged for her and shook her and pummeled her with fists or books or empty bottles and we'd try to grab him, to stop him, to protect her, to defuse the desperate situation, but the madness always bounced us from wall to wall, breaking furniture, bursting clothes at the seams, bruising all of us from head to toe. On more than one occasion he actually got a hold of her sleeve or her wrist or her hair, and he dragged her kicking and screaming o'er the hearth into the fire. But before the flames could catch, somehow, somehow she was always able to claw her way clear of his drunken grasp, or one of the older boys would jump in to pull her out and slap away the sparks that smoldered on her clothes or hair or skin.

'Til they started drinking, too.

They changed when they started drinking, the boys. They stopt being mischievous lads who teased and taunted me and became violent men who tortured and tormented me. The drink took away their inhibitions, it took away their shame, and it left behind frustration, remorse, and limitless quantities of self-loathing.

Every time my father sobered up, he'd hang his head and scuff his feet and beg my mother to forgive him. He'd cry and cling on to her and tell her she was his everything, his whole world, all he had left. He said he'd be lost without her. And she always forgave him and she always ended up pregnant and she always took out all her anxiety and resentment on us. And then we huddled together, we children, waiting with bated breath for the next binge, the next blow-up, and the next terrifying level of descent on the swirling downward spiral that was our lives. We fought each other just to keep a hold on our tenuous positions as we all slid e'er down and down and down.

Everything about my early life stank of rum. We lost our furniture, we lost our houses, we lost everything we e'er owned—but we ne'er lost that steady supply of intoxicating spirits. That dreadful May day on which I was raped, that day when Syawa claimed he had "seen" me, that day when I crawled into my family's wagon to cry and nurse my wounds, the only place I could find to lie down was sprawled out across four barrels of rum.

So when Hector looked at me and raised that jug to his lips, my head exploded, I saw red, and I hated him as much as I have e'er hated anyone or anything. Perhaps the main reason I had agreed to come with Syawa in the first place was that I thought I was getting away from the drunks, because I was determined—absolutely determined—not to be victimized by alcohol the way my mother had been. But here it was again, and here was I—pregnant and wholly bound to a man who would not say no to the offer of a drink.

I lay back down with my arm o'er my face, trying to control my rage. The thought occurred to me that I had a way to stop him. I had an easy way to stop him. All I need do was lie—tell him Syawa was speaking to me, commanding him not to drink the bad water. Hector might defy me, but he would ne'er defy Syawa. All I need do . . .

"Ah, but men'll drink, Katie," I heard my gran's voice sigh in my head. "Men'll drink 'n' women'll suffer. What can ye do?"

I heard raised voices, which snapt my attention back to the present moment. The men were no longer laughing. They were shouting and growling at one another, angry spittle flying. I gritted my teeth, my lips presst in a thin, tight line. This was how it always went. First they laughed and sang, then they argued and fought, then they slobbered and gushed o'er one another before eventually passing out. I was surprised by how quickly we had passed from step one to step two, but, then again, I had no idea how much they'd had to drink.

The raised voices turned into a physical confrontation before I had time to get fully vexed. Alarmed again, I craned my neck to look o'er at the altercation and saw that Hector and the flathead were rolling in the snow, apparently trying very hard to kill one another. The half-breed was still sitting with the jug, laughing and laughing, and the third man was nowhere to be seen.

This had gone way beyond a simple bout of rowdy drinking. Hector was not playing the way he had once wrestled jokingly with Syawa—his face was contorted, his teeth were bared, and he was fighting the way he'd fought in Three Bulls's camp. I sat up and dug frantically in his pack for the French hatchet. I pulled it out with shaking hands.

By the time I had the hatchet, the half-breed was on his feet, unsteady, shouting sloppily in his language. Of course his words had no effect, and by that time it was too late anyway. Hector had knocked the flathead down onto his belly and now sat astride his back. He grabbed the man's head and twisted it violently, snapping the neck like a dry stick. I gasped, horrified.

But I was e'en more horrified to see the half-breed pull a large metal blade from his waistband, raise it o'er his head, and stumble in the direction of Hector's unprotected back.

Hector was rising slowly, wobbling, panting, facing the body of the man he'd just killed, unaware of the man reeling toward him with a raised knife. I had no choice. In one sweeping motion I jumped out from under the canoe and threw that hatchet with all my might. Because the distance was short, it lodged squarely in the back of the half-breed, who fell forward from the impact onto Hector, who fell forward, too. Both of them landed on the dead flathead, and I gasped again, afraid I might have just killed my husband.

I lifted a foot to run to him only to find both my feet suddenly off the ground. The third man had grabbed me from behind in a deadly bear hug. I screamed wildly and kicked with my feet, my arms pinned against my sides as the man squeezed and squeezed.

He shook me like a rag doll, back and forth, back and forth, but he was pretty drunk, so my wild kicking eventually had an effect. He fell sideways, taking me with him.

We hit the ground hard, but I knew I had no time to recover my breath. I rolled away, scrambling toward Hector, who still had not moved. I planned to snatch the hatchet from the half-breed's back, but just before I reached it, my pursuer grabbed my ankle. I screamed Hector's name repeatedly as the drunk savage somehow managed to stagger to his feet without losing his grip on me, after which he lurched this way and that, pulling me 'round the campsite the way I'd seen a dog drag the rotting haunch of a dead deer.

He was unbelievably strong and there was naught I could do to stop him from scraping my face through the snow and mud and sticks and rocks of the riverbank. Because I was struggling so furiously against him, kicking at his wrist, he stopt at one point to jerk my leg like a whip, thereby dashing my head against the ground again and again. When he resumed dragging me, I clawed at the muddy snow to try to pull away from him, 'til finally he stumbled and lost his grip, giving me a chance to escape. I leapt toward the river, diving into the water at a full-on run so that I was halfway to the sandbar by the time my forward motion slowed.

There was ice on the river. 'Twas thin, but I felt it crack against my face as I desperately swam the hundred feet or so to the sandbar. I was floundering in the rushes before I dared turn to see if the man was following me, but as soon as I did, I could see I was safe. Hector had been roused by my screams and was fighting with the man at the river's edge. Their silhouettes loomed large in the wavering light from the fires, the steaming clouds of their breath roiling 'round them. Hector must have taken the knife from the half-breed, for, as I watched in dismay, he thrust that knife deep into the belly of the man who had dragged me. He pushed the blade up, then pulled it down and gutted the man like a fish.

From my hiding place amidst the chattering rushes in the icy water, I vomited forcefully, heaving 'til I thought I had gutted myself. As soon as I could manage, I looked back up to see Hector standing alone on the littered bank, the knife still in his hand, the clouds of his breath swirling in hysterical circles as he panted and drunkenly surveyed his surroundings. The flickering flames of the firelight made it seem as if the shadows were doing a wild dance 'round him.

He shouted for me. I was too terrified to respond. I had just seen him kill two men for no apparent reason and I do not believe it was strange for me to think he might, in his drunken madness, kill me. He shouted again and again, his tone growing frantic. He dropt the knife and dug through the buffalo robe under the canoe, then crawled out and fell down a few times as he stumbled 'round the fire, looking everywhere, shouting my name. He staggered into the river, screaming my name like a lamentation, splashing 'round in the water as if he feared he would find me floating there, face down.

I was trembling so violently I almost couldn't speak, but I knew I must say something or he would, in all probability, do himself harm. How could I just sit there and watch my husband die? "I'm here!" I called, and he looked up so suddenly that he fell over again.

"Where are you?" he wailed from the lapping water at the river's edge, and I yelled for him to stay where he was, that I would come to him.

The very last thing I wanted to do in all the world was swim back across that ice-cold channel, but I had no choice. It was either do it or watch Hector drown. At this point the water was warmer than the air anyway, so I plunged in.

The first time I swam I was filled with fear and driven to survive, so I was strong. But the second time I was numb, depleted, exhausted, and terrified of what awaited me on the other side. I sank into the depths several times and spluttered and coughed before slowly continuing to make my way across. I might not have made it had not Hector spotted me and met me near the middle. E'en in his state of inebriation he was a better swimmer than I, and so he grabbed my arm and pulled me the rest of the way back to camp.

We crawled out of the water, both on hands and knees. I slowly stood up, but he stayed down, saying, "Something is wrong with me. Everything is moving."

I called him every foul name I'd e'er heard in English, pacing back and forth as I yelled at him. He tried to look up at me, but fell over in the process and just lay there in the lapping water, clearly unable to rise. I raised my face to the black sky and screamed. That roused him, and I grabbed his arm and pulled him 'round to push his face into the river. "Drink!" I shrieked at him in his language, determined to purge him of the rum. "Drink the water, you dog!"

He obeyed me without question, drinking/inhaling enough river water to achieve the effect I desired—he was soon vomiting up the contents of his stomach right there beside the bloody fragments of the belly of the man he'd disemboweled. I held his head up, remembering all the family members whose heads I'd seen held thus at one time or another. When he was done, I washed his face with river water, then grabbed his arm and dragged him, moaning, the way the man had dragged me, stopping beside our fire. I dug under the canoe for the bearskin, but as I rolled Hector into it, I heard a noise from the other fire and whirled 'round.

The half-breed was not dead.

He was still on his belly, but either he had moved or Hector had moved him when he crawled out from under him, for he was not where he had been before. I walked slowly over to have a look and saw the hatchet was embedded in his spine a good two inches, but, with a sick feeling in my empty stomach, I realized the wound was not necessarily a fatal blow. With proper care, this man could survive, tho' with his spine severed he would probably ne'er walk again.

What was I to do? I stood there looking down at him, at the dark pool of blood spreading out and deepening exactly like the one I'd seen 'round the deer, the one I'd crawled from, the one that spooked me into getting lost. I looked down at that blood pool and recognized it and wondered about it—could that have been a Vision? Was it a sign I should just let this poor man lie here and bleed to death?

He must've heard me, because he whimpered something in a language I did not know. I was already shivering violently because of the cold, but upon hearing his torment, I shivered in another sort of way. For a moment I numbly watched the blood pool seeping out across the muddy snow. Then I turned and went back to Hector.

When he felt my touch, he moaned and mumbled and tried to get up, but I told him to stop struggling and go to sleep. He obeyed me instantly. With him taken care of, I knew I had to get myself warmed up or I was very likely going to freeze to death.

I added wood to the fire, then crawled under the canoe and wrapt myself in the buffalo robe. Hours passed before I stopt shivering severely enough to make my bones ache. I cried endlessly, and for much of that time the half-breed cried with me. At one point he began begging me in French to help him, but I knew there was naught I could do save put him out of his misery, which I just could not bring myself to do. I covered my ears with my hands and cried louder, to drown him out.

It snowed all night, tapering off at dawn. By then the half-breed had finally fallen silent, but I was still suffering immeasurably, thinking about what I'd done. I kept remembering how excited the young man had been to prove himself to his father. Now he was dead, by my bloody hand. And why? Why? I didn't understand anything that had happened. I just couldn't figure it out.

I coughed now and then through the night because of all the icy water I'd inhaled, and when I got up shortly after dawn to add wood to the fire, my fit of coughing woke Hector. He moaned and tried to sit, then clutched his head and fell backwards, moaning some more. I knew exactly how he felt, because I myself have been stumbling drunk a time or two, but I had little sympathy for him. He tried to tell me he was sick; I assured him it was the bad water. I told him he must sip some good water now—slowly, just a bit. He crawled to the river and did as I advised.

It took a while for him to be able to look 'round, but when he finally did, sitting at the river's edge, he had a baffled look on his face. "What happened?" he asked, gaping at the bloodbath all 'round.

I stood fully enwrapt within the buffalo robe and told him it mattered little—what was done, was done. The important thing, I said, was what we were going to do next.

"Well," he mumbled, rising stiffly to his feet, "we must go."

I was flabbergasted. Here we were, in the midst of a carnage he himself had created, and Hector not only had no remorse, no contrition, no sympathy, but apparently not the slightest concern at all. Just a few weeks earlier he had been rackt with guilt because he believed he had somehow *wisht* his friend dead, but now he cared not a whit about people he had viciously slaughtered in cold blood! When I pointed this out to him, he shrugged and said they had clearly threatened us, and so forfeited their lives. They were, he said, responsible for their own deaths.

As Hector and I argued, he packed things up. I remained motionless, encased in the buffalo robe, hurling invectives at him every time he walked by. At some point he glanced at me and the light was strong enough by then that he could see inside the buffalo robe. He dropt what he was carrying to come grab my shoulders, but I gasped and shrank from him, which stung him far more than any of my angry words had done. My movement caused the buffalo robe to fall away from my face, and the blood drained from Hector's. E'en when Syawa died, Hector was not so stricken, so shocked, so destroyed.

I'm sure I looked awful. I had a split lip, which was swelling e'er larger, and the whole right side of my face was a swollen mass of dried blood and bruises. I couldn't open my right eye, the socket of which was no doubt blackened, and I had a large knot on my head. I didn't e'en mention the awful pain in my side I believed was a crackt rib.

But I was so angry I wouldn't let him look at my wounds. I jerked out of his grasp and said that by putting me in danger he had forfeited his right to touch me. He stood there with an open mouth, his eyes devastated. Glaring with my good eye, I watched as his face turned to stone. Then he lifted his chin and went to gather the rest of our things.

As he finisht breaking camp, I dug through the trader's packs. Hector told me to leave their things alone, but I ignored him. Considering all the fighting I'd done recently, I decided I needed more weapons than just a hatchet, so I took a hide bundle of knives, a sword, some tools, and a pouch full of metal arrow and spear points. I don't know why, but I also pulled out the leather satchel containing the beaverskin-wrapt ledgers. I guess I felt bad about killing that poor man and because the ledgers meant so much to him, I just couldn't leave them to rot on the riverbank. It was bad enough I had to leave him.

When Hector asked about the satchel, I told him it was something he was too stupid to understand. His delicious lips compressed into a bitter line, and I lifted my own chin, glad I had hurt him.

Before we left, I insisted on doing something about the bodies. Hector said wolves would take care of them, but I would not get into the canoe 'til he dragged the corpses into the river. I'm sure it was foolish on my part, but I was inordinately worried about someone finding the carnage and coming after us to hang us as murderers. I reckoned if the dead men were in the river, at least our crimes would be more difficult to trace. Besides—it seemed appropriate to me their misery should end in the Misery.

Pulling the eviscerated man into the water took Hector only a moment, and the flathead, too, was soon swallowed by the current. But when he went to the half-breed and saw the hatchet in his back, he stopt and stared. He looked up at me, his eyes narrowed. I met his gaze unhappily, accusatively, and he turned to drag the body to the river. He cleaned off the hatchet and packed it away without meeting my eyes again.

Hector and I got into the canoe and set off in silence.

~ 30 ~

THE SKY WAS DULL gray and my hair was still quite damp. By afternoon the wind picked up again, and e'en inside the buffalo robe I was numb from head to toe. When my hands grew so numb I dropt my paddle, Hector grabbed it from the water, pulled the canoe to shore, started a fire, and bade me sit under the canoe behind the flames. "I know you do not want me to touch you," he said in a strained voice, "but you must allow me to warm you." He took off his shirt and wrapt his body 'round mine before pulling the buffalo robe 'round us both.

I leaned the uninjured side of my face against his chest, sucking in his body heat the way a chimney sucks up smoke. "I want you to touch me," I whimpered. "I was just so frightened . . ."

"Of me?" he asked, incredulous.

"Yes."

Saying he could remember little from the night before, he asked me to tell him what happened. I told him what I knew, his fingers gently exploring the swollen parts of my face. When I described the way the man dragged me, Hector's hand stopt in mid-air and began to shake. Suddenly he writhed out of the buffalo robe and crawled across the riverbank to vomit. After he finally stopt heaving, he remained on his knees with his head in his hands, saying he had failed me and could never, ever ask me to forgive him.

And then a very strange thing happened, a thing I ne'er imagined, a thing I could not believe e'en as it was happening to me. I suddenly understood my mother.

All those times she forgave my father, all the times she took him back—I always thought she was insane. But now I understood. There was nothing else she could do. She needed him, and, what was worse, she actually *wanted* him. When he was sober he was charming, smart, funny, fun. Of course she wanted him. She loved him. And so she forgave him. Time and time and time again. Just the way I was going to forgive Hector. Just the way I must, sooner or later, finally forgive my mother.

I was so much worse than she had e'er been. Her husband did what—made drunken threats, blustered, bullied, lost a few fortunes? Mine snapt people's necks and tore out their intestines. My father had turned my mother into a screaming harpy who beat and tormented defenseless children. My husband had turned me into a loathsome murderer. But none of this mattered. I still loved him. I still wanted him. And I would forgive him, whether he asked me to or not.

Because just like my mother, I had no choice.

I begged Hector not to dwell on my injuries. "I've been beaten more times than I can remember," I reminded him. "It truly means nothing to me." He moaned that it meant everything, everything to him, and he would not look at me, he would not come back to me 'til I said that seeing him suffer this way hurt me much more than any beating. At that he looked up sharply, nodded, and went to wash his face and get a long, slow drink. As he came back to wrap himself 'round me again, I told him he must not blame himself for what happened—it was all because of the bad water.

In a raspy voice punctuated with coughs, I told him how the intoxicating spirits had devastated my life long before I was born. I told him about my father and my mother and my brothers and myself and all the ways demon rum had tormented us. He listened silently, his cheek against my hair, his hand absent-mindedly rubbing my arm. Whilst I talked, I couldn't stop thinking about how those gentle hands which touched me now so tenderly could snap my neck as easily as they had snapt the neck of that flathead. I couldn't stop thinking about how he had been prepared to accept permanent exile when he thought he broke some petty rule, but he evinced not a flicker of remorse or regret after eviscerating another human being. I understood so little about this man, and yet here I was, commending myself entirely into his hands, body and soul.

What a leap of faith is love.

When I, at long, long last, exhausted myself in talking, Hector quietly asked why my people made the bad water if they knew it was bad. I sighed. It was a reasonable question. "I wish I knew. It's almost as if we *must* make it now, as if . . . as if it *makes* us make it somehow. It makes us do so many things we do not mean to do . . ."

Hector nodded, saying that was the way of Evil Spirits. If he had known the water contained an Evil Spirit, he said, he would have tossed it in the fire.

By this time my shivering had subsided, tho' my chest was beginning to burn and my cough was getting thick. Hector left me rolled in the buffalo robe as he went to heat some of our dried meat. He warmed water in the drinking horn with hot rocks, then tossed in shredded bark. Nothing e'er tasted better to me than that warm beverage, but I wasn't much interested in the meat. I ate enough to satisfy Hector, then lay down and closed my eyes as darkness settled in.

Suddenly I was a child again, sick in bed with some combination of my siblings. Throughout my childhood, one or another of us was always sick, and as bad as it was for us to fight each other when we were well, it was much worse to struggle against one another when we were ill. One disease after another, year after year, left us perpetually rolling back and forth in alternate chills and fevers, trying to create a space for ourselves in the crowded bed so we could lie in our own bodily fluids instead of those of someone else.

The worst was the pox. This was, far and away, the most traumatic memory of my early years, the most wretched experience I'd known before that fateful day in May some ten years later. I was in the sickbed with four or five others, somewhere in the middle of the straw ticking, which was ne'er a comfortable place to be, filled as it was with elbows, knees, and feet kicking from both sides. I was gruesomely ill, but for me, at least, the burning pox were confined mostly to my hands and feet, with only a few erupting on my face. My sister Ellie was not so lucky—her face literally bubbled with the vile pustules. Ellie was seven to my five, and we had formed an alliance against the others, fighting always as a team, side by side. Now we fought the illness together, and I held her close e'en tho' it made me feel sicker each time I looked at her pox-covered countenance.

Day after day we petted each other and murmured loving encouragements. After moaning and tossing in feverish dreams for more than a week, I dissolved into delirium, regaining my senses a day or two later when my fever finally broke. I awoke in a prodigious pool of sweat and immediately felt bad about befouling the bed. I turned my head to look at Ellie to commiserate, but she was lying on her side, staring at me with vacant, glassy eyes. The curled hand beside her cheek was like a door latch, the ice-cold fingers stiff and hard. I screamed and screamed.

As I lay under a canoe somewhere in the middle of a wild continent, I found myself, once again, face-to-face with the cold cadaver of my dead sister. Her eyes were icy blue, exactly the same as mine, but hers were empty, dead, abandoned, and the pustules on her face bubbled, burst, and oozed; from every one of those popping pox an evil liquid dript and from every sizzling drop of evil liquid a Demon Spirit erupted and writhed and danced. I screamed and screamed, trying to get away, but the flood of dancing demons had fallen upon me, pinning me to the ground. I screamed and kicked and rolled helplessly under the weight of them, which felt like the entire universe of stars sitting on my chest. Then I realized it was the buffalo robe I was kicking and it was Hector I was trying to get away from as he hovered o'er me, his face pale with fear. He said a string of things I could not understand and my head flopt back and forth because I could not keep my eyes open, I could not make myself wake up, and I was hot, hot, so hot with fever. I heard a sob— from Hector or Ellie, I knew not which—and then there was only silence and softness and nothing . . .

. . . and then it was bright daylight and Syawa was sitting beside me, smiling as I opened my eyes. I looked 'round, startled, expecting to see the riverbank and the canoe, but we were in a beautiful woodland meadow and it was spring and there were flowers everywhere. I rose up on one elbow to look 'round, marveling at the vivid colors of the flowers, the golden sunshine, and the blue, blue sky. I looked back at Syawa, my mouth open in wonder, but he just smiled that smile of his, that enchanting smile . . .

"Am I dead?" I asked, a wave of anguish rising in me. I so very much did not want to be dead.

"Not yet," he said, smiling.

"Am I going to die?" I was shaking, shivering, in spite of the wondrously warm spring air.

"Everyone dies."

"Like you . . ." I mumbled, which made Syawa chuckle.

"Not everyone dies like me. But, of course, not everyone has a Spirit Keeper."

I sat up, momentarily struck by the fact this conversation was in English. When did Syawa learn English? Then I smelled the glorious perfume of all those flowers, which was so intoxicating, so invigorating. I turned back to Syawa and momentarily lost myself in the intensity of his eyes, his eyes. Oh, I had forgotten how bewitching were his eyes.

I looked unhappily into my lap. "You have made a liar of me! You made me lie to him!"

"Did I?" Syawa seemed confounded. He lightly touched my hair the way he used to do, as if he knew he shouldn't but just couldn't stop himself.

I looked at him, surprised how different it felt when he touched me compared to when Hector touched me. "Of course!" I said. "He believes this Spirit Keeper nonsense, and you know it isn't true!"

"Do I?"

"Damn it! I'm sick of the way you play with me! You know damned well I'm not a Spirit Keeper because you know damned well there is no such thing. And don't say 'Do I?'!"

Syawa laughed. I had forgotten how warm and bubbly his laughter made me feel. It felt good, so good. My anger disappeared. He said, "You say there is no such thing. Do you know every thing that is?"

"No." I saw him lift an amused eyebrow and tip his head, and I looked away. "But I know I am lying to him. And I know I have to tell him the truth!"

From the corner of my eye I saw Syawa nodding thoughtfully as he sat amidst the flowers, but when I turned my face we were walking shoulder to shoulder under the enormous leaf canopy of the great eastern forest. "Do you know what the truth is?" he asked gently.

I stopt and looked 'round, confused. I gaped at him. He smiled. My shoulders slumped as I hung my head. "No." I thought for a moment, then looked up hopefully. "But I know I love him. I know that is definitely true."

Syawa grinned broadly as we walked. "Then that is what you should definitely tell him."

I frowned, distracted by the amazing detail of the sticks and leaves on the ground, but when I looked up again the leaves on the trees were gone and the sun was beating down on me, hot, hot, so hot. I looked mournfully at Syawa, who was pensive, quiet, and I said, "I'm going to lose this baby, aren't I?"

He gave me a sympathetic smile. "There will be others."

I stopt walking and started to cry. "But I wanted this one!"

He took my hand and squeezed it, and my entire body felt suddenly weightless, filled with light, like a warm breeze. "It is hard, I know, but you will see. You will learn. Then will come acceptance."

I wafted my face in his direction, only to find we were sitting now before a raging fire, with darkness surrounding everything but us and the snapping flames. I whimpered, "I took a life so I must give a life, yes?"

Syawa made a face as he shook his head. "No. You must give a life because you refused to use the gift I gave you. You were supposed to protect him, the way he always protected me, the way he now protects you."

"But what was I supposed to protect him *from*?" I asked, looking uneasily at the darkness.

The darkness began spinning, spinning. Frightened, I looked to Syawa, whose eyes were so much blacker than the darkness and absolutely, perfectly still. He said sadly, "It was you."

"Me?" I asked in disbelief.

"It was your people. You should have stopt him from drinking."

I drew my breath in so sharply a rush of flames from the fire entered my mouth and nose, seering my throat and lungs. I coughed and coughed and coughed as I said, "But I tried to stop him! I told him to stop! He wouldn't listen to me!"

Syawa's eyes burnt into me even hotter than the flames had done, flickering yellow and orange and red. "He would have listened to *me*!"

I stared at Syawa, stupefied, but now he was lying on his sleeping robe, dying, and I was leaning o'er him. "That's not fair!" I shouted. "I didn't know!"

He was weak, fading, slipping away from me again. "Make it fair," he croaked. "Accept your gift. Protect him. You have much to learn, Katie. Learn it. One day you will understand, and when you do . . ." He smiled ruefully at me, the very same way he did before he died. "Well, knowing changes nothing. But at least, until then, you can enjoy the ride."

I screamed at him, hysterical—"Syawa! Syawa! Don't leave me! Please don't leave me!" and I heard him murmur he would not just before he was gone and so was I and all was quiet again and nothing, floating formless and weightless and free . . .

I awoke sometime later, confused to find myself in the canoe. It was moving very quickly and I opened my good eye with great difficulty. I tried to raise my head to look 'round but could not. I gave up and worked on focusing my eye instead. Hector was paddling like a madman, in a full panic. I felt so sorry for him, so guilty for failing to protect him.

"I can hear your thoughts," I said in a raspy voice. Oh, it was hard to breathe!

Hector glanced down at me, tight-lipped. His face was grayer than the sky; his eyes were bloodshot. His hair was covered with snow.

"You will not have to watch me die," I croaked. "He says I will be fine."

Hector glanced at me again, and tho' his eyes met mine only for a moment, I saw a glimmer of hope. As he continued paddling, I watched him and loved him and wisht I could help him. After a long moment, he glanced down again. "The baby?" he asked, the tremor in his voice betraying the fact that he already knew the answer.

I blinked as I became aware of the warm liquid pooling between my legs. "He says there will be others."

I saw the spasm on Hector's face, but then it became stone. He swallowed hard, nodded, and tried with all his might to keep his voice steady. "Do not talk. You must save your breath."

It was true that every inhalation was excruciating, but I gave him a reproachful look. I started to say, "I need you more than I need air to breathe . . ." but my lips stopt moving, my eyelids wouldn't stay open, and the darkness came again . . .

The next thing I knew I was being pulled from the canoe. I tried to fight off all the hands grabbing at me, but there were too many and

I had no power. My good eye flickered 'til I found Hector's face at last, swimming in a sea of strange faces. He was exhausted, gray, nigh dead himself.

I was taken to a hut where women tended both my pneumonia and my needs following the miscarriage. Again and again a large woman forced liquid down my throat and I choked and spluttered and tried to fight her off, but she was exceptionally strong and she silenced me by wearing a mask, shaking rattles, and blowing smoke in my face. She put compresses on my chest, as others rubbed oils into my hands and feet. I went in and out of consciousness for days, all the while strangely detached from my body, floating, without substance or sensation.

I've been sick many, many times in my life, so this was nothing new for me. I knew what to expect, how to endure. I let my body heal itself whilst my mind just left, taking this opportunity to relive every precious moment I'd spent with Syawa. During those days of illness-induced oblivion, I experienced it all again, right from the beginning, enjoying our brief Journey in every exquisite detail. I watched his pantomimes and listened to his stories. But this time I accompanied him all the way to the end, again and again, until eventually, instead of crying, I was able to smile gratefully as he gave his final message, the words of which I was at long last able to understand: *It was worth it.*

I vowed to make it so.

I have a vague memory of being carried from the women's hut to a much larger, lighter dwelling made of earth and animal hides, but once there my stupor returned. During this time I dreamt of Hector, only Hector, and I awoke one morning desperate to see him, to touch him, to smell him, to wrap myself 'round him. I tried to sit up, but an old woman put her hand on my chest and held me down, speaking rapidly to people I could not see. I realized how awfully weak I must be if I could not o'ercome this gray-haired grandmother. In a moment she had a wooden bowl in her hand, from which she dug two fingers-full of gruel. When she placed this in my mouth, it seemed the most heavenly ambrosia, and I savored it, swallowed, and opened my mouth for more. The old lady's face crinkled in a smile as she said something to the unseen others. She scooped more gruel into my mouth, and I sucked her fingers, rolling my eyes in appreciation. She laughed.

Then Hector was beside me, and the old woman backed away. He looked me over anxiously without touching me; I would've grabbed him, but I was too weak e'en to lift my hand. "How long have we been here?" I croaked. Hector said seven days. I made a noise of amazement. "No wonder I'm so hungry!"

We both tried to smile, but when our eyes met, our smiles melted and we both looked away. "I'm sorry we didn't make it to the village you wanted to reach by winter," I mumbled. It was something Hector had striven for every single day I'd known him, yet here we were, his goal unmet—all because of me.

"That is nothing." He dismissed my words with a shrug. "These people are kin to those I hoped to reach, and I speak some of their language. They are kind and generous. They have cared for us well."

The "us" struck me, making me look at him more closely. He was haggard, gaunt, grim. When I asked how he fared, he shrugged again, but I would later learn he himself collapsed shortly after our arrival. From the morning he found me delirious, he paddled all that day, all that moonlit night, and on into the next day without eating or sleeping. It was a miracle he did not die.

Of course I did not yet know this. All I knew was that every time our eyes met, we both wilted in an agony of guilt. Our dead baby swirled between us in the tears we were both too afraid to cry.

O'er the next few days that dead baby haunted me. No longer feverish or delusional, my dreams were now my own, and they were filled with dead babies—my mother's, my sisters', my brothers', mine. All the dead babies, piling up like discarded shoes. How little sympathy I'd had for Mother when we wrapt those ice-eyed carcasses. How cold I myself had been, condemning her always with icy eyes of my own. But now it had happened to me.

I wondered what my dead baby would have looked like. I imagined it a boy, tall and well-built, like his father, clever and conversational, like me. Hour after hour, day after day, I lived that child's whole life in my head, gently laying it to rest at last only after it had lived a long, happy, incredibly productive life in my imagination.

Did my mother go through this, I wondered? Did she give all her unborn, stillborn, or short-lived babes entire lives of their own in her head? No wonder she was crazy. How could anyone live so many imaginary lives and successfully live a real one? And no wonder my mother had always hated me. How could I begin to compare to all those brothers and sisters who were perfect because they ne'er existed, children who disappointed her once and only once—when they failed to cling to life?

Through this melancholy period, Hector oft came to check on me, but his face stayed stony, his jaw clenched, his eyes sunk inside his face. He ne'er stayed for more than a few moments.

As I gradually crawled out of my own head, I found we were living in the lodge of the Holywoman who saved us, along with her mother (the grandmother who fed me) and three others. The lodge was large, and I was as comfortable as I could be, under the circumstances. Save for that period of blissful isolation with Hector, I had always lived in quarters much more crowded than this.

I was, at first, intimidated by the Holywoman, for she was big, strong, and strange in many ways, but I owed her my life and I was glad, at least, she was not a man. Probably twice my age, she tended me with a well-practiced, maternal warmth; I wondered if the other people in the lodge were her children, and, if so, what had become of her husband. Her name meant something like "fox running across a log," so I thought of her as Running Fox. Her aged mother, of whom I became quite fond, I called Gran.

When I grew strong enough to be unwilling to use the wood bowl Gran provided as chamber pot, Running Fox helped me stand and walk outside, whereupon I very nigh turned right 'round—the snow was deeper than my knees! She urged me onward, however, and by the time we returned, Hector was at the door, holding aside the hide for us. After Running Fox settled me back in my furs, she turned to speak to Hector. He shook his head to whate'er she said, then slipt out the door without coming to me. I pulled my furs o'er my head and wept.

Whilst I was recovering, I was situated in the middle of the lodge by the fire, with Hector and all our things tucked off to one side. But the day after I first went outside, Running Fox said I was well enough to move back with my husband. Tho' Hector was not there when we rearranged things, he soon returned, and when he saw I was by his bedding, he froze. He turned to ask a question of the Holywoman, who replied in a firm voice. He then bowed his head and came to join me.

He sat a few feet from me, his face to the wall. Without looking at me, he asked how I fared. Assuming he was angry I lost the baby, I kept my own eyes on the ground and mumbled I was fine.

I heard Running Fox sigh, and when I glanced her way, she gestured that my husband and I must share our grief if we e'er hoped to o'ercome it. I stared at her 'til she raised an eyebrow and tipt her head. Then I turned to Hector and released my anguish in a flood of words. I told him I was sorry I lost the baby, so, so sorry, and I knew he'd tried to tell me this would happen but I wouldn't listen and made him act against his better judgment by enticing him and now our baby was dead, like all my mother's dead babies, and it was all my fault and I was sorry, so sorry, and I didn't blame him for hating me now because I hated myself more than he could possibly hate me.

When I finally took a breath, Hector insisted my words made no sense—the fault was his, he said, for he was the one who failed to protect me and he understood why I didn't want him to touch me now, why I shrank from him and screamed when I was ill, why I kicked at him and pushed him away, and he said he understood my revulsion and would not impose himself on me further because he had no right to touch me e'er again and he turned away and held his head in his hands.

I grabbed his arm and pulled him back 'round, telling him he had it all wrong, that my screams and flailing had been on account of my dead sister and I told him about the pox and her death and how my fever had taken me back there and made me go through it all again and it was horrible and I wept and trembled and begged him to hold me, saying the only way I could survive the loss of our child would be if I could please be wrapt in his arms forever.

The rest of our conversation took place with him clutching me to his chest, rocking me gently as I cried. After a time he murmured again that he had failed me, failed me, because he did not recognize the Evil Spirit when it appeared at our campfire. The baby died inside me, he said, because it could not bear to be born to such a stupid, stupid father.

If Hector had talked thus of Evil Spirits only two weeks earlier, I would've laughed in his face and explained how such a view was childish and just plain wrong. But by this time I had learnt that in the weird world in which I found myself, Evil Spirits were very real and only a drooling fool would doubt their power.

Which is not to say I've come to believe in Evil Spirits. I do not. But I understand now that *these* people believe in them. And I understand that e'en tho' I *know* those poor traders were murdered by us for no reason other than that they got drunk with the wrong man, I can ne'er explain that to Hector. Nor will I try. It matters not. What matters is he believed he was protecting me and now he believes he failed me, and I love him too much to allow him to condemn himself for something that was in no way his fault.

After all, I have done a much, much worse thing than fail him—I have lied to him all this time, I am lying to him e'en now, I lie to him every time I open my lying mouth to lie, lie, lie. How dare I judge him harshly? How dare I judge my mother harshly? For that matter, how dare I judge myself harshly? Life is very hard. We all do the best we can.

"The Seer said the fault was mine, Hector," I whispered. "He told me how to fight the Evil Spirit, but I hesitated because . . . because I did not understand him. *I* was the stupid one, the one who failed. That's why our baby died."

I could feel Hector listening intently, understanding what I said, accepting it. "We were both stupid, Katie," he soothed. "We both failed. But the Seer always told me failure can be a good thing, if we learn from it. We will not make the same mistakes again."

I nodded, for I had no intention of making the same mistake again. From now on, I planned to follow the advice of my delirium-induced dream and use my power as Spirit Keeper for all it was worth—*if* I could figure out what this alleged "power" was supposed to be.

Whilst we sat in silent thought, Hector tenderly moved his fingers along the scars on my face. I had forgotten them, but realized now those scars were at least part of the reason he couldn't look at me. "They're not my first scars," I reminded him gently. "I doubt they'll be my last."

"But these are *my* scars," he said, his voice trembling. "And every time I look at you, they taunt me with my failure. You have suffered so much in your life. I wanted to save you from that. I was sure that's why the Seer put you in my hands—so that *I* would be the one who gets the scars from now on. I was so sure."

Ah, yes. How well I recognized that stunned feeling of disbelief, that shocked frustration. I looked up at my beloved and murmured, "I've been sure of things, too, Hector, only to find out I was completely wrong. But when you look at these scars, please do not think of our failures—think of how lucky we are to have found each other. Let these scars remind us both of the one thing we *can* be sure of, the one thing we can ne'er be wrong about—we are supposed to be together. The Seer said so. We can be wrong about everything else, but not this, ne'er this. We're stuck with each other, you and I."

Hector frowned at my scars for a long moment before looking sadly into my eyes. "I do not want you to stay with me only because you are stuck with me."

I half-smiled as I lost myself in his deep, dark gaze. "It matters not what you want, Hector. And it matters not what I want. All that matters is what *he* wants—at least until we fulfill his Vision." I waited for him to consider the truth of these words before adding, "And, honestly, I'm relieved we're stuck with each other, aren't you? Who else could put up with either one of us? We're both so stupid it's a wonder we can walk without tripping o'er our own feet!"

The unexpected jibe made Hector laugh, which gave me a surge of joy almost as strong as if we were engaged in a bout of passion. He held me tight, his face in my hair, and out of the corner of my eye I saw Running Fox glance our way with a smug smile. I gave her a long blink of thanks. She nodded before bending o'er her sewing.

In the months we have been here, Hector has oft been gone from me, out hunting or fishing or helping the villagers in one way or another. To cope with my loneliness, I dug through our packs 'til I found the leather satchel containing the beaverskin pouch with the two ledgers. I asked Running Fox if I could use some black paint and asked Gran for a large goose feather.

I tried to explain about writing. I told Hector I hoped to send this first ledger back east someday, to whate'er remains of my family, but he could not comprehend how marks I make on paper can reveal my thoughts to people who are not here. Everyone has concluded it must be some sort of magic my people use to recover from illness, and I let them think what they will.

I'm not sure why I wanted to write my story down. Part of my motivation, I know, has been to create a private space for myself in these close quarters. When I write, everyone stays well away from me, leery of my supernatural powers, and I am in my own little world. For that I am grateful. Another reason is that this past year has been so incredible, so providential, that I needed to get it all out of my head, to organize it, to control it, to put it down on paper to see if I could somehow make it all make sense. In a very literal way, filling this ledger with my thoughts *has* healed me, because it has helpt me establish some small isle of sanity in the swirling madness of this crazy savage world.

Shortly after I began writing, Running Fox was out late one night, tending a sick baby. As she arose in the morning to get dressed, I glanced up from my writing and happened to see that she had male organs. I immediately looked back at my ledger, dumb-founded. Running Fox is not a woman after all. She's a man.

She must've seen my face—or is it *he* must've seen my face? At any rate, she came to me when she was dressed and looked at me inquisitively. She gestured, saying I seemed disturbed.

I gestured that I was just tired of being stupid. "I think I know how things are. Then I find out I am wrong, always wrong!"

She laughed as she gestured, "Getting tired of being stupid is the first step to wisdom!" She said that because I have the Spirit of a man inside me, we are alike, she and I, and she believed I had been sent to her for a reason. I could not argue with that. Then she said something that will stick with me for the rest of my days. "Rules do not apply to people like you and me," she gestured. "Our power comes to us because we go where others cannot go, see what they cannot see, and know what they cannot know."

I stared at Running Fox as understanding began to dawn. Being a Spirit Keeper is like having a Guarantee of Safe Passage signed by the King himself. I can go where I please, do what I want, say what I will, and no one can stop me. My power is limited only by my imagination.

And so I have spent the rest of the winter learning many, many things from Running Fox. She is teaching me to be a Holyman, a Spirit Keeper. Many things are clear to me now that were not clear before, but one truth stands out above all others:

In a world full of scrupulously honest people, my greatest power is my ability to lie.

When I am not writing or learning the Sacred Ways, I talk in gestures with Running Fox's mother; she is the only person other than Running Fox who isn't deathly afraid of me. One day in mid-winter, after Hector set off for an overnight hunting trip, I asked Gran to help me with something. She did so happily, and when Hector returned, Gran and I exchanged giggling glances when he came into the lodge. We waited in breathless anticipation as he went to put his things away. He suddenly froze, staring at the beautiful new pair of shoes perched on his sleeping fur. He looked at me, his eyes filling as he grabbed me and buried his face in my hair. I think e'en Running Fox was crying by the time Hector had the shoes on his feet.

Every day I yearn to be alone with Hector, but the weather is far too cold for me to spend much time outside and the lodge is oft filled with people eager to hear my strange tales. Hector has encouraged me to tell about my chickens and cows and big dogs. After watching Running Fox and other storytellers gesture their stories, I have e'en dared to act out Hamlet's tale again, as well as that of Romeo and Juliet. My storytelling ability has improved with each tale I tell, and the villagers clearly appreciate the diversion on these long, dark winter days.

338 K. B. Laugheed

The only time Hector and I are truly alone now is when we are wrapt in the buffalo robe. Then we lean our foreheads together and whisper for hours. It has been good for us, I think, to talk again instead of always wrestling in lust, and we enjoy sleeping together as we ne'er could before. We hold each other as we sleep, and if I roll outside my husband's grasp, he snaps awake, looking for me.

The night after I gave him the shoes, I presst myself against him and moved my hands upon him, but he pulled away, gently holding my wrists, and said we must not do that. He said he would not do it. Touching my scarred temple with his fingertips, he said, "Katie, I will not risk your life again. I will not risk putting you through what you have already been through, and, in any case, I could not go through it again myself. We must wait 'til we are home and you are safe."

"But I miss you!" I said pitifully, nuzzling his chin with my face.

"I am right here," he whispered, e'en as he held me firmly away.

I flopt onto my back, breathing heavily. "So we must wait for what—a year?" He murmured an affirmation, and I gasped. "But Hector—I *need* you! You know I go crazy without you!"

Hector put his fingers on my mouth and felt my lips slowly, sensuously, in such a way that I knew he wanted nothing more than to touch them, to kiss them, to lose himself in them. That's when I knew I had him. He might protest, and he might feel bad, but if I wanted him I would have him, and there was not a damned thing he could do about it. All I need do is say "If you truly love me, you will do this for me!" and he would give in. How could he not give me what I want if he truly loves me?

Then he spoke again, and my reason was undone.

"I know this will be hard for you, Katie, but you are not alone.

I am right here with you, suffering the same way you are suffering. All I can do is ask you to have mercy on me. Before I met you, he told me how smart you were, how strong, how brave. You must be strong now, and, as you love me, you must not torture me. I am not as strong as you, and if you entice me, I will fail, and then I will hate myself. Please do not make me hate myself. Love me enough to be strong for both of us."

How was I to argue with that? In my world, love was manipulation, a power struggle, an endless cycle of self-gratification and guilt. In his world, love is trust, mutual support, and a willingness to put the needs of another before your own. I rolled o'er and wept 'til I fell asleep, as he gently stroked my hair. E'er since that night I have buried myself in writing so that I do not succumb to temptation, entice him, and thereby destroy everything we have.

Sometime thereafter, Hector repaid our hosts for their hospitality by taking a group to the site of our battle, where they recovered the traders' canoes and all the goods therein. They had to drag the canoes back here, for the ice on the river was thick. But then, just yesterday, Hector reported the ice is breaking, and we will soon be able to resume our Journey. I was terribly excited, 'til he added that he has convinced three of his new friends to travel with us to the perilous mountain passage. We need their help, he said, because, as he put it, "You may keep the Spirit of a man inside you, Katie, but your body is definitely that of a woman." His eyes twinkled as he said this.

I knew I should be happy about this news, but I had been looking forward to being alone with my husband again. However, when he pointed out this plan should cut many months off our journey, I agreed it was an excellent idea. I am ready to leave the moment the river allows.

It has been a year now, since Hector and Syawa burst into the loft and took me away from the miserable life I had been living. I have suffered greatly on this Journey, but I have also experienced exquisite joy, far more than I knew existed. As I look back thru the ledger I have filled with my words, I am struck by an obvious question: how is it possible for someone to know almost nothing, yet every day feel as if she knows less and less? Clearly no one could be as stupid as I seem to be and yet survive. Therefore, it cannot be that I am so stupid; it can only be that I truly am in a different world than the one into which I was born.

Things are different here. I understand that now. Everything is different. Consider, for example, my delirious dream of Syawa. Was that a message from the Spirit I keep, or was it merely a delusion, spawned by fever and fear? In this world that question itself is a joke, for e'en if I knew the answer, which I do not, I have it on good authority it wouldn't matter anyway. *Knowing*, I've been told, doesn't change a thing.

Indeed, what good is *knowing* in a world where time and space themselves are strange—always shifting, transforming, swirling 'round and 'round like the relentless current of a river? As I bob along, subject to the whims of those whirling circles, only one thing remains constant regardless of the world I am in, only one truth remains inviolable no matter how much I lie and lie and lie. Love. I love Hector—he loves me. Love is all we have to keep our heads above the water, and it is all we need. I understand now that it is love and only love which enables us to whisper at the end of our Journey: *It was worth it.*

So, Syawa, if you can hear me and e'en if you can't—I understand my mandate now. I will do whate'er I must to keep your friend, my husband, safe and sound. If, in order to protect him, I must lie to him, then I will ne'er again hesitate to lie. And tho' I may fret about what the future holds, I intend to enjoy the ride in any case, because life itself is, after all, such a glorious gift.

I thank you, Syawa, for the great gift you have given me; I will use it well. I will be your Spirit Keeper. And I will see you safely home.